Elias Nason

Lives and Labors of Eminent Divines

Charles H. Parkhurst, Dwight Lyman Moody, Ira David Sankey, Philip P. Bliss and Eben Tourjée; accounts of their labors of reform and evangelization and sketches of their lives

Elias Nason

Lives and Labors of Eminent Divines
Charles H. Parkhurst, Dwight Lyman Moody, Ira David Sankey, Philip P. Bliss and Eben Tourjée; accounts of their labors of reform and evangelization and sketches of their lives

ISBN/EAN: 9783337329402

Printed in Europe, USA, Canada, Australia, Japan

Cover: Foto ©Raphael Reischuk / pixelio.de

More available books at **www.hansebooks.com**

LIVES AND LABORS

OF

EMINENT DIVINES

CHARLES H. PARKHURST

DWIGHT LYMAN MOODY

IRA DAVID SANKEY

PHILIP P. BLISS

AND EBEN TOURJÉE

Accounts of
Their Labors of Reform and Evangelization
and
Sketches of Their Lives

BY

REV. ELIAS NASON

AND

J. FRANK BEALE, Jr.

ILLUSTRATED

MDCCCXCV.
JOHN E. POTTER AND COMPANY
PHILADELPHIA
NEW YORK, BOSTON, CHICAGO

CONTENTS

———

CHAPTER IV.

MR. MOODY AS A PREACHER.

CHAPTER V.

LABORS IN GREAT BRITAIN.

CHAPTER VI.

EVANGELISM IN BROOKLYN AND PHILADELPHIA.

CHAPTER VII.

NEW YORK, AUGUSTA, AND CHICAGO.

CHAPTER VIII.

CONTINUATION OF THE WORK IN CHICAGO.

CHAPTER IX.

THE REVIVALISTS IN BOSTON.

IRA D. SANKEY.

HIS BIRTH, BOYHOOD, EDUCATION, AND MISSION.

LIFE OF P. P. BLISS.

THE BIRTH AND EDUCATION OF MR. BLISS. — HIS MUSIC, WORK, AND DEATH.

SACRED SONG IN EVANGELISM.

THE POWER AND RESULTS OF SACRED SONG IN EVANGELISM. — REMARKS ON THE PSALMODY OF THE CHURCH.

ILLUSTRATIONS OF MR. MOODY.

CHOICE SAYINGS, INCIDENTS, STORIES, AND ILLUSTRATIONS OF MR. MOODY.

THE LIFE OF CHARLES H. PARKHURST.

CHAPTER I.

Dr. Parkhurst's Conspicuous Position.—His Ancestors and Parents.—As a Boy.—As a Youth.—As an Educator.—His Residence Abroad.—Choosing a Profession.—His Pastorate at Lenox.—The New Field in New York.—His Growing Fame.—A Sermon on Reform.—Personal Investigation of Crime and Sin.

To Rev. Charles H. Parkhurst, D. D., pastor of the Madison Square Presbyterian Church of New York City, belongs a more contradictory fame than that of any man, public or private, contemporary with him. His method and manner of reform have been such that the vituperate utterances of those whose misconduct he has been either the primary or secondary cause of exposing, are as natural a consequence as the unstinted praise of his constituents, of whose full sympathy he is possessed.

No man can be engaged in a conspicuous capacity as a reformer, either of religion or government, and escape the criticisms, whether just or unjust, and the slander of those against whom his crusade is directed. On the other hand, such a man's following, intensely sympathetic and enthusiastic at first, will sooner or later divide itself into two classes, one of which considers it its individual and collective duty to express doubts, utter suspicions, and make use of suggestions, because perchance the great reformer elects to pursue his own methods.

In the following pages we shall see in what Dr. Parkhurst has merited the esteem of his associates of the Society for the Suppression of Vice and the City Vigilance League of New York City, for the untiring zeal he has displayed in suppressing vice and in endeavoring to raise the standard of New York's municipal government. We shall also see the animus of the many attacks made upon him, either by or at the instigation of those whose criminal operations he exposed.

*   *   *

As the botanist traces with care the facts concerning the existence of the rare flower, so we shall be interested in glancing back at the boyhood, youth, and early manhood of the great reformer, Parkhurst, and note the influences and heredities that fitted him for the conspicuous and honorable position he holds to-day.

The Parkhursts were an English family of no small distinction in their native land. They came to America and made their home in New England several generations ago. The particular branch of the family of which Charles H. Parkhurst came, settled in South Framingham, Mass. Dr. Parkhurst's father was an eminent member of the second generation of American Parkhursts and was a thorough New Englander—fond of his family, his books, his fellows, and his God, living a serene and happy life,—a model citizen. Into this atmosphere the baby, Charles H. Parkhurst, was born one beautiful spring day in 1842. He was a ruddy, rugged child, reared in that peculiar New England way that lays the foundation for a true and useful manhood.

It cannot be said of Parkhurst as a boy that he was " remarkable " or " gave evidence of a career of usefulness and honor," as biographers are wont to write of their subjects. He was a bright, studious lad, however, whose natural inclinations were toward literary pursuits —philology, and in fact higher education. It is said of Spurgeon, Beecher, Talmage, Conwell, and other noted clergymen, that they were " born preachers." Not so with Parkhurst. As a lad he began to trend by inclination to the scholar's life and work. He gave that same untiring application to his studies and his youthful duties that has characterized his later work as preacher and municipal reformer. Almost unconsciously was bred into his soul the intense spirit of fire that lay smouldering until by chance it was fanned into a fierce flame of indignation and horror by a visit to the slums of New York one wintry night in 1886, when Castle Garden, Water Street, the Bowery, and almost the entire vicinity of New York Harbor was a pest-hole of ribaldry, debauchery, obscenity, and shame.

*   *   *

Young Parkhurst entered Amherst College in 1862, and was graduated with honor, but without special distinction, in 1866, at the age of twenty-four. A year after graduation he took charge of Amherst High School, which position he held for two years. During this incumbency he formed an attachment for one of his pupils, a lovely young woman of New England birth and parentage, whom two years later he married. Upon his return from East Hampton, where he went as an instructor to several special classes of young men, Dr. Parkhurst once said : "I firmly believe I learned much more during those two years at East Hampton than my pupils were able to gather from my tuition."

The Parkhurst finances were always in that state which the parlance of to-day describes as "easy." Dr. Parkhurst as boy and man has probably never known a desire that he has not had the means to gratify. This, however, is as much due to the fact that his wants have always been simple and in keeping with his unostentatious mode of living, as to the comfortable dimensions of his purse.

Although his engagements as an educator were probably only sufficiently remunerative to enable him to purchase what books he needed for the prosecution of his pet studies, philology and metaphysics, his inherited wealth enabled him to spend a year in Germany at the University of Halle, shortly after leaving East Hampton.

His residence abroad was a great benefit to him, making him, in the true sense of the term, "a man of the world." He became acquainted, and a thorough sympathizer, with the great efforts of mankind, both contemporaneous and past, and imbibed that high purpose and sense of duty to mankind that has animated his later life. As he studied and familiarized himself with the work of the world's great reformers during that year of his residence abroad, by intercourse with great men of great minds and by recourse to the literature of the ages, he unwittingly prepared himself for that grand struggle for home, purity, and honor which he so nobly made a quarter of a century later, in the second city of the world—our country's great metropolis—New York.

On his return to his native country in 1871, he took the chair of Latin and Greek in Williston Seminary, East Hampton, Mass., and delved still deeper into the history and literature of his two pet studies. He seemed to have no settled idea as to his vocation in life. His object, happily, was not to make the world serve him, but to serve the world. Occupation he did not look upon as a means of bread-winning, but as a means of directing those activities, of which he felt himself possessed, into channels that would lead to the highest good of his fellow-men.

At this period in his life, young Parkhurst began to see the necessity of choosing a profession to which he should devote his life-work. Upon consultation with Dr. Seelye, then president of Amherst, he decided to enter the ministry. Although he had no predilections toward that profession, and had scarcely given it a thought, so highly did he value the advice of his teacher and friend that he went into the necessary preparations for the ministry with that zest and earnestness that have ever characterized his undertakings as a man and crusader.

Dr. Parkhurst once said to a brother of the cloth: "I recall with mingled wonder and thankfulness the night I decided to take the advice of my good old friend and 'preach.' In any other calling I should never have met even with that moderate degree of success which has been my good fortune as a minister of the gospel." This is truly Parkhurstian simplicity. His iron will and steadfastness of purpose would have lifted Parkhurst head and shoulders above "the rank and file" of humanity in any avocation. Parkhurst's place could never be with the mediocrity.

In 1874, at the age of thirty-two, Parkhurst became pastor of the Presbyterian Church of that lovely Berkshire town, Lenox. This was an important link in the chain that drew and bound him to New York, for it was while spending a portion of a summer at Lenox that John E. Parsons, the great lawyer, conceived the idea of transplanting the earnest, sincere Christian worker from the mountain town to a larger field of usefulness in the great metropolis. This was in 1880.

Parkhurst went to the Madison Square Presbyterian Church, in New York City, with the record of six years of successful, though not brilliant, work at Lenox. To some of his new congregation he was known; with a few he was on terms of intimate friendship and regard; to the majority he was barely known.

Like all wealthy and aristocratic congregations, the people of the Madison Square Church received the new man from the popular summer resort with very evident expectations. He was not a trained preacher nor a learned theologian. As a traveler, pedagogue, and student of secular history and literature up to the age when most of his fellow-clergymen had completed their preparation for ecclesiastical duties, he labored under difficulties, more being expected of him than was just under the circumstances. Parkhurst began his preparation for the ministry at the time when most clergymen assume the cloth.

Had he fallen into the rut of conventionalism, he would not have occupied the proud position he to-day holds. Humanity was his chief concern, and his doctrines and theories were only those that had to do with making men and women more pure and wholesome. His sermons were appreciated as having the true ring of high purpose, and he immediately won the hearts of his people. "Right Living" was the motto that shone out bold and resplendent in all his sermons. Like the Alpine youth who struggled up the dizzy heights crying, "Excelsior!" this modern advocate of purity shouted from pulpit, platform, and printed page, "Reform! Reform! in society and municipality," as he ascended the avenue of fame.

It must be remembered that Dr. Parkhurst's fame was gradual in its growth. It will therefore be the more lasting. Perhaps the first direct evidence of the popular attention he gradually attracted was the establishment of a rule in his church that pew-holders must arrive early at the evening service if they wished their seats reserved. This rule was made necessary by the ever-increasing crowds that thronged to hear the ser-

mons of the man who dared to criticise the existing
local evils, having first investigated the things of which
he spoke. It was made imperative by increasing congregations, attracted in a large measure by the first
utterings of the crusade of this comparative "new-
comer." Learned doctors of divinity looked askance
upon the New Englander who dared to preach to re-
fined and cultured people of vice, immorality, and corruption existing at their very doors. These were matters for the police and the courts. They beheld with
wonder Dr. Parkhurst's congregations swelling with
non-church goers and no small number of truants from
their own folds. As Parkhurst became the object of
general attention, he also became the subject of much
unfair criticism of both person and methods. He was
characterized as a man struggling for personal ag-
grandizement and notoriety—a sensationalist. However, criticism seemed to act rather as a tonic, and he
pursued the even tenor of his way oblivious to abuse,
criticism, or threat.

It was evident to the few favored ones who were near
to Parkhurst in those days that he was preparing for a
battle royal against sin, and particularly that phase of
sin we are wont to call "the social evil." It is sufficient to say that neither the great reformer himself
nor his friends anticipated his instrumentality in the
overturning of the greatest organization of power and
the most stupendous corporation of crime the century
has known. The man who had spent his life in the
pleasantest places of New England, in delving in Con-

tinental libraries, and in familiarizing himself with facts in history and the great achievements of literature, now began to investigate local conditions which he had just begun to realize.

It was now about January, 1887, and the press of New York City was ablaze with descriptions of the corruptions and vice of her slums. Occasionally a feeble note was heard from the pulpits of those clergymen whose sense of obligation to mankind in the lower strata was scarcely as well developed as their love of oratorical efforts and fear of offence to hypersensitive audiences.

Not being a city man, Dr. Parkhurst found it hard to realize the possibility of such a state of affairs as the newspapers depicted. He gave the matter much thought and resolved to investigate personally. Many matters of creed he could accept on faith, but he well knew if he was to deal in a successful measure with the hydra-headed monster of iniquity, he must see personally the conditions which he wished to alleviate.

One blustry winter night, accompanied by an ex-police commissioner, one of the few men who had held that position and retained his self-respect and integrity, he made a tour of the darkest dens of vice the city knew. He saw vice and crime as it existed in its lowest and most revolting forms. Later, accompanied by another person, he investigated vice as it existed in higher forms, and at the same time proved to his own mind the profitable and protective connection existing between crime, vice, and debauchery on the one hand,

and the executive branch of the law and the officials of
the municipal government on the other. Nothing
escaped his thoroughly aroused and horrified mind, not
even the most minute detail. The scenes he witnessed
stamped themselves upon his mind indelibly. Almost
before he began to realize the enormity and strength of
the alliance between vice and the law, he began to study
out a remedy.

Dr. Parkhurst's election to the presidency of the
Society for the Prevention of Crime occurred on April 30,
1891, immediately after the death of Dr. Howard Crosby,
its first president. He made it a condition when
he accepted the position that the society's operations
must be on the line which has been followed out with
much success since he has been its president. Before
Dr. Parkhurst's connection with the society, it had
worked in conjunction with the police. Dr. Parkhurst's
fundamental principle was that the Society should
henceforth deal with the police as its arch antagonist.
He believed the police department to be thoroughly
rotten and not fit for his society to lean upon.

As the congregation was largely composed of young
people, many of them young men, his solicitude was
ever to keep them from those forms of sin which too
soon lead to crime and ruin. His struggle was to be
doubly objective—for the best interests of the young
people to whom he is devoted, and for the good of the
city at large.

GRAPPLING WITH THE MONSTER.

CHAPTER II.

A Corrupt City.—Attacking the Social Evil.—Befriending Fallen Women—Discrediting Dr. Parkhurst.—Superintendent Byrnes' Attack.—An Open Letter.—Dr. Parkhurst's Idea of a Citizen's Rights.—How He Exercised His Right.

Dr. Parkhurst was beginning to realize more fully that the "social evil" was playing a most important part in the corruption of the city, and that the unlawful connection between the salaried officers of the city, who were supposed to protect the city, and the wholesale panderers to vice, was probably more noted and more open in this instance than in others. Probably it was because he commenced his crusade by visiting disorderly places, principally houses of ill-repute, that the public press was led to criticise him and to mislead the public into a misapprehension of his work and what he intended to do, whereas he began his work in that way because he thought it was the best means of opening the eyes of the people to the blatant crime to which the city was given over.

Dr. Parkhurst's strides in his attacks upon the evil of which the unfortunate and fallen women were victims, were rapid and aimed right at the heart of the thing. While his crusade was naturally the means of throwing large numbers of women and girls on the charity of the city, he did everything he could personally and by influencing others, to alleviate their condition. His house was literally besieged by poor unfortunates, who, in many instances, came to curse but went away to bless. The girls seemed to think that their being driven out into the cold, dreary streets by the officers of the law, who were unwillingly performing their duty, was the direct work of Dr. Parkhurst, whom they looked upon as a man trying to crush them from the earth. Most of them, however, were soon led to see that in Dr. Parkhurst they had a greater friend than in those corrupt " servants " of the people who were protecting them for a monied consideration. Dr. Parkhurst was not aiming at that end, but at the vice of which they were victims. He was always ready and willing to do anything in his power to help them. In many cases where they appealed to the officers to whom they had paid large sums of money for protection, asking for a little assistance in the hour of need, they were referred to Dr. Parkhurst and told that he would give them what assistance was necessary.

However, the whole matter worked about its own reaction. It soon became known and appreciated that Dr. Parkhurst and the City Vigilance League were not persecuting the women themselves, but were after the police, and they, in turn, were being persecuted by the police. The movement was greatly helped by the fact that even the distressed class was beginning to understand its spirit.

It soon became evident to the police, for whom the investigation was growing too warm, that something would have to be done. They therefore set about to discredit both Dr. Parkhurst and Mr. Gardner, the society's detective. Superintendent Byrnes, of the police department, launched out through the medium of the press of New York City statements to the effect that all Dr. Parkhurst's attacks on the police department were absolutely without evidence to support them, and that he did not really believe in them himself. He claimed that the crusade was started by Dr. Parkhurst and several members of his congregation, because one of his (Byrnes') policemen had refused to testify to suit them in a divorce case in which a member of Dr. Parkhurst's congregation was concerned. He insinuated that there was a band of members of the Madison Square Presbyterian Church, with Dr. Parkhurst at its head, whose avowed intention was to compromise the highest officers of the city, from motives that were only revengeful. He did not seem to think that men with important duties daily claiming their attention could ill afford the time, trouble, and expense necessary to making such an attack merely as spite work, or revenge, and he also seemed to think that the people of the city would overlook the unimpeachable character of Dr. Parkhurst and his associates and take it for granted that their object in making such a crusade was only selfish.

Tricky and dishonest methods, of which Dr. Parkhurst and his associates were incapable, were attributed to them by Mr. Byrnes in interviews with reporters from several daily papers. Direct statements were not made, unless they were couched in terms which could easily be construed as having some other meaning than that which was really intended. An effort was made to discredit the movement of reform, by questioning the motives which led to it, almost from its inception. Dr. Parkhurst replied to all these attacks by an authorized interview in one the leading papers. It read as follows:

"For the sake of argument, I am going for an instant to plead guilty to his (Byrnes') entire indictment; I am going to assume that my motives have been villainous from the start; that, as he intimates, I have been actuated by a sheer spirit of revenge; that something that transpired in a certain 'divorce case' so embittered me that I have been spending all these months in the attempt to square myself with the police department. Supposing all that is true, how does it help Mr. Byrnes? Does that fact close up any of the gambling-houses that he has been allowing to run? Suppose I have been dealing in French pictures, and that my pockets are full of them, does that fact suppress any of the vile dens of infamy in this city which exist because Mr. Byrnes and his department are viciously neglectful of their duty?

"Supposing I have availed myself of members of my congregation and have been putting them upon the track of the city officials and set them to study up the unwholesome record of any who are to-day in the position of municipal authority, and have arranged with all my elders, deacons, and deaconesses to discover the facts as to the domestic life of the police commissioners. magistrates, and captains—what of it? How does that help Mr. Byrnes? In what way does it operate to neutralize that other fact of the recognized existence in this city of institutions for the practice of unnatural vices? Mr. Byrnes is trying to shift the issue from his shoulders to mine. He thinks that by showing the community what I am doing he will make the community forget what he isn't doing. I have only to say that I have exercised my right as a citizen to watch the municipal service. If exigency arises again, I shall put the detectives on the track of the officers again, and if I think circumstances are such as require it, I shall put the detective on Mr. Byrnes. If he is doing right, it won't hurt him ; if he isn't doing right, he ought not to object if it does hurt him. Mr. Byrnes is in our municipal service, and I am helping to pay his salary. His opposition to having our public officers watched has a bad look.''

This open letter was highly characteristic of Dr. Parkhurst. It was a plain statement of his position, which thinking people must see is thoroughly reasonable. In this authorized interview there were clauses which that portion of the newspapers who were in sympathy with the police department, wilfully misconstrued into meanings entirely foreign to Dr. Parkhurst's stand in the matter. By almost all the tricks known to newspaperdom, efforts were made to discredit Dr. Parkhurst. Notwithstanding this, the majority of the intelligent and law-abiding portion of the community gave him their support. Some idea of the character of this support can be gleaned from the account in the following chapter of the banquet given in Dr. Parkhurst's honor.

CHAPTER III.

The Banquet in Dr. Parkhurst's Honor.—General Horace Porter's Speech.—Remarks by Dr. Parkhurst.—An Address by Bishop Henry C. Potter.—Remarks by Charles A. Schieren, Mayor of Brooklyn.—Mr. Goff's Address.—The Crusade to be Continued.—Dr. Parkhurst's Work Benefiting Other Cities.

FIVE HUNDRED members of the City Vigilance League and their friends gathered in Jaeger's Banquet Hall on the evening of November 27th to honor Dr. Parkhurst. General Horace Porter, who presided, made the following remarks:

"I have been conjuring my brain to know just why one brought up in the military service should be called to preside over this memorable festival in honor of a rising divine. It may be because in a recent campaign the two professions were equal belligerents, because the church outfought the army, and there was found to be more potency in St. Peter than in salt-petre. The great champion of this campaign had some critics and made some enemies at the start, but he might well say, as did one of Napoleon's marshals when some one told him, now that the war was over he ought to forgive all his enemies, 'Haven't any, killed 'em all,' he replied.

"Now, while he did not fight with wild beasts at Ephesus, he fought with that ravenous beast, the Tammany tiger. For a series of years there were many excuses made for not fighting that tiger; there was not courage to do it until there was a person came along who fought him in his cage. Our champion began as the Tammany mentor; he became the Tammany tormentor. There is nothing which so captivates the human mind as the contemplation of the achievements of distinct individuality, of what can be accomplished by marked personality.

"We read of the mighty hosts of the armies described in the Old Testament, but they do not create that same emotion which we experience when we read of the single-handed combat of the young David against the giant. We read with interest of the mighty battles of great fleets upon the ocean, but they do not thrill us and arouse us to that pitch of enthusiasm which we experience when we recall that scene in Hampton Roads during the war when the enemy's ironclad came out, a formidable engine of destruction, and sent our navy reeling to the bottom.

"There came to New York not many years ago a quiet Monitor, also clothed in sombre black. He found that ravenous beast in New York devouring our substance, destroying the fair fame of our city. He trained his gun upon it and drove it crippled and helpless to its lair. It was because he had the courage of his convictions. He never took counsel of his peers; his was a faith that saw a bow of promise; he could proceed when others could not; he looked neither to the past with regret, nor to the future with apprehension ; he was ready to leave all the efforts to man, the results to God. He will address us this evening—the Rev. Dr. Charles H. Parkhurst."

Three cheers were here given and Dr. Parkhurst made the following remarks :

" Nothing could touch me more deeply and tenderly than the kind and magnificent tribute involved in this dinner, and in your personal and interested presence. As I looked over this gathering of earnest, sympathetic friends, I have tried to realize to myself the actual personal pressure which it all implies. I never looked upon an assemblage of men whose manly personality seemed to me so full of significance and so fraught with great possibilities. Every fibre of every one is a fibre of earnestness and sincerity. I cannot look upon such a gathering and feel any particular anxiety as to the future of New York.

" We have, however, to remember that it is one thing to win a victory, and it is quite another thing, and a far more difficult one, wisely and concertedly to utilize that victory. There is nothing on earth that you and I and our friends working together cannot do, provided we see and move shoulder to shoulder, forgetting ourselves absolutely in the interest of our common and blessed municipality. I feel strong to-night in my faith in God, and my faith in the members of the City Vigilance League.

" You and I, my friends, represent rather a large idea.

Sometimes it has not been thoroughly understood. Some of you allied yourselves with us in its days when it was not considered reputable or respectable to be in any way identified or associated with myself." The doctor was interrupted here by bursts of laughter from those who well remembered the criticisms aimed at them and their connection with the Parkhurst movement. Dr. Parkhurst, resuming, said: "Yes, it is funny now, but it was not funny then. You and I understand very well that we have from the first occupied a platform that is purely non-partisan, non-political. We have learned to understand that, however many may be the questions into which politics may enter as an ingredient, there are questions that stand up above purely political ones, as the great hills and high mountains lift themselves above sea and valley.

"We are banded together, you and I, not because we are Republicans, for in these matters we are not; or Democrats, for in these matters we are not; Hebrews, Protestants, or Catholics, for on these questions we are not. There are principles that rise higher than any one or all of those in our relations to our municipality, and it is along those lines that we hold ourselves.

"You and I, dear friends, are not in this business for the loaves and the fishes, and in that lies ninety-nine-one-hundredths of our power. We do not care a rap for office. The men who belong to this League have a business of their own. We know that as young men it rests in some measure upon our shoulders and upon our hearts to stand thus just a little aloof from official position, to keep a sharp eye and a watchful thought upon everything that is transpiring in our municipality, and, however hard you and I together have jumped upon Tammany Hall, we are going to jump just exactly as hard on the Republican party if they need it. We do not know that they will need it. Still, they are liable to."

In referring to the victory that had been won, Dr. Parkhurst said:

"Now, friends, let us present to our minds in great brevity three or four things that still remain to be done. Do you realize that notwithstanding 40,000 or more majority by which we recently won over Tammany Hall, there are more than 100,000 men inside of this city that believe in a municipal government, as represented by such men as Divver, Sheehan, and dirty Koch? That is a fact that you and I have to take home and have sanctified to us. We cannot afford to forget the strength that lies in 100,000 men, even though they are defeated men, when they have time to gather together and rally for new effort. A hundred thousand is a good many. Now, one thing we have to do—you and I working together—we have got to go and help to convert them. I am not using the word in the evangelical sense, that would be a good deal too much—we have got to go to work and help to convert that 100,000 men, and taking the word convert in the sense I have intended, it is not such an impossible task."

The following portion of Dr. Parkhurst's speech shows that he was fully aware of the continued corrup-

tion of the police department, both during and after the
sessions of the Lexow Committee.

" We now come to a point or two that is a little more
touchy, but I think the easiest way to treat a difficult
question is to treat it frankly We have been afraid
that good use would not be made of our victory There
are sly enemies that are standing in our paths. Let us
drop the generalities and take the facts. You know
that more attention has been given by the Lexow Committee to the police department than any other I
suppose there is no question but that the searching inquisition that has been applied to the police department
should be applied to every other department in this
city. Now, here is a chance to do good work in a manner to secure permanent results I am speaking now
of the police department only as an illustration. The
temptation always is to mix that which is good with
that which is bad. We are to-day in a situation to do
work that shall reach all the way from the top clear
down to the bottom—for heaven's sake, why not do it?
Here is a department of our city government that has
been demonstrated to be rotten from the top down.
Notwithstanding the severe inquisition to which it has
been subjected, and notwithstanding the vote of repro-
bation which was passed on the 6th of November, that
department, all the way through from the top to the
bottom, is just exactly as rotten to-night as it was three
years ago. I wonder if you are aware of the fact that
since the 6th of November there has been a remarkable
and phenomenal outbreak of crime throughout many

precincts of the city. That is not exactly what you would call bringing forth fruits meet for repentance, is it?

"I trust when it comes time for Mr. Lexow and his Committee to frame a bill that shall be adjusted to the necessities of the case, they will see their way to legislate the entire force, from top to bottom, out of office. If you preserve any of the old virus, rely upon it that in a comparatively short space of time you will have the infection extending through the department. I know the answer is made that there are many honest men in the force, so there are. Legislating the force out of existence, however, does not rob us or deny us the possibility of taking those men and re-admitting them into the police department. And it is a far more simple and thorough way to sweep them out of existence, and then start fresh and replace in the force as many as it is thought best.

"There is another thing we want to see. I have always had to earn the salt of my porridge. I want to see a municipal administration that will make its employés earn the salt of their porridge. It is an undoubted fact that one great reason why there is always so much in the way of applications for positions under municipal, State, and National administration, is because it is understood there will be a maximum of pay and a minimum of work. I do not know why a man in the employ of this city should not earn his salary just as well as the rest of us.

"When the time comes that it is understood that the

employé of the city government has to earn his salary by conscientious and consecutive work. I believe the number of applicants for positions under such an administration will be wonderfully reduced.''

Dr. Parkhurst then made reference to some details of the work of the League. After that his remarks drifted to political bossism. He said: '' There were two points which, if made during the last campaign, were always sure to elicit a response from an audience, whether that audience were made up of Americans, Germans, Bohemians, Poles, Russians, or what not. These two points were, first, reference to Tammany Hall; and the second was reference to bosses. We have nothing to say in regard to the personal boss. We are not going to refer to Richard Croker or Thomas C. Platt. As I have remarked repeatedly, I do not know as there is much difference between a boss of one political complexion or the other. They are both of them unmitigatedly, unqualifiedly, and thoroughly destructive. I believe that the safety of our American institutions lies in the clear and honest appreciation on the part of each man that he has a right to stand up on his own feet, that he has a right to his own opinion, and that he has a right to express it. And I believe that one great object toward which we have to labor is the building up of that appreciation in the minds and hearts of each growing young man. There is a broad line to be drawn between a leader and boss; there always will be a leader. The leader is he who has the power of reproducing his own conceptions, his own ideas, in the minds of those that are in any way subordinated to his influence. The boss is the most sagaciously devised scheme that has yet been originated for the purpose of crushing out, weakening, and drying up individual personality, and therefore you and I, to our dying gasp, are going to fight the boss, whatever may be his professions of respectability. The more respectable he is, the more damnably dangerous he is."

During the doctor's remarks on political bosses there were numerous expressions of interest from all sides, and he was frequently interrupted by applause.

"You send your representatives to Albany," continued Dr. Parkhurst. "I think there is a good deal of a feeling that when our representative has been elected and is at Albany, the link of connection between himself and us is broken. Here is a very practical work you can do—never forget what that word representative means—the man who is a representative represents you and not himself. That being so, he is treasonable if he maintains ideas that are out of tune with those lying in the minds and hearts of his constituents. Therefore, count it a part of your religion to keep your eye on him, and remind him of the fact that he does not represent himself, but you. If you do not know, find out who is the representative of your district. Here is something definite you can do, and you can commence doing it to-morrow if you will, and you can make yourselves felt at Albany." In concluding, the doctor said : "Out of a heart that is tender, I do thank you for the wonderful way in which you have shown to me the kindness and tenderness of your own feeling. As long as God allows us to stand shoulder to shoulder, casting aside our own personal ambitions, thinking of one another and not of ourselves, thinking not of our own individual advancement, but thinking of the weal of our own town, thinking of the possibilities of our own municipal future, we will go on, more and more wisely I hope, more and more appreciatively I hope, but go on the same straight path, rejoicing in the privilege that is ours, of laying ourselves down, not dying, but living sacrifices upon the altar of our municipal good."

One of the features of the evening was an address by Rt. Rev. Henry C. Potter, Bishop of New York, and vice-president of the City Vigilance League, which is reproduced in full. Bishop Potter said: " We have assembled to honor Dr. Parkhurst : the letters we have read and what we have said have very imperfectly asserted what is in our hearts. And yet if you follow as I have the address which Dr. Parkhurst has just delivered, you must have felt, what has been a fact, that which he himself disclosed.

"I suppose Columbus was proud when he discovered America. I am not here to-night with such a great claim, but I discovered Dr. Parkhurst, and I will relate an incident which I do not think he himself has heard : One night at the Century Club—that place to which all good men go sooner or later—I was addressed by a deacon, who said, ' Bishop, we are looking for a minister down at the Madison Square Church, can you suggest anyone?' I said that I thought I could. I told him that I had visited Lenox, Mass., a few weeks before, and had heard while there a man who would, in my opinion, fill the bill. A committee was sent to Lenox and Dr. Parkhurst was called. I shall always therefore regard myself as his spiritual father. I would to God I had other sons of whom I could feel as proud. My brother, whose service to this city—yes, and to this country, for the value of what he has done can never be reckoned—my brother, whose service to this city has been so large, has often been challenged and criticised, as you well know, because it has been said he has stepped out of his calling. I wish to say to you that from first to last I believe he has held himself rigidly within it. No word that he has ever spoken, no act that he has ever done, has been inconsistent with his office and ordination as a minister of Jesus Christ. If we want justification of the course of our good brother here, we have it in the early John the Baptist, of whom he is the true successor. Let us hope that the heroism and prophetic foresight with which God has crowned him will make us willing always to follow his lead."

Bishop Potter's remarks were followed by great applause, after which Hon. Charles A. Schieren, Mayor of Brooklyn, made an address. Among other things, Mayor Schieren said: "I see the earnestness in your faces, I see that you realize what there is before you. You have only plowed the ground—the doctor has sowed some seed—but watch, the rains of heaven may come down, and they may prosper that ground. But with it will grow also the tares, they will spring up again. It is for you to see that the tares do not out-grow the good wheat.

"We are met here to-night to do honor to a hero of our day and time, one whose name is now a household word for purity in high places, and a just regard for that which is honest in sight of all men. He exposed a system of blackmailing and evil-doing that would have done credit to Sodom and Gomorrah in their palmiest days. In the face of discouragements and against the wish of his friends, he persevered until a moral senti-ment, which had long slumbered, was aroused, and he was hailed as a deliverer, and to many, many poor down-trodden outcasts he proved a savior. To him we are indebted for the ending of a system which had fastened itself upon the very vitals of our body-politic. The name of Dr. Parkhurst will be honored by this generation, and those yet to come will be roused up by his earnestness and manliness of Christian character."

Mayor Schieren was followed by Charles Stewart Smith, who made a few direct and pertinent remarks.

John W. Goff, the attorney of the Lexow Committee, made a few remarks, following Mr. Smith. He said:

"In my opinion, the best thing I ever did in my life was to ally myself with Dr. Parkhurst. He tries to ac-complish what the divine Master himself did. Some believe that men and women can be made virtuous by law, a thing that has always failed. What Dr. Park-hurst tried to do is to keep the enforcers of the law from combining with the breakers of the law. He has been called bigoted, low-minded, etc. Those who know

him know that in emergencies his heart is deep, and
throbs with softness and pity for those in distress. No
kinder heart ever beat in the breast of man for poor
fallen humanity than beats in the breast of Dr. Parkhurst."

Mr. Goff then traced the operations of the City Vigilance League from its inception, dwelling at length on
Dr. Parkhurst's great personal work.

Other speakers of the evening, all of whom referred
to Dr. Parkhurst in terms of highest praise, were Father
Ducey, Joseph H. Choate, and James C. Carter.

*   *   *

Dr. Parkhurst has told his friends that in speaking
as he continues to, and with earnestness and direct-
ness, he is simply continuing his warfare by agitation. He says that it may be necessary to continue
it for several years. He believes that in the past,
reform movements have failed because it has been
thought sufficient to make a revolution in the offices, to
turn one party out and put a new party in. His belief
is that revolutions of that kind are apt to do more
harm than good. Therefore he proposes to agitate, and
still to agitate, until he creates and maintains a public
sentiment which will be all-powerful. He declares that
the politicians never dare to disobey public sentiment
when they understand it, and he feels sure that after two
or three years of agitation they will so understand it as
not to stand in the way, but, on the contrary, to serve
it. With this knowledge of Dr. Parkhurst's purpose,
it is easy to see that he does not mean to allow his past

efforts to be wasted. He has still behind him powerful organized influences, and there is no doubt that on the whole public sentiment supports him, although there may have been some disposition to criticise the severity of some of his utterances. The good people of every community owe the great reformer a debt of gratitude. His crusade in New York was but the beginning of a series of investigations in which the *people* must win. Other cities of our fair land, though they have no Parkhurst, can follow Parkhurst's example and methods and free themselves from the grasp of the monster.

Long live Charles H. Parkhurst! His monument is erected while he lives!

THE PARKHURST HOME AND ITS MISTRESS.

CHAPTER IV.

Mrs. Parkhurst Her Husband's Counsellor and Helpmeet.—Her Early Life.—Her Education.—Her Administration of Manifold Duties.—Her Belief in Her Husband.—Her Methods of Helping Him.—The Administration of Her Household.—Her Charitable Projects.—Her Many Womanly and Wifely Characteristics.

WE cannot pass from a description of the life and work of the great crusader without a few remarks on the beautiful life of his wife, who we have seen was once his pupil and whom he married two years after severing his connections with the seminary of which he was a professor at the time she was a student.

The noble woman who has been Dr. Parkhurst's counsellor and helpmeet, in the true sense of the term, was born in the small and beautiful town of Charlemont, in Western Massachusetts. Her father and mother, Luther and Philena Bodman, were the sort of sturdy New England stock that believed in bringing up their children to a life of usefulness. and to live in the enjoyment of good health, good mind, and good morals, rather than idleness, pomp, and ostentation.

The home life of Ellen Bodman was particularly happy, and all its influences were those that tended to bring out the lovable and sunshiny side of her character. She was made thoroughly familiar with household duties in detail, and thus prepared for the arduous task of managing the household of a popular metropolitan pastor, which was to be hers in later life.

During her early life Mrs. Parkhurst was quite ill, and on this account her studies were interrupted, but her receptive brain and naturally bright intellect enabled her to make rapid acquisitions, so that, notwithstanding the interruption, she was as well educated at eighteen as any of her girl friends at that age. It was her aptness and fondness for study and her persevering application in the effort to make up what she had lost, that first attracted the attention of the young man Parkhurst while he was an instructor of Williston Seminary, which she attended. He was not slow to see the lovable side of her character as well as the practical. As we have seen, the attachment soon became mutual, and their marriage took place shortly after her graduation.

Mrs. Parkhurst was an active second to her husband's undertakings in his pastorate at Lenox, and when their work became more exacting in the larger field in New York, Mrs. Parkhurst seemed fully equal to the demands of increasing church duties and of charity, as well as the requirements of society and the administration of her household.

One of Mrs. Parkhurst's most sensible traits, and the one which has in no small degree contributed to the success of her husband, is her thorough sympathy with him in all he does. Her whole-souled faith in him leads her to so implicitly believe in all he undertakes, that her capabilities for good advice and practical assistance are most effectively exercised. From the beginning of Dr. Parkhurst's active life in the Society for the Suppression of Crime, down to his latest work in behalf of the City Vigilance League, and his independent work as an individual reformer, Mrs. Parkhurst has suffered to a degree that no one but the devoted wife of a public man against whom are hurled the threats and anathemas of a large and powerful body of unprincipled and almost unbridled law-breakers, can truly appreciate. Scarcely a day has passed since that first sermon, in which Dr. Parkhurst aroused the entire country to a realization of the corruption existing in New York, that threats and letters of harsh criticism have not been received in the Parkhurst daily mail.

Almost all of Dr. Parkhurst's mail passes through his wife's hands, and she, anxious to save her husband the humiliation of reading the criticisms of those whom he naturally looks upon as his friends and supporters, and any worriment which might be occasioned on account of profane and blasphemous threats, reads all his mail carefully, allowing him to see only those letters requiring his personal attention, answering or consigning to the fire those of which she feels capable of disposing. She also, to a considerable extent, regulates his newspaper reading. Parkhurst is not a man to be easily influenced, either by criticism or threat, but the bravest man is apt to falter if he finds his friends deserting him. It is safe to say that he has not seen one-half the criticisms that have been published concerning his personality, his purposes, and his work.

The Parkhurst home on Thirty-fifth Street, New York, is truly characteristic of its mistress. One can almost imagine he sees written above doors, "Welcome." There is an air of gentle hospitality which permeates the entire house. One cannot visit the Parkhurst home without a feeling of restfulness and ease. Mrs. Parkhurst has neither time nor inclination for what we call "fashionable society." Anyone is welcome to her drawing-room who comes in a respectful, honest spirit, come they in homespun or ermine. The amount of spiritual help and good advice which goes out daily from the Parkhurst house is a great and enduring monument to this truly good woman. She is also a liberal dispenser of charity at her home, though her high appreciation of the possibilities of organized charity leads her to devote the most of her time and means to several charitable organizations with which she is connected in an official capacity.

Her interests are more especially with the common people in her immediate vicinity. Hence her work in the Third Avenue Mission House, which is connected with her husband's church, is particularly enthusiastic. This institution is modeled to some extent after similar European organizations. A garden, employment bureau, sick visitation committees, and a soup kitchen are prominent features. There are also committees on other branches of parish work.

She has no children of her own, and many a little

waif unconsciously has this fact to thank for some special act of kindness on her part. All the warm affection of her womanly heart, which might otherwise have been lavished upon her own children, seems to go out to the children of the poor.

Mrs. Parkhurst is president of the American McCall Society. She is also president of one of the auxiliaries of the society, which is located in New York City.

Personally, Mrs. Parkhurst is hard to describe, unless we use that word so dear to the feminine heart—"lovely"—which, after all, means so much. On her quiet face are mirrored common-sense, and with it a singular sweetness. From her dark-brown eyes beams that womanly sympathy which has made many a poor unfortunate "take heart" and renew a seemingly hopeless struggle. There are no visible evidences in her handsome face of the strong will-power she possesses, and her manner does not suggest all that great executive ability which has enabled her so ably to second her husband and yet find time and improve opportunity for personal work.

Her uniformly good health has been a great blessing to her and her husband in the prosecution of that work to which their lives are devoted.

In summing up this brief sketch, which can only give a faint idea of the lovely life of this lovely woman, it is but suitable to say that she is in every sense womanly and wifely—characteristics which endear her to all American hearts.

LIFE OF DWIGHT LYMAN MOODY.

THE LIFE OF DWIGHT LYMAN MOODY.

CHAPTER I.

THE MOODY AND THE HOLTON FAMILIES. — THE TOWN OF NORTH-
FIELD, MASS. — THE BOYHOOD OF D. L. MOODY.

Lineage of the Moodys and the Holtons. — Description of Northfield. —
The Aborigines. — The House in which D. L. Moody was born. —
Mr. Edwin Moody. — His Death. — Impression on his Son. — Mrs.
Moody's Character and Trials. — Her Pastor. — Traits of D. L. Moody
in Boyhood. — A Trial to Mr. Everett. — Love for his Mother. —
His First Prayer. — His Work on the Farm. — His Boyish Pranks. —
He attempts to buy a Yoke of Oxen. — His Oldest Brother leaves
Home. — Anxiety of the Family. — Early Education. — Influences
under which Young Moody's Character was developed. — The Re-
mark of an Old Man. — The Story of a Money-loving Farmer.

"What manner of child shall this be?" — ST. LUKE.

"A mother's love is next to God's love." — D. L. MOODY.

THE celebrated evangelist Dwight Lyman Moody,
who now has gained a world-wide reputation as a herald
of the gospel, was born on the 5th day of February,
1837, in the beautiful town of Northfield, Franklin
County, Mass. His paternal grandfather, Isaiah Moody,
was born in 1772; went to Northfield about the year

17

1796, and it may have been from Hadley, where his brother Jacob lived, before he removed to Northfield. The whole fortune of Isaiah, it is stated, was "the horse he rode on, and his kit of tools in a bag." He was a mason by trade. He married Dec. 15, 1799, Phila, daughter of Medad Alexander, and died Feb. 20, 1835; Phila his widow died Nov. 1, 1869, aged 89. They had nine children, — five sons and four daughters. Their eldest son and child, Edwin, was born in Northfield Nov. 1, 1800, and died there May 28, 1841. He married Jan. 2, 1828, Betsey, daughter of Luther Holton. They, like his parents, had nine children, — seven sons and two daughters, — as follows: 1, *Edwin J.*, born Oct. 8, 1828, and died young; 2, *Cornelia M.*, born Feb. 26, 1832, and married Bigelow Walker of Worcester; 3, *George F.*, born June 17, 1833, and married Julia Johnson, (2) Harriet Brown; 4, *Edwin J.*, born June 26, 1834, and settled in Chicago, Ill.; 5, *Luther H.*, born Aug. 27, 1835; 6, *Dwight Lyman*, the subject of this memoir; 7, *Warren L.*, born Oct. 23, 1838, and settled at Elmira, N.Y.; 8, 9, *Samuel H.* and *Elizabeth C.* (twins), born June 24, 1841: the latter married Bryant Washburne.

We have not been able to connect this branch of the Moody family with those of the name in Hadley, though probably they belong to it. About the year 1660, Samuel Moody went from Hartford, Conn., to Hadley, where he died Sept. 22, 1689. His widow Sarah was a daughter of John Deming of Wethersfield, Conn., and died Sept. 29, 1717. This Samuel is supposed to have been the only child of Deacon John Moody of Hartford, Conn., who was son of George Moody of Moulton, County of Suffolk, Eng.; "a man," says the Candler MS., "famous for his housekeeping and just and plain dealing." This John Moody[1] came to New England in the year 1633, with his wife Sarah; and settled in Roxbury, Mass., where they became members of the church. He was made freeman Nov. 5, 1635. Sarah, widow of John, died at Hartford in 1671.

[1] The following is a verbatim copy from the Roxbury Church Records, p. 10, in the handwriting of the "Apostle Eliot," minister of the First Church in Roxbury : —

"John Moody. he came to the Land in the yeare 1633: he had no children * — he had 2 men servants y[t] were vngodly, especially one of them, who in his passion would wish himselfe in hell: & vse desperate words, yet had a good measure of knowledge — these 2 servants would goe to the oister bank in a boate, & did, against the counsell of theire governo[r], where they lay all night; & in the morning early when the tide was out they gathering oysters, did vnskillfully leave theire boate afloate In the verges of the chañell, & quickly the tide caryed it away so far in to the chañell y[t] they could not come neare it, wch maide them cry out & hollow, but being very early & remote were not heard, till the water had risen very high upon them to the arme hols as its' thought, & then a man frō Rockbrough meeting house hill heard them cry & call, & he cryed & ran wth all speed, & seing theire boate swam t᠎o it, & hasted to them, but they were both so drowned before any help could possibly come. a dreadfull example of God's displeasure against obstinate servāts.

Sarah Moody, the wife of John Moody."

* His son Samuel was subsequently born, It is supposed, In Hartford, where the father resided as early as 1639, as the following from the Colonial Records of Connecticut, under date of Aug. 1, 1639, shows: "Jno. Moody had an attachment graunted vppon the g[oods of Thomas] Gaines, in the hands of Mr. Stoughton, for a debt [of 5lb weight of Tobacco]."   T.

Betsey (Holton) Moody, the mother of Dwight Lyman Moody, was born in Northfield Feb. 5, 1805. She was the daughter of Luther and Betsey (Hodges) Holton. She was descended in the seventh generation from William Houlton, who in 1634, at the age of twenty-three, came from Ipswich, County of Suffolk, Eng., in the ship " Francis ; " was an original proprietor of Hartford, Conn., and in 1654 was of Northampton, Mass. He was ordained deacon of the first church in Northampton in 1663 ; was a representative to the General Court five years from Northampton, and one year from Hadley. He made the first motion in town-meeting to prohibit the sale of intoxicating drinks, and was the first commissioner to the General Court in Boston in that temperance effort. He died in Northampton, Aug. 12, 1691, at the advanced age of eighty years ; and his widow Mary, in the month of November following. His son John [2] was the father of William [3], whose son William [4] had a son Lemuel [5], born in 1749, and died Oct. 1, 1786 ; " a very worthy and valuable man," says the church record of Northfield. Luther [6], son of Lemuel [5], born in 1777, died Sept. 24, 1835 ; he married April 2, 1801, Betsey Hodges, who died Jan. 30, 1845, aged sixty-three. They had thirteen children, among whom were *Fanny*, born Aug. 6, 1803, married Oct. 16, 1825, Simeon P. Moody : *Betsey*, married Jan. 3, 1828, Edwin Moody ; these were the parents of Dwight Lyman Moody : *Martha* and *Mary* (twins) born June 11, 1809 the former married May 20, 1838, Zebulon Allen; the latter married Jan. 14, 1841, Lewis Ferrell of Greenfield: *Calvin*, born Oct. 11, 1811, married Susan, sister to Anson Burlingame: *Samuel Socrates*, married (1) October, 1843, Elizabeth J. Clapp of Boston, (2) Tryphenia S., her sister, (3) Nov. 24, 1859, Georgiana D., another sister: *Lemuel*, born Feb. 21, 1822, married in 1848 Maria Brown, (2) Amelia Smith.   Samuel S. and his brother Lemuel have long been engaged in business in Boston.[1]

The town of Northfield, in which the evangelist had his birth, is situated in the north-easterly part of Franklin County, Mass., and is noted for its picturesque and varied scenery.

The Connecticut River winds gracefully through a rich alluvial soil in the westerly section of the town; while various mountain-peaks, with charming valleys intervening, present delightful scenic views upon the right and left.   Several mountain streams, as the Squakeag and the Mill Brook, on the latter of which are the celebrated Glen Falls, glide through the landscape, set in motion here and there a saw-mill, and then enter the main river.

The principal street of Northfield extends along an elevated plain on the left bank of the river; and the

---

[1] The above sketches of the Moody and Holton families have been compiled chiefly from that excellent work, the History of Northfield, by J. H. Temple and George Sheldon, published by Joel Munsell, Albany, N.Y., 1875; and the chart of a portion of the Holton family, by David Parsons Holton, M.D., of New York City.

dwelling-houses, ornamented with gardens, fruit and forest trees, present a scene of quiet rural beauty such as a Shenstone or a Goldsmith might admire.

The population in 1875 was 1,641. The men are mostly farmers, — healthful, robust, independent; and their extensive herds, as well as ample barns, attest the

NORTHFIELD VILLAGE LOOKING NORTH.

fertility of the soil in this part of the beautiful valley of the Connecticut River.

The Massachusetts and Vermont Railway follows the direction of the main street; and at the centre, near the station, may be seen the two churches of the town, and the rural cemetery where the ashes of the Moody family repose. The Indian name of the place was *Squakeag;* and people from Hadley and Northampton

began to settle here as early as 1663.   Being, however,
on the frontier, they suffered greatly from the savages,
who saw with no good-will the encroachment of the
whites upon their territory.

Several assaults were made upon the settlement; and
the memory of one of them, in which Capt. Richard

NORTHFIELD VILLAGE LOOKING SOUTH.

Beers was killed, is perpetuated in the name of a
mountain in the southerly part of the town.

Some remains of the aborigines still appear, among
which are two Indian mounds about fifteen feet in
height, in the vicinity of the Moody place.   There is
also a ledge between the Moody place and the centre
of the town, which marks the spot where Mr. Aaron
Belding was killed by the Indians as late as 1748.

The town was incorporated Feb. 22, 1713, and is

noted as the birthplace of the Rev. Caleb Alexander
D.D. (1755–1828), author of several schoolbooks; and
of Joel Munsell, well known as a writer and an anti-
quarian publisher.

It is also noted as the residence of Timothy Swan,
composer of the original tune " China," who died here
July 23, 1842, at the advanced age of eighty-two
years.

The first minister of the place was the Rev. Benja-
min Doolittle, ordained in 1718; and among his parishioners were the Holton family, of whom William
Holton had been one of the committee appointed by
the General Court to lay out the town.

The house in which Dwight Lyman Moody was
born, and which is still occupied by his venerable
mother, is of two stories, and stands at a little distance from the main street, about a mile north of the
centre of the town, and about one-fourth of a mile east
of the Connecticut River. It is a plain, commodious
farmhouse, well shaded by some fine old rock-maple
trees, and having near it a pleasant garden and an
apple-orchard.

The view from this point is superb. The fair Connecticut River is seen for several miles sweeping along
down through the luxuriant meadows, and spanned
by a distant bridge; the grand old mountains raise
their wooded sides and isolated peaks on either hand;
while smiling valleys, in which flocks and herds are
feeding, serve to heighten the enchantment of the

scene. If delightful Alpine prospects have some tendency to invigorate and inspire the mind with vivid
and original ideas, then certainly to the early home
of the evangelist, may we not ascribe something of the
vigor and strength of thought which he now manifests?

The house was built by Mr. Lyman P. Moody, who
married Fanny Holton, sister of Mrs. Betsey (Holton)
Moody; and the parents of Dwight Lyman Moody came
to live in it soon after their marriage on the 3d of
January, 1828.

The little district schoolhouse, painted red, stood
near it; and a short distance northerly the Squakeag
Brook speeds merrily along into the river.

The house was then supplied with water by an aque-
duct from the mountains.

Mr. Edwin Moody, father of the evangelist, was a
strong, active, sensible man, who gained his livelihood
by working at stone-masonry and at farming. In form
and size his celebrated son resembles him. His wife
was a good manager, and noted for her sterling womanly
virtues; so that for some time after marriage their home
was prosperous, and they indulged the hope that the
wants of their increasing family would be well supplied. But by an unfortunate speculation Mr. Moody
lost a large part of his property; and while engaged in
laying stone on the twenty-eighth day of May, 1841,
he was suddenly seized with illness of which in a few
hours he died, — leaving a widow with six sons and a
daughter, the oldest of whom was but thirteen years of

BIRTHPLACE OF DWIGHT LYMAN MOODY.

age, and a homestead of a few acres which was heavily encumbered with debt.

About a month subsequent to the decease of the father, a boy and a girl (twins) were added to the family.

Dwight Lyman, who had been named from a friend of his father, was then a little more than four years old. "The first thing I remember," says Mr. Moody in an impressive sermon on the Prodigal Son, "was the death of my father. It was a beautiful day in spring time, when he fell suddenly dead. The shock made such an impression on me, young as I was, that I shall never forget it. I remember nothing about the funeral; but his death has made a lasting impression on me."

It was fortunate for him that he had a good mother. Almost all great men have had good mothers. Lamartine, Cowper, Wayland, Washington, had good mothers. It is the mother's gentle hand that traces the key-words of its destiny on the heart of the little child ; it is the mother's approving voice that wakens aspiration in the soul.

But, with nine small children in that fatherless home, what could Mrs. Moody hope to do?

With no income, with the burden of such a family, with no visible means of sustenance at her command, how could the very best of mothers keep from sinking under the oppressive weight? Whence were the food for so many little mouths, the shoes for so many little feet, to come?

To the God of the widow and the fatherless Mrs Moody went: and he sustained her.

Some of her friends advised her to give a part of her little ones away. But a good mother loves to have her children at her side; and so this noble woman determined to keep them all at home, and by rigid economy feed and clothe them as she could.

This period of her life was one of care and trial, such as the daughters of ease and affluence learn only from the fashionable romance; but out of such experience comes that nobility of soul that forms the fairest jewel in the crown of womanhood.

She kept the older children steadily employed in cultivating the garden, picking berries, apples, and chestnuts, which are abundant in that region, or in rendering assistance to the farmers of the neighborhood, who made the boys a fair compensation for their labor. She found in her pastor, the Rev. Oliver Capen Everett,[1] a sympathizing friend who took a lively interest in the welfare of her family. Her brothers and sisters kindly aided her in her struggles to sustain the household; and thus by her own incessant toil and forethought, by some assistance from the hands of the older children, by the encouraging words and aid of

---

[1] He was the son of Otis Everett, and was born Aug. 20, 1811; H.C. 1832; settled over the church at Northfield March 8, 1837, and was dismissed Nov. 26, 1848. He married May 25, 1837, Betsy, daughter of Daniel Weld of Boston, by whom he had Oliver Weld, Edward Franklin, Moses Williams, and Oliver Hurd. He was subsequently a minis ter at large in Charlestown, Mass.

her benevolent pastor, and the benefactions of her kindred, this brave woman managed to keep her fatherless group of boys and girls together, to send them to the little school near by, and to appear with them on the Lord's day in decent apparel at Mr. Everett's church and sabbath school.

It was the custom of Mrs. Moody to read and explain to her little ones the books which they brought home with them, and to instil into their tender minds the simple precepts of the gospel. She often repeated to them, as they were seated around the scanty board, some verse of Scripture, or of sacred poetry, which they said over till it was fairly fixed in memory.

If quarrels arose among them, she would go away and pray for them; and returning, as she subsequently said, "I found they would be all again good children."

In such a pious, indigent mountain home, and under the counsel of such a mother, the great evangelist of these modern times passed his boyhood.

In the hard school of poverty he had his early training; and for some minds this is the very best school.

As he advanced in age he became more helpful to his widowed mother, and was in the main obedient to her commands.

His health was good, his complexion ruddy, and his love of sport and play unbounded. Fearless and self-reliant, he used to climb the apple and the chestnut trees, coast down the hillsides, and engage in snowball contests with the larger boys, of whom he always longed to be the leader.

For work or books or music he evinced no specia. inclination. He learned to read, he worked upon the little farm to please his mother. His genius lay concealed beneath the ebullition of his animal spirits; and no one thought of him in his boyhood but as a rugged, headstrong, frolicsome lad, afraid of nothing, and always ready for some new prank or sport by which his wit or skill might be made manifest.

At one time Mr. Everett invited him to come and live with him as a boy of all work about the house; but the worthy minister soon found his patience tried by the innocent pranks and capers of his not very hopeful sabbath-school pupil, and returned him, after a few months' trial, to the counsels of his mother. Her heart was sometimes sorely tried with him; yet he sincerely loved her, and, when the moment for reflection came, was grieved at any pain he might have, in the exhilaration of his spirits, caused her.

This affection for his mother was the golden chain that saved him. He seems in boyhood to have had but little regard for any of his teachers, or but little faith in God. He believed only in himself and his dear mother. "He used to think himself a man," said she, "when he was only a boy." Yet, though he was so self-reliant, he esteemed that mother as the loadstone of his early life.

Once at least in those days he called on God for

help. An old fence had fallen upon him when alone, and was holding him a captive. "I tried and tried," said he, "but could not lift the heavy rails. I hallooed for help; but nobody came. Then I thought I should have to die away up there on the mountain all alone. But I happened to think that maybe God would help me, and so I asked him; and after that I could lift the rails."

This is his first recorded prayer. How faithfully he used to perform his work in boyhood, may be inferred from one of his illustrations of the manner in which some people read the Bible.

"When I was a boy," said he, "I worked on a farm; and I hoed corn so poorly that when I left off I had to take a stick, and mark the place, so I could tell the next morning where I had stopped the night before. If I didn't, I would, likely as not, hoe the same row over again."

He evidently was not fashioned for a farmer. His leading propensity, said one who knew him well in boyhood, was for sport; and to be first in this, was ever his constant aim. It is related of him, that on the death of an old cat he determined to honor its remains by holding funeral services over them; and so, inviting the children of the neighborhood together, he had the body borne into the schoolhouse near his home, and then performed himself the obsequies with an official dignity becoming the occasion.

Another juvenile freak may here be mentioned in attestation of the buoyancy of his young blood.

Following one day, with other boys, an honest farmer who was riding leisurely along, and noticing that he raised a jug of molasses-and-water to his lips to drink, young Moody hurled a ball, as quick as lightning, at the horse, which starting suddenly broke the vessel by the shock, and spattered the contents over the poor man's face. The mischievous boy, however, immediately commiserated him on the mishap, and atoned for the offence by asking pardon, and promising not to commit the same again.

At one period he spent several months with his aunt, Mrs. Lewis Farrell, in the neighboring town of Greenfield; and while living there he actually bargained for a yoke of oxen for the homestead, under the impression that he could easily borrow money enough to pay for them.

But his young life was not all sunshine. Unremitting labor, interrupted only now and then by a brief attendance at the district school, and by the sweet repose of the sacred sabbath, was the imperative necessity of his early days; and sometimes the sickness of his beloved mother, or some other sad event, would cast a gloomy shade over the humble home, repressing levity, and leading even the most buoyant to solicitude and reflection.

Among the most painful occurrences in the history of this family was the sudden departure of the oldest son from home. Mr. Moody most touchingly relates the circumstances in illustration of the parable of the Prodigal Son.

"My eldest brother, to whom my mother looked up to comfort her in her loneliness and in her great affliction, became a wanderer: he left home. I need not tell how that mother mourned for her boy, how she waited day by day, and month by month, for his return. I need not say how night after night she watched and wept and prayed. Many a time we were told to go to the post-office to see if a letter had not come from him; but we had to bring back the sorrowful words, 'No letter yet, mother.' Many a time have I waked up, and heard my mother pray, 'O God, bring back my boy!' Many a time did she lift her heart up to God in prayer for her boy. When the wintry gale would blow around the house, and the storm rage without the door, her dear face would wear a terribly anxious look, and she would utter, in piteous tones, 'O my dear boy! perhaps he is now on the ocean this fearful night. O God, preserve him!' We would sit round the fireside of an evening, and ask her to tell us about our father, and she would talk for hours about him; but, if the mention of my eldest brother should chance to come in, then all would be hushed: she never spoke of him but with tears. Many a time did she try to conceal them, but all would be in vain; and, when Thanksgiving Day would come, a chair used to be set for him

"Our friends and neighbors gave him up; but our mother had faith that she would see him again. One day, in the middle of summer, a stranger was seen approaching the house.

"He came up on the east piazza, and looked upon ny mother through the window. The man had a long beard; and, when my mother first saw him, she did not start or rise. But, when she saw the great tears trickling down his cheeks, she cried, 'It's my boy, my dear, dear boy!' and sprang to the window. But there the boy stood, and said, 'Mother, I will never cross the threshold until you say you forgive me.' Do you think he had to stay there long? No, no: her arms were soon around him, and she wept upon his shoulder, as did the father of the prodigal son. I heard of it while in a distant city, and what a thrill of joy shot through me! But what joy on earth can equal the joy in heaven when a prodigal comes home?"

An aptitude to learn the elements of literature at school in early life is by no means a sure indication of superior genius in the pupil. Many a boy, pronounced a dunce by his dogmatic teachers, has arisen to commanding intellectual eminence. There are higher lessons than the grammar and arithmetic afford; there are more potent voices than the schoolroom ever sends into the listening ear of boyhood. A mother's love, for instance, touches chords within the soul which even the most faithful teacher never reaches. Then, too, the book of this grand, living, mysterious nature, so fresh, so varied, and so charming, wakens thought and aspiration in the plastic soul, and gives to it the elements of such an education as the most assiduous drilling in the schools can never, of itself alone, impart. The schools can make a doctor of divinity, but never a divine.

It is a mistake to say that Dwight Lyman Moody is uneducated. Of scholastic training he had, indeed, not much, for the lessons of his school-teachers — Mr. Bruce and others — were generally unheeded; yet even in his earliest boyhood he was a quick and keen observer of the strange and busy world around him. The tender lessons of his mother were not lost on him; the sorrows of his family sunk through the effervescence of his spirits, deep into his heart. The tolling of the death-bell, the roar of the mountain wind, the fall of the snowflake, the germination of the seed in springtime, the flight of the birds, the rustling of the leaves in autumn, the current of the noble river, the flowing tide of busy life in Northfield, bright in hope, or dark in sorrow, made indelible impressions on his mind.

He received such teachings, pondered over them till they became a part of his own being. He was a learner in the higher sense, — taking his instructions fresh and free, instead of second-hand through books, from life and nature. Hence his originality and power. His apt allusions to the scenes and incidents of his early days, his fine illustrations drawn from memories of childhood, clearly show that he was then a learner, — I had almost said *the* learner of that period, — and that something higher and nobler than what the schools alone can teach is needed for the attainment of commanding power over the minds of men.

This he acquired in part while nurtured in the pinching penury of his mountain home.

Though joyous in his temperament, restive and surcharged with the love of fun and frolic, young Moody was not really vicious; and it is erroneous to suppose that he had no deep religious impressions in his early days. The atmosphere he breathed was flavored with religion. The words of his dear mother were choice seeds of truth sown in his heart. The instructions of the sabbath school, the prayers of Mr. Everett, with here and there a word of Christian counsel, the vicissitudes of life, and the doings of death around him, served sometimes to turn his thoughts to serious things, to awaken aspirations after goodness, and to enrich his soul with imagery and emotions which he now recalls with fine effect for the illustration of religious truth.

"I remember when I was a boy," said Mr. Moody in one of his effective sermons, "I went several miles from home with an older brother. That seemed to me the longest visit of my life. It seemed that I was then farther away from home than I had ever been before, or have ever been since. While we were walking down the street, we saw an old man coming toward us; and my brother said, 'There is a man who will give you a cent. He gives every new boy that comes into this town a cent.' That was my first visit to the town; and when the old man got opposite to us he looked around, and my brother not wishing me to lose the cent, and to remind the old man that I had not received it, told him that I was a new boy in the town The old man,. taking off my hat, placed his trembling hand on my head, and told me I had a Father in heaven. It was a kind, simple act, but I feel the pressure of the old man's hand upon my head to-day."

The impression which the village bell, when tolling out the number of the years that any one deceased had lived, made on his mind, is thus vividly referred to: "I well remember how I used to look on Death as a terrible monster; how he used to throw his dark shadow across my path; how I trembled as I thought of the terrible hour when he should come for me; how I thought I should like to die of some lingering disease, such as consumption, so that I might know when he was coming. It was the custom in our village to toll from the old church bell the age of any one who had died. Death never entered that village, and tore away one of the inhabitants, but I counted the tolling of the bell. Sometimes it was seventy, sometimes eighty, sometimes it would be away down among the teens, sometimes it would toll out the death of some one of my own age. It made a solemn impression upon me. I felt a coward then. I thought of the cold hand of Death feeling for the cords of life. I thought of being launched forth to spend my eternity in an unknown land.

"As I looked into the grave, and saw the sexton

throw the earth on the coffin-lid, 'Earth to earth, ashes to ashes, dust to dust,' it seemed like the death-knell to my soul. But that is all changed now. The grave has lost its terror. As I go on towards heaven, I can shout, 'O death! where is thy sting?' and I hear the answer rolling down from Calvary, 'Buried in the bosom of the Son of God.'"

The flower-bud of religion had not then appeared in his heart; but the sod was broken, and the seed was germinating.

A story told to young Moody by a farmer working with him left a very serious impression on his mind. and may be considered as one of the many influences that led to his conversion.

"Before I left the farm," says the evangelist, "I was talking one day to a man who was working there, and who was weeping. I said to him, 'What is the trouble?' And he told me a very strange story. When he started in life, he left his native village, and went to another town to find something to do, and was unsuccessful. The first sabbath he went to a little church; and the minister preached from the text, 'Seek ye first the kingdom of God;' and he thought the text and the sermon were for him. He wanted to get rich; and, when he was settled in life, he would seek the kingdom of God. He went on, and the next sabbath he was in another village. It was not long before he heard another minister preach from the same text, 'Seek ye first the kingdom of God.' He thought surely some one must have been speaking to the minister about him; for the minister just pictured him out. But he said, when he got settled in life, and had control of his time, and was his own master, he would then seek the kingdom of God.

"Some time after, he was at another village, and here went to church again; and he had not been going a great while when he heard the third minister preach from the same text: 'Seek ye first the kingdom of God, and his righteousness, and all things else shall be added.' He said it went right down into his soul; but he calmly and deliberately made up his mind that he would not become a Christian until he had got settled in life, and owned his farm. This man said, 'Now I am what the world calls rich. I go to church every Sunday; but I have never heard a sermon, from that day to this, which has ever made any impression on my heart. My heart is as hard as a stone.' As he said that, tears trickled down his cheeks. I was a young man, and did not know what it meant. When I was converted I thought, when I should go back home, I would see this man, and preach Christ to him. When I went back home, I said to my widowed mother, naming the man, 'Is he still living in the same place?' My mother said, 'He is gone mad, and has been taken away to the insane-asylum; and to every one that goes to see him he points his finger, and says, "Seek ye first the kingdom of God."' I thought I should like to see him; but he was so far gone it would do no good.

The next time I went home he was at his home, idiotic. I went to see him. When I went in I said, ' Do you know me ? ' He pointed his finger at me, and said, ' Young man, seek ye first the kingdom of God.' God had driven the text into his mind, but his reason was gone. Three years ago, when I visited my father's grave, I noticed a new stone had been put up. I stopped, and found it was my friend's. The autumn wind seemed whispering that text, ' Seek ye first the kingdom of God.' "

CHAPTER II.

> "God is able to make him stand." — ST. PAUL.

> "Oh, happy day that fixed my choice
>   On thee, my Saviour and my God!
> Well may this glowing heart rejoice,
>   And tell its raptures all abroad." — DR. DODDRIDGE.

IN the midst of such circumstances, and under such influences, this country lad grew up till the age of seventeen years. He was compactly built, robust and vigorous, self-reliant, reckless; yet attentive to his mother's wishes, and always ready to confess his errors

During his last term at the winter school, he had an altercation with his teacher, who decided to expel him, but, his mother interceding in the matter, he promised to amend, and so for the first time applied himself to study. He continued docile until the session, and with it his scholastic education, closed.

He then determined to seek his fortune in the world.

Elate with hope, he invested himself in his best clothes, bade his mother good-by, and, with a few dollars in his pocket, left the beautiful scenes of his boyhood, and took the cars for Boston. On arriving in the city, he made his way to the shoe-store of his uncle, Samuel S. Holton, who then was doing business at No. 43 Court Street. On a visit to Northfield the preceding winter, Mr. Holton had declined to receive young Moody into his establishment, fearing that his waywardness under the temptations of the city might result in trouble: his surprise was therefore great on seeing the verdant youth before him at his counter. He inquired kindly as to the welfare of the family, but did not offer Dwight a place; and he himself had too much pride to make again solicitation. Disappointed in his expectations, he set himself to searching through the city, as many a youth has done in vain, for some kind of employment. Every place seemed to be filled; and the hard word, " No one wanted here," met him at every application.

He went over, and tried the City of Lowell with no better success. He then resolved to travel on foot (for his funds were running low) to New York City, in which perhaps he might find fortune more propitious; when happening to discuss the matter with another uncle, Mr. Lemuel Holton, in whose house he lodged at night, a conversation similar to this ensued: "Why don't you ask your uncle Samuel for a situation?"— "Because," replied the high-spirited youth, "I think he ought to make the offer himself."—"But," continued his uncle, "if you consider the place worth having, then certainly it is worth asking for. Go and ask for it."—"He ought to ask me," rejoined the boy; but, his pride somewhat abating by the recollection of his unsuccessful efforts, he added, "I'll go and see him." He went; and his uncle Samuel, who felt the liveliest interest in his welfare, agreed to take him into his store on these four conditions: namely, that he should board in such a family as Mr. Holton, who had then removed to Winchester, should approve; that he should attend the Mount Vernon Church and sabbath school; that he should not visit questionable places of amusement; and that he should be guided by the advice of his employer. These were reasonable requirements; to them Mr. Holton's wayward nephew readily assented, and commenced his labors as a boy of all work in the store. He boarded for a while with Deacon Levi Bowers, in Allen Street; and afterwards with Mrs. David Beal, a pious lady, then living at No. 5 Eaton Street.

A photograph of the young clerk, taken at this

period, is preserved. He appears in an overcoat buttoned up to the neck, and a high cloth cap, with a beardless face expressive of the satisfaction which his good looks and his handsome dress afforded him.

In the store he soon made himself decidedly useful, and became a salesman. He exhibited the three prime qualities of a good clerk, — obedience, honesty, activity; and his uncle had no reason to complain to him of any failure to fulfil the four conditions under which he received him into his employ.

His wages were but small; and, with his love of dress, he often found his pockets empty.

His home at Northfield he kept constantly in memory; and his greatest source of comfort was the reception of a letter from some member of the family.

"I remember," says he in one of his most characteristic sermons, "when I first left home, and went to Boston, I had spent all my money; and I went to the post-office three times a day. I knew there was only one mail a day from home; but I thought, by some possibility, there might be a letter for me. At last I got a letter from my little sister, and I was awful glad to get it. She had heard that there were a great many pickpockets in Boston; and a large part of that letter was to have me be very careful not to let anybody pick my pocket. Now, I had got to have something in my pocket in order to have it picked. So you have got to have salvation before you can work it out."

Young Moody attended the Mount Vernon Church,

then one of the most progressive in the city, and listened with more or less attention to the sermons of its
eloquent pastor.   He also entered a sabbath-school
class taught by Mr. Edward Kimball, an earnest and
intelligent Christian.   For some time he was a silent
pupil; but one day he arrested the attention of his
teacher by the odd question, " That Moses was what
you call a pretty smart man, wasn't he ? "   Mr. Kimball then resolved to visit his country pupil at his
place of business.   He entered Mr. Holton's store, and
in his friendly manner laid his hand on young Moody's
shoulder.   The touch went to his heart.   " I can feel,"
says the evangelist, " the touch of that man's hand on
my shoulder even yet."   After some inquiries, Mr.
Kimball said to him, " Will you not give your heart to
Jesus ? "

That question moved the soul of the attentive clerk :
it led him to desire to be a Christian.   It was the pivot,
as it were, on which his destiny was hinging.   " Yes,"
mused he with himself, " I will consecrate myself to
the service of my God ; " and that decision, made in
earnest, was soon followed by a declaration of his
intent to live a Christian life, and to induce other men
to follow his example.

Of the kindly interest Mr. Kimball manifested in his
spiritual welfare, Mr. Moody always speaks with deep
emotion ; and nothing ever gave him more pleasure
than to see two of his sabbath-school teacher's children
come to Christ through his own persuasion.

MOUNT VERNON CHURCH.

"I am glad to see you," said Mr. Moody after one of his services, to a young man who introduced himself as a son of Mr. Kimball. "Are you a Christian ? "

"No, sir."

"How old are you ? "

"Seventeen years."   .

"Just my age when your father led me to the Saviour; and that was just seventeen years ago this very day. Now I desire to pay him by leading his son to Christ. Come, let us pray together." Soon afterwards the son of Mr. Kimball became a Christian.

When young Moody had decided on a religious course of life, he at once resolved to let his light shine forth. He commenced speaking in the social meetings, but his ungrammatical words and broken sentences were not always acceptable; he had more in his heart than he could express in language. He met with many obstacles in the beginning of his life in Christ. His uncle Samuel and his excellent aunt Holton, however, encouraged him to continue in the course that he had chosen: so he went on telling his friends what Christ had done for his soul, as he had opportunity, and on the 16th of May, 1855, applied for admission to the church. He was examined by the committee; but, failing to satisfy them as to the genuineness of his conversion, he was kindly advised to wait a while in order that they might give the subject more consideration. In the roughness of the setting, the diamond was not discovered; and he certainly at that time had but a limited knowledge of the principles of Christianity. The committee acted wisely, and courteously proffered to him instruction for which he is ever grateful. This delay in receiving him into fellowship Mr. Moody now considers one of the most fortunate circumstances of his life. He was again examined March 12, 1856, and admitted to the church.

One of the committee said recently, in a letter to a friend, " I am glad to sit at his feet, and learn now how to serve our Lord and Master." [1]

[1] The record of Mr. Moody's examination is copied from the church register. The language here used indicates more knowledge of religion than he then possessed; for the statements were put in the form of questions by the committee, to which he replied in general by the monosyllables " yes " or " no."

" No. 1079. Dwight L. Moody. — Boards 43 Court St. Has been baptized. First awakened on the 21st April [16th May]. Became anxious about himself. Saw himself a sinner; and sin now seems hateful, and holiness desirable. Thinks he has repented. Has purposed to give up sin. Feels dependent upon Christ for forgiveness. Loves the Scriptures. Prays once a day. Desires to be useful. Religiously educated. Been in the city a year. From Northfield, this State. Is not ashamed to be known as a Christian. 18 years old.

" No. 1131. March 12, 1856. — Thinks he has made some progress since he was here before, — at least in knowledge. Was then very ignorant of the Bible. Has maintained his habits of prayer and reading the Bible. Believes God will hear his prayers. Does not think of Christ as often as he ought. Believes Christ has suffered a great deal for us, but does not feel it much. Is fully determined to adhere to the cause of Christ always. Feels that it would be very bad if he should join the Church and then turn. Thinks he cannot live without sinning. Must repent of sin, and ask forgiveness for Christ's sake. Will never give up his hope, or love Christ less, whether admitted to the Church or not. His prevailing intention is to give up his will to God.

" Admitted May 4, 1856.

It is related by Dr. Savage of Chicago, that at the close of one of Mr. Moody's great meetings in Exeter Hall, London, he exclaimed in his blunt way, —

" I see in the house an eminent Christian gentleman from Boston. Deacon Palmer, come right forward to the platform: the people want to hear from you." Reluctantly the deacon came upon the platform, and began by saying that he had known Mr. Moody at home, and, had, indeed belonged to the same church with him; when Mr. Moody, suddenly interrupting him, cried out, " Yes, deacon ; and you kept me out of that church for many months, because you thought I did not know enough to join it."

When the laughter of the audience had subsided, Deacon Palmer happily replied, that " all must agree with him that it was a great privilege to have received Mr. Moody into the church at all, even though with great misgivings and after long delay."

It is not true that Dr. Kirk or any member of his church advised Mr. Moody not to speak in the meeting. In a letter referring to this point, and signed by Messrs. A. Cushing, J. W. Kimball, J. M. Pinkerton, J. S. Ward, J. D. Leland, and J. C. Tyler, members of that church, they say, " We have no reason to believe that either the pastor or any member of the church ever by word or act discouraged his efforts." The first time Mr. Moody spoke in public, after his conversion, was at a city mission meeting among the poor at the North End. It was after his removal to Chicago, that he was advised not to speak in public.

On seeing the work of the evangelist in Chicago, several years ago, Dr. Kirk said on his return to Mr. Samuel S. Holton, "I told our people last night that we ought to be ashamed of ourselves for our inactivity. There is that young Moody, who we thought did not know enough to be a member of our church, exerting a greater influence for Christ than any other man in the great North-West."

Still it must be borne in mind, that Mr. Moody gave the church but little reason to hope that he would become an eminent Christian worker. " I can truly say," writes Mr. Edward Kimball, " and in saying it I magnify the infinite grace of God as bestowed upon him, that I have seen few persons whose minds were spiritually darker than was his when he came into my Sunday-school class; and I think the committee of the Mount Vernon Church seldom met an applicant for membership more unlikely ever to become a Christian of clear and decided views of gospel truth, still less to fill any extended sphere of public usefulness." Mr. Moody remained in my class about two years, till he bade me good-by on leaving Boston for Chicago.

Boston proved to be a very good school for this rustic youth. In body, mind, and manners, he arose during his two and a half years' residence here to a higher standard. He also acquired the art of selling goods with alacrity, and in accordance with the Golden Rule. His uncles, Samuel S. and Lemuel Holton, were men of probity and piety. He was led by their example, as well as counsel, to deal honestly, to live soberly, and to cherish an aspiration not only to do good, but also to be good. The eloquence of his pastor, Dr. Kirk, enchanted him; and Mr. Kimball's kind solicitations for his spiritual welfare touched his heart.

The anti-slavery question, then intensely agitated in the city, awakened his attention; and he boldly advocated in his way the liberation of the bondman. During the presidential campaign in 1856, he took a lively interest in the contest, and was often seen in front of Mr. Holton's store distributing or selling the portrait of John C. Fremont to the people as they passed along the street. His companions, Palmer, Gale, and others, exercised a benign influence over him; his rude attempts at speaking in the social meetings quickened his intellectual faculties; and the whole tenor of Boston life, as he beheld it, tended to the improvement of his manners and his heart: so that when he left the city for Chicago he had reached a much higher level than he occupied when he went forth from his widowed mother's home, in 1855, to seek his fortune in the world. He was, moreover, a Christian with a will to dare and a hand to do any thing to which the Lord might call him. Under one point of view, Boston was the university in which he studied: it is the place where he was converted, and where he began to exercise his wonderful gift as a public speaker. Nor were his rude utterances here entirely fruitless; for he says in one of his recent discourses: —

"I remember once, when I was first converted, I spoke in a sabbath school, and there seemed to be a great deal of interest, and quite a number rose for prayer; and I remember I went out quite rejoiced. But an old man followed me out: I have never seen him since; he caught hold of my hand, and gave me a little bit of advice. I didn't know what he meant at the time, but he said, 'Young man, when you speak again, honor the Holy Ghost.' I was hastening off to another church to speak; and, all the way over, it kept ringing in my ears, — ' Honor the Holy Ghost.' "

Though his heart beats warmly towards the city of Chicago, where so much of his life's work has been accomplished, Mr. Moody will ever love Boston as the spot where he first gave himself to the service of his Master; and he doubtless feels in the hearty welcome which he now receives, and in the eagerness with which all classes throng to hear him, ample compensation for any want of sympathy he might have once experienced. From 1856 to 1877, perhaps no living man has made a change so unexpected and so wonderful.

Of Boston he would now perhaps in spirit say, " In a certain sense, I look upon it as my home. Entering it when a boy in search of an occupation, and gaining here my first knowledge of men and business, as well as of that religion which has since been such a joy to me, I cannot hear the dear old city named, but that some memories of my early life will come to me that

I shall always cherish. Though, during many years past, other places and other associations have occupied my mind, still neither these, nor the lapse of time itself, have lessened the deep interest I feel in Boston."

It was in September, 1856, that young Moody, then in his twentieth year, made up his mind to seek his fortune in the rising city of Chicago; and on his arrival there he easily found a situation as a salesman in the boot and shoe store of Mr. Wiswall on Lake Street. It has been stated that the unkindly criticisms he received in Boston led him to go West; yet the love of adventure, coupled with the hope of making money, was undoubtedly the real motive.

Soon after his arrival in Chicago he united by letter with the Plymouth Congregational Church, and began to speak in the sabbath school and social meetings. Though his uncouth language sometimes gave offence, his originality and force were at once admitted. He hired four pews in the Plymouth Church, and hunted up young men and boys to fill them. This was the commencement of that missionary work of which he subsequently became the apostle in Chicago. But he longed to be a teacher, and he soon opened himself the way for it.

Entering a little Sunday school in North Wells Street, he said to the superintendent, —

"Would you, sir, like to have another teacher here?"

"No, I thank you," he replied: "we have almost as many teachers now as pupils."

" There is, then, no chance for me ? "

" Yes, indeed there is, if you will bring your pupils
with you."

The face of the young salesman brightened as he left
the school; and on the following sabbath he returned
to it, attended by nearly a score of ragged children that
he had recruited from the lanes and highways of the
city; and with this motley group he began his work as
a teacher in the sabbath school, averring, that, since
these neglected ones had souls to save, it was the duty
of the Christian " to go in for them."

CHAPTER III.

"Go out into the highways and hedges, and compel them to come in."

JESUS CHRIST.

"Only an armor-bearer, now in the field,
Guarding a shining helmet, sword, and shield;
Waiting to hear the thrilling battle-cry,
Ready then to answer, ' Master, here am I.' " — P. P. BLISS.

THE city of Chicago, then containing about 175,000
people of various nationalities, little dreamed of the
benison it was receiving when the young Christian
clerk, Dwight L. Moody, entered it. Rough and ignorant, to be sure, he was; but his counsellor was the

Lord, his guide the Bible. This precious book he carried in his bosom; he studied it as a message sent direct to him from heaven. He received its teachings, not as questionable or mythical, but as real, practical, and obligatory. It was the voice of God speaking into the innermost chambers of his soul. It meant precisely what it said; and this he felt must be translated by him, just as far as he had power, into immediate practice. He was and is emphatically a man of ONE BOOK, and this the best one. By it his ends were shaped, by it his mental powers were quickened, by it his steps were guided.

It is true that Mr. Moody at this period was but a novice in religion, but a tyro in the study of the Scripture; but he had found out and felt the grandeur of the truth that every man, however abject and immured in sensualism, had an immortal soul in need of cleansing, and that he himself was sent into the world to labor as he could, and where he could, to bring any that would hear him to a knowledge of the Saviour.

His time, however, was mostly engrossed as a salesman in the Lake-street store, where he evinced that good practical common sense and capacity for business which secured the approbation of his employer. On being promoted to a position in the jobbing department of the store, Mr. Moody found, while seeking customers at various public places in the city, more opportunities to work for Jesus; and, happening to make the acquaintance of J. B. Stillson in the spring of 1857, the two, as Paul and Silas, toiled together for the Lord; and visiting, as they could, the poor and destitute, assisted in establishing or augmenting many mission sabbath schools during the ensuing season.

But this was not enough for the irrepressible evangelist: he desired to have a sabbath school of his own; and so, plunging in amongst gambling-dens and other vicious haunts of the notorious "Sands" in the northern section of the city, he hired a wretched old saloon for a school on Sundays and for meetings in the evening.

This was the roughest section, the "Five Points," of Chicago: the people were rude, intemperate, degraded; the children ragged, rollicksome, and unmanageable. They could be brought into the school only by the distribution of sugar-plums, toys, and other kindred allurements; they could be kept in school only by the most dexterous management. As to order, that was at first out of the question. They could neither read nor write; they knew nothing of restraint or of good behavior. They came together a disorderly mob of mischievous urchins, unwashed, unkempt, uncivilized, and ready for any kind of roguery. What could be done in that old rickety building, destitute of seats or any of the furniture of the modern sabbath school? Well, the tact and energy that gathered them from their miserable homes controlled and gradually interested them. Mr. Moody in his heart loved children: he understood them; he had patience to bear with them; and he soon found the means of making them love him. By the aid of music from his friend Tiudeau, of stories by himself, of prayers when he could keep them still enough to hear, of maple sugar, of pictures and apt speeches from good Mr. Stillson, he by degrees succeeded in bringing order out of chaos, in gaining the affection of his pupils, and in making his mission-school the sensation of that degraded section of the city.

"The first meeting I ever saw him at," said Mr. Reynolds recently, "was in a little old shanty that had been abandoned by a saloon-keeper. Mr. Moody had got the place to hold a meeting in at night. I went there a little late; and the first thing I saw was a man standing up with a few tallow candles around him, holding a negro boy, and trying to read to him the story of the Prodigal Son; and a great many words he could not make out, and had to skip. I thought, 'If the Lord can ever use such an instrument as that for his honor and glory, it will astonish me.' After that meeting was over, Mr. Moody said to me, 'Reynolds, I have got only one talent; I have no education; but I love the Lord Jesus Christ, and I want to do something for him: I want you to pray for me.' I have never ceased, from that day to this, to pray for that devoted Christian soldier. I have watched him since then, have had counsel with him, and know him thoroughly; and, for consistent walk and conversation, I have never met a man to equal him. It astounds me to look back and see what Mr. Moody was thirteen years ago, and then what he is under God to-day, — shaking Scotland to its very centre, and reaching now over to Ireland. The last time I heard from him, his injunction was, ' Pray for me every day; pray now that God will keep me humble.' "

Mr. Moody looked upon every boy and girl, however rude and ragged, as a jewel for him to seek, save, and finally present to his Lord and Master. Hence he entered fearlessly the dens of infamy in search of them; he induced some of his Christian friends to do the same; his school continued to increase in numbers and in popularity; a larger room was needed, and at length permission was obtained of Mayor Haines to occupy the ample hall of the old North Market. This was used for dancing, and there were in it no chairs nor benches; so that the motley group was obliged to stand beside the walls, or sit promiscuously, as in the Eastern climes, upon the floor. A prominent Christian merchant, Mr. John V. Farwell, lent his aid to furnish the hall with seats; and, on visiting the school the ensuing sabbath, was surprised to hear himself nominated by Mr. Moody, and appointed by the clamorous throng, their superintendent. He had the grace to accept the office. This enabled Mr. Moody and his co-worker Stillson to scour the wretched region called " the Sands " for raw recruits; and so effectually did they labor in this line, so persistently did they hold prayer-meetings in every shanty and saloon to which they gained access, so wisely did they select instructors, and so admirably, in conjunction with their generous superintendent and Mr. Trudeau the sweet singer, did they manage the school, that within a year it had an average number of more than six hundred pupils. These were divided into as many as eighty classes, which teachers from the various churches in the city volunteered to instruct. The school became a curiosity, and at every session there were persons present who had come from far to see it. " The city missionary," says Mr. Stillson, " began to be alarmed for it, lest, being worked at such a high pressure, it should blow up." But the sterling sense of Deacon Moody, as the children called him, was a guaranty for that. During the six years of its existence, it is estimated that an average of about two thousand children annually belonged to it; and who but God can tell the fruit that seeds of truth there sown shall bring ?

The history of that North Market Mission School is more like a romance than a reality. It was carried on by men who had burning in their hearts the principle that Christ came to save the lost, and that it is the duty of the follower of Christ to go and seek for them. The stirring incidents in that special work would fill a volume. Of Mr. Moody's energy in his school, one writer says, " I have rarely beheld such a scene of high-pressure evangelization. It made me think irre-sistibly of those breathing steamboats on the Missis-sippi, that must either go fast or burst. Mr. Moody himself moved energetically about the school most of the time, seeing that everybody was at work, throwing in a word where he thought it necessary, and inspiring every one with his own enthusiasm. As soon as the classes had been going on for a specific number of minutes, he mounted a platform, rang a bell, and addressed the children. He is a keen, dark-eyed man, with a somewhat shrill voice, but with thorough earnestness of manner and delivery. His remarks were few, but pointed and full of interrogation."

As Mr. Moody could not hold evening services in the hall, he repaired to his old saloon; and calling the abandoned and the lost together, and placing a policeman at the door, he by heartfelt appeals, suited to their various capacities, implored them to leave their vicious courses, and commence a new life in Jesus.

It is to be remembered, that while Mr. Moody was carrying on this efficient work for Christ, he was still performing his full share of business in the jobbing department of the Lake-street store. He was ever on the alert for customers, and as sharp as steel at a bargain, although no one ever charged him with dishonesty. One of his old employers said, —

"We regarded him as an excellent salesman, but a poor judge of credits. In one particular instance he sold goods amounting to over two hundred dollars, to a man whom we found rated as 'doubtful' in the Mercantile Directory; and we therefore refused to send the goods. But Moody at once came to the rescue of his customer, declared him to be as good as the Bank of England, and offered to be responsible for the bill. Or, this we sent the goods; and when the money was due, sure enough, it was Moody who paid it."

In 1858 he entered the store of Mr. C. N. Henderson, and became to some extent a commercial traveller; always arranging his business, however, so as to be at home to manage his beloved mission-school on the sabbath. In the mean time he continued to study, as he could, the Bible. Other books, such as "The Life of Trust," were recommended to him : he would turn over a few pages, and then again take up his precious Bible.

When not engaged in business in the store, he was often still and thoughtful; but, on entering the room occupied by himself and several other clerks at night, he would engage with them in practical jokes and lively conversation, always, however, advocating total abstinence, and denouncing any amusement that might lead to habits of dissipation. On retiring to rest, he used to open his well-worn Testament, and read himself to sleep. "This," said one of the number to the writer, "was then, with us (bad grammar excepted), his only singularity."

After the death of Mr. Henderson, Mr. Moody went into the store of Buel, Hill, and Granger; but, finding his love of missionary work increasing, he at length concluded to devote his whole time to it, trusting in the Lord for his support.

" I have decided," said he to Mr. B. F. Jacobs, " to give to God all my time."

" But how are you going to live ? " replied his friend.

" God will provide for me, if he wishes me to keep on ; and I shall keep on till I am obliged to stop."

" He left our house," said Mr. Hill, " under the pleasantest circumstances, having maintained his Christian character unblemished ; and we all bade him God-speed in the work to which we believe he was called."

Not money, not emolument, not fame, but the North Market Mission-School, was the object of his thought ; the recovery of the lost, his spring of action. The incidents connected with that school are, as I have already said, almost romantic. Although the barefooted and ill-fed children soon came to love their benefactor, and to speak of him as *their* " Deacon Moody," the parents sometimes interfered with his benevolent plans, and caused him to escape from their wretched haunts for his life. Three ruffians once confronted him as he was looking after the wild urchins, and resolved to kill him.

" Look here," said he to them, " just give a fellow a chance to say his prayers, won't you ? "

" Oh, yes ! go on," they shouted ; and, kneeling down, he prayed so earnestly, that they left the room and in it the children for his sabbath school.

On another occasion, while soliciting children from a Roman Catholic family, a strong man made an assault upon him with a deadly weapon ; when Mr. Moody sprang away, and saved himself by flight.

Once, when threatened with violence at a miserable den, he brought in music to subdue his enemy.

"We are your friends," said he to the ruffians "come, let us have a song." Mr. Stillson then with his sweet voice sang, —

> " Oh, how happy are they
> Who the Saviour obey,
> And have laid up their treasures above ! "

and Mr. Moody followed with prayer. The rough men were moved by the gentle words, and allowed the children to be taken to the mission-school, in which they subsequently were all converted.

It was by such kind of work, hunting among the wrecks of humanity, seeking for lost souls as the pearl-diver for the treasures of the deep, that Mr. Moody re-enforced his mission-school. " I made up my mind," said he on one occasion, " that I would go on as if there were not another man in the world but I to do the work. I knew I had to give an account of stewardship. I suppose they say of me, ' Oh ! he is a fanatic, he is a radical ; he has only one idea.' Well, it is a glorious idea. I would rather have that said of me, than to be a man of ten thousand ideas, and do nothing with them."

In one of his recruiting expeditions, Mr. Moody met an old infidel who kept a gin-shop. " Well," said he to him, " you are talking about the Bible : I will read the New Testament, if you will read Paine's ' Age of

Reason.'" — "Agreed," said Mr. Moody; but he soon found he had the worst of the bargain. On inviting the infidel to go to church, he said to him, "You can have a meeting in my saloon, if you desire it." — "Well," replied the evangelist, "to-morrow morning at eleven o'clock I'll be with you." — "But," returned the infidel, "I want to do part of it myself." — "Very well," said Mr. Moody: "you and your friends may take the first forty-five minutes, and I will take the last fifteen." This was satisfactory; "and that Sunday morning," says Mr. Moody, "I took a little boy with me, that God had taught how to pray. I remember how weak I felt as I went down to that infidel saloon. The owner had gone to a neighboring house where he had engaged two rooms with folding-doors, and had them filled with infidels and deists. They first began to ask me questions; but I said, 'Now, you go on for forty-five minutes, and I shall listen.' So they got to wrangling among themselves. Some thought there was a Jesus, some not. When the time was up, I said, 'Now look here, my friends, your time is up: we always open our meetings with prayer.' After I had prayed, the little boy cried to God to have mercy on these men. They got up one by one, — one going out by this door, one by another. They were all gone very soon. The old infidel put his hand on my shoulder, and said I might have his children. He has since been one of the best friends I have had in Chicago. So you see it must be personal effort with us all."

This kind of labor Mr. Moody with untiring zeal put forth; and fruit in golden clusters sprang from it.

Going with a friend into a drinking-den one Saturday night, they ascertained that the keeper was the son of Christian parents, and then said to him, "Do they know that you are selling liquor?"

They left him meditating on the subject, but had not proceeded far when it occurred to them that they had not thought to pray with him. Returning, Mr. Moody knelt upon the sawdust of the saloon, and presented the rumseller at the seat of mercy.

"I never," said Mr. Stillson, "heard Moody pray like that before: it seemed as if the baptism of the Holy Ghost was upon him." The prayer was answered; and soon the man declared that he would rather die a pauper than to gain his livelihood by selling rum.

"I believe in that Sunday school," said another man, throwing down a piece of silver from an attic window as Mr. Moody passed along, "and I want to take a little stock in it."

The missionary had, a few days before, discovered the poor fellow drunk, and his wife and children starving in their wretched home. Help for the body and the soul was rendered; and subsequently this wretched man through his little investment in the Sunday school became the owner of a happy home, and, what is better still, an earnest worker in the vineyard of the Lord.

Amongst the many annoyances which Mr. Moody

met with in his mission-work, was the occasional breaking of the windows of his schoolroom by the boys of
the Roman Catholic families, who were very numerous
in that neighborhood. He went and laid the case
before the Roman bishop, who promised to attend to it
if he would join the Catholic Church.

"But that might hinder me," said Mr. Moody, "in
my work among the Protestants."

"Oh! not at all," replied the bishop.

"What! do you mean to say that I could go to the
noon prayer-meeting, and pray with all kinds of Christian people, just as I do now?"

"Oh, yes!"

"Then Protestants and Catholics can pray together,
can they?"

"Yes."

"Well, bishop, no man wants to belong to the true
Church more than I do. I wish you would pray for me
right here, that God would show me his true Church,
and help me to be a worthy member of it."

The bishop knelt and prayed with him; he stopped
the breaking of the schoolroom windows, and became
his sincere friend.

On hearing this incident in London, a Catholic priest
said to Mr. Moody, "If you would only join the true
Church, you would be the greatest man in England."
This Mr. Moody had no desire to be.

Sometimes this earnest worker held at his old saloon,
or "rookery" as they called it, a Thanksgiving jubilee,

— not for the sake of feasting, but simply to recount the favors God had shown to them. On one of these occasions, a poor scholar who had been converted rose and said : —

" There was that big fellow Butcher Kilroy, who acted so bad that nobody would have him, and he had to be turned out of one class after another, till I was afraid he would be turned out of school. It took me a long time to get him to come, and I begged for him to stay. I used to pray to Jesus every day to give to him a new heart; and I felt pretty sure he would, if we didn't turn him out. By and by Butcher Kilroy began to want to be a Christian, and now he is converted ; and that is what makes this Thanksgiving the happiest one in all my life."

A notable event in the history of this school was the visit made to it by Pres. Lincoln after his election in 1860. He was received with deafening cheers by the delighted pupils; and he then made to them one of his characteristic little addresses, telling them they were in the right place, and learning from the Bible those things which, if observed, would make them good and honorable men and women. Subsequently sixty of those pupils joined, in answer to his call, the Union army.

The end and aim of Mr. Moody's life was the conversion of souls to Christ. No fitting opportunity was neglected. In the dens of infamy, the hospitals, among the boatmen, the mechanics, the traders and teachers, in the railway-car, on the steamer, wherever he was, wherever he went, in season or out of season, he had his word to say for Jesus.

"I was in a railway-train one day," said a good Christian, "when a stout, cheery-looking stranger came in, and sat down in the seat beside me. We were passing through a beautiful country, to which he called my attention, saying, —

"'Did you ever think what a good heavenly Father we have, to give us such a pleasant world to live in?'

"'Yes, indeed,' said I.

"'Are you a Christian?'

"'No.'

"'But you ought to be one at once. I am to get off at the next station,' he continued. 'If you will kneel down right here, I will pray to the Lord to make you a Christian.'

"Scarcely knowing what I did, I knelt down beside him there in the car filled with passengers; and he prayed for me with all his heart. Just then the train drew up at the station; and he had only time to get off before it started on again.

"Suddenly coming to myself out of what seemed more like a dream than a reality, I rushed out on the car-platform, and shouted after him, 'Tell me who you are!'

"'My name is Moody.'

"I never could shake off the conviction which then took hold upon me, until the strange man's prayer was answered, and I had become a Christian."

The Young Men's Christian Association, instituted in 1858, appointed Mr. Moody chairman of its visiting committee, and found in him an efficient worker and supporter. He purchased an old pony, and mounted thereupon was often seen riding through the miserable lanes and alleys of the North Side, a bevy of ragged children hanging to his saddle, and rejoicing in the loving words of their own "Deacon Moody." The number of families visited the first year was 554; and $2,350 were dispensed for the assistance of the needy. Mr. Moody could not be induced to receive any compensation for his services; and, though holding money in reserve for others, made his bed of the benches in the room of the noon prayer-meeting, and lived upon the simplest fare.

On the breaking out of the civil war in 1861, the energies of the evangelist were directed to the alleviation of the sufferings and the advancement of the spiritual welfare of the soldiers. As chairman of the devotional committee of the Young Men's Christian Association, he commenced holding prayer-meetings at Camp Douglas, and had soon the pleasure of seeing a chapel raised, at a cost of $2,300, for the accommodation of the troops. It was the first camp-chapel erected.

In the camp-meetings it is said that Mr. Moody seemed almost ubiquitous. He was in his proper element. "He would hasten," says a friend, "from one barrack and camp to another, day and night, week days and Sundays, praying, exhorting, conversing personally with the men about their souls, and revelling in the abundant work and swift success which the war had brought within his reach."

Mr. Moody was sent as the first regular delegate to the army from Chicago; and after the battle of Fort Donelson, Feb. 15, 1862, he went with others from Chicago to minister to the sick and wounded on the field. He was the same earnest, sympathizing worker there; and many a dying soldier's heart was comforted by his kindly sympathy and fervent prayers. The scenes he witnessed made a deep impression on his mind; and he now frequently recurs to them in illustration of religious truth.

"At last," said he on one occasion, "I went into the battle-field, and helped to bear away the sick and wounded; and, after I had been over one or two battle-fields, I began to realize what it meant. I could hear the dying men, and their cry for water; and, when I heard of a battle, the whole thing was stamped upon my mind; but I tell you how the Son of God suffered, and some of you will go out laughing."

Resting briefly, Mr. Moody was married on the twenty-eighth day of August, 1862, to Miss Emma C. Revell, an estimable lady who had for some time assisted him in his mission-work, and who has shown herself to be in spirit and in deed most worthy of her noble husband. They have two children, Emma and

Willie, to both of whom the father often refers in his discourses. "One day," says Mr. Daniels in his instructive life of Mr. Moody, "he found his little boy with an elegantly illustrated Bible on his lap, digging out the eyes of a picture of Judas Iscariot with a pair of scissors. On being asked why he was doing such mischief, the little fellow referred to the lesson read at prayers that morning, which had been the betrayal of the Lord; and his indignation at the conduct of Judas had taken this form of expression."

Mr. Moody was with the army, laboring to the utmost limit of his strength, at the battles of Shiloh, Pittsburg Landing, and of Murfreesboro'. "One day," he said, "at Nashville a great strong, wicked-looking soldier came to me trembling. He said he had got a letter from his sister six hundred miles away, and she said that she prayed to God, night after night, that he should be saved; and he said that he could not stand to hear that, and he had come to give himself to Christ. And there and then we knelt down together in prayer to God, he crushed and broken in heart."

Many such instances of answer to prayer came to his observation during his eventful army-life. One of the most remarkable is thus related : —

"One night a party of our men found themselves on the battle-field in charge of a great many wounded soldiers, who, by the sudden retreat of the army, were left wholly without shelter or supplies. Having done their best for the poor fellows, bringing them water from a distant brook, and searching the haversacks of the dead for rations, they began to say to themselves and one another, ' These weak and wounded men must have food, or they will die. The army is out of reach, and there is no village for many miles: what are we to do?' — 'Pray to God,' said one, ' to send us bread.'

"That night in the midst of the dead and dying they held a little prayer-meeting, telling the Lord all about the case, and begging him to send them bread immediately; though from whence it could come, they had not the most remote idea. All night long they plied their work of mercy. With the first ray of dawn, the sound of an approaching wagon caught their ears ; and presently through the mists of the morning appeared a great Dutch farm-wagon, piled to the very top with loaves of bread. On their asking the driver where it came from, and who sent him, he replied, —

" ' When I went to bed last night, I knew that the army was gone, and I could not sleep for thinking of the poor fellows who always have to stay behind ; something seemed to say to me, " What will those poor fellows do for something to eat?" It came to me so strong that I waked up my old wife, and told her what was the matter. We had only a little bread in the house; and, while my wife was making some more, I took my team, and went around to all my neighbors, making them get up and give me all the bread in their houses, telling them that it was for the wounded soldiers. When I got home my wagon was full; my old wife piled her baking on the top; and I started off to bring the bread to the boys, feeling just as if the Lord himself was sending me."

Although Mr. Moody was so intently engaged in ministering to the wants of the soldiers in the army, he by no means neglected his beloved mission-work at home. Feeling the need of a chapel for his converts, he raised by subscriptions about twenty thousand dollars, with which a neat and commodious building was raised in Illinois Street in 1863, and a church on independent principles organized.

After the long and sanguinary work was done, Mr. Moody was one of the first to enter Richmond; and no one saw the stars and stripes float over it with greater joy.

"I had not been long there," said he in one of his discourses, "before it was announced that the negroes were going to have a jubilee meeting. These colored people were just awakening to the fact that they were free; and I went down to the African Church, one of the largest in the South, and found it crowded. One of the colored chaplains of a Northern regiment had offered to speak. I have heard many eloquent men in Europe and in America; but I do not think I ever heard eloquence such as I heard that day. He said, 'Mothers, you rejoice to-day: you are forever free.

That little child has been torn from your embrace, and sold off to some distant State, for the last time; your hearts are never to be broken again in that way: you are free!' The women clapped their hands, and shouted at the top of their voices, 'Glory, glory to God!' It was good news to them, and they believed it. It filled them full of joy. Then he turned to the young men, and said, 'Young men, you rejoice to-day: you have heard the crack of the slave-driver's whip for the last time; your posterity shall be free. Young men, rejoice to-day: you are forever free!' And they clapped their hands, and shouted, 'Glory to God!' They believed the good tidings. 'Young maidens,' he said, 'you rejoice to-day: you have been put on the auction-block and sold for the last time: you are free, forever free!' They believed it, and, lifting up their voices, shouted, 'Glory be to God!' I never before was in such a meeting. They *believed*: it was good news to them.''

CHAPTER IV.

* "This one thing I do; forgetting those things which are behind, and reaching forth unto those things which are before, I press toward the mark for the prize of the high calling of God in Christ Jesus." — St. Paul.

"It does not take God a great while to qualify a man for his work, if he only has the heart for it." — D. L. Moody.

Mr. Moody founded a free and independent church, consisting at first of about three hundred members, on the simple, unsectarian, and fraternal principles of the gospel. "This body of believers," one of its organic articles declares, " desire to be known only as Christians, without reference to any denomination. While

76

the common evangelical doctrines are fully recognized, the plan is to unite in one all who are willing to co-operate in carrying on the work of the common Master.

Mr. Moody was the heart and soul of the enterprise; and it soon became an institution of remarkable power for the dissemination of the gospel amongst the poorer classes in the city of Chicago. Acting on the Napoleonic motto, " To every one his work," he suffered no member of the fold to rest in idleness. He infused his own progressive spirit into his congregation, so that each and every one was led to make the winning of souls to Christ the objective aim and end of life. The church-bell which some good friend had given to him sent forth its pealing notes for some kind of meeting every evening in the week; and so earnest were the pastor's appeals, so prevalent his prayers, so personal his work, so numerous the conversions, that one continuous revival was the grand result.

The sabbath school soon numbered about one thousand pupils; and a quickening influence was sent into the other churches of the city. The amount of labor performed by Mr. Moody in visiting the poor, the sick, and the degraded, in holding extra meetings, in exhortation, and in prayer, seems almost incredible. His iron constitution, and the ardor of his soul in the good work, alone sustained him.

" I am used up. I can't think, or speak, or do any thing else," said he after morning service, one Sunday noon, to his friend Col. Hammond. " You must take my meeting to-night: I have nothing left in me."

Col. Hammond went to church prepared to lead the service. The house was full; and, just as he was rising to speak, Mr. Moody came rushing in with a large company of young men he had induced to follow him from the saloons, and then delivered one of the most affecting sermons that gentleman had ever heard him preach. Wherever he goes he has a kind word for whomsoever he meets, and also the happy faculty of giving every one something to do for Jesus. "Here, take this pile of papers, stand at that corner of the street, and give one to everybody that goes by," he has said to many an idler in the city; and, by thus setting him at work, has interested him in his church, and finally brought him as an active member into it.

Mr. Moody's manner of making calls upon his people on the first day of the year is thus happily described by Mr. Hitchcock, superintendent of his sabbath school: —

"On reaching a family belonging to his congregation, he would spring out of the omnibus, leap up the stairways (for many of the families lived in garrets), rush into the room, and pay his respects as follows: 'You know me: I am Moody. This is Deacon De Golyer, this, Deacon Thane, this is Brother Hitchcock. Are you all well? Do you all come to church and Sunday school? Have you all the coal you need for the winter? Let us pray.' Saying this, Mr. Moody would offer earnest, tender, sympathetic supplication that

God would bless the man, his wife, and each one of his children.

"Then, springing to his feet, he would dash on his hat, dart through the doorway and down the stairs, throwing a hearty 'good-by' behind him, leap into the omnibus, and off to the next place on his list: the entire exercise occupying only about one minute and a half.

"Before long the horses were tired out, for Moody insisted on their going at a run from house to house: so the omnibus was abandoned, and the party proceeded on foot. One after another, his companions became exhausted with running up stairs and down stairs, and across the streets, and kneeling on bare floors, and getting up in a hurry, until reluctantly, but of necessity, they were obliged to relinquish their attempt, and the tireless pastor was left to make the last of the two hundred calls alone; after which feat he returned home in the highest spirits, and with no sense of his fatigue, to laugh at his exhausted companions for deserting him."

Mr. Moody himself occupied a small cottage on the North Side; and, as the good and faithful Müller of Bristol, Eng., trusted in God for his support. Nor was the trust in vain. "We need a barrel of flour," said his wife to him one morning, as he was going out to work for Christ: "will you attend to it?" The request was soon forgotten; but, on returning in the

evening, Mrs. Moody said to him, " I thank you for
that barrel of flour."—" What barrel of flour?" he
answered: " did a barrel come?"—" Yes."—" Well,"
he said, " I haven't thought of it since you spoke of it
in the morning." But the Lord had thought of it;
and so his wants, though he receives no salary, have
been till now supplied.

In addition to Mr. Moody's earnest labors in his
church, and in sabbath-school conventions far and near,
he infused by his untiring energy new life and spirit
into the noon prayer-meetings of the Young Men's
Christian Association; and then induced that body to
erect for its use a noble structure upon Madison Street.

" The only way to get a building," said a young
member after several schemes had failed, " is to elect
Mr. Moody president of the Association." He was,
against strong opposition on the conservative side,
elected. He planned the work judiciously, and had
the pleasure of seeing the beautiful structure dedicated
on the 29th of September, 1867, under the name of
" Farwell Hall." In his address on the occasion, Mr.
Moody said, " When I see young men by thousands
going in the way of death, I feel like falling at the feet
of Jesus, and crying out to him with prayers and tears
to come and save them, and to help us to bring them
to him. His answer to our prayers, and his blessing on
our work, give me faith to believe that a mighty influence is to go out from us, that shall extend through
this county and every county in the State, through

every State in the Union, and finally, crossing the waters, shall help to bring the whole world to God."

These words were prophetic. Through the personal energy of Mr. Moody, sabbath-school conventions were held in every county in Illinois; a wave of Christian influence was sent swelling through the country; and millions in lands beyond the sea have been converted, or wakened to a higher life in Christ.

Mr. Moody held meetings sometimes in the open air, and in general with great success. Visiting a certain town for the purpose of reviving the work of God, a pastor said to him, " You might better have staid at home: winter is the time; in summer people here are too busy." Mr. Moody then went into the public square, took his stand upon a box, and began to address the few persons who had followed him. A crowd of people soon came up, and some of them were moved to tears by his deep earnestness. He held another meeting at the church. It was not large enough to contain the people. Other meetings followed; and a grand awakening led the pastor to exclaim, " I see, dear sir, that summer is just the time for a revival."

In his daily walks, this brave and tireless laborer would neglect no opportunity to address his fellow-men on the subject ever glowing in his heart; saying to a stranger waiting for the train, " Are you for Jesus?" to a conductor, " Are you all right with God?" to a doctor of divinity, " How does your soul prosper?"

"He seems," says one who knew him well, "to be always carried along on a sea of inspiration. He passes his life tossing on its waves, where he is as perfectly at home as the stormy petrel on the ocean."

"Though earnest in his piety, and full of religious conversation," says the Rev. David Macrae in "The Americans at Home," "Mr. Moody has no patience with mere cant, and wants everybody to prove his sincerity by his acts. At a meeting in behalf of a struggling charity, a wealthy layman, loud in his religious professions, offered up a prayer that the Lord would move the hearts of the people to contribute the sum required. Mr. Moody rose and said that all the charity wanted was the sum of two thousand dollars; and that he considered it absurd for a man with half a million to get up and ask the Lord to do any thing in the matter; when he could himself, with the mere stroke of the pen, do all that was needed and ten times more, and never feel the difference."

"In private intercourse," says the Rev. Dr. Clark of Albany, "I have always found Mr. Moody as full of gentle courtesy towards others, as he was of tender love for his Saviour. I never knew a man so free from selfishness or self-seeking as he. His friendship is as pure as crystal, and his generous love flows out toward all whom he can serve or benefit. A nobler soul was never formed by grace or spiritual culture. His very presence as a guest is a blessing in any house."

In his early evangelical efforts Mr. Moody used to

blame the ministers for the inactivity of the churches. At a certain meeting for the promotion of a revival, one good brother rose and criticised him severely for his uncharitableness, when Mr. Moody said with deep emotion, "From my heart I thank that brother. I deserved it. Will you, my brother, pray for me?" All hearts were touched by his repentance; and his course in respect to the clergy ever since proves it to be sincere.

The Sunday-school conventions held by Mr. Moody and his helpers were characterized by remarkable solemnity; and under the impressive appeals of the evangelist, who was gaining every year in spiritual power, thousands were turned from darkness into light. Though rough in speech, the common people heard him gladly; yet he was not satisfied with himself. The boy preacher, Harry Moorhouse of Manchester, had been in Chicago, and had spoken with great acceptance in the pulpit of the Illinois-street Church. He had evinced surprising knowledge of the Scriptures; he had revealed a new method of studying them. One passage was to be interpreted by another passage, one revelation to be examined under the light of another revelation, and the golden thread that held all parts together as an harmonious whole pursued from the commencement to the close. Mr. Moody saw that he had read the Bible hitherto only by piecemeal, and without any consistent plan. He was intensely interested in the system of Mr. Moorhouse; and in 1867 visited England for the purpose mainly of learning what to him was a new way of finding out the riches of the word of God. In London he met the late celebrated evangelist Henry Varley, who said to him, "It remains for the world to see what the Lord can do with a man wholly consecrated to Christ." These words sank deep into his soul. He gave himself more heartily than ever to the study of his Bagster's Bible and to the work of leading wanderers in sin to Jesus. During his brief visit to London he preached almost one hundred sermons, and succeeded in establishing a daily union prayer-meeting in that city. Though the time had not yet come for him to do much for London, some fuel was added to the flame in his own soul by the Christian men he met there, and his aggressive power as an evangelist was augmented.

"Is this young man all O O?" said a Christian from the city of Dublin to another in London, pointing to Mr. Moody. "What do you mean by O O?" said the one to whom the question was directed. "Is he out and out for Christ?" replied the other. "I tell you," said Moody, "it burned down into my soul. It means a good deal to be O O for Christ."

On returning from England, Mr. Moody with renewed vigor carried on his work, preaching in his church in the morning, infusing fresh life into his beloved sabbath school now numbering almost a thousand pupils, and addressing vast audiences at Farwell Hall in the evening. He introduced more of the Scripture into his sermons, and spoke as a lawyer to a body of jurymen — intent on the conversion of one at least to the truth as it is in Jesus.

"How did you prepare that sermon on the compassion of Christ?" said Dr. Roy to him one day. "I took the Bible," answered the evangelist, "and began to read it over to find out what it said on that subject. I prayed over the texts as I went along until the thought of His infinite compassion overpowered me, and I could only lie on the floor of my study, with my face in the open Bible, and cry like a little child." Sermons so composed could hardly fail to move an audience to tears.

Mr. Moody continued during four successive years to hold the office of president of the Young's Men's Christian Association; and at one time he was, as he himself has said, " president, secretary, janitor, and every thing else." Here is an instance of the kind of outside work he was constantly performing.

"Are you a Christian?" said he to a man leaning against a lamp-post. He answered the question with a curse. "Maybe," said Mr. Moody to himself, " I am doing more harm than good." One night he heard a knock on the door, and the man who swore at him at the lamp-post, appearing to him on the door-step, said, " Do you remember the man you met about three months ago at a lamp-post, and how he cursed you? I have had no peace since that night. Oh, tell me what to do to be saved!"

" We just fell down on our knees," said Mr. Moody, "and I prayed; and the next day he went to the noon prayer-meeting, and openly confessed the Saviour How often have I thanked God for that word to that dying sinner! "

In January, 1868, the beautiful building of the Young Men's Christian Association was reduced to ashes; but there are large-hearted, noble Christian men in the city of Chicago. John V. Farwell, B. F. Jacobs, and others came immediately forward, and commenced on the same site another and a better building, which, the ensuing year, was dedicated to the service of the Lord.

On New Year's Day, Mr. Moody and his family were taken into a carriage, and driven to a new house, which had been built and elegantly furnished by some liberal friends for his abode. It was filled with old acquaintances who greeted him with cordial welcome, while Dr. Robert Patterson in fitting words made the presentation of the lease and furniture to the astonished preacher, who in the fulness of his heart could offer only broken sentences of gratitude in reply.

Mr. Moody was very happy in his new home. " His delight was to play with his children," says one of his friends, " and to entertain strangers. He loved to see his whole household in a roar of laughter; and yet, when a passage of the Bible came up suddenly to his mind, he would turn to them with his usual word, ' Come, let us pray!' and then all would kneel, and listen silently to the outbreathings of his fervent soul.'

" The spirit of his companion," says the Rev. Dr. Clark in an excellent sketch of Mr. Moody, " harmonizes perfectly with his spirit; and her sympathy and tenderness are among Heaven's choicest gifts to him. A stranger who was visiting his sabbath school noticed a lady teaching about forty middle-aged men in the gallery. Looking at her and then at the class, he said to Mr. Moody, ' Is not that lady altogether too young to teach such a class of men?' He replied, ' She gets along very well, and seems to succeed in her teaching.' The stranger did not appear to be altogether satisfied. In a few moments he approached the superintendent again, and with becoming gravity continued, ' Mr. Moody, I cannot but feel that that lady must be altogether too young to instruct such a large company of men. Will you, sir, please to inform me who she is?' — ' Certainly,' replied Mr. Moody: ' that is my wife.'"

The Bible readings now held by this man of one book became the engrossing topic of conversation among Christians in Chicago; and hundreds joined his classes for the purpose of obtaining a key to the hidden wealth of Holy Writ. His plan is to take one word or doctrine, and, by the aid of a concordance, to trace it through the various books of Scripture, and thus examine it by the light of inspiration under all its meanings and relations. " I remember," says he, " I took up the word ' love,' and turned to the Scriptures and studied it, and got so that I felt that I loved everybody. I got full of it. It ran out of my fingers. Suppose you take up the subject of love, and study it. You will get so full of it that all you have got to do is to open your lips, and a flood of the love of God flows out upon the meeting. Take the 'I ams' of John,— 'I am the bread of life;' 'I am the vine;' 'I am the water of life;' 'I am the way, the truth, and the life; 'I am the resurrection.' God gives to his children a blank, and on it they can write whatever they most want, and he will fill the bill."

In order to aid his eye and memory, Mr. Moody connects by a fine hair-line drawn in his Bagster's Bible, which he carries in a pocket made expressly for it, words, names, or passages co-related, and introduces many other marks of reference.

In the early part of 1871, this untiring servant of the Lord had the good fortune, while attending a convention at Indianapolis, to make the acquaintance of Ira David Sankey, who has since become so celebrated as " a sweet singer of the gospel." Mr. Moody is himself no singer; but, aware of the power of sacred music over the hearts of men, he determined wisely to secure his services. A kind of co-partnership in evangelization was soon formed between them; and now Mr. Moody with his Bible, and Mr. Sankey with his song-book, move together in fraternal concord, publishing the glad tidings of salvation through the world.

The mighty conflagration of the city of Chicago commenced in the evening of the 8th of October, 1871, and swept over an area of four square miles, leaving but a mass of blocks and smouldering ruins in its course. Aroused by the uproar of that night of terror, Mr. Moody and his family fled for shelter from the flames. "Every thing I have is lost," said he, "except my reputation and my Bible."

To his wife, who solicited him to take his portrait with them, he replied, "Wouldn't I look well carrying my picture through the streets?" His beautiful house, his beloved church, and Farwell Hall, the evangelical centre of Chicago, were consumed; and most of his parishioners were left in destitution. As soon as Mr. Moody's family were safe, he hurried back to assist the sick and wounded in their efforts to escape from peril. In one of his discourses, he thus speaks of the dreadful scene : —

"It was my sad lot to be in the Chicago fire. As the flames rolled down our streets, destroying every thing in their onward march, I saw the great and the honorable, the learned and the wise, fleeing before the fire with the beggar and the thief and the harlot. All were alike. As the flames swept through the city, it was like the judgment day. Neither the mayor, nor the mighty men, nor the wise men, could stop these flames. They were all on a level then, and many who were worth hundreds of thousands were left paupers that night. When the day of judgment comes, there will be no difference : all sinners will suffer."

On the evening of the great fire Mr. Moody spoke to an audience of three thousand persons in Farwell Hall, exhorting them to become Christians. During the meeting Dr. Thomas Hastings's hymn, —

> " To-day the Saviour calls :
> Ye wanderers, come;
> Oh, ye benighted souls !
> Why longer roam ? "

was sung by the congregation, and ten persons remained to express their determination to follow Jesus. As they went out into the street, the flames were seen approaching, and three of the number perished in the conflagration.

Mr. Moody has a brave heart, sustained by confidence in God. After rendering to the sufferers what relief he could, he went to Philadelphia with the view of raising funds for the erection of a temporary building for religious services.

" If I had a thousand dollars I could build," said he to George H. Stuart and others, " a great box that would hold my Sunday school." — " You shall have three thousand," was the prompt reply. With this money he commenced a rough tabernacle a hundred and nine feet by seventy-five, of boards, in the burnt district; and by aid of the hands of poor men, women, and children, who sometimes toiled by night, the rude structure was within eight weeks after the fire completed. At the dedication more than a thousand children were present. The tabernacle presented a most singular appearance, rising as it did thus solitary among the ruins; and it served the triple purpose of affording shelter to the homeless, of storing supplies for the destitute, and of being used as a religious temple. Mr. Moody and his family made it the place of their abode, and from it charitable distributions were continually extended to the poor people of the city. Religious services were often held in it; and by the powerful preaching of Mr. Moody, whom the fire had brought into closer union with his Lord and Master, and by the sweet and touching songs of Mr. Sankey, many wandering souls were led to Jesus. Never was there a livelier or a busier scene of varied labor, such as sewing, mending, arranging, and distributing, than that low, tar-covered tabernacle presented for a long time subsequent to the memorable fire ; and the services for the sabbath were, according to the Rev. Mr. Daniels, conducted in the following order : —

" The Lord's Supper every Sunday at nine in the morning; preaching by Mr. Moody at half-past ten, at the close of which he waited at the door to greet the people as they passed out; then dinner in the class-room, at which a number of the Sunday-school teachers were present to talk over the work of the day; immediately after dinner, a teachers' meeting for the study of the lesson; at three o'clock the Sunday school, with Mr. Moody for superintendent; following it a teachers prayer-meeting, also led by him; then supper in the class-room; then the yoke-fellows' prayer-meeting; preaching again at half-past seven; after which Mr. Moody held a meeting for inquirers, which sometimes lasted far into the night.

Though left entirely destitute by the fire, Mr. Moody toiled, regardless of his own necessities, for the salvation of the masses who came in their poverty to listen to his heartfelt exhortations. His own pocket-book was often empty while he was engaged in the distribution of the alms of others to the needy. Having preached for the Rev. Dr. Goodspeed one day, ten dollars were tendered to him by the pastor, who at the same time said to him, ' This is all I have.' — ' Then,' replied the self-denying Moody, ' I won't take but half of it, though I have not one cent.' "

At the solicitation of three gentlemen, Mr. Moody, after some profound religious experiences, determined in 1873 to revisit England; and, on being asked why he came to this decision, his quick reply was, " To win ten thousand souls to Christ."

He made his preparations for the voyage, leaving his church in the hands of long-tried and efficient laborers; but up to the eve of his departure took no thought for the money, even to pay his passage. He literally abided by the words of Christ, " Take no thought for the morrow;" and his simple trust in God was not in vain. Just as he was about leaving with his family, his liberal friend John V. Farwell came to him, and, bidding him good-by, placed in his hand a check for five hundred dollars, saying he perhaps would need it after reaching England.

On the 7th of June, 1873, Mr Moody and his family, together with Mr. Sankey, sailed for Liverpool, at which city they arrived upon the seventeenth day of the same month. The prayers of thousands followed these gifted messengers of good-will to men; and the Spirit of Jehovah, speaking through their voices, moved the hearts and tongues of millions in Great Britain to declare for the Redeemer and his kingdom.

CHAPTER V.

"Poor, but making many rich; having nothing, and yet possessing all things."
ST. PAUL.

"Attempt great things for God, and expect great things from God." — CAREY.

THE 17th of June is a memorable day in the history
of England and America.   On that day the brave and
well-disciplined soldiers of England met in deadly conflict, on the slopes of Bunker Hill, the hastily gathered

and raw militia of Boston and the adjoining towns. The contending forces found out by that day's experience that they were kindred in blood and soul. It was a lesson they have never forgotten. The world knows that to all intents and purposes the English and Americans are one.

It was a fitting coincidence, that Messrs. Moody and Sankey in their evangelistic visit to England should land upon her shores on the 17th of June. They were not invaders with hostile intent, but friends and helpers of all good men and women in saving the perishing multitudes, who, living in the midst of the light of the gospel, were yet rejecting its offers of mercy.

They did not go to England because there were no living, working Christians there; for there is, and has been since the days of Wesley, a vital type of Christianity in that country equal to any the world has ever known. They did not visit England for the reason that there was no work for them to do at home; for in all our great cities there are vast multitudes yet unreached by the gospel. They did not go as religious adventurers, but because, like Paul of old, they had heard a cry for help, which they could not resist. They went forth on their mission as evangelists, and they carried their divinely given credentials with them. They were not of the class who send themselves, men, and sometimes women, of small natural abilities, a narrow range of thought, a meagre supply of common sense, and not much religion. They were rather men of holy lives they enjoyed experimental piety; they were not covetous of wealth or honor; they had walked with Christ until their hearts were all aflame with his quenchless love for a dying world; they had known the fellowship of the sufferings of the world's Redeemer, the bitterness of sin, the peace of pardon, the comfort of hope, the joy of adoption, the victory of an abiding faith, and the unspeakable glory of personal communion with the Triune God.

If Mr. Moody had been going into a country where there were no Christian people, then of course his work would have been entirely among the unconverted; it would have been to preach repentance and faith, and to call men to a knowledge of Christ. In England Christianity had been planted for many centuries, and there were many Christian churches already organized, many professing Christians, and many devout and earnest souls bent on the spread of the Redeemer's kingdom. Besides these, there were vast masses of the unsaved, with more or less knowledge of the gospel, who were living in neglect of the great salvation. Under these circumstances the work of Mr. Moody was twofold in its character. He would first unify and intensify the individual activity of all Christians, and then with their help proclaim the gospel to the entire community.

When the two evangelists landed at Liverpool on the 17th of June, 1873, they were met with the disheartening news that one of the principal men who had invited them had died. Seeing no other course -to pursue, Mr. Moody sent a telegram to the secretary of the Young Men's Christian Association at York, another friend who had invited him to England, that he was ready to begin his work. He was informed in reply, that religion was at a very low ebb in York, and that it would require at least a month to get ready for a revival. The communication closed by asking Mr. Moody when he might be expected, to which he returned immediately the despatch, " I will be in York to-night."

If one might judge of the character of the people by the number of their churches, as Paul of the Athenians by the number of their gods, the conclusion would be that the inhabitants of the famous old city of York were very religious. Three hundred years ago York had nearly sixty parish churches and chapels, together with an ample supply of monasteries and nunneries. At present, with a population of about fifty thousand, there are, besides the cathedral, twenty-nine churches and about half as many Dissenting chapels. If all the people of York, from the oldest to the youngest, were to choose some fine Sunday to go to church, there would be room in the churches for them all, and nearly half as many more. A harder place than this could not be found for the commencement of the labors of the American evangelists. Religiously educated, wealthy church-goers, with an archbishop and many clergy employed and unemployed, — what could the citizens of York want of uncultivated revivalists who had never been ordained, nor even licensed to preach the gospel?

It may be supposed that it was in the divine order that they should go to this unpromising field in the beginning, that their faith might be strengthened for the difficulties yet to come.

The first of the meetings held in York was on Sunday morning, in one of the small rooms of the Young Men's Christian Association; and the number present was but eight. Four churches had been opened for them, and amid great discouragement they held meetings through the week. There was no apparent sympathy on the part of Christians, and no movement on the part of the unconverted. There was no decided opposition; yet the ministers both of the Dissenting and Established churches rendered them no active co-operation. The result of a month's unremitting labor was the conversion of about two hundred and fifty persons, the awakening of some Christian people in the city, and, what was of very great importance, an impression made upon the public mind outside of York, that these two earnest workers were the servants of the Most High God.

From York they went to Sunderland, a seaport in the North-west of England, with a population of about eighty thousand people. Here on Sunday, July 27, they began their labors; but still were destined to encounter many obstacles. The English mind is slow to accept new ideas; nor does it look on foreigners with any special favor. These evangelists were plain men, without wealth, social position, or diplomas from the schools. They were perhaps curious specimens of the Yankees, who had come over to the Fatherland on purpose to make money. Mr. Moody was blunt in his manners; he understood so little of the science of red tape, and went at things so abruptly, that the English did not exactly understand what to do with him. But they learned in time to love him and to trust him as a servant of the living God, tremendously in earnest to do his Master's will.

Meeting with but limited success in Sunderland, the evangelists went next to Newcastle-upon-Tyne. Here had lived one of the men who had invited them to England; but he had gone to his reward, without beholding the work he had so much desired to promote. "We have not done much in York and Sunderland," said Mr. Moody on his arrival, "because the ministers opposed us; but we are going to stay in Newcastle till we make an impression, and live down the prejudices of good people who do not understand us." This purpose he adhered to with the most encouraging results. The ministers and laymen gradually came to his help; and their united efforts were honored of God, by the conversion of many precious souls. "We are on the eve of a great revival," said Mr. Moody, at one of the meetings at which almost a thousand Christians were present, "which may cover Great Britain, and perhaps make itself felt in America. And why," continued he, "may the fire not burn as long as I live? When this revival spirit dies, may I die with it!"

On Wednesday, Sept. 10, an all-day meeting was held in Rye Hill Chapel, where about seventeen hundred people were present, all manifesting the profoundest interest in the novel services. The first hour was devoted to the reading of the Bible and to prayer; the second to the promises, when Mr. Moody said, "These promises, like precious gems, are to be found in every book of the Bible, and to-day we may get into the company of all God's great men who have passed away, and hear what things they have to tell us about our Father's love. We may summon the patriarchs, the prophets, the priests, the kings; we may listen to the historians, the biographers, the poets, of the Bible; and they will all give us some of the precious promises spoken by God through their lives to the ears of the whole world. The meeting is to be quite open and free; not for speeches about promises, but for the reading forth of these good words of God to our souls." Then from every part of the audience came passage after passage, — for the people had their Bibles with them, — which set forth the fulness of God's love to man. During the last hour, Mr. Moody spoke of heaven; and well it could be said of him, "The pure, full-orbed truths of God's word came in close and certain succession from his lips, and fell with telling power on the hearts of the throng."

Mr. Sankey sang his sweet songs with touching pathos, and thus deepened the impression made by the outspoken words of Mr. Moody. The memory of that meeting, said a minister present, " will live till the last year of our lives ; and many a soul travelling home to God will think of it as one of the deep poo s by the way, dug by the hand of a loving God for the refresh-ment of his children."

By the labors of these two evangelists in Newcastle, the churches were awakened, sabbath schools increased, and Bibles circulated. A new style of religious life was introduced into Northumberland. " Never shall we forget," said a person present, " Mr. Moody's fare-well address to the delegates who had come from dis-tant counties to take leave of him. He would not say ' Good-by,' — no, ' Good-night ' rather, and meet them all in the morning in the dawn of the eternal day. Then strong men bowed and wept out their manly sorrow like children, — blessed children, as they were, of the same great Father."

Passing through Carlisle, where the Briton and the Scot had so often met in sanguinary conflict, the two evangelists arrived on the 22d of November in the celebrated city of Edinburgh, Scotland. Mr. Moody had some fears lest his visit here amongst the learned and wary Scotchmen, set as they were in their own theological opinions, might turn out to be a failure. " What," said he, " can such a man as I do up there amongst those great Scotch divines ? " The work was indeed derided by some and vilified by others, while many good men were sorely perplexed at the methods of the evangelists and the agencies they employed. It was shocking to a real Scotchman to praise God with an organ; and the simple heart-songs of Mr. Sankey were not by any means to be allowed to supplant the grand old psalms sung by the sainted Covenanters, and the long succession of holy men and women since worship had been free in Scotland. But the power of God was with the evangelists. The difficulties one after another disappeared, and thousands were happily converted to God in the capital city of the North. The day after the arrival of the evangelists, Music Hall, which seats two thousand people, could not hold the crowds that thronged to hear them. A noon prayer-meeting was begun the following day, and inquiry-meetings followed almost every public service. Mr. Moody's constant reference to the Bible, and Mr. Sankey's beautiful songs, as " Hold the Fort," " Jesus of Nazareth passeth by," and " The Prodigal Child," greatly pleased the Scottish people. " One of the first things that impressed us," says the Rev. John Kelman, " was the extraordinary voracity of Mr. Moody's faith. We had been accustomed to go to the meetings, hoping God would bless us; but Mr. Moody always said, ' We *know* that he will bless us.' " " We are all delighted with them " [Moody and Sankey], wrote another, under date of Nov. 28, 1873; " ministers of all denominations are joining cordially in the service, and God is indeed working graciously. About two thousand are out every night hearing. Two churches are to be opened simultaneously each night next week. The singing of Mr. Sankey lays the gospel message and invitation very distinctly and powerfully on the consciences of the people; and Mr. Moody's gospel is clear, earnest, and distinct."

On the 2d of December Mr. Moody made a most impressive address on " Where art thou ? " in Broughton Place Church; and at an inquiry meeting nearly three hundred, embracing students from the University, soldiers from the castle, old men of seventy years, the intemperate and the sceptical, listened as for life to the pointed words of the revivalist. At one of these meetings Mr. Moody said to the chairman of an infidel club, —

" Would you like to have me pray for you ? "

" Oh, yes ! I have no objection to your trying your hand on me, if you like ; but I think you will find me a match for you."

Mr. Moody knelt down and prayed for him in earnest, and had the pleasure of knowing subsequently that this chairman and eighteen members of his club were converted to Christianity.

The Free Church Assembly Hall, the largest public building in Edinburgh, and the established church, Assembly Hall, were crowded every evening to hear the urgent appeals of Mr. Moody, and the affecting gospel songs of the sweet singer. The secular press proclaimed the progress of the revival; and people came from distant towns to share in its blessed influ ence. Denominational distinctions were forgotten, and never before was the city so intent to hear the tidings of salvation. The theme of conversation everywhere was Jesus, and many souls were daily born into his kingdom. At the meeting on Sunday night, Dec. 29, in the Corn Exchange, Grass Market, about three thousand people of the poorer classes were present, and the most profound attention was paid to the pathetic stories and the hallowed songs. About six hundred men came up to the Assembly Hall from one of these meetings, fell on their knees, and professed themselves willing to serve the Lord.

The meeting at the Tolbooth Church, Dec. 31, was perhaps the most interesting one held in Edinburgh. The house was thronged. The ministers and all were deeply affected. " The intense interest," says one who was present, " increased as midnight neared. Kneeling or with bowed heads, the whole great meeting with one accord prayed in silence; and, while they did so, the city clocks successively struck the hour. The hushed silence continued five minutes more. Mr. Moody gave out the last two verses of the hymn, —

' Jesus, lover of my soul.'

And they all stood and sung, —

' Thou, O Christ, art all I want.'

"The gates were ajar, and our hearts were pressed close to the heart of God. After a brief prayer the benediction was pronounced, and all began like one family to wish each other ' a happy New Year.' "

The revival spirit, awakened in Edinburgh, spread through the whole of Scotland; and constant applications were made to the evangelists from ministers in other cities to come and aid them. A letter signed by all the leading pastors of Edinburgh was sent to every church in the country, urging it to make the great work of the American revivalists prominent in their supplications during the week of prayer. From this, many wonderful results ensued. Messrs. Moody and Sankey continued their labors in Edinburgh until Jan. 21, 1874; and the whole city, as it were, came out to the slopes of Arthur's Seat to bid them an affectionate farewell. So greatly had this intelligent city been moved by these two humble men, that not less than three thousand converts were received into the churches; and Dr. Horatius Bonar said that almost every Christian household had been blessed with one or more conversions.

Mr. Moody was steadily gaining spiritual and intellectual strength, while his success in Edinburgh emboldened him to go forward in his glorious mission.

The manufacturing city of Glasgow, forty-two miles west of Edinburgh, and containing half a million people, was prepared to receive with open arms the evangelists. They commenced their labors here on the 8th of February, 1874, by addressing a meeting of about three thousand sabbath-school teachers in the City Hall. The Bible readings of Mr. Moody met with great acceptance, while the soul-moving songs of Mr. Sankey sent the word home to the heart. Helpers came from Edinburgh, the churches entered zealously upon the work; and conversions, more especially among the educated, multiplied every day, so that soon the whole city became alive to the revival.

Three large churches near the City Hall were opened for simultaneous services, and vast assemblages received the glad tidings in the open air. At the first noon prayer-meeting fifteen hundred persons, some of them coming from distant towns, were present. At the meeting in the City Hall on Thursday evening, Mr. Moody spoke with wondrous power on the text, "Except a man be born again;" and, when he invited those on the Lord's side to remain, more than a thousand people kept their places. On Sunday evening, Feb. 15, he addressed a vast assembly of men at the City Hall; and when Mr. Sankey sung in his touching style, —

> " In the promises I trust,
>   Now I feel the blood applied;
>   I am prostrate in the dust,
>   I with Christ am crucified," —

not a head in that great throng was seen to move. More than a thousand remained for prayer. On Monday evening, Feb. 16, as many as seven hundred Christian young men at the Erving Place Chapel agreed to meet every night to watch and pray for the conversion of the souls of their companions. On Sabbath morning, Feb. 22, Mr. Moody spoke in the City Hall to about three thousand Christian workers, from the text, "Send me." At the Erving Place Chapel, Feb. 24, a party of young men numbering one hundred and one took sides for Jesus; and at the noon prayer-meeting on Thursday Mr. Moody said he had once, after most urgent solicitation, preached in a rude church on the prairies, where one Christian woman continued praying day and night for the pleasure-loving young people whose only enjoyment seemed to be the song and the dance. A letter received that morning brought the cheering tidings that in that same spot thirty-two young men were now on the Lord's side and working for him.

On Sabbath morning, March 1, he spoke with his usual power to three thousand young men of the Glasgow Christian Associations, Mr. Sankey singing with great effect, —

"Hold the fort, for I am coming."

It is the aim of Mr. Moody to lead Christians to work for God, as well as pray to him. "Now," said Mr. Sankey in one of the assemblies, "is the time for working. I saw on a tombstone at Stirling this word deeply carved in the stone, 'WAITING.' There will be time for waiting by and by, but now is the time for *working*." He then sang with great effect, —

> " Hark, the voice of Jesus crying, —
> Who will go and work to-day?
> Fields are white, and harvest waiting :
> Who will bear the sheaves away? "

While meetings of children, of mothers, of young men, working-men, teachers, students, ministers, were held in almost all of the one hundred and forty churches of Glasgow during March and April, thousands and thousands were laboring personally for the conversion of souls. At one of the great meetings for children, the boys, who were delighted with the simplicity of the preaching and the sweetness of the songs, climbed up the stairs, filled the pulpit, and hung as bees in quest of honey around the speaker. So large was the attendance at the churches that the Crystal Palace was at length opened to the eager multitudes; and, after seven thousand five hundred tickets had been distributed, hundreds applied in vain to gain admission. At one time the crowd, amounting to about twenty thousand, filled the whole space between the Palace and the Botanic Gardens, intent on hearing the words of the American evangelists. In his preaching Mr. Moody, unlike most revivalists, was business-like, unpoetical, often very blunt, but thoroughly in earnest; and his power was felt not only in every family in Glasgow, but, through the press and telegraphic wires, in every part of the United Kingdom.

The writer was in Glasgow a year after the departure of the evangelists, when ample time had elapsed for

measuring the magnitude of the work of the evangelists.
Noonday prayer-meetings were still sustained, in one of
which a Lutheran pastor from the South of Germany
testified that a year before he had been in Glasgow, and
attended the meetings. He had been wonderfully blessed
of God; and, when he returned home to his work, the
Lord.in an extraordinary manner poured out his Spirit
upon the people. Many in the villages in the neighborhood of his church were earnestly seeking salvation;
and he had returned to Glasgow for the reception of a
new baptism, so that he could the better lead his flock.
In private conversation with several of the most distinguished clergymen of the city, one of them remarked
that at that time, or within a space of a single twelve-
month, more than three thousand people had joined the
evangelical churches, and many more were ready to
unite with them; another said that Mr. Moody had
done more for the cause of temperance in Scotland than
all the lecturers for the last twenty years, and that in
Glasgow alone more than seventeen thousand had
signed the pledge; another averred that " dear auld
Scotland had never seen such a year of blessing in all
her history; " and still another testified that Messrs.
Moody and Sankey had done more to revolutionize the
service of song in the churches, to liberalize the hard
features of Scottish Calvinism, and to save Scotland
from the terrible curse of strong drink, than had been
done by any twenty men in the last three hundred
years.

Besides all this, the revival in Glasgow took a practical turn; and, as never before, efforts were made to save the vicious and to help the worthy poor. So great was the activity of Christians, that they could not content themselves with ordinary church work; but in the long evenings, when daylight lingers in this high latitude, in the open squares, on the bridges or at the corners of the streets, alone or in little companies, devoted Christian men and women might be seen engaged in prayer, or making brief addresses to groups of listeners, or leading the company in singing some of the favorite gospel hymns.

In May the evangelists returned to Edinburgh, where on the 21st one of the largest assemblies ever seen in that city was gathered in the Queen's Park to hear for the last time the living words and touching music of the beloved heralds of salvation.

During the summer of 1874, they visited most of the large towns in Scotland, and their names became as household words from the Cheviot Hills to John O'Groat's. Wherever they went, the pillar and the cloud went with them; the work of God spread and prevailed, while Christians and happy converts rejoiced at the glorious manifestations of divine power. It was indeed a time of gladness to that land of many saints and martyrs; and it seemed as if the hour were near at hand when the prayer of John Knox — "Give me Scotland, or I die" — was about to be fully answered.

The first week in June, Messrs. Moody and Sankey

spent at Perth, on the river Tay, where they spoke to crowded meetings. " It seemed," said one, " as if God had sent his servants to unlock the floodgates of his grace, and the water of life has swept out in deep and steady currents, leaving no place for the breaking waves of excitement and mere feeling." At Dundee a blessed work was done. At Aberdeen they spoke, June 14, in the natural amphitheatre of the Broadhill, to some twenty thousand anxious people. The songs " Almost Persuaded," " Come Home," and " The Lost Sheep," greatly affected them. Many conversions followed. They arrived at Tain, having about two thousand five hundred people, on the 13th of July. The church was densely crowded. About five hundred stood up for prayers, and tearful eyes testified to the power of song. At Huntley as many as fifteen thousand were present at the meeting in the open air; yet Mr. Moody spoke so as to be heard by every person.

An outdoor meeting was held at Elgin, July 23, which was said to be the largest ever seen in that city. It was on Lady Hill, and the spectacle was most imposing. " Thousands," says a writer, " hung spellbound on the speaker's lips. One often hears doubts as to the possibility of producing an impression in the open air, but there is no mistake this time. No, there is no mistaking these long concentric arcs of wistful faces curving around the speaker, and these reluctant tears which conscious guilt has wrung from eyes unused to weep. Oh the power of the living Spirit of God! Oh the fascination of the gospel of Christ! Oh the gladness of the old, old story to these men and women hurrying to eternity!"

The last meeting which the evangelists held in Scotland was at Rothesay, Sept. 3. This town has about seven thousand inhabitants, and stands at the head of a beautiful bay. The service was held by the seashore on the esplanade, as many as three thousand persons being present. Mr. Moody spoke with remarkable energy. The exercises were continued into the evening; the stars shone out brilliantly over the bay; and the Spirit of God seemed present, turning the hearts of the spell-bound multitude to make ready for a joyous meeting in our Father's home on high. A mighty work had been accomplished in Scotland; and the tide of religious feeling still rolls on to the praise, not of the human agents, but of the Son of God, who selects the weak things to confound the mighty.

On the 6th of September, the two earnest workers began their labors of love in the industrial city of Belfast, Ireland. Success at once attended them. A daily prayer-meeting was commenced; addresses were made to Christian workers; the largest churches were densely crowded; and, at an outdoor meeting in the Botanic Gardens, it is thought that as many as twenty-five thousand persons were present. Many were converted. On Sunday, Sept. 13, an open-air meeting was held for the people working in the mills, where from ten to twenty thousand were present.

While Mr. Sankey was singing, —

"Jesus of Nazareth passeth by," —

many people manifested their emotion by sighs and tears. At a meeting held on the 27th, more than two hundred young men came forward to acknowledge Jesus. "It was a sight," says one present, "which would have drawn tears of joy from any heart." On sabbath morning, Oct. 4, the people waiting to hear the evangelists stood closely packed over a field of about six acres. The impression made upon the multitude was very deep. On the 15th of October, Mr. Moody presided over the noonday prayer meeting in St. Enoch's Church. It was held for those beginning to seek Jesus, and about twenty-four hundred persons were by tickets admitted. On the 17th the evangelists held their last meeting in Belfast. About three thousand were present. "It was," a writer says, "like the sound of many waters, to hear this multitude sing the new song. As all stood and sung in one burst of praise, —

'Oh, happy day that fixed my choice!' —

the effect was overpowering, filling the soul with a sweet foretaste of the praises of heaven."

After a brief visit to Londonderry, where they won some trophies of grace, the revivalists commenced laboring in the city of Dublin, which contains about two hundred and fifty thousand people, on the 24th of October, and continued there until the 29th of November. Many prayers had been offered there for their success; tracts concerning the glorious work in Scotland had been distributed, noon prayer-meetings held, and the splendid glass building called the Exhibition Palace had been engaged for the assemblies. Day after day and night after night this vast edifice was crowded with anxious listeners, seeking to know the path of life. The evangelical ministers with one accord assisted in the various services, and people came from the distant counties to enjoy the refreshing from on high.

" We have never before," wrote an Episcopal minister, " seen such sights in Dublin. One feels that the Spirit of God is present, and that a wave of prayer is continually going up to the throne from the Lord's people. What is the magic power which draws together these mighty multitudes, and holds them spellbound? It is the simple lifting up of the cross of Christ, the holding forth the Lord Jesus before the eyes of the people in all the glory of his Godhead. It is deeply instructive to see the things new and old which Mr. Moody draws in rich profusion from the treasury of God's word." " It is becoming," said the Rev. J. G. Phillips, "a more personal thing with many. It is not simply what Messrs. Moody and Sankey have to say, but it is, What have Christ and Christianity to do with ME?" Sometimes as many as seven hundred inquirers would remain after the ordinary services had closed, to learn what they must do to be saved. One old gentleman of more than threescore years and ten at one of these meetings fell upon his knees, sobbing like a child. "I was utterly careless about my soul till last night," cried he; "but I have been so unhappy since, I could not sleep. I seemed to hear ringing in my ears, 'Jesus of Nazareth is passing by;' and, if I don't get saved now, I never shall be.' Four of the daily papers published full reports of the different meetings, and the seeds of truth were thus sown broadcast over Ireland. Noblemen, military men, professors in the university, as well as ministers, lent their influence to carry on the revival; and in many instances the Roman Catholic priests were present at the meetings. Such cordial unity of sentiment had never before been known in Dublin. The straightforward, off-hand style of Mr. Moody, and his flashes of real mother-wit, combined with the heartfelt pathos of Mr. Sankey's singing, fairly captivated the Irish people; and if the two could have remained long enough it is possible that St. Patrick might have been supplanted by them. A convention of three days, attended by more than eight hundred ministers and others from all parts of Ireland, closed the labors of the evangelists in Dublin. "Aged ministers," says one present, "bowed their gray heads and wept at times with joy. At one point during the discussion of Ireland, the central subject of the day, and when Mr. Sankey, seizing the opportunity with his usual tact, sang 'Hold the Fort' alone, and the ministers and people lifted up the chorus in a mighty shout, the enthusiasm was overpowering and altogether indescribable. It was the first time that all those ministers had met on a platform broader than their churches; and it is easy to see already that the impression on the country is very deep."

Leaving Ireland, the evangelists spent the month of December in the great manufacturing city of Manchester. It is a sad confession, but none the less true, that the factory system of England tends to the demoralization of the people. The blood and brains and muscles, if not the souls, of multitudes of the men and women of Manchester are used up in the production of cheap yarns and cloths for the various markets of the world. Thousands and thousands of poor, uncared-for people here, who had heard but few words of encouragement, and fewer still of love and blessing, received the good news of salvation from the lips of the revivalists, and caught a glimpse of heaven that will help them on till they behold the King in his beauty.

Proceeding from Manchester to Sheffield, a city of about two hundred and fifty thousand people, and famous for its cutlery, the two co-workers began their services on the last night of the year, and remained in the place, speaking to immense congregations in Albert Hall and other places; the interest continuing to increase until the departure of the evangelists, on the 17th of January, 1875, for Birmingham. This city of four hundred thousand people has been called "the toy-shop of the world." It received the gospel gladly, and was the scene of the most wonderful triumphs of the grace of God. The revival was the theme of conversation in every home, every office, every manufactory; and multitudes were brought to confess allegiance to Jesus Christ.

The people of these manufacturing cities are noted for their liberal and republican ideas; they have often listened to the eloquent orations of the great modern English statesmen; but the simple utterances of Mr. Moody pleased them more than the studied rhetoric of their ablest speakers. His honest Saxon way of stating Bible truths produced conviction, and led many to declare for Jesus.

"On a dull, raw, and inclement Sunday morning in January, such is the magic of their names," said "The News," "that they can crowd a large hall in the centre of a practical, industrial town, with worshippers, at an hour which would be considered early even on a week-day. That same evening they attract to a still larger edifice crowds which would be unusual in a period of intense national excitement. Again at noonday, when the bench and the desk chain their workers with the strongest bonds, thousands after thousands throng to meet them at the prayer-meeting until the Town Hall presents the appearance of a gigantic beehive, swarming with masses of people. Nor does the story close here. In the evening at Bingley Hall is gathered together an assembly which equals the population of many towns. A small harmonium, a few simple hymns, and short, stirring addresses on religious topics, comprise all that the public see or hear; yet the influence of Messrs. Moody and Sankey is overwhelming." The results mentioned were greater love and activity among believers, many conversions, and many drawn to listen to the gospel.

In the mean time, zealous Christian men were raising a vast structure capable of holding eleven thousand persons, and called Victoria Hall, in the heart of Liverpool, for the use of the evangelists. This was the first one built for them. Here from the 7th of February to the 7th of March they labored with their wonted fervor, and with even greater success than they had previously seen. The Young Men's Christian Association was very active, Christians were united, the tabernacle was capacious, and every thing conspired to make the meetings most effectual in bringing souls to Christ. Being in Liverpool three months subsequent to the departure of the evangelists, the writer found that at least two meetings a day had been, up to that time, held in Victoria Hall, and that, while he was attending service there, several persons were awakened and resolved to seek the Lord.

Leaving Liverpool on the 9th of March, the evangelists went at once to London, and commenced their mission in the great metropolis, not only of the British empire, but of the world. It is a nation of itself, made up of all kinds of peoples, languages, and religions. It abounds in churches, schools, museums, and places of amusement. It is the home, for half the year at least, of the royal family, and most of the nobility of the realm. It has vast masses of the poorest of the poor, more than one hundred thousand known and recorded criminals, and is demoralized to a lamentable degree by the use of strong drink. At the same time, its wealth is immense, and nowhere on the face of the globe is there greater indulgence in luxurious living. To gain the attention of four millions of such people, scattered over a territory twenty miles in length by ten in width, is no mean undertaking. Yet Messrs. Moody and Sankey did this; or, rather, God did it through them.

As London, like the city spoken of in Revelation, lies four-square, the plan was to reach in order every section. Four centres for operation were selected, — first, the great Agricultural Hall in North London, capable of seating fourteen thousand; second, the Royal Opera House at the West End, the aristocratic part of the town; third, the Bow Road Hall in East London, a building created for revival services, and holding about ten thousand; and, fourth, the Camberwell Hall in South London, erected for the use of the evangelists. In these several centres of aggressive work, the two men of God labored with unremitting devotion from the 9th of March till the 12th of July. The results were such as to surprise all beholders, and bring delight to all who love the cause of Christ. From my own personal observation and from inquiries, the conclusion reached was that the city in all its history had never before seen such displays of the power of God in the conversion of men of all classes and conditions. The number of the saved was far above the anticipation of the most hopeful.

In conversation with the well-known Newman Hall, he made the remark that never before had any Christian minister of the dissenting churches succeeded in getting the ear of the titled nobility of England, who, as a class, were in sympathy with the Established Church. "But," continued he, "your American evangelists have brought us all together, and now the most common thing is to see the highest people in the land at these meetings. Many times they are seen sitting side by side with the poorest."

Eternity can alone reveal the influences of these London meetings; and doubtless they will be felt as long as time endures. One of the grandest of English pulpit orators has said, "The moral state of England is of immeasurable importance to the whole human race;" and this we know to be true, because the relations of England extend to every part of the globe. Hence the mighty reformation in London has been world-wide in its bearings. It has swept across the Channel, and is a living power in France and Germany; it reaches every other nation in Europe; it touches Africa; it is felt in India, China, and far-off Australia. The songs of Mr. Sankey, and the sermons of Mr. Moody, are translated into the language of Madagascar, and are enjoyed by those most recently converted in the lands of heathenism.

The universality of the revival work in Great Britain was continually manifesting itself to the writer, during a long-extended tour through that country. Mr. Moody was quoted and commended in a sermon preached in the cathedral before the Archbishop of York. The press, almost without exception, was in sympathy, more or less pronounced, with the movement. Mr. Moody's addresses and sermons were printed and scattered broadcast over the whole United Kingdom; and the hymns sung by Mr. Sankey were circulated by the million. It was a pleasure never to be forgotten, to hear ten thousand Londoners singing heartily "Hold the Fort," and other familiar songs. Everybody seemed to know them; and in the cars, the homes of the people, as well as in the churches, they were heard. It was almost impossible to get out of the reach of these holy, heavenly melodies. The hearts of the old and young were filled with them.

In various places not visited by the evangelists, devout Christians were full of zeal for God, and were doing the best they could to hold revival meetings after the style of the men whose fame had entered every hamlet in the land; and their efforts were in many instances attended with success. It was especially pleasant to observe that the labors of these two earnest men had a tendency to bind England and America in closer bonds. No plans of diplomates, no carefully digested treaties, no congresses of the advocates of universal peace, have ever done so much to unify the two nations, as these two God-gifted men. The kindness of feeling existing, especially among the middling and the lower classes, towards America and the Americans, was simply marvellous. The cause of this, to a very marked extent, is attributable to the direct or indirect influences of Mr. Moody's words and Mr. Sankey's songs. Millions of English Christians felt themselves strangely in love with American Christians, full of good-will to our country and her institutions, and desirous of her future welfare; and though they might not love their own form of government any the less, nor abate their loyalty to their Queen, yet it was evident that they were ready to fraternize most cordially with their fellow-disciples across the sea. There was enough Christianity in the two nations ten years ago to enable them to forego a bloody quarrel, and afterwards to settle by arbitration a case that seemed almost beyond honorable and peaceful adjustment. But there is more of real Christlikeness in both nations now, and we can hardly conceive of circumstances in which their kindred people should resort to war. American evangelism in England and English evangelism in America antedate the dawn of the millennial glory destined soon to break upon this long-benighted world. The Christians of the British Isles, standing shoulder to shoulder with the Christians of America, and marching beneath the folds of the radiant banner of the Prince of peace, shall right speedily fill the world with their pæans of victory.   May God hasten the time, and bless all who pray and labor for a consummation so much to be desired!

CHAPTER VI.

THE EVANGELISTS RETURN TO AMERICA.—THEIR WORK IN BROOKLYN.—IN PHILADELPHIA.—IN NEW YORK.

Farewell to England.—Mr. Moody visits Northfield.—His Bible.—How he is Supported.—His Brother Converted.—Begins to preach at Brooklyn.—The First Meeting.—A Battle-Field.—The Singing of Mr. Sankey.—Conversion of an Infidel.—The Interest deepens.—"Hold the Fort."—How God forgives Sin.—Dr. Cuyler's Account of the Work.—Meeting of Ministers.—Letters to Converts Abroad.—"Only Trust Him."—Mr. Moody's Activity.—Conversion of a Lady.—Preparations in Philadelphia.—The Old Freight Depot.—The Opening Service.—The Classes of People attending.—How a London Lady works for Christ.—Cause of the Success of the Revivalists.—Thanksgiving Day.—President Grant.—Midnight Watch-Meeting for Sabbath-School Teachers.—George H. Stuart's Letter—Results.—Closing Words to Converts.—The Orange-Tree.—Visit to Princeton.

"I am not ashamed of the gospel of Christ; for it is the power of God unto salvation to every one that believeth."—St. Paul.

> " What means this eager, anxious throng,
>   Which moves with busy haste along, —
>   These wondrous gatherings day by day?
>   What means this strange commotion, pray?
>   In accents hushed the throng reply, —
>   Jesus of Nazareth passeth by." — Emma Campbell.

After a farewell meeting of great interest held in Camberwell Hall, July 11, in which the Earl of Shaftesbury said that if the American evangelists had done no more than to teach the people to sing as they did such hymns as —

"Hold the fort, for I am coming," —

they had by this alone conferred on them an estimable blessing, the party left for Liverpool, where an enthusiastic assembly of seven thousand persons greeted them, and received their parting benediction. Many followed them in the tender to the steamer "Spain," in which they took passage for America, arriving at New York on the 14th of August, 1875. During the voyage the passengers enjoyed the songs of Mr. Sankey, who, on being asked how he and his co-laborer had been able to do such a wonderful work in Great Britain, replied, "God was in it."

Mr. Moody repaired at once to the old homestead in Northfield, where he received a most cordial greeting from his beloved mother and the family circle; and in the seclusion of that quiet town wrote sermons, and pursued for a while the study of the word of God. His Bible is a curiosity. These words on the flyleaf, " D. S. Moody, Dublin, December, 1872. God is love. W. Fay," — indicate the donor, and the time and place where it was given. It is full of lines and references made with ink of different colors ; and the margins of almost every page are covered with written comments, annotations, and the heads of sermons, all evincing close and critical searching for the honey of the sacred volume. As an heir examines the will conferring a grand inheritance, so intently Mr. Moody studies the Bible. "What would you know," says he, "of your boy's letter, if you were to read the superscription on Monday, look at the signature on Friday, and read a little of the middle of it three months afterwards? I get tired towards the end of July, and I go away to the mountains. I take the Bible with me. . I read it *through*, and I feel as if I had never seen the book before. I have spent most of my life in reading and expounding it, yet it seems as if I had never seen it. It is so new, so rich, so varied, the truth flashing from a thousand unexpected and undiscovered points, with a light above the brightness of the sun. That summer reading of the Bible is what I call tuning the instrument." Mr. Moody has bought a little place near that of his mother, overlooking the fair valley of the Connecticut River, with the Sugar-Loaf Mountain on the south, and the Green Mountains on the west; and in this sylvan home he reposes and refits himself for his evangelistic labor. His sister, Mrs. J. Bigelow Walker, is now occupying the house. But, as this lay preacher takes no compensation for his services, how is he supported? In answer to this question, it is said that his friend John V. Farwell and other liberal Christians once remarked to him, " We know you want to go out and preach: you ought to do it. Go ahead, and we will see that you have the means." It is fortunate for Mr. Moody that he has such **noble** friends, since that **anxiety** for temporal support, which disturbs the peace

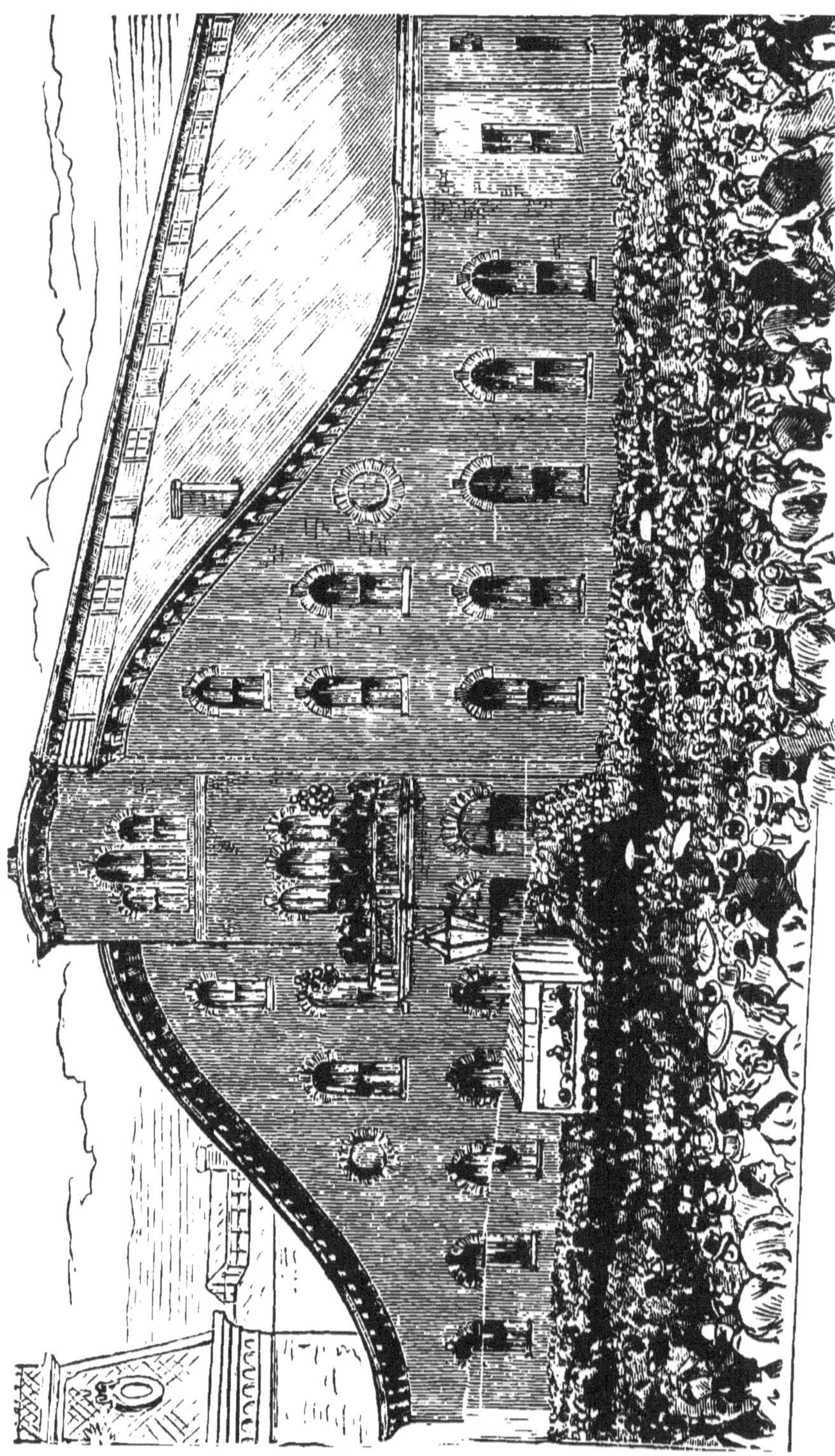

of so many servants in the Lord's vineyard, being removed, he can give himself wholly to the revival-work. While at Northfield many people came from distant towns to hear him preach; and among the conversions which he had the pleasure of seeing was that of his beloved brother Samuel. " He became," says Mr. Moody, " an active Christian; and, when they decided to have a Young Men's Christian Association for that town, they elected him for a president. Oh, that was a blessed day for me, when my brother, converted to God after twenty years of prayer, took charge of that little band! I heard him make his first speech, and that seemed the happiest day of my life. He searched for souls on both sides of the Connecticut River. More conversions took place after I left than when I was there. . . . No one knows how I loved him, and how I rejoiced with great joy."

The surprising results of the labors of Messrs. Moody and Sankey in Great Britain led some progressive Christians in the city of Brooklyn, N.Y., to secure their services towards the close of the year 1875. The public curiosity was excited, and extensive preparations, temporal and spiritual, were made. Subscriptions in money were obtained, the Rink on Clermont Avenue, capable of seating about five thousand, was provided for the preaching, and Mr. Talmage's Tabernacle for the prayer-meetings. Ministers and laymen with remarkable unanimity engaged in the good work; union meetings were held for prayer; and a new book of songs was published for the use of the worshippers.

Some fears, indeed, were entertained, lest the revivalists would fail to make the same impression here that they had done abroad, since there the songs and sermons were a novelty. But on the 24th of October the evangelical co-partners came up to the contest in the panoply of God; and the expectations of their most zealous friends were more than realized.

"Ah, Lord God! behold, thou hast made the heaven and the earth by thy great power and stretched-out arm," said Mr. Moody as he commenced his work in Brooklyn; "and there is nothing too hard for thee." So by His strength they won the public ear, and many hearts to Jesus.

The services at the Rink began at half-past eight o'clock on Sunday morning; but long before that time arrived, the streets were thronged with people eager to see and hear the men of whom such marvellous accounts had come from England. They surged into the building, which was quickly filled; and the doors were closed upon the disappointed crowd. Messrs. Moody and Sankey appeared upon the platform (on which a choir of two hundred and fifty singers was seated) at the appointed hour; and silence reigned in the vast congregation. Mr. Moody then rose, and gave out from the " Gospel Hymns,"—

"Rejoice and be glad ! the Redeemer has come,"—

which was sung by Mr. Sankey and the choir. Some one then present describes Mr. Moody as having "a ruddy, almost English face, covered to the cheek-bones with a heavy brown beard and moustache;" and as having also a husky tenor voice which he sent forth with earnestness and power. After a prayer by one of the ministers present, Mr. Sankey sung or rather chanted with great effect, —

> "Hark, the voice of Jesus crying, —
> Who will go and work to-day?"

when Mr. Moody rose, and delivered a thrilling address from Num. xiii. 30, " Let us go up at once, and possess it." The intense earnestness of the speaker held the audience breathless. " I say to you to-day," said he, " there is only one obstacle to a revival ; and that is the unbelief in the churches. Sinners and the Devil cannot stop a revival: it is only the unbelief of the Church that can do it. If we will trust God, we need not fear the rumsellers nor the sabbath-breakers. It is not we who fight, but God through us. You would laugh at seven priests marching. around the walls of Jericho, blowing ram's horns. If the doctors of Brooklyn were to blow trumpets, you would say they should be silver or gold. But God's way is not our way. I would like to speak through a ram's horn to the forty thousand ministers of the United States to-day, and ask whether they are ready to fall into line and go up and possess the land." — " We are all ready," cried Mr. Stuart of Philadelphia. " Then," continued Mr. Moody amidst great sensation, " let us go up and possess the land." When Mr. Moody closed, his coadjutor sung most appropriately and affectingly the song by Mr. Bliss, —

> " Only an armor-bearer, proudly I stand,
>   Waiting to follow at the King's command."

Of this first meeting Dr. Cuyler said, " It has been a great awakening for the Brooklyn people. There is not another man in the world but Moody who could have got them out of bed at such an hour on Sunday morning." The most rapid phonographic reporters found it impossible to keep pace with Mr. Moody in his most impassioned utterances, sometimes at the rate of two hundred and twenty words a minute ; but his most important thoughts were taken, and by the public press disseminated through the world. In the afternoon, thousands were unable to gain access to the Rink, and what are called " overflow-meetings " were held in several of the neighboring churches. Mr. Moody's theme was from 1 Cor. i. 1, " I declare unto you the gospel," which, after the singing of " The Ninety and Nine " by Mr. Sankey, he developed with surprising earnestness and power; closing with this telling illustration : —

" A friend of mine in Paris said that, when Prussia was at war with France, they went out one night to bring in the wounded men. They were afraid to take out lights, for fear of getting bullets from the enemy. When they thought they had taken up all the wounded, and all was silent on the field, a man from a high spot of ground cried in a loud voice, asking if there were any who wished to be taken into Paris, and telling them that the ambulance was ready. Before he spoke it was silent; but the moment he ceased speaking, and the men knew that there was help, there was a cry all over the field. Now, I come to-day to tell you there is One willing to save, that there is help. Let a cry go up, Shepherd, save me from death and hell! This is the gospel. We have no new gospel. Some will say that 'it is the old story; we thought we were going to hear something new:' but we have nothing new; we have only the old gospel. This to me is as fresh as it was twenty years ago: and, when I give up preaching this gospel, I shall go to farming or something else; for I know not what else to do." Thus the work of the evangelists in the "City of Churches" was most auspiciously begun.

It was arranged that during the week meetings should be held at the Tabernacle, commencing at eight o'clock in the morning, and in the evening at the Rink. At the first meeting in the former place, every seat was filled, a great number of ministers being present. The beautiful hymn, "Sweet Hour of Prayer," was sung by the vast audience, and Mr. Moody spoke with telling effect upon the theme that "Nothing is too hard for God." In the evening at the Rink, which was densely crowded, and after singing "I need Thee every Hour," "Free from the Law, Oh! Happy Condition, " and "Jesus of Nazareth passeth by, " Mr. Moody spoke from Rom. iii. 22, " There is no Difference ; " showing by apt illustrations how Christ brings us out by substitution from the penalty of the law.   The singing of Mr. Sankey was so felicitously adapted to the subject, and so touchingly pathetic, that a profound impression was made upon the audience.   Mr. Moody treats spiritual themes in a business-like and practical manner, without any sort o' cant or affectation.   His language frequently is very plain, sometimes ungrammatical : hence the songs of Mr. Sankey, which are characterized by a certain Scottish tenderness, come in to complement what is wanting in the speaker.   It is certainly the fitting union of the two that makes the whole complete.

In his Tuesday morning's service, Mr. Moody said, "I have hopes of the work in Brooklyn, not from the crowds at the Rink, but from these throngs at the morning prayer-meetings.   Let us unite in this work, that a wail may go up from this city, ' Lord, what can I do to be saved?'   We must shut ourselves up in our closets every day, and pray until his gifts are bestowed.   In London I knew a woman who had an infidel husband. She prayed every day for him, for a whole year; not succeeding, she resolved to pray every day for six months longer.   One day on going to her room, she found him there praying, ' O God, be merciful to me a sinner!'   He t a great business man in Europe, and has built a to tah at his own expense."

It was evident that the special presence of God was in the meetings, kindling the hearts of ministers and people, producing unity of sentiment among Christians, and bringing many of the unconverted, especially young men, to seek salvation. Many requests were made for prayer, many inquiry-meetings were held, and many churches were quickened in the revival work. Day after day, week after week, the religious interest deepened, and Mr. Moody said, " I have nowhere found more impressionable audiences than in Brooklyn; and the most encouraging feature is the union of the churches."

On Sunday morning, Oct. 31, Mr. Moody preached with his usual fervor to a vast concourse of people in the Rink, on courage and enthusiasm, and in his sermon said, " I would rather have a man with zeal and wanting in knowledge, than a man of much learning and little zeal. The former may do much good in the world: the latter helps no one but himself;" and when he prayed, " May God give us the holy fire of heaven!" the "amens" from the audience testified to the impression which he made. In giving out the hymn, " Hold the Fort, for I am coming," he said that during the Rebellion one of the Union officers in command of a fort closely invested by Gen. Hood was by the distress of his men almost persuaded to surrender the position, when he received a despatch from Gen. Sherman to this effect: " Hold the fort, for I am coming. — W. T. Sherman." It inspired the soldiers with confidence: they kept up courage, and were saved. " Mr. Sankey," says a writer, "produced a remarkable effect by the manner in which he rendered the last line, 'Victory is nigh,' and dwelt with redoubled force upon the word 'Hold' until the vast chorus of singers had caught the spirit and action of the leader." In the afternoon at the Rink, services were held exclusively for women, when more than six thousand were present; at the same time Mr. Needham, a well-known Irish revivalist, held an "overflow-meeting" in one of the churches. At the prayer-meeting on Monday morning following, Mr. Moody appointed a fast for Nov. 12; and in the evening at the Rink he preached his celebrated sermon on the "Lifting-up of the Son of Man," in which he said with great emphasis, "If there is any one here who will be lost, it will not be because Adam sinned six thousand years ago, but because he fails to accept the religion of Jesus Christ, which can save any man." During the prayer-meeting, at which the writer was present, Wednesday, Nov. 3, Mr. Sankey sung with exquisite tenderness Miss Fanny J. Crosby's beautiful song, —

> " Pass me not, O gentle Saviour!
>   Hear my humble cry :
> While on others thou art smiling,
>   Do not pass me by," —

and Mr. Moody commented interestingly on the one hundred and third Psalm, saying : —

" If the Lord forgives at all, he forgives all our sins.

Ezekiel says they are not even mentioned. They are rolled into the sea of forgetfulness. We greatly dishonor God by bringing up our sins after he has forgiven them. Hundreds of Christians are all the time doing this. Suppose my little child has disobeyed me, and comes to me and says, 'Papa, I did what you told me not to do I want to be forgiven.' She has deep and genuine repentance. I kiss away her tears, and forgive her. She then comes to me the next day, and wants to talk about it. 'No,' says I, 'it is all forgiven.' The next day she says, 'Papa, won't you forgive me for that sin I did two days ago?' I think it would grieve me. Suppose she came to me every morning for six months: would it not grieve me and dishonor me? God has not only forgiven our sins, but removed them for time and eternity. Ought one to dishonor and grieve him by bringing them up before him every day?"

Mr. Moody's remarks were pointed and logical, closing with an unstudied but effective climax. His Bible-readings in the afternoon were numerously attended, and served to deepen the revival spirit. In the evening at the Rink he preached on, " The Son of man is come to seek and to save that which was lost," and closed with a prayer so affecting that many of the audience wept, and his own voice was choked by his emotion. In the evening service at the Rink on Friday, Nov. 5, Mr. Moody spoke on " Where art thou?" and said in his discourse, " Oh that God would wake up the slumbering church of to-day, when men count themselves good Christians if they attend church and criticise the sermon!"

At the last of the three meetings on Sunday, Nov. 7, t.ckets were issued to those not professing religion; but many were unable to gain admission. At this service about three thousand copies of the gospel were distributed; and Mr. Moody, after prayer and the singing of "The Ninety and Nine," preached with much feeling on the tender compassion of Christ. During the service a woman fainted, when some one called out for a physician. Improving the occasion, the preacher said, "I have the Great Physician to offer you: he will cure your sins, and wipe out the stains of your soul, as well as heal your body." At the close of the second week's work, Dr. Cuyler wrote, "God's people keep in sweet unison. The press, secular as well as religious, continues its good behavior. Many souls are rejoicing in a new birth. . . . One of the grandest blessings of the week has been Brother Moody's three afternoon lectures on 'Studying God's Word.' He has made the Bible a new book to hundreds."

The revival meetings continued through the third week with deepening interest. Five meetings were held on Thursday, at one of which a German pastor spoke of a young man who was converted by hearing Mr. Sankey sing Mr. P. P. Bliss's hymn, "Almost persuaded." In the Bible-reading upon "Grace," Mr. Moody said he believed John Bunyan would thank God for Bedford Jail, and that the Devil found a match in him. On Friday, Nov. 12, the day appointed for fasting, nearly one hundred ministers were present at the early prayer-meeting in the Lay College; and many of them fell upon their knees, confessing their jealousies and hard-heartedness. At the meeting in the Tabernacle, which was crowded, after the singing of "Hold the Fort," Mr. Moody said, speaking of Daniel, "He held on to prayer until he heard from heaven. So let us hold fast at this hour until we get the desire of our hearts." It was a precious season to all present.

Mr. Moody wrote this day to his converts in Great Britain a very affectionate letter, in which he says, "Pack your memories full of passages of Scripture, with which to meet Satan when he comes to tempt or accuse you; and be not content to know, but strive to obey, the word of God. Never think that Jesus has commanded a trifle, nor dare to trifle with any thing he has commanded. I exhort the young women to great moderation. . . . Keep one little thought in mind, — I have none but Jesus to please. And so make your dress as simple as you know will please your Lord; make your deportment as modest as you know will commend itself to him."

On Sunday afternoon Mr. Moody preached exclusively to the women admitted on tickets, taking for his subject "Trust." After many earnest appeals to his audience, he invited those who were willing to trust the Lord to rise. Most of the congregation did so, and he then gave out the hymn, "Only trust Him," asking those who had arisen to sing the chorus, —

"Only trust him, only trust him," —

which they did.

"Now," said Mr. Sankey, "can't we sing it, 'I will trust him'? and at the end he said, "Now let us sing it, 'I do trust him!'" — "Yes," interrupted Mr. Moody, "sing it if you can, but don't lie." New voices were added to the chorus, when Mr. Moody cried impetuously. "Sing on! we're making heaven glad this afternoon; but don't sing a lie." After it had been several times repeated, he continued, "Now we'll sing it as a doxology, and then go home."

The revivalists closed their labors in Brooklyn on Friday, the 19th of November, the demand for tickets of admission and the tide of religious interest continuing to rise until the last. During their brief stay in the city it is estimated that as many as three thousand persons attended the inquiry-meetings, and as many as twenty thousand persons heard the gospel daily from their lips. During the last twelve days the committee issued a hundred and twenty-five thousand tickets of admission; and the desire to hear the co-laborers became more intense as the time for their departure drew near.

The activity of Mr. Moody during his stay in Brooklyn was amazing. From it ministers who complain that preaching one day in seven is above their strength may learn a salutary lesson. He conducted daily a great morning meeting at the Tabernacle, a Bible meeting in the afternoon, preached a sermon in the evening at the Rink, attended an inquiry-meeting after it, and then, returning to the Tabernacle, addressed at nine, P.M., a congregation of young men. Few preachers know what they can do until the Holy Spirit moves them to bring forth all their power for the conversion of their fellow-men.

When the revival was at its height, a very wealthy, cultivated, and sceptical lady from New York went over to hear Mr. Moody preach. She was amazed and a little disgusted by his style of oratory. But for some reason, which probably she could not have defined, she went again; still again. On her fourth visit she passed into the inquiry-room, and said to Mr. Moody that she would like to hear from him, directly and privately, his argument why she should become a Christian. He answered her, saying, " Madam, I know of no surer way to reach your heart than through prayer. Let us pray." Mr. Moody knelt. His manner was such that the lady could not choose, but knelt beside him. He asked her to repeat after him his prayer. In low, earnest tones, and with all the tender and pathetic phraseology of which on occasions he is master, he uttered his supplication, pausing after each sentence for his companion to follow. The prayer concluded with the vow, —

" And now, O Lord, I give my life to thee ! "

"Mr. Moody," said the lady, in a hard, painful whis per, "I cannot say that: truly I cannot."

Mr. Moody made no reply, nor did he change his position. There was a pause of half a minute. Then again he uttered the words, —

"And now, O Lord, I give my life to thee."

The lady, trembling, did not respond. The evangelist paused for about the same space as before, motionless. And now, with a voice still more resolute and fervid, he repeated for the third time the pledge. After a momentary interval of silence, the new convert said, —

"And now, O Lord, I give my life to thee."

Mr. Moody rose, took his weeping charge by the hand with the words, "Madam, I devoutly thank God," and led her quietly to the door. She has ever since been actively employed in religious work.

It is impossible to tell numerically the results of the revival: but while many conversions, manifesting the gracious presence of the Lord, occurred from day to day, the sacred flame of love to God and man was made to burn more radiantly in many a Christian heart; and thousands of ministers and teachers who had come from afar to catch new inspiration for their work went home to infuse fresh life into the spirits of those whom they instructed. The press, too, spread the living words of truth among the people, reaching millions daily who could not personally come within the magnetic influence of the great evangelists.

Arrangements were made for Messrs. Moody and Sankey to commence laboring in Philadelphia on the 21st of November. An old freight depot on Thirteenth and Market Streets was hired for two months, and fitted up at an expense of about twenty thousand dollars, by the liberality of the noble Christian, John Wannamaker; and a choir of six hundred singers, under the direction of William S. Fischer, was well trained for the occasion. The vast auditorium was provided with more than ten thousand chairs, and mottoes from the Bible were inscribed in large scarlet letters on the walls. Lighted by about a thousand gas-burners, and filled with people, this immense room presented a magnificent appearance.

The Philadelphians are proverbially sober, staid, and quiet; the ministers and churches undemonstrative and averse to change. It was, then, with many a serious question whether the revivalists would ever fill the building, or make any durable impression on the public mind. The clergymen were not very well united, nor had there been any such preparatory prayer as opened the way for the work in Brooklyn. But the words of the Bible and the hearts of men are everywhere the same; and, when brought together by the burning tongue of some God-appointed prophet, the result is ever the same. Great expectations had been raised on the part of the friends of the movement, for the opening of the work on Sunday, Nov. 21. But the rain came down in torrents; the seats in the churches

THE OLD DEPOT, PHILADELPHIA.

generally were vacant. At the morning service in the Market-street Tabernacle, however, there were at least nine thousand people present. The aim of Mr. Moody here, as in other places, was to awaken Christians to the necessity of personal labor for the salvation of their fellow-men. After prayer by the Rev. Dr. Richard Newton, the reading of the Scriptures, and the singing of the hymn by Mr. Sankey, —

" Ring the bells of heaven," —

Mr. Moody said, "Some ask, 'What is the object of these special meetings? are there not churches and ministers enough in Philadelphia? We have come just to help. In the time of the harvest, extra help is needed; and harvest time is now. I have been in the school of Christ for twenty years, and I have never seen a better time than the present. We are right in the midst of the blessings from heaven. Three classes attend these meetings, and I wish the first class might be brought over to the third. The first class, some of whom are Christians, come out of mere curiosity: they come to criticise, but it does not take brains nor heart to find fault. To such I say, 'Can you do better? If so, take hold and show us how.'

" The second class come just to enjoy themselves; and when they leave they say to each other, ' Didn't we have a good meeting?' They always come early, and take all the good seats. They are always ready to receive, but have nothing to give. We do not want such people here: we want ten thousand workers The third class consist of such. They come to watch and pray for souls; and, when they find one by their side weeping for sins, they take him to the inquiry-room, and show him the way to life. A lady in London," said he in conclusion, "succeeded in converting one hundred and fifty persons, and in speaking of it she said, ' We did not work: we just laid ourselves out for Christ.' That's the way to do it: don't count your strokes, just lay yourselves out. Go ye into the vine-yard: don't wait for the harvest, for — hark!" and after the breathless assembly had waited a moment, hearing only the rain-drops pattering on the roof, he added, —

> " ' Hark ! the voice of Jesus crying,
>   Who will go and work to-day ? "

when Mr. Sankey sung the song with marvellous pathos and effect. No such singing had ever before been heard in the churches of the " Quaker City."

The services in the afternoon commenced at four o'clock; but an hour before, the entire building was crowded, and thousands failed to gain admittance. Mr. Moody spoke on moral courage and enthusiasm, with his usual force; and his appeals were sent home to the heart by the spirited hymns, " Hear ye the Battle-Cry," and " Hold the Fort," as sung by Mr. Sankey, with the well-trained choir upon the chorus.

Thus was the revival work inaugurated. The plans adopted and the sermons preached were almost the same as those in Brooklyn, and week after week the surging crowd continued to fill the Tabernacle. The speaker had a blunt, ungraceful manner, an unstudied diction, and a husky, high-keyed voice. What, then, drew out the people in such numbers? what enchained as by an enchantment their attention? One attributed the interest to the reputation of the revivalists; but how had they gained that reputation? Another said it was their way of putting things; but many ministers in the city had more eloquent ways of putting things. Still another said it was by hammering at the heart with a sublime persistence; but some others did this without making an impression. The revivalists themselves said, "It is because the Spirit of God is moving the hearts of men;" and this undoubtedly was the true solution of the problem.

On Thanksgiving Day the auditorium was decorated with the national banners, and as many as eleven thousand people listened with rapt attention to the fervid utterances of the two great modern apostles of the gospel. "If you want to praise God," said Mr. Moody, "go and do some work; lift up somebody, relieve the sick, and comfort the heart-broken. By so doing it will be the best praise that we can give to God. . . . Oh that we may have live churches! Oh that we may get rid of these dead churches, with their cold forms and ceremonies, and have them filled with live, happy people!" Then the choir and congregation broke forth into the song, —

> " We praise thee, O God! for the Son of thy love, —
> For Jesus who died and is now gone above," —

after which Mr. Sankey, having told a touching story of a prodigal son, sung with sweet expression, —

> " There were ninety and nine that safely lay
> In the shelter of the fold,
> But one was out on the hills away,
> Far off from the gates of gold."

Mr. Moody's Bible-readings proved to be a great attraction to the Philadelphians, as many as five thousand being sometimes present to hear his felicitous interpretations of Holy Writ.

At the evening meeting, Dec. 19, President Grant, some members of his Cabinet, and some Congressmen, were present, and at the close expressed themselves as well pleased with the services, and especially with the singing of Mr. Sankey. " Mr. Moody," said Ex-Speaker Blaine, " is a wonderful man." At the inquiry-meeting that evening, Mr. Moody said, " It was the best service we have ever had in America or in Europe: it was perfectly marvellous; it went beyond all my faith."

" These are golden days for Philadelphia," said Mr. Wannamaker at one of the meetings : " to-night let this vast congregation join in the solemn prayer for the great and glorious work that is now progressing amongst us." And then the hymn, —

> " Rejoice and be glad ! the Redeemer has come," —

was sung so touchingly that a gentleman on the platform rose and exclaimed, " I have frequently heard it said that Jesus loves a musical heart more than a musical voice. If that be so, I tell you that here we have learned how both can be united."

At the close of the year 1875 a midnight watch was held, when after various solemn services Mr. Moody invited the whole congregation to unite in silent prayer. While all heads were bowed in supplication, Mr. Sankey sang in a low and broken voice, " Almost persuaded," then Dr. Newton recited the Lord's Prayer; " Praise God from whom all blessings flow," was sung; and the silence of profound meditation reigned until the clock struck the knell of the old year. Dr. Plumer of South Carolina then pronounced the benediction; and, after Mr. Moody had bid them all a " happy New Year," the meeting was dissolved. On the 6th of January, 1876, he tenderly addressed a great assembly on the subject of the sabbath school, urging teachers to labor personally for the salvation of their pupils. " ' Now let us go to work,' said I one day to two of my teachers, ' and see if we cannot win those three young ladies in the school to Christ. You take Margaret, you take Sarah, and I will take Henrietta; and we will give them books, write to them, visit them, and pray for them, work personally with them.' Within a month two of them were led to Christ; and since I have been in Philadelphia I have learned that Margaret has been converted."

On Fridays he spoke to the inebriates; and about a hundred and fifty of them were reformed during his stay in the city.

On the 14th of January, George H. Stuart wrote to "The Tribune," "The last service of the eighth week of Moody and Sankey's labors in this city was attended this evening by over thirteen thousand persons, filling the great depot building to its utmost capacity. Many thousands were turned away, unable to obtain even standing-room. The interest in these services has from the first steadily increased, and the labors of the evangelists have been and continue to be the all-absorbing topic of conversation."

The regular services of the revival were brought to a close on the 16th of January, when the throng of worshippers was still augmenting, and the religious interest deepening. It was estimated that since the work began on the 14th of November, the total attendance had been as great as seven hundred thousand, the number of converts four thousand, and the expenses of the revival were about thirty thousand dollars. No orator probably ever addressed in an equal space of time such a large number of people. The immediate effects were grand; but who can estimate the magnitude of the work as bearing on the future destiny of the mighty throngs that heard the word proclaimed with such convincing power?

Returning to Philadelphia on the 4th of February, the evangelists met the clergymen and the converts in the depot building, which was densely crowded; and after Mr. Sankey had sung with unusual tenderness Mrs. Emily S. Oakey's fine hymn, —

" Sowing the seed by the daylight fair,
Sowing the seed by the noonday glare," —

Mr. Moody prayed that God would bless the work accomplished, and that "on the golden shore of the Beyond, all who had found Christ might clasp hands without missing the face of one lost brother." He then addressed some earnest and affectionate words to the converts, taking for his theme, "God is able to hold you." In the course of his remarks, he used this beautiful illustration : " Every Christian's life should be like the orange-tree. In Florida I saw these trees growing in dry sand; and, when I asked how they lived, I was told that every tree had a tap-root which went right down until it struck water. We, too, must find a fount so pure and revivifying that no surroundings can injure our spiritual growth." " Let word and work," he also counselled, " be our watchword. If you neglect either the one or the other, you cannot be successful. But he who holds the word in one hand, and works with the other, must advance nearer and nearer to the throne." In closing he said with deep emotion, "I do not like the word 'farewell.' I'll bid you good-night, and by the grace of God I want to meet you in the morning."

Many eyes were moistened as " The Sweet By-and-By" was sung; and many a silent prayer ascended to

the mercy-seat as the audience left the building in
which so many brave words had been spoken, and so
many hearts won from ways of error to the love of
Jesus.

YOUNG MEN'S CHRISTIAN ASSOCIATION BUILDING, PHILADELPHIA.

In one of the meetings Mr. Moody took up a collection for the building of the Young Men's Christian
Association, which amounted to about a hundred
thousand dollars. He himself put in a diamond ring,

which came to him enclosed in this letter: "Dear Mr. Moody, — Through the instrumentality of the blessed meetings now closing, my darling son, a prodigal, and his wife, are now resting in a Saviour's love. The accompanying ring, the gift of one dearly loved, and so long worn it seems a part of myself, I now offer to my dear Lord and Master as a thank-offering for his unspeakable blessing. Do with it as the Holy Spirit directs." The ring was sold for a thousand dollars, and assisted in paying for the noble structure of which a picture is here given.

At the sale of the furniture of the depot building, Mr. Stuart gave fifty-five dollars for the chair of Mr. Moody, and Mr. Field the same for that of Mr. Sankey.

The same day, Feb. 5, Mr. Moody addressed the students of the college at Princeton, taking for his subject, "What Christ is to us." In the course of his remarks he said, "Some think we are getting wiser than the Bible; but I always say to those people, 'Bring me a better book than the Bible, and I will throw it away.' You might as well say, 'What splendid gas we have now! Let us build all our houses and churches without windows: we don't want the sun any more.'" The students were deeply impressed by the discourse.

At the conclusion of his address on "There is no Difference," the next day, fifteen of them rose for prayers; and before the month closed about one hundred were converted.

CHAPTER VII.

"Let him know that he which converteth the sinner from the error of his way
shall save a soul from death, and shall hide a multitude of sins." — St. James.

"In the cross of Christ I glory,
Towering o'er the wrecks of time:
All the light of sacred story
Gathers round its head sublime."

JOHN BOWRING.

THE two evangelists began their glorious work on
Monday evening, Feb. 7, 1876, in the city of New
York. The Hippodrome, a huge structure on Madison
Avenue, had been engaged for them, and divided into
compartments, one seating six thousand, and the other

154

about four thousand people. The space between them had been separated into rooms for inquiry and other purposes. As many as eight hundred singers and six hundred Christian workers had been trained for the revival. Union meetings had been held, in which earnest Christians of various denominations assembled to pray for the outpouring of the Spirit of God upon the people. The ministers were in living sympathy with the movement. Never, perhaps, before had preparations on so grand a scale been made in any city for the advent of an evangelist. Nor were the friends of religion disappointed in their expectations.

"Too much machinery about all this," said some who doubted. But for the diversion of the public in that same building, Mr. Barnum had used a great deal more. Might not the followers of Christ employ means to lead the erring to him? did he not himself use means to win them? and should not the means be in proportion to the work to be accomplished?

The audience that awaited Mr. Moody and his compeer was the largest ever convened in the metropolis, while thousands pressed in vain to gain admittance. As the speaker came upon the platform, and looked over the vast throng, he said, "Let us all bow our heads in silent prayer." The stirring songs "Hold the Fort," and "What shall the Harvest be?" soon followed, and then, choosing for his theme the power of weak things to confound the mighty, he spoke as one whose lips were touched with fire from heaven; and

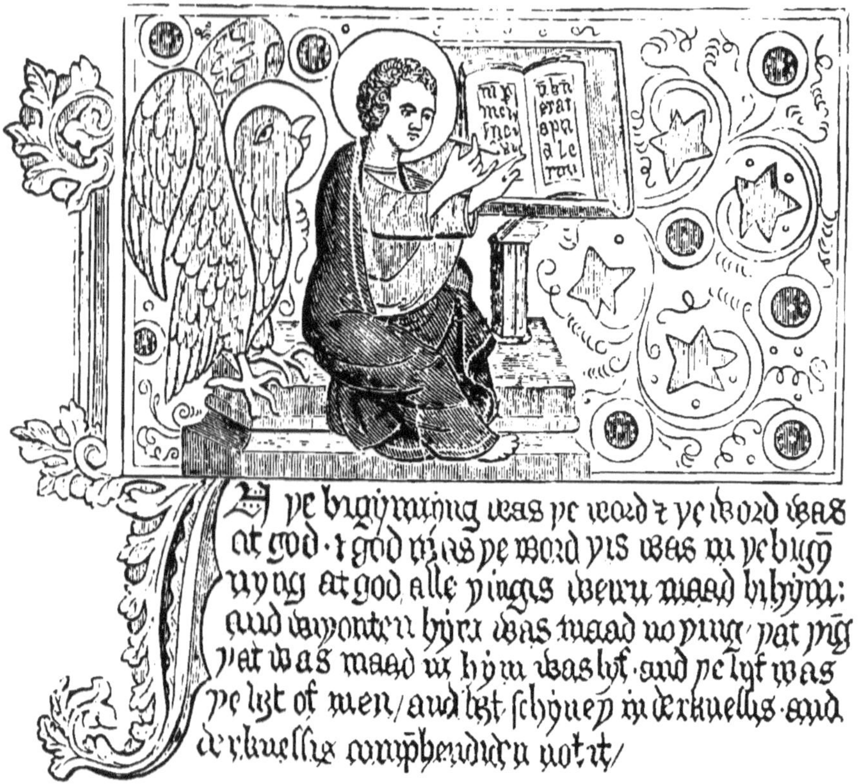

FAC-SIMILE FROM WYCLIFFE'S BIBLE.

From the first chapter of St. John's Gospel, Wycliffe's Version, Fourteenth Century. Engraved from the original.

moved, as no other living man could do, the hearts and consciences of the vast assembly. Instead of lessening, his incessant toil in Philadelphia seemed to have re-doubled both his physical and mental energy. In his style of delivery he had much improved, and never had he in any city before commenced his work with such a powerful sermon. God was evidently with him. All things were ready, and a great awakening was antici-pated. Mr. Moody closed his sermon by saying, " The mighty spirit of Elijah rests upon us to-night. Let us go to our homes, and cry to the God of Elijah, ' Here I am, God, use me,' that we may be ready for all his services." Here was the key-note of the awaken-ing.

On Wednesday evening, Feb. 9, the Hippodrome was, in spite of the rain, densely filled; and Mr. Moody, after the singing of " Only an armor-bearer " and other hymns, spoke on moral courage with such point and impetuosity as made a profound impression on the audience, so that many —

" Who came to scoff, remained to pray."

On Thursday, Feb. 4, five distinct meet'ngs were held at the Hippodrome, at which there was un aggre-gate attendance of about twenty thousand people. Many were moved to tears, and about two hundred inquirers remained to converse with the Christian workers. Mr. Moody's theme for the evening was, " To every man his work." His sermon abounded in felicitous illustrations, and riveted the attention of the audience to its close.

In his preaching during all the work, his chief aim was, to convince Christians that each and every one has a personal work to do in bringing souls to Jesus. "There are many," said he, "that are willing to do great things for the Lord; but few are willing to do little things. The mighty sermon of our Lord on regeneration was preached to one man. Many are willing to preach to thousands, but are not willing to take their seat beside one soul, and lead that soul to Christ."

It is the habit of Mr. Moody to write out a sermon carefully, and then, surcharging his mind with its spirit, to deliver it *extempore*, varying the illustrations so as to suit the character of his hearers. Most of his discourses he has repeated, it may be, forty or fifty times: yet such is the force and fervor he throws into them, such is the magnetic power of his person, that they are heard over and over again with unabated interest. The lively anecdotes and touching stories he has told so often have been a thousand times published and circulated through and through Great Britain and America. So many of them refer to his own life and experience that his biography might to a great extent be woven out of them; yet we love in him this frank, Pauline egotism, revealing as it does the honesty of his soul, as well as the noble ardor which inspires him to go forward in his glorious work.

"Mr. Moody must have great executive ability,"

wrote to me an attendant on the meetings at the Hippodrome, "for he controls his audiences seemingly without any effort; and you know in many cases there are rough men and boys, and women too, but there is never any disorder, and hardly ever any inattention. He is entirely devoted to his work: he thinks rapidly, and expresses himself as rapidly as he thinks. In the inquiry-meetings he is never at a loss for a reply, and that a good one. 'I don't think I have a soul,' said a lady there to him one day, 'any more than a dog.' —'Then why, madam, did you come to me? I can't reason with a dog,' he instantly replied."

The second week of the revival opened with the interest still increasing. On Sunday afternoon, Feb. 13, Mr. Moody preached on "the Gospel" to an audience of about six thousand women. Such a congregation had perhaps never before been seen in America. The novelty of the spectacle was almost as great when in the evening he preached the same discourse exclusively to men. "I have spoken," he said, "a great many times in this city; but I believe I never preached the gospel here but once. That was twelve or fifteen years ago, down in the Tombs. . . . I believe I was converted years before I knew what the gospel meant. Now, the word 'gospel' means 'good spell,' or in other words 'God's spell.'" Referring to the interest of Christ in the wandering, he said, "I noticed on my way down this morning not less than four or five tramps. They looked weary and tired. I suppose they had slept on the sidewalk last night. I thought I would like to have time just to stop and tell them about the Son of God, and how Christ loved them."

On Friday, Feb. 18, the noon prayer-meeting was attended by more than six thousand persons, the subject discussed being — as afterwards on this day — intemperance; and in the evening Mr. Moody preached his great sermon on " What is Christ to us?" In the course of his remarks he said, "I was once speaking on this theme in Europe, and said to a Scotch friend, as we were going home, I was much disappointed that I did not get through with the subject. He looked at me with astonishment, and said, ' What, my friend! did ye expect to tell what Christ is in half an hour? Ye need never expect to tell it in all eternity: ye would never get through with it.'"

In the audience were seen sometimes eminent merchants, lawyers, judges, and statesmen of the city. Gov. S. J. Tilden, Cyrus W. Field, and Dr. John Lord have been attentive listeners. Mr. Moody said he had never before received such cordial aid and sympathy from the ministers. Among those actively engaged with him were Messrs. Taylor, Tyng, Hall, Chambers, Anderson, Armitage, Ormiston, and Rogers. The latter said that during a ministry of more than thirty years he had never witnessed scenes of such solemnity and power.

On Sunday, Feb. 20, about four thousand Christians were present at the morning service; about ten thousand women listened to Mr. Moody's sermon on the text, "Where art thou?" in the afternoon, and about the same number of men in the evening. The Hippodrome continued to be crowded through the week; and in the streets, the offices and homes throughout the city, such words as "Have you heard Moody?" "Does he not send solid shot into his congregation?" "Did not Sankey sing most touchingly?" "Were you ever at such grand, good meetings?" continually met the ear. The secular papers spread abroad the truths spoken by the evangelists; and thousands of ministers from a distance, catching the inspiration of the great meetings at the Hippodrome, carried something of the flame back to their churches. Never since the apostolic times had the voices of two unlettered men so moved the world.

In his address on "Grace," Feb. 25, the speaker gave this pointed illustration: "'Moody,' said a man to me some time ago, 'have you got grace to go to the stake as a martyr?'—'No! what do I want to go to the stake for?' Another said to me, 'Moody, if God should take your son, have you grace to bear it?'—'What,' said I, 'do I want grace for? If God should call me to part with my boy, he would give me strength to bear it.' 'As thy days, so shall thy strength be.'"

Thus these two remarkable men proceeded day after day and evening after evening, Mr. Sankey with his melodeon, and Mr. Moody with his Bible, singing and preaching to undiminished audiences in the centre of New York City, quickening the hearts of the clergy, and turning many people to righteousness. Mr. Moody's sermons — among which those on " The Divine Compassion," " The Blood," " Heaven and its Treasures," " Men's Excuses," " God's Love," " How to study the Bible," " Work of the Holy Ghost," and " Trust," awakened great attention — were always direct, pointed, Biblical, catholic, and hopeful. They were all enriched with apt scriptural citations, touching anecdotes, pertinent illustrations, and epigrammatic points, that went directly to the heart.

In one of his addresses on the Good Samaritan he said, " A great many people ask us, ' What are you going to do with these young converts when you get them? where will you put them, into what church, — Methodist, Baptist, Episcopal?' Well, we don't know; we have not thought of that: we are trying to get them out of the ditch first."

The emperor Dom Pedro was present when Mr. Moody preached his thrilling sermon on " What shall I do with Jesus which is called Christ?" and paid the strictest attention, bowing his head in assent to the remark, " Even a great emperor cannot save his soul, with all his wealth and power, unless he bows himself at Christ's feet, and accepts him."

On the 29th and 30th of March a revival convention was held in the Hippodrome, at which there were 3,350 pastoral and lay delegates.

In reply to the many questions proposed to him, Mr. Moody evinced good common sense with not a little native wit. In respect to prayer-meetings he said, "They ought to be short. I find a great many are killed because they are too long. The minister speaks five minutes; and a minister's five minutes is always ten, and his ten minutes is always twenty. The result is, you preach everybody into the spirit and then out of it before the meeting is over."

To the question, "Why was the Lord not able to do any thing at Nazareth?" his quick reply was, "On account of their unbelief; but that was the world, not the church."

On being asked if he would encourage women preaching in the pulpit, he replied, "That is a complicated point, and we will leave it. I don't care about my wife going around and preaching."

To the question, "Would you stop a man's prayer by a bell?" he answered, "If a man's prayer don't seem to go higher than his head, I should not hesitate to ring him down."

To one asking him, "What is the best book for inquirers?" he said, "Well, the book written by John is about the best I have ever seen."

"Suppose none of the congregation understand music?" asked another: "how are you going to have it?"—"Well," said he, "I don't understand music, but I can sing, as well as Mr. Sankey. I can sing from my heart. The fact is, people have gone to sleep. Larks never sing in their nests: it is when they get out. A little boy who had been converted was constantly singing; while his papa was reading the paper one day, he came up to him, and said, 'Papa, you are a Christian, but you never sing.' Says the father, 'I have got established.' Not long after, they went out to drive, but the horse would not go. The father got vexed, and said 'I wonder what ails him.'—'I think,' said the boy, 'he has got established.'"

To the question, "How can you make sinners feel their sinfulness?" he answered, "That is God's work: you can't do it."

During the meeting of the convention, Mr. Sankey sung with great tenderness Miss Fanny J. Crosby's sweet hymn, —

> " Rescue the perishing,
>   Care for the dying, " —

Saying as he came to the third stanza, that it contained one of the most blessed truths referred to by the speakers : —

> " Down in the human heart,
>   Crushed by the tempter,
> Feelings lie buried that grace can restore:
>   Touched by a loving heart,
>   Wakened by kindness,
> Chords that were broken will vibrate once more."

The services of this great revival in New York, during which so many hearts had been rescued from perishing, so many believers brought nearer to God, were closed on Wednesday evening, April 19, 1876, when Mr. Moody during his affectionate address to the

Christian workers made this fine comparison : " You say you are in the world. Well, you may be in the world but not of it, just as a ship is in the water but not of it. The moment the water begins to get into the ship, it sinks. You are in the world, but don't let the world be in you." In his address to the converts, of whom about thirty-five hundred were present, he urged every one to serve Christ, saying, " It is not too much to expect that each one of you should bring twelve more to him. One young man came to me, and said he was converted on the 3d of February ; he had a list of fifty-nine persons, with the residence of each, whom he had since that time been instrumental in leading to Christ. Now, if he has led fifty-nine to the Saviour, each of you ought to be able to reach some. Let each of you go to work, for that is the way to grow in strength." As he bade the audience good-night he said, " We have received nothing but kindness since we came here, and the Lord has abundantly blessed our work. May God bless all the policemen, the reporters, the choir, the ushers, and all who have aided the Lord's cause since we came here ten weeks ago! May he bless all the ministers who have worked so nobly with us for Christ, and may the good work go on when we are far away!" Many were bathed in tears, and the benediction was pronounced by Dr. J. Cotton Smith.

It was estimated that as many as a million and a half of people had attended the various meetings at the Hippodrome, of whom as many as ten thousand different persons had been present at the meetings for inquiry. Large accessions were subsequently made to many of the churches; but what the grand harvest will be, what tongue can tell?

In taking leave of him, one of the leading New York journals said, "Make him the best-read preacher in the world, and he would instantly lose half his power. Put him through a systematic training in systematic theology, and you fasten big logs of fuel to the driving-wheels of his engine. . . . We shall not soon forget his incomparable frankness, his broad undenomination-alism, his sledge-hammer gestures, his profuse diction which stops neither for colons nor commas, his true-ness which never becomes conventional, his naturalness which never whines, his abhorrence of Phariseeism and of ecclesiastical Machiavelism, his mastery of his subject, his glorious self-confidence, his blameless life, and his unswerving fealty to his conscience and to his work."

At the conclusion of their ministry at New York, Mr. Sankey repaired to his home in New Castle, Penn.; while Mr. Moody, without taking rest, proceeded to Augusta, Ga., where he held, April 25, in the grove of the Presbyterian Church, a meeting at which about six thousand persons, white and colored, were pres-ent. The Southerners were delighted with his afflu-ence of illustration, and profoundly moved by his pathetic appeals. While referring to the healing of the woman by touching the Lord's garment, in his sermon of the next day, he said, "Jesus had more medicine in the hem of his garment than all the apothecaries in the land."

On Sunday, April 30, as many as fifty, moved by his magnetic power, rose up for prayers.

He left Augusta on the 9th of May, highly gratified with the kindness he had received, but more especially with having some good evidence that through his preaching many hearts were led to rejoice in the Redeemer.

Returning by the way of St. Louis, where he held several meetings of great interest, he became, on reaching Chicago, the guest of his benefactor John V. Farwell.

For the better accommodation of his church and society, Mr. Moody, prior to his visit to England in 1873, planned and commenced an edifice on the corner of Chicago Avenue and La Salle Street; but, owing to the depression in business, it was not completed till the summer of 1876. It is built of brick and stone in the Gothic style, and will seat about two thousand people. The whole cost of the structure, and the land on which it stands, was about eighty-nine thousand dollars, towards which sum about five hundred thousand sabbath-school children contributed their mite. The building was opened for service in June; but Mr. Moody then said that it should not be dedicated until it was entirely paid for. It was a bad thing to be in debt. He could not bear to look one in the face if he owed him any thing. A collection was then taken which amounted to thirteen thousand dollars, and the whole sum required to pay for the church was soon afterwards obtained. The edifice was dedicated on the 16th of July, the sermon on the occasion being preached by Dr. James H. Brooks of St. Louis. In the completion and dedication of his church, Mr. Moody had a long-cherished desire gratified; and he then soon repaired to his quiet home in the valley of the Connecticut River, for a little study and repose. But rest he could not find; for the desire to hear him was so intense, and solicitations for his services in the neighboring towns came in to him so urgently, as to admit of no refusal. On Tuesday, Aug. 15, he preached on revivals, to as many as a thousand people in the Congregational church in Greenfield; the next day he spoke in Northfield, and on Sunday following, again to a crowded house in Greenfield. On the 22d he delivered his great sermon on "To Every One his Work," before an audience of above three thousand people in the City Hall at Springfield. He was to have spoken at half-past seven, P.M., in the First Congregational Church. At four, P.M., it was packed with people; and when it was announced three hours later, that the services would be held in the hall, well-dressed women leaped from the windows of the church in order to secure seats in season. He also, with Mr. P. P. Bliss, held services on the 10th of September in Brattleboro', Vt.

In the mean time earnest Christian workers of various denominations were engaged in the construction of a tabernacle with seats for eight thousand persons, and standing-room for about two thousand more, in the business centre of Chicago, for the especial use of the evangelists. The structure, which was substantially built, costing about twenty thousand dollars, was of two stories, with galleries on three sides, and a platform in the rear of the speaker's stand, intended for the accommodation of about three hundred singers. During the construction of this commodious edifice, meetings were frequently held in the different churches of the city for the purpose of invoking the presence and Spirit of God upon the place, and of more fully preparing the hearts of Christians for carrying on the evangelical movement. A delightful spirit of harmony prevailed amongst the ministers, who spoke and labored as with one accord for the advancement of the work.

Chicago was the scene of Mr. Moody's early evangelical success; in that city his character as an aggressive herald of the cross had been established. The clergy had in him full confidence; the churches and the people needed the burning words of an accredited evangel to awaken them from slumber to the realities of religion and of the world to come. But a prophet has not honor at home. Men love novelty. The manner, voice, ideas, and methods of Mr. Moody were well known in the great city of the West. Here he had been prominently identified with the work of the

Young Men's Christian Association, into which he had infused a new energy; the erection of the beautiful hall of the Association being chiefly due to his labors.   But would the people come to hear him?   Would the expectations of his friends who had made such perfect preparations for the accommodation of the multitude

be met?   The anxiety on the part of Christians was intense, yet prayer for the outpouring of the Spirit of God continually ascended to the throne of mercy.

Mr. Moody began his evangelical labors at the new tabernacle in Chicago at eight o'clock on Sunday morning, Oct. 1, 1876; and the sea of upturned faces which then greeted him at once allayed the fears of Christians in respect to the result.   On the platform, supporting Mr. Moody, were many clergymen of different denominations, sitting side by side.   The choir of three hundred singers, led by Mr. Stebbins, opened the services by singing from leaflets, the Rev. W. P. Mackey's spirited hymn, —

> " We praise thee, O God! for the Son of thy love,
> For Jesus who died, and is now gone above," —

after which Mr. Moody said, " If we are going to have a blessing in the North-west, it must be from the throne of God."

From the " Gospel Hymns," Mr. Sankey sang several songs, as, -

> " Only an armor-bearer, proudly I stand,
>   Waiting to follow at the King's command," —

with a voice of winning sympathy; when the great evangelist rose, and in his impetuous and effective style, unlike that of any other living speaker, delivered his sermon on " Rolling away the Stone from the Door." The three great stones to be rolled away before the revival would succeed were unbelief, prejudice, and a sectarian spirit. " If I thought this morning," said he under the last topic, " that I had a drop of sectarian blood in my veins, I would open them and let it out before dinner. On the great day of Pentecost there was but one mind and one spirit."

At four o'clock in the afternoon Mr. Moody preached his sermon on the " Reward of the Faithful," to an audience of nine thousand people, every available spot in the Tabernacle being occupied. An immense overflow-meeting was also held in Farwell Hall. As Mr. Moody went on with his discourse he specified four classes — the ministers, the sabbath-school teachers, the young men, and the mothers — from whom he desired assistance in the revival. While speaking of the first class, he touchingly said, " There was one thing that pleased me

INTERIOR VIEW OF FARWELL HALL, Y. M. C. A. BUILDING, CHICAGO.

this morning, and that was the eight thousand people who came to this building, and the large number of ministers who seized me by the hand with the tears trickling down their cheeks, and who said to me, ' God bless you!' It gave me a light heart.''

Others had happy hearts that day; for some were turned to Jesus, and Christian workers felt assured a movement so auspiciously inaugurated would eventuate in success. The field was white for the harvest; the reapers had put in the sickle; and the aim of Mr. Moody's sermons, as in other places, for the first week or two, was to urge them to lay their hands with vigor to the work.

On Friday, Oct. 6, the evangelist was startled by the intelligence that his youngest brother, Samuel Holton Moody, had died at his home in Northfield in a fit; and, leaving his work so well begun, he came home immediately to weep with the afflicted family over the remains of the loved one passed away. He was buried on Tuesday, Oct. 10; and fifty young men whom he had been instrumental in converting followed him to the grave.

In a sermon preached on his return to Chicago, Mr. Moody said, " My call to mourning was the deepest I have ever known; for next perhaps to my wife, my two children, and my aged mother, I loved none so dearly as this youngest brother."

The first night on which rooms were opened for inquirers, a large number, especially of the neglected and the poor, were present; and when Mr. Moody, Nov. 6, met the young converts at Farwell Hall, he had the pleasure of addressing at least three hundred who had just set out to run the Christian race. Every day the tone of religious feeling was deepening in the city. Men and women of every class were seeking for salvation and crowding to hear the living word of God as sung or spoken by the revivalists. The noon prayer-meetings at Farwell Hall were well attended, meetings for the intemperate were crowded, and the meetings at the Tabernacle, especially on Sunday evening, were thronged with people who under the impassioned eloquence of Mr. Moody were swayed just as the sea by the deep ground-swell.

In his service on Sunday morning, Nov. 2, Mr. Moody said, --

" I will tell you how I got my first impulse in this personal work for souls. I hadn't got hold of the idea; there was no one to teach me, and I was going on with the general work of my school in 1860, when a man who was one of my Sunday-school teachers came into my place of business one day, looking very ill. I asked him what was the matter, and he replied, ' I have been bleeding at the lungs, and the doctors have given me up to die.'

" ' But you are not afraid to die, are you ? '

" ' No, I think not,' he answered ; ' but there is my class, — I must leave it, and there is not one of them converted.'

"It was a class of young girls that gave me more trouble than any other class in the whole school; and he had hard work to get along with them. 'Well,' said I, 'can't you go and call on them before you go away?'

"'No,' he said: he was too weak to walk.

"So I went and got a carriage, and took him round to see those careless scholars; and he pleaded with them and prayed with them, one by one, to give their hearts to Christ; he spent ten days at this work, and every one of that class was saved. The night before he left the city for his home at the East, where he was going to see his mother and to die, we got the teacher and the class together; and such a meeting I never saw on earth. He prayed and I prayed; and then the scholars, of their own accord, without my asking them, — I didn't know as they could pray, — prayed for their teacher, and for themselves that they might all be kept in the way of life, and by and by all meet again in heaven.

"I have thanked God a thousand times for those ten days of personal work."

An immense audience listened to Mr. Moody at the Tabernacle in the afternoon as well as evening. As many as a thousand persons presented themselves as seekers of salvation during the day. In the interim between the usual services, Mr. Moody preached a brief sermon to the Germans in Farwell Hall. After

Mr. Sankey had sung to them " Where are the Nine?
the Rev. Mr. Hager rose and said, " The secret of the
great success of these evangelists may be found in
three little words, — ' God, Virtue, Immortality.' "

CHAPTER VIII.

"Thy statutes have been my songs in the house of my pilgrimage." — DAVID

> "Strong in the Lord of hosts,
> And in his mighty power,
> Who in the strength of Jesus trusts
> Is more than conqueror." — CHARLES WESLEY.

A MOST impressive meeting was held in Farwell Hall, Thursday, Nov. 16, for the outpouring of the Holy Spirit. It was continued on Friday, and drew from Mr. Moody the remark that it was the most profitable one he had ever held in Chicago. The songs of Mr. Sankey in these assemblies seemed to soften the hearts of the people, and prepare them for the reception of the seeds of truth as sown by Mr. Moody. A gentleman from Elgin, who had been awakened by reading the reports of the revival in "The Chicago Tribune" came up to the meeting to-day, and on being asked by Dr. Thompson, —

"Are you willing to confess Christ to your friends?' replied, —

"Yes, I am."

"Will you kneel down here, and promise it to God?"
"Yes."

The two then kneeling joined in prayer, and rose rejoicing in the Lord. This is but one instance among many like it constantly occurring. God was there in the midst of them, speaking in a still small voice to thousands. Christian women organized themselves into a society in aid of the revival, and visited those parts of the city out of the usual line of evangelical effort. They were not a little surprised to find some who had never heard of the revival meetings.

"What," said these people, " is Mr. Moody a star actor?"   "Do they have dancing at the Tabernacle?" But many were induced to go and see for themselves; and some were led by the sweet influences of the house of prayer and praise up to a better life.

At a grand meeting for the business men of the city, many rose and testified to the good hope they had obtained of pardon and adoption.

On the 21st inst., a great Christian convention was held, when about twenty-five hundred clerical and lay delegates from the churches in the North-west were present. The meetings, conducted as in Philadelphia and New York, were characterized by fervor and solemnity. Mr. Moody illustrated what he considered the best method of carrying on evangelization by referring to the work as it was then proceeding in Chicago. At the close of the convention, Nov. 24, a large number of delegates entered into a covenant to pray for the special presence of the Spirit on their respective fields of labor.

On Thanksgiving Day, Nov. 30, Mr. Moody gave a dinner to the reformed inebriates, in his own church on the north side of the river, where about two hundred and fifty partook of the feast.

An old Scotch woman once kept the noon prayer-meeting alive in Chicago, by performing all the exercises by herself and to herself. The next day Messrs. Moody, Farwell, and Jacobs came to her rescue ; and the noon prayer-meeting became an altar where the sacred fire burned most steadily in that city. But so wonderfully had religious interest deepened, that on Friday, Dec. 8, as many as seven thousand were present at that meeting, and the most reverent attention was given to the solemn services. In the afternoon Mr. Moody continued his Bible-readings ; and in the evening, though a storm was raging, had as many as four thousand at the Tabernacle, to hear his sermon on the " Rich Man " spoken of in the twelfth chapter of Luke.

In his effective sermon to young men, on " Your sin will find you out," at the Tabernacle, Dec. 13, Mr. Moody said, —

"A man was cursing me on the street to-day for sending a poor fellow back to the penitentiary in Ohio, to meet the just punishment of his theft and his perjury; but, if he had not done that thing, he never could have stood before God in judgment. He must confess his sin; and, though it meant three years in prison, still he must reap what he had sown. I have received a letter from that man, and he says that he is a happy man in spite of his prospect of a prison. God is with him, and is helping him bear his punishment, now that he has confessed and given his heart to Christ."

At the Friday noon prayer-meeting on the 15th, the exercises were opened by the singing of Horatius Bonar's familiar hymn, —

> " What a friend we have in Jesus,
>   All our sins and griefs to bear!
> What a privilege to carry
>   Every thing to God in prayer!"

After which Mr. Moody spoke to about seven thousand people on temperance, who, rising at the conclusion of his address, pledged themselves to abstain from the use of wine and other intoxicating beverages at their receptions on New Year's Day. During his address Mr. Moody related the following affecting incident as an illustration of God's readiness to answer prayer: Six weeks ago the speaker had read a letter from parents in Scotland, begging him to find their wandering boy Willie. For six weeks Mr. Sawyer, who has charge of the temperance work, sought in vain to find the boy; but a week ago last Friday a young man came up to Mr. Sawyer accidentally, and addressed him.

"What is your name?" said Mr. Sawyer.

"Willie ——," he replied.

"Is it, indeed? I have been seeking for you the last six weeks."

"How can that be?" answered Willie. "You do not know me."

"Yes," said Mr. Sawyer. "We have a letter telling of your mother's love and prayers for you."

"That," said Mr. Moody, "broke his heart; and on Friday he stood up and told a story that melted the whole audience to tears. Years ago he married a beautiful girl, a minister's daughter. Already he had begun his downward course. His wife, who had been his guardian angel, soon died. They had a little girl. He left her, and became a homeless wanderer. When about to start for Australia, his little girl, kissing him good-by, said, 'You will not be gone long, papa.' He had not seen her since. He had gone the world around, — a very prodigal, full of sin and shame. But now prayer had been answered; God had brought the lost one home." "Strong men," says The Interior, "fairly sobbed, and the whole audience was in tears. Mr. Moody, with a voice broken with sobs, gave thanks for answered prayer, and cried to God to keep the boy, by his grace, unto eternal life."

The revival influence had now spread out from

Chicago into many cities in the North-west, and helpers went forth to assist the pastors. Messrs. Whittle and Bliss carried on the good work at Peoria, Mr. Harry Morehouse at Racine, and Messrs. Needham and Stebbins at Fort Howard in Wisconsin. Mr. Moody was to have closed his labors in Chicago, Dec. 17; but such was the manifestation of divine power on the hearts of the people that it was deemed advisable for him to continue one month longer. He wrote, Dec. 20, an appeal to the churches of the North-west, in which he said, "The work in Chicago ought to be regarded as only a small part of a great general awakening," and urged them to unite and seek for it in importunate prayer.

In his sermon on Christmas Eve Mr. Moody made this point, which moved the vast audience as if the angel notes were pealing over it: "You are in debt to God, and you have nothing to pay; but Christ offers to pay it all if you will accept him. Set down all the sins you can think of, and then write underneath, 'The blood of Jesus Christ his Son cleanseth us from all sin.' There it is over there, painted on the gallery-front. I am glad they painted the 'ALL' in big letters. That is the gospel: all your sins are washed away in the blood of Jesus Christ. Surely that is the very best news you could hear."

The intelligence of the death of Mr. P. P. Bliss and his wife in the terrible railroad accident at Ashtabula Bridge, Dec. 29, filled the hearts of the evangelists with profound sorrow. On the sabbath following, the choir at the Tabernacle sung several of the hymns of Mr. and Mrs. Bliss; and when Mr. Moody came upon the platform he repeated with intense emotion the words of David, "Know ye not that there is a prince and a great man fallen in Israel?" He then said, "Let us lift up our hearts to God in silent prayer," and proceeded afterwards to speak in eulogistic terms of the deceased. He subsequently raised ten thousand dollars by subscription for the children of the departed singers, and also had money contributed for a stone to perpetuate their memory.

It were utterly impossible to measure by numerical signs the mighty influence of this evangelical enterprise in Chicago. As well might we attempt to make a record of the sunbeams dancing over the waves of ocean. The hearts quickened, the eyes opened, the homes gladdened, the kind words spoken, the prayers answered, the seeds of truth scattered, the trains of influence started, can be counted only in the land beyond the river. "It has been," says The Interior in speaking of the revival, "a great day in Chicago, in many respects the greatest our city has ever seen. It has been the day of her merciful salvation. Unlike her day and her nights of fire and sackcloth and ashes, it has been a day of joy and gladness; it has been a day of Pentecost, a day of extraordinary privileges, a day of great and blessed opportunities. It has brought salvation to many hearts and many homes, to the splendid mansions of the rich and to the humble dwellings of the poor. There are many who have been able to say during these three months, as they have never said before, ‘The Lord hath done great things for us, whereof we are glad.’ Our churches are revived, our ministers are revived, our sabbath schools are revived, our Christian homes are revived. In many new homes the voice of prayer and praise is now heard where it was never before.

If ever any thing was put forward by system, it has been this revival movement; one man performing one kind of labor, and another, another kind of labor; Mr. Moody and the ministers and the workers sounding out more and more warmly the great battle-cry. The instrumentalities have been short prayers, short sermons, pathetic gospel songs, Bible readings, hard work, common sense in an unusual degree, and a zeal and faith which grew stronger every hour up to the close.”

After the foregoing pages had been written, the following interesting account of the revival in Chicago was received from the Rev. Mr. Pentecost : —

“ The ordinary seating-capacity of the Tabernacle was eight thousand ; but on Sundays and special occasions two thousand extra chairs were introduced to accommodate the great throngs of people. Those who are accustomed to see only the ordinary six hundred or one thousand persons who make up an average city congregation can have but little idea of the imposing effect produced by witnessing that vast audience of ten thousand people, all with eager, interested faces, listening to the rapid and oftentimes impassioned utterances of the evangelist. Yet this great, and in this country unprecedented audience, was sustained night after

INTERIOR OF TABERNACLE, CHICAGO.

night for nearly four months; and three times each Lord's day was the building filled, — at eight A.M., and at four and eight, P.M. But the meetings in the Tabernacle were not the only ones held. Twice every day

Farwell Hall, with a seating-capacity of twenty-five hundred, was filled to overflowing. At noon the people gathered in it to spend an hour in prayer, and at three o'clock, P.M., again to listen to a Bible-reading by Mr. Moody. Beside these main meetings there were held every day a men's meeting and a women's meeting In addition to the union meetings there was, as a result of the work of Messrs. Moody and Sankey, an unusual interest awakened in nearly every evangelical church in the city, so that almost daily the various pastors held inquiry-meetings in their churches.

"It would be a great mistake to suppose that this awakening was confined to Chicago. Such was not the case: it was felt throughout the entire North-west. By twos Mr. Moody sent out evangelists, one to sing, and one to open the Word; and in all the leading towns and cities round about the truth was preached with power and in the Holy Ghost. Of this great work in the North-west, it may be said in the language of one of the sweet gospel hymns, —

' The half was never told.'

The noonday prayer-meeting in Farwell Hall was thrilled again and again, as the reports came in from the churches, and by telegram from the outlying cities, where the evangelists were at work, of the great things God was doing in righteousness.

"One of the most blessed results of the meetings in Chicago was the fusing together of the evangelical churches. Sectarianism seemed for once to have been laid low in the dust; and it will be impossible in this generation, if ever again, to revive it. It was "the church which is in Chicago." One had to make diligent inquiry to find out to what denomination the min isters who were in constant daily attendance belonged. This alone must result in good unspeakable.

"The mere casual observer might not have noticed any distinct plan in the meetings; but a little close observation reveals the fact that never did a general plan a campaign with more method and precision of detail than were those meetings and the work in connection with them pre-arranged.

"As near as can be indicated, the results aimed at were as follows : —

"First, To bring about union of effort on the part of the evangelical churches and ministry. This Mr. Moody makes a grand condition of success. At first the union may have been more apparent than real; but as the work proceeded, the beauty, power, and blessedness of real union, in the effort to promote results dear alike to all evangelical believers, were realized. The ministers worked together as brothers; and, catching Mr. Moody's spirit, they seemed to realize that 'the church which Christ purchased with his blood,' was of more importance than any sect within the church; and, as a consequence, sect and sectarianism took their proper and subordinate places. It is pretty certain that hereafter the walls between Methodists, Baptists,

Congregationalists, Presbyterians, &c., will be regarded as walls that bind together, rather than as those that separate.

"Second, The next general movement was upon the Christian people themselves, and the work was thus divided. First, Christians were taught the sin and misery of living in doubt respecting their relationship to God. The finished work of Christ was urged as an all-sufficient ground for coming into absolute assurance of salvation. Frames and feelings were made to give place to assurance based upon the promises of God, . which cannot be broken. When the question was put, 'Are you a Christian?' or 'Are you saved?' the doubtful 'I hope so,' or 'I think so,' were made to give place to the simple 'Yes,' or the assured 'I am;' and this was not the language of presumption, but simply that of faith. The 'verily, verilies,' of Christ to believers were made prominent; and, throwing themselves upon the word of God, Christians were lifted into confidence. 'These things,' says John, 'have I written to you that believe, that ye may *know* that ye *have* eternal life' (1 John v. 13), 'I *know* whom I have believed, and am *persuaded* that he is able to keep that which I have committed unto him against that day' (2 Tim. i. 12), and other scriptures of the same import, were brought forward. The result was joy, gladness, and liberty among the believers. That snare of Satan, that to have assurance is presumption, and to be in doubt is humility, was entirely broken; and scores of Christians who had been raised, it is true, out of their grave of trespasses and sins (Eph. ii. 1), but who came forth bound hand and foot with their grave-clothes, and who had been living for years thus bound, were loosed and set free (John xi. 44). It was most refreshing to be in company with these Christians, walking in confidence, and yet in great humility. Their very presence, with happy voices and shining faces, were living sermons. Truly that was seen again which is recorded: ' Then were the churches edified, and walking in the fear of the Lord, and in the comfort of the Holy Ghost, were multiplied' (Acts ix. 31). Second, a most direct and searching delivery of the word of God was made upon that vast multitude of worldly and formal Christians who have a name to live indeed, but are dead,— who, being in the church nominally, are yet really in and love the world. Truly they came to church once or more on the Lord's day, but beyond that they had apparently no part or lot in the matter. Such persons were plainly taught that, 'if any man love the world, the love of the Father is not in him.' The result of this plain, straightforward preaching to the cold and inconsistent members of the church produced a very marked effect, as the following incident will serve to illustrate: —

" My attention was attracted, in one of the women's meetings, to a remarkably fine-looking woman, past middle life, plainly but elegantly dressed, and evi-dently a person of influence and position. Yet above

all mere dress and bearing there was something in her
face that marked her as being thoroughly devoted to,
and enthusiastic in, the work. On asking who she was,
a friend replied to me, ' That is Mrs. ——. She is
one of the leading women in Chicago, — wealthy and
very influential. A few weeks ago she was found in
the inquiry-rooms; and, when Mr. Moody asked if she
was a Christian, she replied, " Mr. Moody, I am a
member of the —— church; but I am going straight
down to hell. And that is not the worst of it: I am
leading my husband and children down there with
me." She then went on and told a story of early conversion, of removal in early life to Chicago, of the
prosperity of her husband in business, of accumulated
wealth, of worldliness coming with the wealth, of a
mere nominal Christian life, and how for years she had
been plunging headlong into every fashionable pleasure
and dissipation. Now the whole course of her life had
been suddenly brought before her, and she was con-
science-smitten, especially as she believed, that, but for
her sin and folly, her husband and her children might
have been saved. She had no hope for herself, but was
in great distress about her family. She longed to see
them saved. Mr. Moody turned her thought to God's
word to backsliders, and pressed her to come to Him
who said, " Return, thou backsliding Israel, for I am
merciful." The result was, that then and there she
gave her heart back to the Lord, accepting his plenteous
mercy. Going to her home, she confessed to her hus

band and her children the sinfulness of her past life, and, seeking their forgiveness for unfaithfulness, she besought them to turn to the Lord, which they did; and salvation came to all in her house. Then, turning to the Lord for service, she gave herself entirely to it, and became, by reason of her zeal, ability, and position, one of the most efficient workers in Chicago.'

"It might also be mentioned that very many men who had been silent and inactive in the church, except in its business meetings, have been greatly quickened in this revival. Dr. Goodwin gave me this incident, in connection with his church: 'One of our best men, yet one who never took any part in our devotional meetings, went one day to a brother in the church, who like himself was a "silent member," and said to him, "Brother ——, you and I have been in the church a number of years, and yet I never heard your voice in prayer or testimony, nor you mine. Now, I think we have been dumb long enough. We have no trouble in talking to each other on 'Change about our business. What do you say to calling with me upon Brothers A and B and C and D, who like ourselves have been silent so many years, and having a meeting of the *dumb Christians* of our church?" The result was a gathering of the *dumb* for prayer. They had their meeting all alone, and had it again; "and now," said Dr. Goodwin, "we can scarcely get a word in edge-wise." Several of the largest mercantile houses have suspended business during an afternoon, and, calling their employees together, have held prayer-meetings This is notably true of the house of John V. Farwell & Co.. and, I understand, of Field, Leiter, & Company.

"Third, Throughout the entire North-west, and especially in the large towns and cities, there are thousands of men and women, who, having removed from the Eastern and Middle States, have taken no letters from their home churches, or, if so, have failed to ally themselves with any of the churches in their new homes, and from various causes have slipped back into the world, and are known or unknown as backsliders. Vast numbers of these wandering and backslidden Christians have been reclaimed, and restored to the churches.

"Thus has this great awakening gone through the churches. The best have been quickened; doubt and despondency among morbid Christians have given place to confidence and joy; worldly Christians have been led into a new consecration; and many open, sad backsliders have been turned from their backslidings, and restored to God. The work in the church would of itself be an unspeakable blessing. It ought to be added that the influence of these meetings upon the clergy has been most helpful. They have learned new lessons in the work of the pulpit. First they have learned that the most effective preaching is not the most elaborate, and that the best preaching is that which the most simply expounds the word of God; and second, that written sermons are not, for effectiveness with the masses, to be compared, as a general rule, with direct, simple, warm-hearted, extemporaneous address.

"After a week or two spent in stirring up the church, and inciting Christians to consecration and service, the preaching was directed mainly to the unconverted. Mr. Moody's style of speaking is direct and simple. He adheres rigidly to the plain statements of the word of God, — teaching that all men are sinners, that there is no difference as to guilt, 'for all have sinned, and come short of the glory of God;' that 'God commended his love toward us in that, while we were yet sinners, Christ died for us;' that Christ as the Son of God has through incarnation, death, and resurrection, made a complete and finished atonement for sin; that God desires the salvation of all men; that all, even the worst, may come to God through Christ now, and be saved; that conversion occurs the instant the sinner believes. His sermons are characterized by an intense, living earnestness. One feels that he loves the souls of men, that he has a perfect hunger for them, and that he is trying all the time not only to induce them to trust God through Jesus Christ, but also by his own simple and vehement faith to lift them himself into reconciliation with God. He believes thoroughly in the existence of a personal Devil, in future punishment, and that eternal death awaits all who reject Jesus Christ. This makes his preaching terribly earnest. He has, or seems to have, a superabounding love for the very poor and the deeply fallen, especially for the drunkard. His work among the intemperate is especially marked and wonderful. He teaches that drunkenness is not only a misfortune, but a sin ; that it can be dealt with effectually only by grace ; and that this can and does save drunkards from drunkenness as well as from the desire for drink, as it saves a liar from lying and from the desire to lie. The hope of perfect salvation from the appetite for drink has in it a charm for the drunkard, — who has so vainly striven to break loose from the bondage of the 'rum-devil' as he calls it, — that leads him to seek Christ and salvation from all sin. Many thrilling incidents of salvation coming to life-long drunkards might be related, — how heart-broken families have been lifted up and restored ; how men who have gone home for many years under the influence of liquor have returned at last converted. Several hundred drunkards in Chicago have been thus saved.

"The main work among the unconverted is done in the inquiry-rooms. The sermons are designed mainly to awaken an interest in the things of God, and to induce the unconverted to go into the inquiry-rooms where the work of the meetings is really done. The methods used are substantially as follows : —

" After the sermon, which is always short, all persons desirous of being saved are invited to retire to one of the many inquiry-rooms in the building. Then the benediction is pronounced, a hymn is sung, and the congregation is dismissed. Usually from one to three hundred persons find their way into the inquiry-rooms. Here a brief address is made explaining more fully the way of life, then follows a season of prayer; then at once a Christian finds out some unconverted one, and the two, going together apart from the crowd, sit down face to face, the worker having the Bible in his hand. The sin of the human heart is laid bare, and the saving grace of God held up. Repentance, faith, and the confession of Christ are urged. All over the room, earnestly conversing in suppressed voices, these little groups may be seen, apparently oblivious of the presence of other people. After a while two persons may be noticed slipping quietly from their chairs to their knees, which indicates that the surrender to God has been made, and there upon the bended knees the heart is given to Jesus Christ; sometimes it means that the darkness of the mind is so great that no progress can be effected, and that an appeal is made to heaven for light and pardon.

"The following incident may serve to illustrate the nature of the work:—

"The inquiry-rooms had been crowded all the evening. It was now about eleven o'clock, and most of the 'workers' and inquirers had gone home. A few, however, of both classes were lingering still. I had just left a man — a straightforward German — who had given himself up to God through Jesus Christ; and was about leaving the room, not seeing that there was any thing more for me to do, when I was approached by a young Christian who said,—

"'Mr. Pentecost, before you go won't you come and

speak to that young man ? [pointing to him] I do not seem to be able to meet his need.'

"'Certainly,' said I, and went over to where the young man was seated, and, drawing a chair up to him, said, —

"'Can I be of any help to you, my brother ?'

"'I don't know, I am sure ; but, if you can give me any help, I will gratefully receive it.'

"A few questions developed the fact that he was a cultivated young German, the son of a German rationalistic theologian. He had been but a short time in this country. He was thoroughly conversant with the current Continental sceptical philosophers, he told me that he was fond of study, and especially philosophical study, and gave good evidence of familiarity with the various schools of thought current and past; he said he had been led to think of Christianity as an ingenious mythology, having a very slender thread of historical truth in it, more or less the product of an early enthusiasm that had exalted Jesus into Deity. He confessed that he had never made the New Testament a study, but had imbibed his opinions mainly from Strauss. He went on to say that he had been attracted by curiosity into the Tabernacle, and had been amazed at the vast audiences held together week after week without excitement, simply by the rehearsal of Christian truths and Bible stories. He admitted that he was impressed with the matter of Mr. Moody's preaching, and was convinced from his manner that he was a sincere and honest teacher. Finally he determined to take up the New Testament, and carefully read it. He had done so, and this night he had come into the inquiry-room to seek conversation with some Christian who would explain, if it were possible, some of the chief difficulties that he met with in the New Testament. He was altogether frank and candid, saying that he was free to admit that a careful reading of the New Testament revealed a purer and altogether better system of ethics than any of the philosophers with whom he was acquainted, and that the whole book had an air of sincerity and truth about it. But there were several insuperable difficulties in the way of his acceptance of it as truth.

"I asked him to state his difficulties, which he did in about these words : —

" ' There are three great claims set forth in the New Testament, upon the truth of which it seems to me the whole system must stand or fall.'

" ' What are they ? '

" ' Why, first of all, it is claimed all through the New Testament that Jesus was the Son of God, i.e., God manifested in human nature — a supernatural being. This he claimed for himself, and even died in defence of the claim ; for, if I am not mistaken, that was the charge upon which he was put to death by the Jews that in claiming to be the Son of God he made himself to be equal with God, which is blasphemy. Certainly he believed himself to be God ; and so did his apostles, especially John and Paul."

"'Well, what is your next difficulty?'

"'Why, the next difficulty is that our salvation depends not upon the uprightness of our own lives, but upon the fact of Christ's death, which is represented as a sacrificial act,—what Mr. Moody calls the atonement.'

"'Well, what is the other difficulty?' ⸱

"'Why, the resurrection of Christ from the dead. Every thing in Christianity depends upon that.'

"'Well,' said I, 'now, why are these things difficulties to you?'

"'Why, I cannot possibly believe that Jesus was God: he could not be. And it is not possible for any one who was really dead to rise again: such a thing never was in the world, and it cannot be; and even if it were so I do not see how any one could be saved on account of another's death, and not on account of his own uprightness.'

"I confess that the task before me seemed very great indeed. But he seemed guileless in his desire to know the truth, and so with a prayer in my heart for help I said,—

"'Well, now, let us look at the first difficulty,—the incarnation. As I understand it, you are a theist: you believe in the existence of a personal, eternal, and omnipotent God, who is the author of the universe and our being?'

"'Oh, yes!'

"Very well. Now, with that for a starting-point you

cannot philosophically hold that the incarnation is an impossibility, — that it could not be.'

A very little talk ended in his admitting the possibility of the incarnation, but denying the probability of it; and then he went on to say with the quickness of thought, and the clearest perception of the whole matter, —

"But I think Jesus was himself deceived. I grant that he may have in moments of enthusiasm thought he was the Son of God; and that he did at times make this claim, there is no doubt. But at other times he certainly made such statements as forbid us on his own testimony to believe that he was equal with God; indeed, he admits that he is an inferior being. In fact, Christ's own testimony concerning himself is contradictory; and this leads me to question the truth of the Gospels, and so to reject Christ as the Son of God, and hence Christianity itself; for Christianity is nothing but a beautiful delusion if Christ is not what he claims to be. Now, he says in one place, "I and my Father are one;" and again, "He that hath seen me hath seen the Father;" and as I have before said, when on trial before the high priest, he still claimed, and that in the face of certain death, that he was the Son of God. But he said on another occasion that his Father was greater than he. Now, he can't be one with God, and at the same time inferior to God. And he says, "All power is given unto me." Now, that is an admission that he did not have power himself, but it was given to him;

and surely he that receives power is inferior to him
that gives it. Now, are not these contradictions in
his own testimony? and do not they destroy the worth
of it entirely? It seems to me, that whatever of truth
there may be in the historical existence of Jesus Christ,
he only imagined that he was the Son of God, and that
in speaking of himself he spoke according to the mood
he was in, sometimes believing himself to be the Son of
God.'

"Finally I said, after turning to the passages he had
referred to, and reading them aloud, —

"'Now, suppose that you had been on earth when
Jesus was here, and had heard him make these contradictory (?) statements, and had asked him, saying,
"Master, I do not quite understand you. A little while
ago you said, 'I and my Father are one,' and, 'He that
hath seen me hath seen the Father;' and again you say,
'My Father is greater than I;' and, 'All power is given
me.' How can you be one with the Father, and yet less
than the Father? and how can you be equal with the
Father if your power is given to you and not yours
independently?" And suppose he had said in reply,
"My child, what if for the purpose of your redemption
from sin and the curse of the law, I voluntarily laid
aside my eternal glory, and suffered myself to be made
of a woman, and made under the law, thus limiting my
being to the conditions of your nature, that I might in
that nature offer up to God such a sacrifice for sin as
would enable him to proclaim forgiveness of sins to the

whole world? In such a case can you not conceive that there is no contradiction in these sayings of mine? For indeed I am one with the Father, and he that hath seen me hath seen the Father; but for purposes of atonement I have voluntarily assumed an inferior position, that I might thus take your place and die, which I could not have done unless I had taken a subordinate place. Thus I sometimes speak of my eternal relation to God, and sometimes my relation to him as the messenger of the covenant sent for to redeem.'''

"He listened attentively to this, and then said, as if speaking to himself, —

"'Yes, that might be. I can see how that might be. But [speaking to me] did Christ ever make such an explanation? Is that the theory of Christ's subordination to the Father?'

"I in answer turned to the second chapter of Philippians, and said, 'Certainly this is the explanation of it. For see: Paul was trying to inculcate lessons of humility by exhorting the Philippians to voluntarily take a subordinate place in relation to each other, though they might as a matter of fact and right stand on an equality; and enforced his exhortation by this reference: "Let this mind be in you which was also in Christ Jesus; who being in the form of God thought it not robbery to be equal with God [thought not his equality with God something to be contended for], but made himself of no reputation, and took upon him the form of a servant, and was made in the likeness of men, and being found in fashion as a man he humbled himself, and became obedient unto death, even the death of the cross."' (Phil. ii. 5–8.)

"He took my Bible in his hand, and read the passage over and over himself, and said, 'Wonderful, wonderful!' And, still holding the book in his hand, with quivering chin and moistened eyes he said, —

"'Yes, the Son of God made himself of no reputation for me, and took my nature, and died on the cross for me.'

"And then looking up into my face, said, 'What have I got to do about it?'

"To which I replied, 'Accept him, believe on him, and confess him as your Saviour.'

"'May I?'

"I replied, opening my Bible to Rom. x. 9, 'If thou shalt confess with thy mouth the Lord Jesus, and shalt believe in thy heart that God hath raised him from the dead, thou shalt be saved.'

"'Let me see that.'

"I handed him the book, and he read it aloud, and then said, —

"'I do believe in my heart that God raised him from the dead, and I do acknowledge him as my Saviour.'

"We dropped down together upon our knees (with a little group which had gathered about us), and I offered a little prayer of thanksgiving to God for his conversion, and a little petition for his keeping.

"It will be seen at a glance that there was no attempt

made to meet his objections by an exhaustive argument, but by simply presenting the Biblical statement to him, leaving the work of conviction to the Holy Spirit. As a mere argument, the statement may have been very defective; but God can take his own truth and use it more mightily than the strongest argument man can construct."

"The blessed work went on from night to night, and from day to day, for nearly four months. Nor must it be supposed that the only personal efforts of this kind made were in the inquiry-rooms. Far from it. In homes, in shops, in counting-rooms, all over the city, God was working through his people. There must have been great joy in heaven in the presence of the angels of God during the continuance of this work. At the close of it the names of forty-eight hundred converts who resided in Chicago, to say nothing of those living elsewhere, were recorded. May such a work, yea, a far greater one, be done in Boston!"

CHAPTER IX.

"I think it meet, as long as I am in this tabernacle, to stir you up by putting
you in remembrance." — ST. PETER.

> "Ride on in thy greatness, thou conquering Saviour;
> Let thousands of thousands submit to thy reign,
> Acknowledge thy goodness, entreat for thy favor,
> And follow thy glorious train."
>
> S. F. SMITH.

THE two evangelists commenced their labors in
Boston on Sunday, the 28th of January, 1877, under
the most favorable auspices. Extensive preparations
had been made, and every thing that human foresight

could devise was provided to secure success. A meeting at which seventy-eight churches were represented was held as early as the 8th of May, 1876, when it was voted to invite Messrs. Moody and Sankey to labor in Boston, and to extend to them hearty co-operation and support. On the 28th of June Mr. Moody himself visited Boston, and held a conference with the representatives of about three hundred churches, but came to no decision as to when he might commence his evangelical efforts in the city. At a meeting, Sept. 13, held by the committee before appointed, it was enlarged to fifty members, of which the Rev. E. B. Webb, D.D., was made the chairman. By the 6th of November the sum of thirty thousand dollars had been given or pledged for the construction of a building for the use of the revivalists; the work thereon was immediately commenced, and at the close of the second week in January completed. It is a substantial brick edifice on Tremont Street, with eight entrances, and capable of seating about six thousand persons. It has an ample platform for about eight hundred persons in addition to the choir, together with rooms for inquirers and other purposes. It is well lighted, warmed, and ventilated; and, on the whole, presents without as well as within a tasteful, neat, and inviting aspect. While the workmen were constructing this large tabernacle, earnest prayers in churches, ministers' meetings, Christian conferences, sabbath schools, and domestic circles, were ascending for the baptism of the Holy Spirit on the

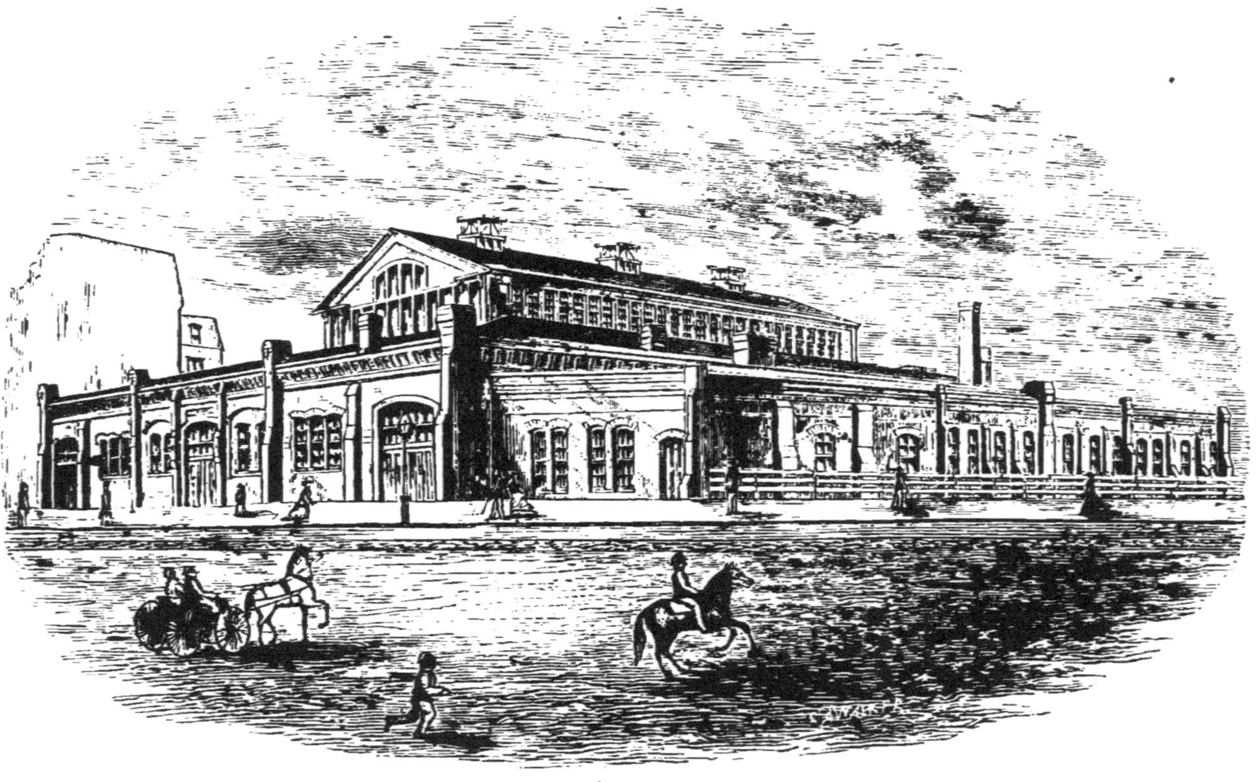

MOODY AND SANKEY'S TABERNACLE, BOSTON.

people. Evangelical ministers were united, spiritual forces were combined, and Christians, forgetting the denominational lines dividing them, held union meetings, and freely gave their talents, time, and money, to help on the preparations. A choir of about two thousand singers under the direction of Dr. Eben Tourjée, and divided into five complete organizations, together with a large company of Christian workers, was trained for the spiritual awakening; ushers were appointed under the direction of Mr. Franklin W. Smith; the new " Gospel Hymns," prepared by Messrs. Bliss and Sankey, were sold by thousands; and other provisions for efficient co-operation with the long-expected heralds of salvation made.

The building was dedicated on Thursday evening, Jan. 25, when addresses were made by Bishop Foster, the Rev. R. Thomas, the Rev. R. R. Meredith, and the Rev. Dr. E. B. Webb; the dedicatory prayer was offered by the Rev. A. J. Gordon; the singing by Dr. Tourjée's large choir was grandly effective, and a profound solemnity prevailed through all the services. A free-will offering of $2,390 was made by the assembly.

Preparations for evangelism on such an extended scale had never before been seen in the metropolis.

But Boston prides itself on being the " Athens of America." Mr. Moody sometimes breaks the rules of grammar: will the people come to hear him ? Boston is æsthetical, fond of literary culture, critical. Mr. Moody has no taste for any thing but the Bible:

INTERIOR VIEW OF MOODY AND SANKEY'S TABERNACLE, BOSTON.

will he command attention? Boston, with its numerous schools and institutions, is scientific, philosophical. Mr. Moody never studied Darwin: will his teachings be accepted? Boston abounds in learned theologians. Mr. Moody never read Hooker, Paley, Hodge, or Channing: will he make an impression? Such considerations filled the minds of some with doubt; but those who knew the man, who had traced his wonderful career in Great Britain and America, felt assured that the Tabernacle had not been raised in vain.

The two evangelists arrived soon after the dedication; the preacher making his home with Mr. Henry F. Durant, the sacred minstrel his at the Hotel Brunswick. All things are in readiness: now what will the opening of their evangelism, what will the harvest be?

On Sunday afternoon, Jan. 28, the Tabernacle was densely crowded with an expectant throng; and the services were opened with singing by the choir, and a prayer by the Rev. Dr. Webb. At length the two evangelists appeared upon the platform, Mr. Sankey taking his seat beside his beloved melodeon, and Mr. Moody at his little desk. The favorite hymns "Ninety and Nine" and "Only an Armor-Bearer" were then sung with sympathetic fervor; after which Mr. Moody rose and delivered in his usual earnest and impetuous tone his oft-repeated sermon on "Going up to Possess the Land," adapting various parts of it, as he went along, to the condition of his audience. His aim was here, as in the beginning of his work in other cities, to

incite Christians to personal consecration and activity.
"When we came to Boston," said he, "some people
thus spoke to me: 'Mr. Moody, we must give you a
little warning. You must remember that Boston is a
peculiar place, and you cannot expect to do the same
here as elsewhere; there are a great many obstacles.'
It is the same old story: Boston is the same as other
places. The enemy cannot hinder God from working,
if we only have faith. This terrible unbelief God can
shake in Boston, as easy as a mother can shake her
little child."

The audience appeared to be highly pleased with the
brusque and earnest manner of the speaker; and many
felt and said, "There is a power here, of God or man,
that cannot be resisted."

In the evening the Tabernacle was again thronged
to its utmost capacity, and "overflow meetings" were
held in Clarendon-street and Berkeley-street Churches.
Mr. Sankey concluded the introductory exercises by
singing in his charming style the popular hymn by
"Paulina" (Mrs. Bliss), —

> "We're marching to Canaan with banner and song," —

when Mr. Moody came forward, and enchained the
attention of the grand assembly by his spirited address
on "Christian Courage," of which he himself might be
cited as an illustrious example. The sermon abounded
in stories, anecdotes, and epigrammatic points, with
here and there a touch of pathos moving many in the

audience to tears. The luxury of doing good he thus vividly set forth : " Suppose," said he, " an angel could wing his way to this world to-night, and should go back to say, ' There is just one solitary child in Boston, whose mother is dead, and whose father is drunk ; and the poor homeless, motherless boy is wandering in the street ; ' and God should call around his throne the angels, and ask if any one of them was willing to live here for fifty or a hundred years to save that little child : I don't think there would be one who would not volunteer. I can imagine each one saying, ' Lord, let me go, and have the luxury of leading one soul to Christ.' And yet the Church has folded its arms, and a great many of us are sound asleep.' " In his closing prayer he used the strong expression, " O Son of God, beat back these dark waves of death and hell, that come rolling down through the streets ; and may the day come when of the city of Boston, as of the city of Samaria, it shall be said, ' There is great joy in that city.' " After this, Mr. Sankey sung, as none but he can sing, " Hold the Fort ; " and the Rev. Phillips Brooks (Episcopalian) pronounced the benediction.

The first noon prayer-meeting was held on Monday in Park-street Church, which was filled to overflowing. In the evening Mr. Moody delivered his sermon on the text " To every man his work," before an immense assemblage at the Tabernacle, — his design being, as before, to bring Christians into earnest personal labor for the salvation of their fellow-men. He regards the

Church as God's great instrument for the conversion of the world, and therefore labors wisely in the outset for its renovation.

In the prayer-meeting held after the close of the regular services, Mr. Moody said, "We are here to-night to pray for one another.   Remember me in your prayers. I do not understand it, but I have many times felt when I have gone from one place to another, and tried to do the work with the grace that God has given me to work in another place, it seems to me that every time we change we need a fresh baptism, a fresh power, a fresh supply of grace ; and, now we have come to Boston, we would like to have you pray for us, that God may bless us with his Spirit, and Christ may enter all our prayers, and be a power in us to preach the simple gospel.   And now, if there are any friends to pray for us and to be prayed for, would you just rise ? "

As many as three thousand people rose, and the Rev. Mr. Pentecost made a fervent prayer.

At the noon prayer-meeting in Tremont Temple on Tuesday, Jan. 30, there was an immense crowd present, and hundreds were not able to obtain admittance. Mr. Sankey sung Mrs. Lydia Baxter's fine hymn "Take the Name of Jesus with you" most effectively, and Mr. Moody spoke upon his favorite theme, " The Character of Daniel."   The large attendance at the various meetings during the week, the heavy blows that Mr. Moody struck into the formalism and indifference of Christians, the hearty response of ministers and others to his appeals for greater personal activity, the effective solo and chorus singing, together with the interest observable in the respective churches, gave assurance that the Tabernacle had not been raised in vain. The long-desired revival had already begun. Hearts which the eloquence of the learned could not reach were moved and melted by the simple and pathetic words of the evangelists.

At the Friday noon meeting, Feb. 2, the Tabernacle was completely filled. The theme was " Temperance ; " and in the course of his remarks Mr. Moody said, " What are we going to do to stem this terrible torrent of iniquity ? We have tried a great many methods: we have had our temperance societies and bands of hope, our lodges and our reform-clubs; we have had the pledge. But I am almost discouraged with these things; I am coming to the conclusion that the only hope is that the Son of God is to come and to destroy man's appetite for liquor." Such is the view of the evangelist: yet he believes in means and instruments ; must we not, then, use them in respect to temperance until the Son of God does come ? In the course of the meeting three reformed inebriates spoke ; and, when the audience began to applaud the last speaker, Mr. Moody rose at once and said, " Let us praise God with our hearts, and keep our hands still."

At the close of the meeting at the Tabernacle another very devotional exercise, at which about a thousand ladies were present, was held in Berkeley-street

Church. At Chicago Mr. Moody gave as a reason for
classifying some of the meetings, that he could thereby
do the most good to the greatest number of people.
" There were a great many good brethren and sisters
who seemed bound to attend every single meeting.
They were always on hand promptly, and always occupied the front seats. When he and Mr. Sankey were
in New York, there was one man who always sat up in
front, and even Mr. Sankey said he got tired of seeing
that same face in the same place every night. When
they went to Philadelphia, they thought they had seen
the last of this brother; but no, he was there every
night, and seemed to have nothing to do but to come
early and get one of the best seats. [Laughter.] When
they returned to New York, there was their old friend
again in his old seat; but he couldn't get into the
woman's meetings, and then at least he had no chance
to crowd somebody else out who didn't have his opportunities for attending."

Although his son Willie was seriously ill, Mr. Moody
presented himself in the evening at the Tabernacle, and
spoke with his wonted vehemence on the text " Who is
my neighbor? " saying with startling effect, —

" I don't think Jericho is far from Boston : I don't
think you have got to travel thousands of miles to get
to Jericho. I think you will find a great many who
have been stripped and wounded and left half dead in
the streets of Boston. Eight or ten Christians came to
me to-day to set them to work. I looked at them in

perfect amazement,—persons who have been living ten and fifteen years in Boston, and yet want a stranger to set them to work! Ah! you will find enough to do if you will keep your eyes open."

On Sunday morning, Feb. 4, Mr. Moody preached to sabbath-school teachers, and said as he went along that he had never had his work open better than in Boston. In the afternoon he delivered his sermon on "Sowing and Reaping" to the ladies, and in the evening, the same discourse to men alone. The inquiry rooms, opened for the first time to-day, were visited by as many as five hundred people, some of whom had just found peace in believing.

In the morning Mr. Moody attended service at the Technological Institute, and listened to an eloquent sermon by the Rev. Phillips Brooks.

The noon meeting at the Tabernacle, Feb. 8, was attended by about five thousand people. A praise-meeting well conducted by Mr. H. L. Whitney, and many requests for prayer, preceded Mr. Moody's service. This was upon the "Necessity of Salvation," and by it many hearts were moved. Although some take exceptions to the methods used in the revival-work,—such as the urgency of appeals to the inquirer, and the presentation of so many special requests for prayer,—the solemnity of the meetings, the numbers converted, and the brightening of the hopes of Christians, are sure indications that the Spirit of God is silently moving the hearts of the people.

To an Irishman who presented himself to Mr. Moody as a Catholic, he said, " I suppose you are an enemy of all righteousness." — " What makes you think so ? " replied the indignant visitor. " I smell your breath," answered the revivalist. He afterwards knelt with the intemperate man in prayer.

Many of the churches in the State observed this day as one of fasting and prayer on behalf of the efforts of the two evangelists in the metropolis. It was also observed in the city of Chicago. The meetings at the Tabernacle still continue to increase in interest, and the awakening is felt in many of the city and suburban churches.

The Tabernacle on the 9th inst. was densely crowded, and the opening prayer was made by the Rev. Phillips Brooks. Mr. Sankey sung, " Free from the Law," and " Hallelujah ! what a Name ! " with his usual tenderness, after which Mr. Moody's strong sermon on " The Spirit of the Lord is upon me," &c., commanded the undivided attention of the audience until its close. He daily gains in power; and few can listen to his fervid utterances and breathe the spirit of his audiences without exclaiming, " God is here ! "

The evangelists began upon the third week of their work in Boston on Sunday, the 11th of February, when five meetings of profound solemnity were held. That in the afternoon was for ladies, that in the evening for men. The Rev. Henry Ward Beecher occupied to-day the pulpit of Mr. Moody in Chicago. The desire to near him was intense, and thousands were unable to gain admission to the church.

It was pleasant to see at the evening service, Feb. 13, as many as fifty clergymen seated on the platform, and listening to Mr. Moody's effective sermon on "The New Birth." More eloquent speakers and skilful singers than these two evangelists we have, but none that so gain access to the interior chambers of the heart, and so unseal the fountain of tears. Mr. Moody preached a very practical sermon on "Faith," at the afternoon meeting, Thursday the 15th, pleasantly illustrating one point by referring thus to the Rev. Dr. Gordon : —

"Some say they are so constituted they cannot believe God. Away with that delusion! What has your constitution to do with it? Suppose Dr. Gordon here asked me to take dinner with him to-morrow, and I said, 'Doctor, I'd like to, but I don't know that I can.' — 'Why, are you engaged?' — 'No,' I reply, 'but I don't know that I feel just right.' — 'Don't feel just right! What do you mean? Don't you want to come to dinner with me?' says Dr. Gordon. 'Oh, yes!' I say, 'but I am so constituted I can't believe you want me to come.' [Laughter.] Ah! you laugh, but yet that is what people are doing when they say they are so constituted that they can't believe the Eternal God. God invites you to the feast, and it is a real invitation. If God sent his Son down into this world, and didn't give you power to believe, and then punished you eternally for not believing on him, he would be an unjust God. But God doesn't do that: with the command to believe, God gives you the power."

Mr. Moody is remarkably prompt in respect to every service, — commencing and closing precisely at the time appointed. He thus not only inspires confidence, but sets a fine example to dilatory ministers and men of business.

On Sunday evening, Feb. 18, Mr. Moody repeated to men his sermon on "The Compassion of our Lord," which he had given in the afternoon to ladies. The praise-meeting under the direction of Dr. E. Tourjée was admirably conducted; and, as the strains of music from the immense congregation rose and swelled and died away, the soul had some sweet foretaste of the harmonies of the golden shore. The praise-meeting is an admirable feature of the service. In his own church to-day the Rev. Dr. Mallalieu preached a sermon on "The Critics of the Evangelists," during which he said that we are learning by this revival that the gospel may be preached effectively by the uneducated, as well as by learned ministers; and that the plain, cheap Tabernacle, with the Lord's work in it, is solving the question, "How to reach the masses in our cities." Of his opponents Mr. Moody takes no notice; but, with an eye single to his Master's service, presses enthusiastically on his way, rejoicing in the luxury of doing good.

The churches are alive, and "evangelical religion in Boston," says a leading journal, "never presented a bolder front. There is no longer any doubt as to the doctrines held by the revivalist. He is an out-and-out believer in the ruined state of man, in the substitution of the blood of Christ for broken law, and in pardon gained through faith in him. He believes in the Trinity, the personality of the Devil, the second coming of Christ, the salvation of those believing in him, and the everlasting punishment of those rejecting him. He also holds that conversion is instantaneous, and that good works follow as a consequence."

Mr. Charles M. Sawyer, a reformed inebriate of Chicago but formerly of Boston, is rendering him assistance in respect to temperance; and many men who have renounced strong drink are among the trophies of this awakening.

On Feb. 20 Mr. Moody preached his famous sermon on "Heaven," repeating it in the evening to an assembly composed largely of young men. The service was opened by the Rev. Robert Lowry, author of "Shall we gather at the River?" and other beautiful hymns. More than three hundred requests for prayer were made to-day; and the eyes of many ministers, of whom there might have been one hundred present, were filled with tears at the reports of a revival of religion in many of the churches. The inquiry-meetings are now kept open from four until nine o'clock, P.M.; and Christian workers are busily employed, with the Bible in hand, leading young and old to Jesus.

On Wednesday afternoon, Feb. 21, the vast assembly at the Tabernacle listened to the revivalist's second great sermon on "Heaven," which was repeated in the evening. Many people from the country were present and heard for the first time the celebrated preacher. The singing was inspiring; and, in the glowing eloquence of the evangelist, all forgot the characteristics of his style or diction. It is the subject, sharply defined, distinct, and luminous, that he presents to the mind's eye of the listener, and not its drapery or himself. At the noon meeting Mr. Sankey, in referring to the "living water" spoken of by our Saviour, told a little story of a girl who had a garden and in it beautiful flowers. After a short time, however, the plants began to droop and fade, and gradually they died.

"Her mother upon questioning her said, 'Did you water the plants, my child?' to which she replied that she did, and took the water from a spring near by That was just the difficulty: the water, being cold and clear as crystal, had eventually chilled the flowers and plants so that they perished.

"That is the very reason why many of our works are not more successful. We shed abroad this cold love of ours, and it has the same effect as the spring water upon the flowers. Let us set it in the sunlight of righteousness, and then apply it, and notice the different result.

"Let us impart more life to our works, and have the word in the heart as well as in the mouth."

The sale of Bagster's Bible has greatly increased this season in the city, while that of the " Gospel Hymns No. 2 " by Sankey and Bliss has been immense.

The meetings on the 22d were largely attended ; and, it being the birthday of Washington, prayers were offered for the country. The singing by the choir, as well as Mr. Sankey's rendering of Mrs. M. A. Kidder's fine hymn on immortality, —

> " We shall sleep, but not forever:
> There will be a glorious dawn," —

was deeply impressive, and will never be forgotten by those present. The Rev. Charles E. Robinson, author of " The Songs of the Sanctuary," made an eloquent address during the closing services.

At the meeting on Friday evening, Mr. Moody in speaking on " Grace " said, " A man came to the Tabernacle Thursday night to hear Mr. Sankey sing. When he had satisfied himself, he wanted to go out before the sermon ; but some one who was with him induced him to remain. When I got to the story of the man in Chicago who spent twenty-one thousand dollars and became a beggar, the Spirit of God found him out. I found him at the young men's meeting.

" When I had told him how he could be saved, he said, ' I wish you would pray for a brother-in-law of mine.' That is grace. The moment a man becomes a partaker, he wants some one else to be saved."

With Mr. A. S. Ackers at the organ and an excellent

choir, Dr. Tourjée's praise-meeting which precedes the regular service is a most fitting and delightful preparation for the preaching and the singing of the gospel by the great evangelists.

On Monday evening, Feb. 26, a grand service of song was held at the Tabernacle, which was filled in every part. Dr. Tourjée led the choir, consisting of more than six hundred voices, which sung the fine old hymns with an effect truly sublime. Mr. Sankey said : —

"I believe there are more ways than one of praising God in singing. There are many, many ways, and it is not exclusively confined to singing hymns. Several hymns are put under the head 'Hymns of Praise,' while there is no praise in them at all. As to singing solos, I am convinced that this kind of singing is not thoroughly understood by most people. If I were to come here and sing a solo of some of these songs, there would be no praise in them ; but yet your prayers often recite, ' As we join together to sing His praises, may his blessings descend upon the preaching of his word in song.'

" Now, there is praising and teaching and preaching in song ; but these missions of song are not fully understood. Take the hymns ' Jesus of Nazareth passeth by,' and ' What shall the Harvest be ? ' they are called hymns of praise often ; and yet there is not a word of praise in them. They are teaching hymns but ' Praise God, from whom all blessings flow,' is a hymn of praise. I suppose many have wondered why I have sung alone. They have thought, ' He cannot offer up praise for all these people.'   Well, I sing alone because I believe that I may reach some heart that could not be reached by the congregational singing. I praise God to-night that he has blessed our service of song."

Brief addresses were made by the Revs. W. O. Holman and H. M. Parsons; the congregation sung, " Trusting Jesus, that is all."

Mr. Sankey closed the musical services by singing in his own sympathetic style, " Waiting and Watching for me."

In speaking of the noon meeting, which was very large, at the Tabernacle on Tuesday the 27th, the " Evening Traveller " says, —

" Notwithstanding the inevitable 'sameness' of the exercises, the crowds still press onward to the Tabernacle to hear the 'word' presented by Mr. Moody, and the 'goodness of his grace' sung by his companion. This blunt man, with his wonderful store of the richest gems of thought, still brings men to a more complete realization of their own sinfulness; and the multitudes sit entranced by the almost magic music of the singer, as at the commencement of the religious movement in this city."

Many instances of conversion have occurred under the influence of the sympathetic singing of Mr. Sankey. One young lady, leaning her head upon her mother's shoulder during the execution of one of his touching melodies, said, while the tears were fast falling,

"Mother, I can hold out no longer: I will be a Christian."

In his able sermon on "Excuses," Feb. 28, Mr. Moody said, "I was over at the young converts' meeting Monday evening, and heard them tell of their joy and happiness. Well, my good friend, after you become a Christian you can talk about happiness. You want a Christian's experience before you become a Christian; that is the trouble: and you are looking for their experience before you have taken God at his word.

"I met an excuse in the inquiry-room the other day; in fact, it was quite common: 'I would not like to be converted, Mr. Moody, in the time of a revival.' If it is really a *bona fide* excuse, you can jump on the train, and drop off at some country town where there is no revival; and if you cannot go out of town I think we can find some churches in Boston where there is no revival. I don't care where you find Christ, as long as you find him. If you come to us we will try and hunt you up some church where they haven't had any revival for years, if you really want to become a Christian."

Miss Frances E. Willard, a lady of rare accomplishments, conducts efficiently the ladies' meetings held at one o'clock, P.M., in a church near the Tabernacle.

The question is often proposed, "How is this unlettered speaker, ignorant of the arts of eloquence, thus able to command the attention of the largest audiences, and produce such wonderful results? Whitefield, Wesley, Finney, had learning to sustain them: how does Mr. Moody produce without it such impressions? What is the lever by which he moves the world?"

Under a human point of view, the secret of his power consists, it may be, in a felicitous combination of these several characteristics : —

1. He uses simple Saxon language. He knows no other. His words are household words, plain, homely, pertinent. They present his thought precisely as it is, unshaded by the diction. The hearer takes his meaning without thinking of the form in which it comes to him. The words are Bible words, familiar to us from our infancy. The idea shines through them as the 'ight through crystal. Perhaps no man since Bunyan has presented grand religious truths in plainer drapery. A child may understand him; and yet the learned are frequently astonished at his sharp, trenchant, and original expressions. A friend of mine once took a dictionary with him to church, in order to find out the meaning of the minister. Mr. Moody's language is not that of science or theology, but of business and the Bible. This is one point.

2. But Mr. Moody is in the higher sense a poet. He has not made rhymes or verse; and yet he has the glowing conceptions of a poet. He sees things vividly, he paints them vividly. His use of tropes and metaphors, to be sure, is but infrequent; yet at times he manifests Shaksperian power in the representation of actual or imaginary scenes. Take for example, as one instance out of thousands, a description of a scene of

sorrow, in a sermon preached at Brattleboro, Vt., Oct 5, 1875: " One of my little scholars was drowned; and word was sent by the mother that she wanted to see me. I went. The dripping body was there on the table. The husband was in the corner drunk. The mother said she had no money to buy a shroud or coffin, and wanted to know if I could not bury Adeline. I consented." What could be more graphic, or better fitted for the pencil of a painter? Mr. Moody is matter-of-fact, to be sure; but still he has a grand imagination.

3. His persistent study of the Bible forms another element of his power as a preacher. He pores over the pages of the sacred volume, not through the spectacles of some learned commentator, but with his own observant eye comparing passage with passage, and text with context. He makes the Bible interpret the Bible. He traces out a line of thought in it, as the miner a vein of gold through the rock-bed of the mountain. He is emphatically a man of ONE BOOK, and that the soul-rousing, the soul-sustaining book of the ages. His intellect has been nurtured, quickened, and magnetized by this word; his weapons are drawn from this word; his positions are fortified by this word; his plans are formed upon this word; and this is another reason why he speaks with such convincing power.

It is surprising to mark his familiarity with the Scriptures. They have been, as with David, his meditation day and night. Their contents are engraven on his heart. His revelation of their meaning shows as well to-day as when inspiration dictated them that they are the power of God unto salvation. When a clerk in a shoe-store in Chicago, and long ere he was known or thought of as a preacher, Mr. Moody used, after spending the evening in joyous recreation, to retire to his bed with his Bible in his hand, and read and pray himself to sleep. He has since made it the intimate companion of his life, — studying it by night and by day, and drawing from it the enginery whereby he breaks the strongholds of the adversary. His sermons on the study of the Bible indicate the origin of a great deal of his intellectual strength.

4. Enthusiasm in his work has much to do with his success. He has a great warm, loving, and unselfish heart. It is in profoundest sympathy with the sufferings of humanity. He sees in every man, however poor and penniless, a brother, and he would help him bear his burden. He is never so happy as when lifting some abject, hopeless mortal to a higher plane in life. His heart is a fountain of sympathy, not pent up by fear and formalism, but open, free, redundant. He believes in his mission; he glories in it. With him Christ is a reality, life is a reality, heaven is a reality. He is on a battlefield with the foe before him: the guns are pealing; he smells the fire; he sees the blood; he hears the peal of victory. Abstractions with him go for nothing: he takes God at his word, grasps the tremendous issues of the future, and speaks of them as present, actual, living verities. Hence he is, because so

fixed in faith, making it the very "substance of things hoped for," profoundly earnest and enthusiastic. With his own spirit thus enkindled, he electrifies the spirits of those who hear him.

5. He has also, as a check to his enthusiasm, an ample fund of good, sound common sense, so that, while the ardor of many revivalists leads them into fanaticism, he is, in the main, self-possessed, and adopts such methods as commend themselves to the good judgment of the people. "Common sense," says a writer "stamps all his earnestness and all his plans; and this wins in a remarkable manner all who come in contact with him. Whatever else may be said of him, no one can call him a fanatic; and this gives to his steady, invincible, untiring self-sacrifice such irresistible power."

6. Though not prepossessing in his voice or gesture, Mr. Moody is intensely natural. This is of great advantage to him as a speaker. He is just such a rugged, whole-souled, unaffected man as nature made him. There is no study, no art, no pretension at all about him. He never stood before a glass to practise attitude or gesticulation; he never stopped to ask himself the question, "Is this movement graceful, or ungraceful?" He never drew, perhaps never saw, Hogarth's Line of Beauty. He is intensely natural, — a little rough sometimes it may be, but characteristic, forceful, and original.

7. It may also be added, that, in speaking, Mr. Moody's rapidity of utterance — it being often at the rate of two

hundred and twenty words per minute — tends to keep up the interest of the audience. The Revs. Henry Ward Beecher, Phillips Brooks, and other eminent speakers, well understand the effect produced by quick enunciation. By the mere velocity of Mr. Moody's tongue something is doubtless done to disarm criticism, and to deepen the intensity of feeling in the assembly.

8. Still with all these varied elements — simplicity of diction, a vivid imagination, long study of the Bible, enthusiasm in his work, good sterling common sense, naturalness and rapidity of speech — combining, it were not easy to account for his wonderful ability to sway the minds and change the intents and purposes of the hearts of such vast multitudes of men. Another and a higher element must be acknowledged. What is it? Not man alone, not the Bible, nor the manner of presenting its sublime instructions, but the Spirit of the living God, co-operating specially with the spirit of the speaker, and preparing the minds of those that hear for the reception of the truth. This untutored evangelist is a man of prayer. He has drunk deeply of the hidden wisdom of God; the mantle of inspiration has fallen upon him; and the doctors of the law, as well as the common people, sit and weep and wonder at his feet. Did the High and Holy One cease to dwell in the hearts of men when the canon of the gospel was completed? May we not, then, admit that over and above and through the points referred to, his special presence is the real, the efficient cause of the surpris-

ing influence that Mr. Moody exerts upon the hearts and consciences of men? " The Holy Ghost is here in power," says he; and this alone is the solution of the problem. " God is with me: this is all the strength I have," he says again; and herein is the real secret of his might.

In person Mr. Moody is of medium size, thick-set and compactly built, with broad shoulders, a round head, ruddy face, and short neck. His eyes are dark and piercing; his nose is very well formed; but his mouth is wanting that fine classic finish which bespeaks the orator. He wears a long, full beard, which, though it may improve his looks, is detrimental to his speech. He dresses plainly, in the style of a man of business. His voice is somewhat shrill and husky, his articulation indistinct; yet his lungs are powerful, and he easily succeeds in making himself heard by as many as ten thousand people. His unstudied gestures are sometimes quite forcible, and his attitudes often lead one to suppose him utterly unconscious of the audience before him.

A SKETCH

OF THE

LIFE OF IRA DAVID SANKEY.

IRA D. SANKEY.

HIS BIRTH AND BOYHOOD. — EDUCATION. — MISSION.

"Speaking to yourselves in psalms and hymns and spiritual songs, singing and making melody in your heart to the Lord." — ST. PAUL.

> "A verse may win him whom the gospel flies,
> And turn delight into a sacrifice." — GEORGE HERBERT.

> "Music speaks the heart's emotion,
> Music tells the soul's devotion;
> Music heavenly harps employs,
> Music wakens heavenly joys." — ANON.

THE delightful and effective singer and composer Ira David Sankey was born in the little village of

Edinburgh, Lawrence County, Penn., on the twenty-eighth day of August, 1840, and is therefore at the present time thirty-six years old. His parents, David and Mary Sankey, the former of English, and the latter of Scotch-Irish descent, are respectable and pious people. They brought up their children — nine in number — in the nurture and admonition of the Lord. They taught them also how to speak our language with propriety. In early boyhood Ira began to manifest a love for sacred music, and the sweetness of his voice was noticed in the sabbath school which he attended. He had a pleasant disposition, an engaging manner, and a bright, sunny smile, which won the hearts of all who knew him. "He was," says one of his companions, "the finest little fellow in the neighborhood." His attention to the subject of personal religion, as he himself relates, was first awakened by an old Scottish farmer of the name of Frazer, living in the neighborhood. "The very first recollection I have of any thing pertaining to a holy life," said Mr. Sankey in addressing a company of children in the city of Dundee, Scotland, "was in connection with that man. I remember he took me by the hand, along with his own boys, to the sabbath school, — that old place which I shall remember to my dying day. He was a plain man, and I can see him standing up and praying for the children. He had a great, warm heart, and the children all loved him. It was years after that when I was converted; but my impressions were received when I was very young, from that man."

On attaining the age of fifteen years he began to compose tunes for his own amusement; and he was soon after led during a revival of religion in Edinburgh, by the entreaties of an old steward of the church, to consecrate himself entirely to the service of the Lord. This brought to him that peace of mind which passeth understanding. Not long afterwards his father removed with his family to the large town of Newcastle, Penn., where the young singer had the benefit of some academical instruction, and obtained the rudiments of a useful English education. He also became a member of the Methodist Episcopal Church. He made the word of God and sacred music his chief study; and the tones of his sweet, silvery voice in the songs of devotion attracted many people to the house of worship. Such was the beauty of his Christian life, such his knowledge of the Bible, that in 1859 the church appointed him superintendent of the Sunday school, and subsequently a class-leader. In training the voices of his school to sing, his own musical taste was improved, his reputation as a vocalist extended; while his discussions as a class-leader with those older than himself led him to a closer examination of the sacred volume. "Tell me your condition," said he to his beloved class, "in Bible language. The Scriptures abound in accounts of religious feeling of all descriptions. There is no state of grace which may not be described by a text." As a leader of the choir, he insisted on the proper deportment of the singers, as well as on the correct expression of the sentiment of the hymn. He believed that song was intended for the dissemination of the gospel; and he early began to sing solos for this purpose. In this way he was making preparation, though unconsciously, for the glorious work in which he is now engaged.

On the call of President Lincoln in 1861, for men to sustain the Government, Mr. Sankey was among the first in Newcastle to have his name enrolled as a soldier. He remained in the army, enlivening the camp and endearing his companions to him by the sweetness of his music and his temper, until the expiration of his term of service, when he returned to Newcastle to assist his father in his office as collector of the revenue. "In the civil service, as in other departments of labor," says one who knew him intimately, "he was noted for conscientiousness, and patient, faithful attention to duty. In his rank he stood first in the district, and had the entire confidence of all the officers and tax-payers with whom he had official dealings. In his long connection with the service, there were never known any irregularities in his accounts, or any loss to the government. On this account he left the service with honor and with the regret of those who were asso-ciated with him."

On the 9th of September, 1863, he married Miss Edwards, a member of the church, a singer in his choir, and a teacher in his sabbath school. She is an estimable woman, and the mother of three sons; of whom Henry, the oldest, is now beginning to assist his father in his evangelism. One of the children was born in Scotland.

While engaged in the civil service, Mr. Sankey found many opportunities, especially in the way of sacred song, to labor for his Lord and Master. His fame as a singer had spread through Western Pennsylvania, and invitation after invitation crowded in upon him to attend conventions, conferences, and other public gatherings, for the purpose of singing his beautiful solos, and of leading other voices in song. These invitations he generally accepted, believing that the gospel should be sung as well as preached; yet his rule was never to receive any compensation for his services.

He had not studied music scientifically, or even as an art. His intention had never been to make the practice of it a profession; but he saw in it a mighty force for the advancement of the kingdom of the Redeemer. He consecrated his power of song, as every other gift, entirely to that noble cause, and God has wonderfully blessed the consecration.

Some time in the early part of 1867, a Young Men's Christian Association was, through the activity of Mr. Sankey and other gentlemen, formed in Newcastle, of which he subsequently was elected president. Through this institution his Christian influence was extended, and he became instrumental in leading many by his voice of prayer and praise into a Christian life. The acquaintance between him and Mr. Moody began in June, 1870, at an international convention held in Indianapolis, to which he had been sent as a delegate. The singing at an early morning prayer-meeting being intolerably dull, Mr. Sankey was invited to take charge of it. Coming forward modestly, he complied with the request; and such was the charm of his manner, such were the sympathetic and flexible tones of his voice, varying so as to express every emotion of the soul, such were the freshness, tenderness, and beauty of his songs, that every heart was won. Though ignorant of music, Mr. Moody understands full well its power; and he saw in Mr. Sankey just the man whom he had long been searching for to aid him in his work. On being introduced to the sweet singer, he said to him in his characteristic way, —

"Where do you live?"

"In Newcastle, Penn.," Mr. Sankey answered.

"Are you married?"

"Yes."

"How many children have you?"

'One."

"I want you."

"What for?"

"To help me in my work at Chicago."

"I cannot leave my business."

"You must: I have been looking for you for the last eight years. You must give up your business, and come to Chicago with me."

"I will think of it," replied Mr. Sankey. "I will pray over it; I will talk it over with my wife."

The result was that the singer of Newcastle, after prayer and consultation with his wife, determined to identify his interests with those of Mr. Moody, to live with him the life of trust, and enter on the work of evangelization in the city of Chicago. In this almost romantic way commenced that Christian fellowship between these two gifted servants of the Lord, which the toils and trials of six long years have cemented as a bond that death alone can sever.

Although Mr. Philip Phillips, author of "I love to sing for Jesus," and other beautiful tunes, had in some measure prepared the people of Chicago to listen to the "solo singing of the gospel," still many supposed it an unscriptural innovation; yet such was the melody, the flexibility, and pathetic charm of Mr. Sankey's voice, that opposition soon changed to admiration, and his services soon came to be justly appreciated by the clergy and the churches. He entered heart and soul into the missionary work of Mr. Moody, and led the great congregation and sabbath school in his church, as well as at Farwell Hall, in the service of song, giving it life and variety by intermingling with the mighty choruses some touching strain, as, "Sweet Hour of Prayer," "He leadeth me," or, "I love to tell the Story," sung tenderly and touchingly by himself alone.

These hallowed and refreshing songs, rising sweetly at the close of some earnest appeal of Mr. Moody's,

would melt the audience into tears; and amidst the
profoundest feeling every tone would touch the heart,
as if an angel's wing were sweeping over it. Mr.
Sankey sings, not for money nor for reputation, but for
the lofty purpose of winning men to Christ. He believes in the power of song to do this. His songs are
Bible songs: he puts his soul, and that an inspired soul,
into them. He makes the music all subservient to the
sentiment, and so, by its heavenly ministry, fixes it in
the listener's mind. Though not an artist, he sings
with such excellent taste that the cultivated ear receives his simple melodies with delight. The gospel
in song thus becomes more charming and potential in
its sway. He himself relates a most touching instance
of its influence : —

"During the winter after the great Chicago fire,
when the place was built up with little frame houses
for the poor people to stay in, a mother sent for me one
day, to come and see her little child, who was one of
our sabbath-school scholars. I remembered her very
well, having seen her in the meetings, and was glad to
go. She was lying in one of these poor little huts,
every thing having been burned in the fire. I ascertained that she was past all hopes of recovery, and that
they were waiting for the little one to pass away.
'How is it with you to-day?' I asked. With a beautiful smile on her face, she said, 'It is all well with me
to-day. I wish you would speak to my father and
mother.' — 'But,' said I, 'are you a Christian?' —

'Yes.'—'When did you become one?'—'Do you remember last Thursday in the Tabernacle, when we had that little singing meeting, and you sung, "Jesus loves even me"?'[1]—"'Yes.'—'It was last Thursday I believed on the Lord Jesus, and now I am going to be with him to-day.'

"That testimony from that little child in that neglected quarter of Chicago has done more to stimulate me, and bring me to this country [Scotland], than all that the papers or any persons might say. I remember the joy I had in looking upon that beautiful face. She went up to heaven, and no doubt said she learned upon the earth that Jesus loved her, from that little hymn. If you want to enjoy a blessing, go to the bedsides of these bedridden and dying ones, and sing to them of Jesus, for they cannot enjoy these meetings as you do. You will get a great blessing to your own soul."

When the conflagration in October, 1871, had swept away that section of Chicago where the two evangelists were laboring, Mr. Sankey returned to his home at Newcastle: but as soon as the rude Tabernacle was erected he came back, and, lodging in a small room in the building, assisted Mr. Moody in supplying the wants of the destitute, and in carrying on the mission work in that quarter. It was at that period that the touching incident just given occurred; and by it Mr. Sankey's soul

---

[1] The words and music of this beautiful song are by the late lamented P. P. Bliss, killed by the railway accident at the bridge over the Ashtabula River in Ohio, Dec. 29, 1876.

was moved to make a profounder consecration of its powers to the service of the Lord. He not only sung, but spoke and prayed, for the conversion of the people; he selected Bible hymns or "spiritual songs" of sterling merit; he adapted them to lively music, sometimes of his own composing; he encouraged others to compose; he conducted meetings, leading in all the services himself; and, during Mr. Moody's visit to England in the spring of 1872, he took charge of the work and worship at the Tabernacle. On his return Mr. Moody found him cherishing the same Biblical spirit which he himself had imbibed in England; and they both, as fitting counterparts in sweet accordance, toiled together, comforting and reviving many churches. In the mean time Mr. Sankey, with remarkable good taste, was selecting from the new stores of hymnology and revival tunes such spirited and popular pieces as would best promote his evangelical work. In addition to the beautiful airs of Bradbury, Lowry, Main, Root, Grape, Phillips, Doane, and Bliss, he composed many excellent tunes himself; and with the fine lyrics of Annie S. Hawks, Fanny J. Crosby, Lydia Baxter, Prof. Gilmore, Ellen H. Gates, Anna Warner, Kate Hankey, Mrs. Bliss, and others, had, as it were, a stock of sacred songs adapted to almost every exigence. His voice, which is a rich baritone, was constantly gaining power, and no singer ever better than he knew how to suit his music to the time and the occasion. The composition of hymns he does not consider within his sphere; yet " For me, for me," the only one of his that has been published, indicates that he is endowed with poetical as well as musical ability. Among his tunes, "The Ninety and Nine," to words of Miss E. C. Clephane, is perhaps the most popular.

Mr. Sankey with his family accompanied Mr. Moody in his remarkable evangelistic tour through Great Britain, and assisted him materially in producing that grand awakening which filled all Christendom with surprise. It was feared at first that his new style of songs, his solo singing, and his melodeon, would meet with great opposition on the part of Christians, especially in Scotland, where Rouse's rough version of the Psalms and the plain old tunes had become so deeply imbedded in the hearts of the people. But the American minstrel put so much of his soul and of the gospel into his song that he soon overcame all prejudice, and made himself the most popular sacred singer in the United Kingdom. In passing from Southampton through mid-England, in the summer of 1875, the writer was surprised, as well as delighted, to see the songs of Mr. Sankey in various forms for sale at almost every station, and to hear them sung by laborers and by children in the streets. America seemed to have filled the heart of England with her music. Of Mr. Sankey's service of song in Edinburgh, Dr. Thompson said, " Those who have come and heard have departed with their prejudices vanquished, and their hearts impressed." The Rev. Mr. Taylor also said, " As Mr.

Sankey proceeded to sing, we felt that it was real teaching. Not only was there his wonderful voice, which made every word distinctly heard in every corner of the hall, and to which the organ accompaniment was felt to be merely subsidiary, but it was the scriptural thought borne into the mind by the wave of song, and kept there till we were obliged to look at it and feel it in its importance and its preciousness."

Mr. Sankey not only sang, but preached the gospel, conducting meetings, and, though not delivering sermons, inviting in simple and persuasive words the people to the cross of Jesus. While addressing a group of inquirers at Glasgow on everlasting life, and emphasizing the word *hath*, a woman listening attentively exclaimed, "That word *hath* has done it all," and went away rejoicing in the Lord. In Paisley he produced a profound impression by singing in his moving way "Nothing but Leaves, the Spirit grieves." At Perth the song, "Go work in My Vineyard," awakened the great congregation to labor more earnestly for the advancement of the Redeemer's kingdom. At Aberdeen he was assisted, as in many other places, by a most efficient choir of male and female voices, and his American melodies produced a wonderful effect. His songs met with special favor in the North of Scotland, where it was supposed that the prejudice against them would be strongest. "In the remote Highland glen," says an interesting writer, "you may hear the sound of hymn-singing : shepherds on the steep hillsides sing Mr. Sankey's hymns while tending their sheep; errand-boys whistle the tunes as they walk along the streets of the Highland towns; while in not a few of the lordly castles of the North, they express genuine feeling."

The Daily Edinburgh Review thus spoke of the singing of Mr. Sankey in Scotland:—

"Why should there be any prejudice? For generations most of the Highland ministers, and some of the Lowland ministers too, have sung the gospel, sung their sermons, ay, and sung their prayers too. The only difference is, that they sing very badly, and Mr. Sankey very beautifully. He accompanied himself on 'the American organ,' it is true; and some of us who belong to the old school can't swallow the 'kist of whustles' yet. It may help us over this stumbling-block if we consider, that, with the finest voice and ear in the world, nobody could maintain the proper pitch of a melody, singing so long as Mr. Sankey does. And then, 'the American organ' is only a 'little one.' When a deputation from the session waited on Ralph Erskine, to remonstrate with him on the enormity of fiddling, he gave them a beautiful tune on the violon-cello; and they were so charmed that they returned to their constituents with the report that it was all right: 'it was na' the wee, sinfu' fiddle that their minister operated upon, but a grand instrument, full of grave, sweet melody.' I'm afraid some good, true Presby-terians will be excusing Mr. Sankey's organ, and them-selves for listening to it, by some such plea as that."

Another wrote: "The admiration of Mr. Sankey's music is enthusiastic. When he sings a solo, a death-like silence reigns in the audience. When he ceases there is a rustling like the leaves of a forest when stirred by the wind. We might apply to him the language of Scripture, 'Lo! thou art unto them as a very lovely song of one who hath a pleasant voice, and can play well on an instrument.' No one can estimate the service he has rendered to the Church of Christ by the compilation of his book of 'Sacred Songs,' and their sweet tunes. They are the delight of all ages. I have heard in Scotland that they are already sung in our most distant colonies. Ere long, I believe, they will be sung wherever the English language is spoken over the earth. Nor will they be confined to that language, for a lady is already translating them into German."

In Belfast the newsboys cried out as they went on their daily rounds, "Hymn-books with songs sung at Moody and Sankey's meetings!" and sold them in large numbers through the city. In Londonderry Mr. Sankey was so well sustained by the local choir, that his co-worker said he had never before heard such sweet music, adding, that he thought they should sing "new songs" as well as old ones, and that they could sing the gospel into many a man's heart.

In Manchester a Mr. Cook, one evening at the Royal Theatre, sung in imitation of the popular song "He's a fraud," the words, —

"We know that Moody and Sankey
Are doing some good in their way," —

and received both cheers and hisses from the audience; but, on repeating the words, the displeasure was so great that he was obliged to leave the stage. This testimony of theatre-going people even, in favor of the evangelists, was noticed in the morning papers, and the fact also that the song was not repeated.

Public sentiment in favor of the evangelists was the same in Dublin. During the performance at the circus, on a certain evening, one clown said to another, "I'm rather *moody* to-night: how do you feel?" To which the other answered, "I feel rather *sankey-monious*." This was met with hisses, and the whole audience joined with grand effect in singing, —

> "Hold the fort, for I am coming,
> Jesus signals still;
> Wave the answer back to heaven,
> By thy grace we will."

The greatest favorite at Birmingham was " Hold the Fort," by Mr. Bliss. The vast audiences joined in the stirring chorus, filling the Bingley Hall with rousing peals of sacred song. In London "The Ninety and Nine" and "Only an Armor-Bearer" appeared to afford the most delight; but other hymns, as, "Almost persuaded," and "The Prodigal Child," by Mrs. Ellen H. Gates, became immensely popular, and were daily heard in all quarters of the city.

While in London, the Princess of Wales, the Duchess of Sutherland, and other distinguished personages, attended the revival meetings, and united heartily in the

choruses of Mr. Sankey's songs. His singing here won
many hearts, and his labors amongst the inquirers were,
as usual, owned and blessed of God. The testimony of
one young man is that of many: "I went," says he,
"into the inquiry-room, and Mr. Sankey walked up and
down with me, and talked with me as if he had been
my own father; and I found Christ." At the close of
the meetings in Liverpool, Mr. Sankey sung as a
farewell song, "Home, Sweet Home," with remarkable
pathos, moving many in the audience to tears.

Mr. Sankey gathered several new and beautiful
hymns and tunes during his mission-tour abroad, with
which he has since enriched his sacred song-books. He
found the words of the song "Ninety and Nine," in
"The Christian Age" of London, and immediately
composed the music for them. They were written (as
he afterwards ascertained through a letter from her
sister) by Miss Elizabeth C. Clephane of Melrose,
Scotland, a short time before the author's death, and
were first published in Dr. Arnott's "Family Treasury,"
in 1868. The hymn commencing, —

> " Beneath the cross of Jesus
>   I fain would take my stand," —

for which Mr. Sankey also wrote the music, is by the
same author. Soon after his return to America in 1875,
Mr. Sankey published, in connection with Mr. P. P. Bliss,
"Gospel Hymns and Sacred Songs," of which an immense number of copies have been sold. It contains

eight of his own musical compositions. At the Tabernacle in Brooklyn, Mr. Sankey was supported by a well-trained choir of two hundred and fifty voices; and the singing during the revival was remarkably good. The pieces sung were familiar to the people, and fears were entertained lest on this account the effect would not be as great as it had been across the sea; but in this all were happily disappointed. One of the first hymns given out was, "Hark! the Voice of Jesus crying;" and, says a reporter, "as Mr. Sankey's magnetic voice and wonderfully expressive singing filled the great auditorium, the sympathy among his hearers grew and increased until it seemed as if, had he continued the sweet melody and earnest supplication, every person in the whole audience would have risen and joined with him in a grand musical prayer of mingled appeal and thanksgiving. The effect he produced was simply marvellous. Many responses, such as ' Amen!' and ' Glory to God!' were heard from all parts of the vast assembly; and at the close a great many men, as well as women, were in tears. Mr. Sankey's voice is a marvel of sweetness, flexibility, and strength. There is a simplicity about his vocalism, that disarms the criticism that would apply to it any of the rules of art. It has a charm purely its own, which attracts and holds one with a power that is gentle but irresistible." In Philadelphia he had the assistance of a choir of five hundred singers under the leadership of Prof. Fischer, and rendered the same effective assistance as before to

Mr. Moody in his evangelical mission. His songs sunk into the hearts of the people, so that such questions as " Did you hear the ' Ninety and Nine ' ? " " Isn't his singing better than a sermon ? " " Wasn't that hymn ' Nothing but Leaves ' impressive ? " as well as the singing of the songs themselves, were frequently heard along the streets of the city.

The Rev. Dr. Sheppard said, " The first song I heard Mr. Sankey sing was, ' Jesus of Nazareth passeth by ; ' and it was the most eloquent sermon I ever heard. It spoke of the opportunity present, soon to pass, and actually past. It was most impressing and powerful."

At a convention held near the close of his labors in Philadelphia, Mr. Sankey said, in respect to church music, — and his words are worthy of attention, " It should be conducted by a good large choir of Christian singers, who should encourage the congregation to join heartily with them in the songs of Zion, instead of monopolizing the service themselves. I would have the singers and the organ in front of the congregation, near the minister ; and would insist on deportment by the singers in keeping with the services of the house of God. The conduct of the choir during the service will have very much to do with the success of the preaching. Instead of whispering, writing notes, passing books, and the like, the choir should give the closest attention to all the services, especially to the preaching of the word. There should be the most intimate relation between the leader of the singing and the pastor. Old familiar hymns and tunes should be used, and now and then a Sunday-school song; so that the children may feel that they have a part in the prayer-meeting, as well as in the Sunday school. All should try to understand the sentiment of the hymn or sacred song, and enter into it with heart and voice, in a prayerful frame of mind, silently asking God to bless the song to every soul."

During the meeting Mr. Sankey spoke of the pleasure he had received in hearing his songs sung in the capital of Switzerland, which he visited before returning to America, — and also on the railways in France, — adding that by God's grace he would keep on singing, and encourage others to sing those sweet stories of Jesus and his love.

In respect to church psalmody, Mr. Sankey at another time said that music occupied a very prominent place in the Lord's work; and that the choirs in the churches should consist of Christian people, and be led by a Christian chorister.

If he could not find sufficient members among the congregation, he would go into the Sunday schools, where they would generally find the gospel songs sung more heartily than anywhere else.

The ministers, also, should encourage the singers. Mr. Spurgeon, in London, never gives out a hymn without telling the people just how he would like it sung; and the result is that the whole assemblage of people partake of his earnestness, and sing it with spirit.

Mr. Sankey hoped that he should be pardoned if he said that ministers did not make as much of the singing as they could. The singing, he thought, should be prayed for as much as the preaching. It has been an important part in the services in all ages. The choir should not be away in the back gallery. The singers should be near the minister, alongside the platform, so that he could be in accord with them. In churches there should not be two parties, one at one end, another at the opposite end of the church.

He did not think there should be any people in the choir whose deportment would grieve the children of God.

Mr. Sankey said he once heard a bishop preach, and during the whole service a young lady, a member of the choir, kept talking and writing notes to a young gentleman, which behavior so distracted his (Mr. Sankey's) attention that he did not know actually what the bishop was talking about.

The man, he said, who leads, should go into the Sunday school and into the prayer-meetings. If he cannot do this, he will exercise no very marked influence for good in the choir. In the Sunday school Mr. Sankey would have a little organ.

He admired the large, the noble instrument; but people did not sing so well with it as with the small one. When a large organ is being played, it drowns the voices, and people just sit and listen without singing. A little organ will only give the singers the key·

note. We do not, in fact, need any instrumental music in the house of God : we only want the key-note.

Then he would insist that the organist should play softly. He had a pretty strong voice, but the strength of some of the organs would effectually drown his voice.

If there are any evangelistic services to be held in your midst, every minister, when he sends in lists of people for our choirs, should send in the very best. When the choir meets, let the exercises be commenced and closed with prayer. He believed four-fifths of the traditional trouble in choirs is because of the ungodly people composing them.

He would not have a man get up and flourish a book or stick in leading. When practising, of course it might be admissible ; but, when we come to worship God, the less the display the better.

Mr. Sankey concluded by touching upon the necessity of a correct pronunciation.

" Owing to a careless reading, people do not understand the words as they are sung ; consequently they cannot take up the hymn and sing in unison with the choir. If the reading were better, there would be a great deal more interest manifested by the congregations."

At the Hippodrome in New York City, Mr. Sankey afforded Mr. Moody essential aid in conducting the long-extended services of the revival, adding to the interest of the meetings not unfrequently, by a pertinent illustration or a story, as well as by his soul-moving songs. "His singing," said one of the religious journals, "contributed much to the inspiration which animated the services, and helped to draw the vast crowds which felt their influence. Every hymn was a gospel message; and the tunes seemed not only to be made on purpose for the hymns, but the expression given to their spirit, and the articulation given to the words, were scarcely less than perfect."

At the conclusion of his labors here he said in a large meeting, "I feel in my heart to-night a sad minor note sounding there, — one of sadness and regret that the meetings which have been so blessed are so soon, so far as we are concerned, to pass away; this is a sad thought and note in the song of my heart to-night: yet still there is a louder note, one of a joyful tone, telling me we shall meet again. I desire to say before giving way to others, that in all our work, both in this and other countries, we have never had more hearty, warm, and efficient help than we have had in New York in all the departments of our labor. We feel that each one, in whatever secluded place, has done his duty; and my heart goes out to each of you with a hearty 'God bless you!'"

After the close of this campaign, Mr. Sankey's health became somewhat impaired: yet feeling the need of new hymns and music, he engaged zealously with his friend Mr. P. P. Bliss in the preparation of "Gospel Hymns No. 2," which contains twelve of his own tunes, together with some by Messrs. Bliss, Doane, Root, Vail, Perkins, Lowry, Phillips, Main, Bradbury, and others, and which is now used at the Tabernacle in Boston.

In the midst of his arduous labors in the city of Chicago, Mr. Sankey was suddenly called to mourn the death of Mr. and Mrs. Bliss, with whom he had been so long associated in the sweet service of song. The assurance only, that through Christ they should beyond the river sing a sweeter strain in company, could assuage his grief.

At the opening of the Tabernacle for the renowned evangelists in Boston, on the 28th of January, 1877, the expectation in regard to the singing of Mr. Sankey was very great; as this city is noted for its knowledge and its love of music. Will Mr. Sankey's simple melodies, his unartistic style of singing, satisfy the public taste? Will the efforts of the Western vocalist with his melodeon be appreciated? The desire to listen to his songs was perhaps as strong as that of hearing the distinguished preacher.

The services opened, and the minstrel who had charmed so many audiences, both in the Old World and the New, came in and modestly took his seat beside his little instrument on the platform. The hymn commencing, "There were ninety and nine that safely lay," being then announced, he arose, and in a clear, distinct voice made the following supplication for a blessing upon sacred song : —

"Our heavenly Father, in the name of the Lord

Jesus we come to thee at this moment, asking that thy blessing may rest upon the singing that has already been done, and shall be done, in this great Tabernacle. Bless, we pray thee, the message of thy love as found in these songs. And we pray, our Father, that thou wouldst bless the singers who have just come here, and will come day after day, to lift up the voice of praise unto thee. And as in days of old, when singers were wont to make a joyful noise unto the Lord, do thou meet with thy people in this temple dedicated to thy service. And, our Father, shall we not ask that ere long we may even see the prodigals being brought home by the Good Shepherd himself; having wandered far away from thee, they will hear that ringing voice of thine, and say, 'I will arise and go to my Father.' Lord Jesus, bless us now in all that we shall do here, and we will give thee the praise for evermore. Amen."

He then in tones of remarkable sweetness sung the celebrated song, enchaining the attention of the great assemblage, and convincing all, that, though he might not satisfy the high demands of art, he had the power to send his voice into the soul, and touch the secret chords of its most profound devotion. This indeed is something higher than art, and captivates when art is powerless. It is not so much by the force, as by the peculiar *timbre*, the searching quality of his voice, that Mr. Sankey produces such effect. Many of his songs, as rendered by very accomplished vocalists, are powerless to move the heart. People hear them thus performed in the social circle, and wonder how and why they ever make such marked impressions. The reason may be that Mr. Sankey sends by an intense sympathy, and by tones peculiarly his own, the sentiment of the song into the hearer's soul. His objective point is the conversion or the sanctification of that soul; the listener then, forgetting the singer and the song, turns his thought inward to himself, and the truth as it is in Jesus wakens the emotions. To know the power of Mr. Sankey's songs, the only sure way is to hear him. He may well be called the Dempster of sacred song. His voice, especially in the middle notes, has a peculiar sympathetic sweetness that steals into the heart, and mysteriously unlocks the fountain of tears. He reveals, as none others can, the sentiment of his hymn, and, enunciating every word and syllable with remarkable distinctness, makes himself heard with ease in the remotest parts of the very largest audience-chamber. He has also the tact of adapting every song to the subject-matter of the speaker, or to the peculiar mood of the congregation, so as to produce the best effect. Sometimes a doubt arises whether he or Mr. Moody draws the greater number to the Tabernacle: certain it is, that neither would succeed so well alone. Persons of a delicate, sensitive, and emotional temperament would undoubtedly prefer the singer; those who love to hear plain truths enunciated fearlessly would prefer the preacher: yet, as the public is made up of both these classes, it finds that in the union of the two evangelists its spiritual demands are satisfied.

"Mr. Moody," says The Inter-Ocean, "startles us and arouses us, while Mr. Sankey soothes and comforts. Mr. Moody, earnest as he is, succeeds without the grace of voice and manner: Mr. Sankey, earnest as he is, succeeds because of grace in voice and manner. He is well fitted to be Mr. Moody's companion, and those who hear him do not wonder at his continued success in this peculiar field."

"Mr. Sankey," says Mrs. Barbour truthfully as well as beautifully, "sings with the conviction that souls are receiving Jesus between one note and the next. The stillness is overawing; some of the lines are more spoken than sung. The hymns are equally used for awakening, and none more so than 'Jesus of Nazareth passeth by.' When you hear 'The Ninety and Nine' sung, you know of a truth that down in this corner, up in that gallery, behind that pillar which hides the singer's face from the listener, the hand of Jesus has been finding this and that and yonder lost one, to place them in his fold. A certain class of hearers come to the services solely to hear Mr. Sankey, and the song throws the Lord's net around them."

Sustained by the efficient choir of Dr. Tourjée, this gifted singer, criticise him as we may, continues to perform admirably his part in the varied exercises of the Tabernacle. The great congregation listens with ever-fresh delight to his well-rendered songs, "I need Thee every Hour," "Hallelujah, 'tis done," "Where are the Nine?" "Hold the Fort, for I am coming,"

"Waiting and Watching," "Have You on the Lord believed?" "Go bury thy Sorrow," "Pull for the Shore," and others of a world-wide reputation, and always joins with united and exultant voices in the chorus.

Mr. Sankey has a pleasing personal appearance. Though not as large as Mr. Moody, he excels him both as to symmetry in form and grace in manner. His hair and eyes are dark; his countenance is open, genial, expressive, and sometimes, when he is engaged in singing, radiant with joy. The artist has in the accompanying portrait presented truthfully and to the life the features of this charming vocalist, and the autograph is copied from a letter in my possession.

Without the force, mental or physical, of his fellow-laborer, Mr. Sankey has more of personal beauty, more of culture, and also of that natural suavity which wins the hearts of all who know him.

May his life be long continued, and his tongue, tuned to still loftier notes of praise, call, by the power of consecrated song, yet mightier throngs of people to rejoice in God their Saviour!

The following lines addressed to him were sent to me by the author for this work: —

> "Sing on, minstrel, heavenward bearing;
> Music moves the world from sin;
> Onward, then, God's truth declaring;
> Faith and works are bound to win, —

Bound to win in every contest,
  Though the odds be ne'er so strong ;
Truth the firmest, hope the fondest,
  Cheer thee in thy "gospel song."

Drones can never rise to glory,
  Doomed to perish in the strife ;
God ordains it, true the story,
  ' Workers reap the joys of life.'

Sing, then, songs new, sweet, and holy ; .
  Lure the world away from sin ;
Lift the burdens from the lowly ;
  Upward, onward, work and win."

ROBERT B. CAVERLY

A SKETCH OF THE LIVES

OF

MR. P. P. BLISS AND DR. EBEN TOURJÉE.

LIFE OF P. P. BLISS.

Birth of Mr. Bliss. — Early Taste for Music. — His Disposition. — Comes to Chicago. — His Wife's Influence over him. — He conducts Musical Institutes. — Effect of his Singing on Mr. Moody. — At a Sunday-School Convention. — His Publications. — His Connection with Major Whittle. — A Notice of one of their Meetings. — A Letter. — "The Gospel Songs." — Style of the Music. — Sources of his Hymns. — "Lower Lights." — "I am so glad." — "Life-Boat." — "More to follow." — "Meet me at the Fountain." — Effects of his Music. — An Incident. — His Mission. — Mrs. Bliss. — The Royalty on "The Gospel Hymns and Sacred Songs." — "Gospel Hymns No. 2." — "Waiting and Watching." — Singing at Chautauqua. — Remarks on Church Music. — A Letter. — A Prophecy. — Disaster at Ashtabula Bridge. — Death of Mr. and Mrs. Bliss. — Telegrams. — Letter of Condolence. — Memorial Services at Chicago. — Boston. — Notice from "The Tribune." — Mrs. Bliss. — Personal Traits of Mr. Bliss. — His Monument. — Birth of Dr. Tourjée. — Education. — His Praise-Meetings. — Conservatory. — Character.

> "Sing unto the Lord a new song." — DAVID.

> "Sing on your heavenly way,
> Ye ransomed sinners, sing ;
> Sing on, rejoicing every day
> In Christ, the heavenly King." — WILLIAM HAMMOND.

> "Sing of Jesus, sing forever,
> Of the love that changes never:
> Who or what from him can sever
> Those he makes his own ? " — THOMAS KELLY.

THE songs of Mr. P. P. Bliss are sung by millions. They are joyous, bright, and hopeful, indicating thus the spirit of the man. Like his name, his life was brief and beautiful. His record is romantic, yet from it many salutary lessons may be drawn. He was born in the little town of Rome, near Towanda, Penn., on the ninth day of July, 1838. His parents were very poor; and their only son was early inured to labor, which, instead of injuring, tended to develop both his physical and mental constitution. In his boyhood he evinced a love of music, but had then no opportunities to study it as an art. He, however, remembered well the sabbath-school and martial songs that met his ear, and often amused himself and others by singing and whistling them at his work. He had, as it was said, a good ear for music, and, what is better, a bright and genial turn of mind. He was, though penniless, a light-hearted, merry, and obliging boy, — well formed, well behaved, and well beloved. As he advanced in age his voice became more sweet and powerful. He led the music in the sabbath school, and sought, as he was able, for improvement in the "art divine." On coming to Chicago in 1864, he was fortunate in making the acquaintance of the distinguished musical composer Mr. George F. Root, and in coming under his instruction. Entering into the employment of the firm of Messrs. Root and Cady, music-publishers, he found means to gratify his passion for song, and soon learned, as Mr. Sankey, how to play accompaniments on the melodeon to his voice. He began to compose simple songs for the sabbath school, and to arrest the attention of the public by his spirited rendering of the popular tunes of Messrs. Root and Bradbury, which were making then a new departure in the field of sacred melody. He had a charming voice, a joyous temper, and his services for sabbath-school and musical conventions gradually came to be in great demand. On his marriage to Miss Lucy J. Young of Rome, Penn., a lady of fine poetical as well as musical taste, he received a fresh incentive to pursue the study of sacred song. Through her influence he became a Christian; and by her his culture of music and of lyrical poetry was encouraged and advanced. He became a member of Dr. E. P. Goodwin's church, in which he was in 1870 appointed chorister, and subsequently superintendent of the sabbath school. While in this capacity he composed many of those beautiful hymns and tunes now sung with gladness by so many millions both at home and across the sea. When Mr. Bliss had gained sufficient knowledge of his favorite art, he began with his wife, who was a charming singer as well as writer, to hold normal musical institutes through the towns and cities of the great North-west, by which he for several years did much towards raising the standard of taste both as to secular and sacred music in that region. He also became very popular as a singer in Chicago, and received merited applause in carrying the bass solos in the grand oratorios of the "Creation" and of "Elijah." But his favorite work was in connection with the sabbath schools, young men's conventions, and evangelism.

It was the hearing of the magnificent voice of Mr. Bliss in Farwell Hall that gave Mr. Moody his idea of engaging a "gospel singer" to aid him in his revival work. He took Mr. Sankey with him to England, because Mr. Bliss had shown him how glorious it is to sing the praises of the Lord.

During the time of the great Sunday-school awakening in Illinois, Mr. Edward Eggleston went out to hold a convention in a certain town, and was much discouraged to find but a very few people present. The services went on heavily for an hour or so, when it was announced to him that Mr. Bliss and his wife had arrived in town.

"Who is Bliss?" said he.

"A music-teacher who is travelling for Root and Cady."

"Bring him in."

In a short time Mr. Bliss appeared, and said that he would sing if he could have his melodeon to assist him. It was a United Presbyterian Church; and the minister said to Mr. Eggleston, "I cannot give you permission to introduce a melodeon, but we have lent to you the church for a convention. If you introduce a melodeon I am not responsible."

The instrument was brought in, and Mr. Bliss and his wife with her fine contralto voice engaged in singing. "And such singing!" says Mr. Eggleston. "Instead of some poor country singing-master, beating out his music as with a flail, I soon found that here was a man with one of the richest voices in the world, capable of putting his own strong spirit into all he sung. He made us forget our Tate and Brady; he sung us into a state of delight, and I saw tears running down the cheeks of the United Presbyterian minister." The house was overcrowded in the evening, and so Mr. Bliss turned what else had been a defeat into a victory.

The first Sunday-school music of Mr. Bliss appeared in Mr. George F. Root's little work entitled "The Prize," which was published in 1870. "Whosoever will," and "Look and Live," with their animated choruses, soon became familiar to the members of the sabbath schools throughout the country. Encouraged by this success, he published himself, in 1871, "The Charm," whose very title indicates the effect which it produced wherever it was used. In the year ensuing he brought out "The Song Tree," indicating in the preface, formed of an acrostic, the design for which the work was published.

> " Sing away dreariness,
>   Tree of my love ;
> Oh, and to weariness
>   Rest may'st thou prove ;
> Nobly endeavor
>   The erring to win,
> Guarding forever
>   From evil and sin."

He next published for the use of sabbath schools, "Sunshine," the title itself showing the spirit in

which it was composed; and then another work entitled
"The Joy," containing music of a higher style.

In the spring of 1874 his friend Major D. W.
Whittle, knowing his remarkable power to "sing the
gospel," invited him to leave his musical institutes and
singing schools, and devote himself entirely to evangelism. He accepted the invitation, and engaged heart
and soul with him in the self-denying work, trusting, as
Messrs. Moody and Sankey, in the Lord alone for his
support. They held successful meetings in various
cities as far south as Mobile, Ala., and as far north as
Minneapolis, Minn., proving that in the union of music,
prayer, and exhortation, there is strength. One of
their notices will indicate their method in evangeliz-
ing : —

"Week of prayer. Major Whittle will preach the
gospel, and P. P. Bliss will sing the gospel, this
Wednesday evening, Jan. 6, at Union Park Congregational Church, Ashland Avenue, opposite the Park.
Seats free; all invited; further appointment. 'He
hath appointed a day in the which he will judge the
world in righteousness by that man [Jesus Christ]
whom he hath ordained; whereof he hath given assurance unto all men, in that he hath raised him from the
dead' [Acts xvii. 31]. Friend, are you ready to meet
this appointment? There can be no postponement."

In the summer of 1874 he wrote to a friend, "Major
Whittle and I are holding protracted meetings. God is
wonderfully using us in every way. Help us to praise

him for it. I am preparing a book of ‘Gospel Songs’ for our special use, and would be right glad to have you send a list of hymns and tunes which have been most successful in your experience. And, above all, pray for the book. All the good in the book must come from God.” This book was published the same year at Cincinnati, and contains as many as fifty-two of his own compositions, among which, “ Jesus of Nazareth passeth by,” “ I am so glad that Jesus loves me,” “ Only an Armor-Bearer,” “ More to follow,” “ Let the Lower Lights be burning,” “ Almost persuaded,” “ Daniel’s Band,” “ Pull for the Shore,” “ Hold the Fort,” “ Go bury thy Sorrow,” “ Meet me at the Fountain,” and “ Roll on, O Billow of Fire,” have become famous both in England and America. The music of these hymns is well adapted to the words, written in some instances by Mr. Bliss himself; and although it evinces not much of originality, consisting as it does of ideas and phrases long familiar to the ear, it still is sprightly, buoyant, as the soul of its composer, and reaches into the innermost chambers of the heart. It is national, and will doubtless live for many years to cheer the sorrowing, and to aid in the dissemination of the seeds of truth. No American music is known so well in Great Britain as that of Mr. Bliss. Many of the hymns of Mr. Bliss are founded on some striking incident, and hence are true to life experience.

“ Let the Lower Lights be burning,” was suggested by a shipwreck thus graphically described by Mr. D. L.

Moody: "On a dark, stormy night when the waves rolled like mountains, and not a star was to be seen, a boat, rocking and plunging, neared the Cleveland Harbor.

"'Are you sure this is Cleveland?' asked the captain, seeing only one light from the light-house.

"'Quite sure, sir,' replied the pilot.

"'Where are the lower lights?'

"'Gone out, sir.'

"'Can you make the harbor?'

"'We *must*, or perish, sir.'

"And with a strong hand and a brave heart the old pilot turned the wheel. But alas! in the darkness he missed the channel, and with a crash upon the rocks the boat was shivered, and many a life lost in a watery grave. Brethren, the Master will take care of the great light-house. Let us keep the lower lights burning."

The very beautiful song, "I am so glad that our Father in Heaven," was suggested to Mr. Bliss by the refrain, "Oh, how I love Jesus!"

"I have sung long enough," said he to himself one day, "my poor love for Christ, and now I will sing of his love for me." He then wrote in his very best style, his soul being filled with sacred emotion, the words and music of this favorite piece. The effect of this song in Scotland was electrical; and it still is sung by high and low, from Solway Frith to John O'Groat's.

The effective lyric, "Roll on, O Billow of Fire!'

written and set to music by himself, and dedicated to
Mr. D. L. Moody, is a graphic description of the burning of Chicago : —

> " Hark, the alarm! the clang of the bells!
> Signal of danger, it rises and swells;
> Flashes like lightning illumine the sky;
> See the red glare as the flames mount on high.
> Roll on, roll on, O billow of fire!
> Dash with thy fiery waves higher and higher:
> Ours is a mansion abiding and sure,
> Ours is a kingdom eternal, secure."

Both in the words and the music Mr. Bliss presents
most vividly the picture of that dreadful conflagration,
and then beautifully contrasts the insecurity of our
earthly habitations with the permanence of our celestial
home. Had he written only this spirited song, his
memory would have been long cherished by the lovers
of sacred melody.

The stirring song of the life-boat, commencing,
" Light in the darkness, sailor: day is at hand," and of
which Mr. Bliss wrote both the words and music, was
suggested by the following graphic description of a
shipwreck : —

" We watched the wreck with great anxiety. The
life-boat had been out some hours, but could not reach
the vessel through the great breakers that raged and
foamed on the sand-bank. The boat appeared to be
leaving the crew to perish ; but in a few minutes the
captain and sixteen sailors were taken off, and the vessel went down.

"' When the life-boat came to you, did you expect it had brought some tools to repair your old ship?' said I. —'Oh, no! she was a total wreck. Two of her masts were gone, and if we had staid mending her, only a few minutes, we must have gone down, sir.'—'When once off the old wreck, and safe in the life-boat, what remained for you to do?'—'Nothing, sir, but just to pull for the shore.'"

Spiritualizing this incident, Mr. Bliss brought forth in a moment of musical and poetical inspiration, his effective song, which with its spirited chorus,—

> " Pull for the shore, sailor, pull for the shore :
>   Heed not the rolling waves, but bend to the oar ;
>   Safe in the life-boat, sailor, cling to self no more :
>   Leave the poor old stranded wreck, and pull for the shore,"—

now goes echoing round the world. Charles Dibdin wrote nine hundred songs, the most of them pertaining to the sea, but none with the Christian ring of this by Mr. Bliss. And sweet it was to hear, on a passage from Liverpool to New York, its cheering notes pealing the tongues of sailors over the deep.

The beautiful song "More to follow," of which he composed both the words and music, was founded on the following incident related by his friend D. L. Moody in one of his stirring addresses :—

" A vast fortune was left in the hands of a minister for one of his poor parishioners. Fearing that it might be squandered if suddenly bestowed upon him, the wise minister sent him a little at a time with a note saying, 'This is thine; use it wisely: there is more to follow.' Brethren, that's just the way the Lord deals with us."

The idea is beautifully spiritualized in the words of the song: —

> " Have you on the Lord believed?
> Still there's more to follow.
> Of his grace have you received ?
> Still there's more to follow."

And the tune in sextuple time finely expresses the hope of the Christian for blessings yet to come.

The charming song, with its effective chorus, —

> " Will you meet me at the fountain,
> When I reach the glory-land ? " —

was suggested to him by the common invitation at one of the Expositions.

How many souls the precious songs of Mr. Bliss, through Christ, have turned and will still turn away from sin ; how many burdened hearts they have most sweetly comforted, and still will comfort, — never can be known till the grand harvest-home. It is one of the tenderest tokens of our heavenly Father's love, to send into this world such harbingers of the felicity of the land of song beyond the river. To cite the instances of the salutary effects of the delightful strains of Mr. Bliss would fill a volume. Such as these are every day occurring: A man had organized a Sunday school in

Missouri. He sung to the little company one day the hopeful song of Mr. Bliss, "I am so glad that Jesus loves me," and then put the question, "Are you glad that Jesus loves you?"

A young man, rising instantly, came and threw his arms around the singer's neck, and sobbing said, "You must not go away till I am a Christian." Praye was offered, when he exclaimed, "Oh that song! I could not get away from it, and it has saved me!"

What if his music does not meet the demands of art? It surely meets the wants of the overburdened and the sorrowful; it moves the hearts of the multitudes to a higher life; and this, I apprehend, is the grand design of song. Mr. Bliss had the genius to give the people what they wanted, what they needed; and so performed a glorious mission.

Mrs. Bliss wrote the hymns, "We are marching to Canaan with Banner and Song," and "I will love Jesus, and serve Him," under the assumed name of "Paulina;" she also composed the music for the latter, as well as the fine air for the "Rock of Ages."

In 1875 Mr. Bliss published, in conjunction with his friend Ira D. Sankey, "The Gospel Hymns and Sacred Songs," which were used in the revival work at Brooklyn, New York, and Philadelphia. An immense number of copies was sold; but the royalty thereon, amounting to about sixty thousand dollars, was by the compilers devoted to charitable purposes. On being urged by Mr. Moody to reserve at least five thousand dollars for himself and family, Mr. Bliss replied, "It must all go for the advancement of the work of the Lord." This book has been in part translated into the Chinese language; and some of the hymns, as, " Hold the Fort," are sung in several of the other Pagan nations. The beautiful hymn by Mrs. Bliss, " We're going Home To-morrow," for which her husband wrote the music, appears in this collection.

"The Gospel Hymns No. 2," compiled by Messrs. Bliss and Sankey, who fed, as it were, on angels' food while working over it, was just completed when Mr. Bliss and wife were called to leave their labors here for the great song-world above. It contains one hymn, " Hold fast till I come," by Mrs. Bliss; and the tune is the last one written by her husband. Mr. Bliss was noted for his gentleness, humility, and fervent piety. His heart was a fountain of good-nature and of spiritual joy. He was wont to pray over his music, and seemed never so happy as when it was moving the souls of men to come to Jesus. His prayer in verse was, —

> " More purity give me, —
> More strength to o'ercome,
> More freedom from earth-stains,
> More longings for home."

To one writing to him in respect to " Waiting and Watching for me," for which he composed the music, he replied, " No, I don't seem to rest much in the hope of seeing a throng of heavenly ones waiting and watching for me. They might be in better business. Nor of hearing echoes of my songs there. I want something better. The best things about heaven, it seems to me, will be eternal freedom from sin, and the immediate presence of Jesus.

> ‘ There we shall see his face,
> And never, never sin.’ ”

Mrs. Bliss was an estimable lady, well educated, and always ready to assist her husband in his studies and his Christian work. They were most happy in their union, as well as in their children, and their modest home which they appropriately called “ The Cottage of Content.”

“ I think the last time I joined in song with them,” says Mr. W. F. Sherwin in “ The Christian Union,” “ we were under the grand old trees at Chautauqua. A sister of Mr. Bliss (a soprano), with Mr. and Mrs. Bliss and myself, made up the quartet. They were about leaving. We turned to his song, ‘ Meet me at the Fountain,’ and Mr. Bliss sung with unusual sweetness the solo, —

> ‘ Will you meet me at the fountain,
> When I reach the glory-land ? ’

And we together responded for the last time, —

> ‘ Yes, we’ll meet you at the fountain.’

The emotions were too deep for utterance, while with uncovered heads we bowed at the rustic seat, and Mr

Bliss offered a fervent but peculiarly sweet and tender prayer, that, if we should not stand to sing again on the banks of the beautiful lake [1] which shimmered in the sunlight before us, we might meet 'beyond the river, by and by.'"

At one of the Sunday-school meetings held in Chautauqua, at which there was an audience of three thousand persons, he sung his beautiful heart-song, —

> " Almost persuaded now to believe,
> Almost persuaded Christ to receive," —

with such effect that the profound silence which ensued was broken only by the sobbing which arose from various parts of the assembly.

At " The Sunday-school Parliament " held on Wellesley Island in the St. Lawrence River, in 1876, Mr. Bliss justly said respecting church music, " That which ought to have the greatest emphasis just now, in regard to sacred music, is the need of greater reverence. While a song is being sung, people will pass up a church aisle or a Sunday-school aisle, whisper to each other, move about the room, distribute or collect library-books, put on overcoats, or do a score of other

---

[1] Chautauqua Lake is a fair expanse of water, eighteen miles long, and from one to three miles wide, in the south-west extremity of the State of New York. It is about seven hundred and thirty feet above Lake Erie, and is said to be the highest navigable sheet of water on this continent. The name signifies in the Indian language, "a misty place," in allusion to the fogs by which, from its elevated situation, it is often covered. It is about five miles distant from Lake Erie.

things that one would never think of doing during any other kind of prayer. When we are offering praise or prayer to God in metre, as much as if we were doing it upon our knees, a reverence of manner and of spir't should accompany it. Another thing to be enforced n connection with singing is a greater thoughtfulness in regard to the meaning of what we sing. Are the words prayer, or praise? Let appropriate thought, as well as appropriate melody, accompany the words."

The following letter, showing the anxiety of Mr. Bliss for his unconverted friends, was written by him to a business man in Chicago whose death had been erroneously reported : —

KALAMAZOO, MICH., Nov. 7.

"*Dear Friend*, — About a year ago I wrote you a personal letter about good things, urging upon your attention what you must know is the most important business in the world, — eternal life. We have been praying for you ever since ; and I believe that in your good-will toward me, you will not be offended if I venture one more letter from my heart. I admire your kindness of heart, and want to thank you for your favors to us. I love you as a brother ; and, having no brother of my own, wish I could have you in every thing to commune with.

" Isn't it business wisdom to lay up abiding riches in the other world, where we must so soon appear? Is it the fair and honest thing not to confess one's faith in Him who has done so much for us? Pardon me if disagreeable; but, dear brother, when I read of your death in the papers last spring, I wished I had done more to bring you to Christ, my blessed Master. Will you be a follower of Jesus?

"Do not feel obliged to answer this to *me*. I have prayed the Lord to follow it with his Spirit, and lead you to answer it to him, as you will be glad through all eternity.

"Your loving brother, P. P. B."

It had been arranged that on the departure of Messrs. Moody and Sankey, Major Whittle and Mr. Bliss should carry on the evangelism at the Tabernacle in Chicago; but this was by a most terrible accident prevented. The last time Mr. Bliss sung at the Moody and Sankey meetings there, he said, — as it afterwards appeared almost prophetically, — "I don't know as I shall ever sing here again; but I want to sing this as the language of my heart, —

> ' I know not the hour my Lord will come,
> To take me away to his own dear home;
> But I know that his presence will lighten the gloom,
> And that will be glory for me.' "

With Mrs. Bliss he went to Towanda, on the Susquehanna River in Pennsylvania, to spend Christmas with his mother. On Thursday, the 28th of December, he with his wife bade their relatives and friends at Towanda and Rome farewell, and started for Chicago. The engine breaking caused them to take a later train, on board of which Mr. Bliss was observed to be engaged in composing, with the Bible and a pencil in his hand, a piece of music. When the train with its two engines, on the evening of Friday the 29th, and in the midst of a terrible snowstorm, was crossing the Ashtabula bridge[1] between Erie and Cleveland, the iron structure and the cars upon it fell with a horrid crash, some seventy feet or more, into the stream below.

The passengers were in an instant buried in the dreadful wreck, to perish by the concussion or the flames which in a few moments left but a mass of black and smouldering ruins in the stream. A few of the people escaped, but the bodies of the most of them were so consumed that it was not possible to identify the remains. It is said that Mr. Bliss rose from the ruins, but returning to extricate his wife shared her untimely fate. The news of the death of these beloved singers brought sincere grief to every Christian heart.

The following telegram was sent from Philadelphia : —

"PHILADELPHIA, Jan. 1.

" MOODY AND SANKEY, — The brethren of the East send tenderest sympathies in overwhelming bereave-

---

[1] This iron-truss bridge over the Ashtabula Creek, near its entrance into Lake Erie, was, like the old Pemberton Mill at Lawrence, Mass., but a mere trap for the destruction of human life. The weakness of both these sham structures was pointed out in the beginning by the architects; but such is the greed for gain, that the public safety is knowingly, constantly and shamefully compromised for the almighty dollar

ment of our beloved brethren. Bliss and wife. 'Only remembered by what I have done.' Sudden death, sudden glory.

"STUART, WANNAMAKER, AND NEEDHAM.'

The next day Mr. Moody received this sad intelligence from Mr. H. W. Stager of Cleveland : —

"ASHTABULA, Jan. 2.

" The last hope is gone of finding any thing of our dear friends Bliss and wife. Every thing has been done that human power can do. There is no other conclusion to be reached, but that all in that car were entirely consumed. I have found nothing but a hand and a few fragments of bodies to-day, but quite a number of articles of wearing-apparel, both male and female, quite a number of which have been identified by friends, but none by Major Whittle as belonging to Mr. Bliss or wife.

" To-morrow will probably end one of the saddest tasks it has been my lot to perform, or to be imagined."

The following tender letter of condolence, expressing the deep sympathy of Christians in Chicago, was forwarded to the widowed mother of Mr. Bliss : —

CHICAGO, Jan. 3.

MRS. BLISS. *Dear Madam,* — As the representatives of thousands of Christian people in this city and its immediate vicinity, permit us to express to you the affectionate and prayerful sympathy with which all our hearts gather about you in this sad hour.

We feel painfully how inadequate the most loving of human words are to lift or lighten the burden of such a grief. We do not seek to do this : rather we commend you afresh, as we have done already in our homes, our prayer gatherings, our sabbath services, to Him who is a refuge from the storm, a covert from the tempest, and whose divine pledge is that none of them that trust in Him shall be desolate. But we have thought that among the tributes to this beloved son's character and work upon which your thought will love to linger, it would be pleasant to you to have a word of testimony as to how dear he had become to us. We feel this affliction to be peculiarly personal to us and to those whom we represent. The songs of this dear brother are in many of our churches, our Sunday schools, our homes : and they are there as among the most precious helps the Lord has given to our Christian life and service. They have given peculiar and blessed inspiration to our gatherings for prayer; for they have rung in our ears so tenderly the call of duty, have urged us so tenderly to reconsecration, have put in our lips petitions so earnest for God's aid, have held up before us so attractively the satisfactions to be realized, the joys, the glory to be won, that doubts and gloom have been often banished, sloth broken up, the things of faith more clearly apprehended and rejoiced in, the life of faith, and prayer, and toil for Christ more zealously taken up, more faithfully carried on.

They have had like ministry in our sabbath schools ; no songs have more quickly reached and more powerfully moved the children. Hundreds and even thousands have been won by them not only to sing for Jesus, but to accept the call of Him of Nazareth, and can say to-day from the heart, as they do with their lips, —

> "Hallelujah, 'tis done !
> I believe on the Son ;
> I am saved by the blood of the crucified One."

And in our family circles these sweet songs have been a perpetual joy. Times without number they have comforted the bereaved, cheered the discouraged, strengthened the weak, brightened as with the light of heaven the faces of the dying.

Dear madam, as we recall these things we cannot but lift up thanksgiving in the midst of our tears for God's gift of this servant to his Church in the latter days; and we feel that God has greatly honored you, as he honored the mother of Samuel and the mother of David, in giving you such a treasure, and through your prayers and Christian nurture preparing him for such a glorious ministry of winning souls. We rejoice also for the work which he is yet to do. Although he rests from his labors, through all the ages to come his works will follow him. Already these gospel songs are sung round the world; yet their mission is only begun. As the years roll on, like the handful of seed dropped in the furrow they shall yield increasing harvest, till from all lands and kindreds and tongues there shall come up a mighty throng to cast their crowns at the feet of that dear Lord whose dying love it was our dear brother's highest joy to magnify.

We do not forget how lonely the way will be unto which you are called by this Providence. But though this beloved son's arm, upon which you hoped to lean in these declining years, has been struck down, a stronger arm, a surer support, still remains; and in the kingdom of the Shepherd of Israel your feet will not stumble. Though the face you had so loved to look upon is withdrawn, the face of One altogether lovely will shine ever in its place. Though the voice so full of music to your ears is hushed, the voice that spake as never man spoke, and to hear which all heaven would keep glad silence, will speak unceasingly to your heart. And evermore before you and the dear children so bereft will be the vision of the beloved gone before, and of the welcome that awaits your coming at the gate of the city.

As we speak these words there comes to us one of the songs, that, like the precious Scripture lyric of which it was born, has been blessed of God to many a weary pilgrim. May its cheering, hope-

ful words minister strength to you as to those who listened to it
from the lips now sealed to human ears! —

> " Through the valley of the shadow I must go,
>   Where the cold waves of Jordan roll;
> But the promise of my Shepherd will, I know,
>   Be the rod and the staff of my soul.
> Even now down the valley as I glide,
>   I can hear my Saviour say, ' Follow me!'
> And with him I'm not afraid to cross the tide:
>   There's a light in the valley for me.
>
> .   .   .   .
>
> Now the rolling of the billows I can hear,
>   As they beat on the turf-bound shore,
> But the beacon-light of love so bright and clear
>   Guides my bark frail and low safely o'er.
> I shall find down the valley no alarms,
>   For my Saviour's blessed smile I can see;
> He will bear me in his loving, mighty arms:
>   There's a light in the valley for me."

We wish also to express through you our most sincere and
prayerful sympathy with the parents of our beloved sister, Mrs.
Bliss. Some of us have known how peculiarly identified with her
husband she was in all his work for Christ. And no testimony
could be more beautiful than that which he so often bore to the
cheerfulness with which she accepted the separations from home
which his evangelistic life necessitated, and the loving encouragement and aid, alike by counsel, pen, and voice, which it was her
delight to render. Lovely and pleasant in their lives, in their
death they were not divided. And through all future years, while
their memories will be alike cherished, their labors will be alike
fruitful.

And now, dear madam, we commend you all, and especially
these dear children, to the tender care, the unfailing guardianship,
of Him whose mercies never fail. May the peace of God, which

passeth all understanding, keep your hearts and minds through the knowledge of Christ Jesus our Lord. And through Him who is the resurrection and the life, may we all be gathered with these beloved in the home where " God shall wipe away all tears from our eyes, and there shall be no more death, neither sorrow nor crying, neither shall there be any more pain; for the former things are passed away."

In the bonds and consolations of the gospel we are affectionately yours,

EDWARD P. GOODWIN,
First Congregational Church.

CHARLES EDWARD CHENEY,
Christ Church.

M. M. PARKHURST,
Clark-street Methodist Episcopal Church.

W. W. EVERTS,
First Baptist Church.

W. J. PETRIE,
Church of our Saviour.

On the sabbath following the disaster, memorial services were held at Chicago in the Tabernacle, which was crowded to its utmost capacity. They consisted mainly of the singing of the hymns of the deceased, interspersed with brief remarks and prayers.

Mr. Moody said, " The hymns of Mr. Bliss are such as he was himself, full of life and cheer. In all the years I have known and worked with him, I have never once seen him cast down: here is a hymn of his I think we may sing. It begins, ' Brightly beams our Father's mercy.' Yet still more brightly beams the light along the shore to which he has passed. My

heart goes out for his mother.   He was an only son,
and his mother is a widow.   Let us just put up a prayer
for this mother.   And there was dear Mrs. Bliss, who
was not one inch behind her husband.   She taught
him how to pray, and encouraged him with his music.
I have often heard him say, ' All I am I owe to that
dear wife.'   It was in the midst of a terrible storm that
he passed away ; but the lights which he kindled are
burning all along the shore.   He has died young; but
his hymns are sung round the world."

The Rev. Dr. Goodwin said, " The other day I received a visit from a missionary in South Africa.   He
said he was going out, some time ago, to establish a
new mission ; and, taking refuge in a Zulu hut, the first
thing he heard was ' Hold the Fort,' sung in the Zulu
language."

Meetings were held in many other cities, commem-
orative of the death and characters of Mr. and Mrs.
Bliss.   Dr. Goodwin (of whose church Mr. Bliss was a
member) preached a funeral sermon at Rome; and in
Boston, Jan. 7, a meeting *in memoriam* was held in the
hall of the Young Men's Christian Association, which
was overcrowded.   Dr. Eben Tourjée led the music,
which was confined to the singing of the hymns of Mr.
and Mrs. Bliss.   Remarks were made by the Rev. M.
R. Deming on the power of the gospel songs which they
had composed, and on the loss to the church by the
death of these gifted singers.   " The Tribune " as
kindly as beautifully paid this tribute to Mr. Bliss : —

"He has been Mr. Moody's right arm; for Mr. Sankey has chiefly sung the songs which the dead singer composed and used to sing. He is dead, but he lives again; lives in the Sunday school, in the church, in the revival, in the foreign missions, in the heart of every man and woman striving for something higher and better, wherever men preach Christ, and sinners seek repentance.

"It takes much from the sadness of the singer's awful death, that his life was so rounded and complete. His work had been so well done that death could not surprise him, and find him with his mission unaccomplished. He had made his mark, and the mark will remain. His life has stopped, but his work goes on in every church and in every home all over the world; and years from now, when even his name may be lost, his songs will still continue to inspire faltering men and women with courage, to bring consolation into the house of mourning, to arouse faith in the human heart. For such a life, so perfect, so successful, so far-reaching in its influences, spent in the most beneficent of labor, and lost at the post of duty, there should be no tears. Other voices will take up his strains, and the work will go on without stop. Their simple beauty is not marred, nor is their wonderful influence upon the popular heart lessened by his death. Noble and impressive in his physique, affable and genial in his conduct with every one, earnest and untiring in his work, he will long be missed as a leader in the evangelical movement which is now stirring the popular heart; but he has left his impress upon the world, with results more lasting than the work achieved by heroes of the battle-field or masters of state-craft. His harp is forever silent, his voice forever hushed; but the songs which he sung can never die. Their melody, like the brook, goes on forever."

He left two children, George G. and Paul P.; the one about two, and the other about four years old. For them Mr. Moody raised at once by subscription the sum of ten thousand dollars, and also a liberal sum for the mother of Mr. Bliss. The father of Mrs. P. P. Bliss is still living, at Rome, Penn.

In his personal appearance Mr. Bliss was remarkably prepossessing; in his manners, affable, obliging, and polite. "He was tall and well developed in his physical frame," says one who knew him intimately, "with clustering black hair and a handsome face; possessing easy and polished manners and a very joyous temperament, together with a wealth of sympathy." His songs and poetry breathe the spirit of his own bright and joyous disposition, the movement of the music being lively, and the minor key but seldom introduced.

"I am so glad that Jesus loves me," —

with its light sextuple measure, well represents his genial and loving nature. It could have come only from a heart aglow with life and joy in the Redeemer. Mrs. Bliss, who died at the age of thirty-five years, was a fitting companion of such a noble man. With fine natural abilities improved by culture, with an affluence

of good-nature, a lively imagination, and a spirit sanctified by religion, she made his home and public life
happy; dividing his sorrow and doubling his joy. In
life they were as one, in death they were not divided.
The pictures which the artist has here given of them,
says Mr. Sankey in a letter lying before me, "are very
good, especially the one of Mrs. Bliss." The scene of
the dreadful accident by which they lost their lives is
vividly presented at the bottom of the portraits. A
penny contribution has been taken up in the sabbath
schools for the erection of a monument in honor of the
lamented singers. But their noblest and most enduring
monument is the beautiful Christian hymns and tunes
they have composed. These will still ring on, comforting and consoling many, and embalming the names
of the authors in the hearts of millions of the heirs of
glory.

In his own sweet words we may say that these two
loved ones, whose rich music fills so many souls with
gladness, are now singing sweeter songs, —

> " Safe in a land immortal,
>   Safe in a country rare,
>   Safe in a heavenly portal,
>   Safe in a mansion fair;
>   Safe with the joys supernal,
>   Safe with the blest to bow,
>   Safe with the Love eternal,
>   Safe with the Master now."

DR. EBEN TOURJÉE.

THIS distinguished musical director, whose services materially enhance the interest of the revival at the Tabernacle in Boston, was born in Warwick, R.I., on the first day of June, 1834, and is consequently forty-two years of age. He is of Huguenot descent, his ancestors having, in company with the Tourtelottes, Mauneys, and other French families, settled in Rhode Island soon after the famous Edict of Nantes by which the Protestants of France were compelled to seek for safety in foreign lands. He is the son of Ebenezer and Anne D. (Ball) Tourjée, and is through Ebenezer[5], Jeremiah[4], John[3], and Peter[2], of the sixth generation from Peter[1], the original settler. He early evinced a re-markable fondness for music. The ringing of bells, the sounds of the fife and drum, the tones of the organ, filled his soul with delight; and such was the correct-ness of his ear that he was generally called upon to give the pitch of the tunes sung in the sabbath school. Having religious parents, and a mental organization keenly alive to good impressions, he was at the age of eleven years converted to Christ, and soon afterwards became a member of the Methodist church of which

the Rev. George M. Brewster was then the pastor. As
an alto singer in the choir, he learned by rote the common psalm-tunes then in vogue, but had no knowledge
of music as an art. The following circumstance, however, led him to determine to make of it a life-study.
A daughter of Gov. Elisha Harris was the organist of
the church at Harrisville (Warwick), and was about to
be married. The governor, who had observed the musical ability of young Tourjée, then thirteen years of age,
and in his employ, said to him on a certain Wednesday
evening, " I wish you would learn to play the organ
soon as possible. Here is the key." The lad had
never played on that or any other instrument; but
the key was in his trembling hand: it was the key
to his fortune. He longed to touch the instrument;
he feared he could not play it.   He did not dare
refuse the governor; indeed, he did not wish to do it,
for his fingers burned to touch the instrument. He
unlocked it, looked at the ivory keys, but knew not
which were high or low. He touched them, and the
tones responded to his wishes. He soon made out the
air of " Greenville," then added to it the bass ; and so
the hope came fluttering over him, that he might possibly prepare himself for the services of the coming sabbath. On the succeeding evenings of the week he
learned to play " Chimes," " Naomi," and " Lanesboro',"
and thus with his four tunes went creditably through
his part of the sacred services. He was soon appointed
organist of the church ; and this enabled him to go to

Providence, thirteen miles distant, and take lessons in music of Mr. Henry Eastcott, who thus had the honor of initiating him into the mysteries of his beloved art. He sometimes walked the whole distance ; and his practice was on the organ in the old Round Top Church. At the age of fifteen years he became a clerk in the music store of Mr. E. W. Billings of Providence, with whom he remained two years, enjoying many facilities for study, and making the acquaintance of many musical people. At the age of seventeen he opened for himself a music store in Fall River, Mass., and at the same time taught music in the public schools, and edited a little paper called "The Keynote," in which he prophetically indicated some of the musical schemes that he has subsequently carried into effect. In 1855 "The Keynote" was merged into "The Massachusetts Musical Journal," which he conducted for one year. On the thirty-first day of October of the same year he was married to Miss Abbie I. Tuell of Warren, R.I., an estimable lady whose death he was called to mourn in 1867. This union was blessed with four children : Lizzie S., Emma (deceased), Clara S., and Homer. For his second wife he married Miss Sarah Lee of Newton, Mass., by whom he had Hattie and Arthur, the former of whom died at the age of two years. Closing his business at Fall River, young Tourjée went to reside in Newport, R.I., where he officiated as organist of the First Baptist Church one year, and then at Trinity Church four years, performing on the celebrated instrument which Dean Berkeley sent over as a present to the town which bears his name.[1]

In addition to his labors as organist, he held musical conventions, and taught music in the public schools of the city.

As early as 1851 he entertained the idea of establishing a musical conservatory on the European plan, in which his favorite art should assume the same position as other branches in our literary institutions, and thus be systematically pursued, so as to give completeness to a liberal culture of the mind. He had not the means himself to establish such an institution; nor were those to whom he applied for aid disposed to advance much money for carrying into effect what they believed to be a visionary scheme. But the reformer clung to his idea: he made it not only the subject of study, but of prayer. For years his mind was brooding over his beloved project; and in 1859 he succeeded in opening at the academy in East Greenwich, R.I., his original conservatory of music, and the first one in America. At the beginning he had but three pupils; yet, moving on persistently, he soon made of it a marked success. In 1863 he visited Europe. He examined carefully the musical institutions there established, and for some time enjoyed the instruction of several of the most eminent masters. At Berlin he introduced successfully

---

[1] The people of Berkeley voted not to receive the gift, declaring that "an organ is an instrument of the Devil for the entrapping of men's souls."

our American style of singing into the sabbath schools, which prior to that time had sung nothing but the heavy choral music of that country. He returned to America, bringing with him many musical curiosities and a rich store of information in respect to musical subjects, gained by intercourse with the most celebrated instructors and composers of the age. In 1865 he established a chartered music school in Providence, R.I.; and on the 18th of February, 1867, opened under favorable auspices, and a charter from the State, the New England Conservatory of Music, at the Music Hall in Boston. Thus was realized the fond aspiration of his early manhood; thus was laid, after years of planning and of preparation, a music school on a grand and liberal scale, embracing in its several departments teachers of the highest skill, and furnishing at a moderate cost a musical education of the highest order. During the ten years of its existence, it has had not less than sixteen thousand pupils under its tuition, many of whom have already attained distinction in the musical world; and from it have sprung many other similar institutions.

In consideration of his eminent abilities as a musical director, the degree of Doctor of Music was in 1869 conferred on him by the Wesleyan University; and ro man in this country is more worthy of the title. In the same year his administrative powers were anew called into action, by the organization of the choruses, consisting of twenty thousand voices, for the grand

Peace Jubilee of P. S. Gilmore. But for the influence of the conservatory in elevating the style of music in New England, and the admirable management of Dr. Tourjée, that great musical festival could not have taken place. It was the outgrowth of an idea cherished by a youth of seventeen while editor of " The Keynote," in Fall River, and having its development in the conservatory at East Greenwich, then at Providence, and finally at Boston. But that is not by any means the measure of the influence of the institution founded by Dr. Tourjée. It has sent the charms of music into thousands of our happy homes; it has raised the standard of musical culture in our public schools and in our churches; it has improved the music of the concert-room; and, either directly or indirectly, it has awakened a taste for music in the minds of millions. During the summer vacation of the conservatory, Dr. Tourjée holds a musical institute at East Greenwich, R.I., where teachers of music from various parts of the country enjoy the instructions of his corps of Boston artists.

Dr. Tourjée holds the office of Dean of the faculty of the College of Music in the Boston University, and was for years superintendent of the sabbath school, and President of the North End Mission; a noble work of charity, which owes its foundation and continued success largely to his self-denying labors. He is an earnest advocate of congregational singing in the churches; and his able address on that subject, delivered in many cities, has contributed in no small degree to produce a favorable change in public sentiment. His excellen. work on psalmody, entitled "The Tribute of Praise," in which all the tunes are so arranged as to be easily sung by the congregation, has also been conducive to the same desirable end. His other publications are, "The Chorus Choir," consisting of classic music from the old masters; "The Lesser Hymnal;" and "The New England Conservatory's Pianoforte Method," which appeared in 1870. The same year, by invitation of the National Teachers' Association, he prepared and read, at their annual convention, a paper upon music and its relations to other studies. At the close of the reading President Fairchild warmly commended it, and asked for its publication, which was unanimously voted.

To Dr. Tourjée the Church is indebted for the conception and plan of the praise-meeting. As early as 1851 he began to hold in Warren, R.I., the home of his first wife, meetings for praise. He called them "sings." The people were interested in the exercises. Subsequently he united the congregation, choir, and sabbath school in these assemblies for singing, and called them, by the approval of Messrs. Webb and Mason, "praise-meetings." The design is to interblend responsive Scriptural readings on any given topic, as "Heaven," "The Advent," "The Promises," with responsive singing by the congregation. A brief prayer is also introduced. A logical order is preserved, so that the mind is not confused by the multiplicity of thoughts presented. Thus, if the theme be "Heaven,' the first part of the exercise may describe the beauties of the place; the second, the occupants of heaven; the third, the joys of heaven: the fourth, the way to heaven; and the whole may close with an invitation to heaven. An exercise so arranged may teach many truths impressively, and be carried on with far more life and spirit than an ordinary prayer-meeting. It tends also to call forth the inert musical ability of the people, and to promote congregational singing in the churches. When the great revival meetings commenced at the Tabernacle in Boston, Dr. Tourjée came forward with a choir of about two thousand voices, separated into five or six sections; and with one of these, under his own or some other leadership, he has directed with great acceptance the music of the immense congregations, — sometimes in the way of a praise-meeting, sometimes in that of the grand old chorals, and then again in that of music by the choir alone. In no city have the revivalists been sustained by better music than in Boston; and it is certainly most gratifying to every Christian in the audience to see the accomplished director of the largest musical conservatory in the world thus lending his own personal influence to swell the tide of song that rises from the mighty concourse to the praise of the Redeemer.

Dr. Tourjée has filled the office of President of the Boston Young Men's Christian Association, is now President of the Boston Missionary and Church Extension Society of the Methodist-Episcopal Church, and was recently elected President of the National Music Teachers' Association.

Dr. Tourjée has a very sweet tenor voice, and is never so happy as when using it for the honor of his God. Indeed, all his plans and purposes are sanctified by prayer, and carried on for the advancement of the kingdom of the Lord. His life-work is Christ-work. He looks on music as the voice of God to lead us heavenward. He employs it for the purposes of praise, and nothing is more beautiful than to behold a man of his executive power and rare endowments consecrating all to Christ, and with warm enthusiasm striving to raise music, one of heaven's serenest gifts to man, to its legitimate design of rendering praises to Jehovah's name. In person this eminent musical director is pre-possessing and agreeable. His countenance is open, frank, and genial; his hair is brown, his forehead fair and well developed; his eye is large and full, his mouth expressive. In manner he is polite and courteous; in speech, graceful and confiding. His conceptions are vivid, and his mental combinations rapid, though distinct and clear. With great suavity, and tenderness of feeling, he at the same time possesses a reserved force equal to any emergency that may arise; and, if life is spared to him, will make a still higher record in the musical world.

The following incident from his pen, and relating to his beloved mission, carried on now for about ten years, will serve as a specimen of his spirit as well as of his style in writing : —

"One Sunday," says Dr. Tourjée, "a man came in to our Sunday school at the Boston North End Mission, drawn by the sweetness of the children's singing. He remained until the close, and came again that evening to our prayer-meeting. When the customary invitation to seek the Saviour was given, he came, forward, and found 'peace in believing.' To a few of us who had remained to pray with the penitent seekers he said, 'My friends, I feel that I'm a saved man ; and *I owe it to your children's singing "Jesus loves me," this after-noon.* I couldn't realize it, I've been such a miserable sinner; but after I went away I thought it over, "Jesus loves me;" and then I thought of the next line, "The Bible tells me so," and I tried to *believe* it ; and I came here this evening to get you to pray for me.' He became a regular attendant at the mission, and while with us gave the clearest evidence of a genuine change of heart.

"This is but one of very many similar instances of almost weekly occurrence at this mission. This same man soon after felt called by the Holy Spirit to prepare himself for the Christian ministry ; and at present he is regularly occupying a pulpit in Massachusetts, spending much of his time during the week in lecturing upon the evils of intemperance."

SACRED SONG IN EVANGELISM.

SACRED SONG IN EVANGELISM.

"Teaching and admonishing one another in psalms and hymns and spiritual
songs, singing with grace in your hearts to the Lord." — ST. PAUL.

> " I would begin the music here,
>   And so my soul should rise;
> Oh, for some heavenly notes to bear
>   My spirit to the skies!" — ISAAC WATTS.

> " Saints below with heart and voice,
>   Still in songs of praise rejoice;
> Learning here, by faith and love,
>   Songs of praise to sing above." — JAMES MONTGOMERY.

THE influence of music on the heart of man is
mighty. There is no sorrow it may not alleviate, no

joy it may not exalt. Hence the military commander the dramatist, and the reformer, have in all ages pressed it into service. Its power lies not only in imparting immediate pleasure, but also in awakening sweet or grand associations, and in breathing into the soul fresh ardor for the accomplishment of its purposes. The battle-hymns of nations have sometimes roused, more than the words of orators, the spirit of the people; and, when all other arts have failed, a simple song has sometimes brought back reason to the mind of a distracted king. Since, then, music has such marvellous power, it is not at all surprising that the servants of God have in every age employed it, not only for the expression of grateful praise, but also as a means for propagating the religion they profess Indeed, the singing of psalms, as David tells us, " was a statute for Israel, and a law of the God of Jacob; " and he also declares in one of his sweet lyrics, that when *all* the people praise God, " then shall the earth yield her increase " (Ps. lxvii. 6).

The disciples of our Saviour sung a hymn at the Last Supper; and Paul and Silas whiled away the hours of their imprisonment, as many others in bonds have done, by singing the inspiring songs of Israel. The early Christians understood full well the power of music, and used it both for consolation and for the advancement of the Master's kingdom.

" How many tears have I shed," says St. Augustine, " when I heard hymns and canticles sung in the church to thy praise, O my God! While the sound thereof struck my ears, thy truth entered my heart; it drew tears from my eyes, and made me find comfort and delight in those very tears."

St. Ambrose instituted the Ambrosian chant at Milan, "that the people might not languish and pine away with a tedious sorrow;" and in the fourth century St. Gregory introduced the Gregorian tones into Rome, which on certain occasions are still chanted. During the mediæval ages many Greek and Latin hymns as —

> " Jerusalem the golden,
>   With milk and honey blest," —

the "Stabat Mater," and "Dies Iræ," were written, and sacred song was practised to inspire devotion and to keep alive the embers of religion in the church; yet it may be noticed that whenever any thing of a revival spirit rose, then with it swelled more fervently the tide of hallowed praise. The great reformation was in part produced by music. Luther knew and confessed its power. "Next unto theology," he said, "I give the place and highest honor unto music." "It is," he also said, "a half-discipline and schoolmistress to make the people gentler, milder, more moral, and wiser." In accordance with this opinion, he introduced new hymns and music, such as the Old Hundredth, to be sung congregationally in the reformed churches. The Protestant armies sometimes sung this and other grand old chorals on the eve of battle. The Nonconformists of

England, as well as the Covenanters of Scotland, alle
viated their burdens and poured forth their praises in
psalms and spiritual songs. "Methinks," said the pious
Richard Baxter, a celebrated Nonconformist, "when
we are singing the praises of God in great assemblies,
with joyful and fervent spirits, I have the liveliest
foretaste of heaven upon earth; and I could almost
wish that our voices were loud enough to reach
through the world, and to heaven itself. Nothing
comforts me more in my greatest sufferings, or seems
more fit for me while I wait for death, than singing
psalms of praise to God; nor is there any exercise in
which I had rather end my life."

Our forefathers appreciated the value of music consecrated to the service of the Lord: it served to lighten
the burdens of life in the wilderness, and give them a
foretaste of joys to come.

> " Amid the storm they sang;
>   And the stars heard, and the sea;
>   And the sounding aisles of the dim woods rang
>   With the anthems of the free."

It is a significant fact, that when, in the days of witch-
craft, religion had declined to the lowest point, the
singing in the churches also became almost intolerable.
The people could execute but three or four tunes, and
those only by rote. During the great revivals under
the lead of the Wesleys and under the eloquent George
Whitefield, sacred music played a conspicuous part. It

was then that Charles Wesley produced his glorious hymns, as, "Jesus, lover of my soul," "I know that my Redeemer lives," "Depth of mercy! can there be?" and insisted on the use of a livelier style of music, which should not only express the sentiment of the hymn, but also inflame the hearts of the congregation. The effect produced by the singing of these new evangelical hymns by large assemblies was sometimes marvellous. Many were converted by hearing them, and continued to sing them alone and in their homes until the close of life.

An actress one day heard some poor people in a cottage singing, —

> "Depth of mercy! can there be
> Mercy still reserved for me?" —

and also a simple prayer which followed it. Her heart was touched, and when first importuned by the manager of the theatre to perform her part, declined to do so, but afterwards consented. When the curtain rose she was to sing a song, and the orchestra began to play the accompaniment; but she did not appear. It commenced again, when, coming forward with her eyes suffused with tears, she sung, instead of the appointed song, —

> "Depth of mercy! can there be
> Mercy still reserved for me?" —

with such effect as to lead some present to consecrate themselves, as she herself had done, to the service of the Lord.

Thousands who cared but little for the spoken word were drawn into the religious meetings just to hear the new and stirring songs of Wesley. Mr. Southey speaks of one instance which he regarded as the most singular case of instantaneous conversion ever recorded. It was in Wexford, Ireland, where, to avoid the violence of the Romanists, the worshippers shut themselves up in a barn. In order to open the door to their opponents, an Irishman concealed himself in a bag; but when the singing commenced, it so delighted him that he decided to remain and hear it through, and after that the prayer. But the service so affected him that he from his place of concealment cried outright. The people then removed him from the sack, and found in him a real penitent.

The preaching of Charles Wesley was indeed effective; yet his glorious hymns, which have now been ringing round the world for one whole century, are a thousand-fold more effective. Every day they bring, by their sweet influence, souls to rejoice in hope of glory.

I would rather have written the grand, comforting, and reviving hymn, —

> " Jesus, lover of my soul,
> Let me to thy bosom fly," —

than to rule a kingdom. Princes die; their graves are seldom visited: but in that hymn Charles Wesley lives forever, and by it he makes others live who love to scatter flowers upon his resting place. The Wesleys,

Dr. Watts, Dr. Doddridge, and Mrs. Steele produced by their inspiring strains a new departure in hymnology; and they still go on singing the gospel songs through the generations.

The revival of forty years ago in this country called forth a certain class of new hymns which were set to lively music, and sung with spirit; yet many of the lyrics, as, —

"Don't you see my Jesus coming ? " —

"Now the Saviour stands a-pleading
At the sinner's bolted heart," —

"When I was down in Egypt land," —

are entirely destitute of any poetic merit, and the tunes are secular. But the excellent hymns of Samuel F. Smith, our best writer of sacred lyric poetry, of Dr. Thomas Hastings, and others, together with the music of Zeuner, Mason, Kingsley, Hastings, and Webb, soon put to silence what were called "the revival melodies." These rich contributions to hymnology and psalmody, in connection with the wealth of hallowed song from Great Britain, especially from the gifted pens of Heber, Lyte, and Montgomery, met for a while the wants of our evangelical churches.

Then William B. Bradbury came, and set the world a little forward by his beautiful songs. He embalmed many new and sweetly devotional hymns, as Walford's "Sweet Hour of Prayer" and Gilmore's "He Leadeth me," in simple yet heart-moving music which the church holds as a precious legacy. While he sings the

beatific song, the pleasant strains he left us cheer
unnumbered pilgrims on their way to join him in the
anthems pealing over the " sweet fields of Eden."

But the kingdom of our Lord is ever rolling on, and
as it rolls demands new men, new measures, and new
songs. Bliss, Phillips, Lowry, Fischer, Sankey, enter
on the stage, and in a style unknown before sing songs
so fresh, so sweet, so cheerful, and withal so evangelical,
as to win the hearts of millions to the Saviour, and to
form a new era in the psalmody of the church.

Never perhaps in the whole course of Christianity
have any songs turned, in so brief a period, so many
hearts to seek the Lord, as those of Mr. Bliss ; never
perhaps has any voice ever preached the gospel so
effectively in song as that of Mr. Sankey. Thousands
and thousands of people attribute their conversion to
some truth sent into the heart, and made to stay there,
by the silver tones of his sympathetic voice. They
were drawn, perhaps, to the place of worship by the
fame of the " gospel singer." They heard unmoved the
fiery appeals, the touching stories, of Mr. Moody ; but
the rare tenderness of some strain of the " gospel singer "
stole into deep recesses of the soul, awakening it, as
the breath of May the flower, to life and beauty. The
burst of song that rises grandly from a vast congregation has the general effect of inspiring all with an
emotion of sublimity: the voice of one alone comes
searching more directly into each individual heart.
Mr. Sankey literally sings the gospel. He makes the

music altogether subservient to the words, and these he enunciates with the utmost clearness. His melodeon sounds more like an Æolian harp than a reed-organ; and he puts his soul in all its trembling delicacy so entirely into his words, his voice, his instrument, that the effect is wonderfully sweet and winning. When the hearer feels the gospel is thus sung for nothing but to save his soul, how can he find it in his heart to reject the message?

The following incidents revealing the effect of Mr. Sankey's and other singing on the heart, and as instrumental in producing conviction and conversion during the revivals, both at home and abroad, will undoubtedly be read with interest, and it is hoped with profit also.

A thoughtless young girl, unable to get into one of the revival meetings in Edinburgh, remained outside; and hearing Mr. Sankey sing in his own affectionate style, "I am so glad that Jesus loves me," said, "I cannot sing that," and at the close of the service went in among the inquirers, and became a Christian.

A gentleman in the same city was in distress of soul, and happened to linger in a pew after the noon-meeting. The choir had remained to practise, and began to sing the song of Mr. Bliss, —

> " Free from the law, oh, happy condition!
> Jesus hath bled, and there is remission," —

when the Spirit of God entered his soul, and led him to rejoice in the removal of his burden.

" Perhaps," says a correspondent, " not a week has passed during the last year, in which we have not had evidence that the Lord had directly used a line of one of these hymns in the salvation of a soul."

Mr. Sankey said to a young minister one time, " I am thinking of singing, ' I am so glad,' to-night." — " Oh, no!" replied the minister : " do rather sing, ' Jesus of Nazareth.' An old man told me to-day that he had been awakened by it the last night you were down. ' It just went through me,' said he, ' like an electric shock.' "

" Many of the most thrilling and marked cases of conversion in Scotland," says the Rev. Mr. Pentecost in a communication to me, " have been attributed to the solos sung by Mr. Sankey. I recall two cases. One of them is that of an infidel, a man past middle life, who for years had been zealously engaged in attacking Christianity and propagating infidelity. He came to the meetings to scoff, and to expose, as he said, the ' humbug.' One night Mr. Sankey sung the exquisitely tender hymn, ' Waiting and watching for me ; ' and when he came to the verse, —

' There are little ones glancing about in my path,
    In want of a friend and a guide ;
There are dear little eyes looking up into mine,
    Whose tears might be easily dried.
But Jesus may beckon the children away
    In the midst of their grief and their glee :
Will any of them at the beautiful gate
    Be waiting and watching for me ? ' —

The memory of an infant's face that once looked up into his, but which had long years ago been ' beckoned away,' came up so vividly, that his heart was melted. That was God's opportunity. The truth entered his soul, and he became one of Mr. Moody's best Christian workers."

I heard one day a man whose hair was white with more than fifty years rise up and tell the story of his conversion. He was a well-known citizen, a prominent politician, yet had led a somewhat dissipated life. He was present at one of the meetings, and heard Mr. Sankey sing "Jesus of Nazareth passeth by." When the last verse was sung, —

> " But if you still this call refuse,
>   And all his wondrous love abuse,
>   Soon will he sadly from you turn,
>   Your bitter prayer for pardon spurn ;
>   ' Too late, too late ! ' will be the cry,
>   ' Jesus of Nazareth *hath passed by.' "*

He said that he had always secretly intended to be a Christian some time before he died; but with the verse and with the words, —

> "Jesus of Nazareth hath passed by," —

the terrible thought came to him, " What if Jesus of Nazareth *has* passed *me* by, and it is too late ? " The thought moved his heart. He went home, fell on his knees, sought the mercy of God, and found peace in believing.

Speaking of the first meetings of the evangelists in Glasgow, Dr. Andrew A. Bonar said, " Mr. Sankey's singing began at once to be felt as indeed ' the gospel ' preached by singing ; impressive, melting, as well as most attractive. Is it another of the Lord's many new ways, in these last days, of graciously compelling men to come in,—like the Grecian mother's agony of desire, expressing itself in the song that lured her wayward child back from the precipice to safety ? "

A wicked young man in a Highland parish was brought to see and abandon the error of his ways by hearing the Rev. W. O. Cushing's simple hymn, —

" When he cometh, when he cometh to make up his jewels," —

for which the music was written by Mr. George F. Root.

While the revivalists were at Manchester, an infidel was converted by hearing Mr. Sankey sing Fanny J. Crosby's fine hymn, —

> " Safe in the arms of Jesus,
> Safe on his gentle breast,
> There by his love o'ershaded,
> Sweetly my soul shall rest."

"I believed," he subsequently said, " only in God and the Devil ; the latter I served well, and sat laughing at the Christians about me, whom I thought to be nothing better than fools." While listening to the song, as touchingly rendered by the singer, a sudden thrill went through his heart.

" There is," said he, " a Saviour. Who is he? where is he?" It is enough to add that the scoffer found him, and with brightening eye exclaimed, " I will now live and work for Jesus."

At a noonday meeting Mrs. Emily S. Oakey's hymn, —

" Sowing the seed by the daylight fair," —

was given out, when Mr. Sankey rising said, " Before we sing this song, I will tell you one reason why we should sing these hymns; and that is, God is blessing them to many a poor wanderer who comes to this building night after night. Last week a man who had once occupied a high position in life came into this hall, and sat down. While I was singing this hymn he took out his pass-book, and wrote out these words, —

' Sowing the seed of a lingering pain,
Sowing the seed of a maddened brain,
Sowing the seed of a tarnished name,
Sowing the seed of eternal shame ;
Oh, what shall the harvest be ? '

Last night that man in the inquiry-room went on his knees, and asked God to break the chain that had dragged him down from such a high position to the lowest of the low. He said he had resolved when he went out of that praise-meeting that he would cease to indulge in the intoxicating cup; but before he reached home he went into a saloon, and broke his resolution. We prayed for him last night. He is now praying that

God may break his chain. I want you to pray that this brand may be plucked from the burning, and that God may use these gospel hymns to turn the hearts of sinful men."

A great many instances of the power of the songs of Mr. Sankey to reach the hearts of men, and turn them to the Saviour, might be presented. At one of the meetings in the Tabernacle in Chicago, Mr. Baxter rose and said that two years ago his mother died, and so intemperate was he then that on his way to notify some neighbors that his mother was dying, he stopped and got drunk. Five weeks ago he came to Chicago from Naperville to put himself in a reformatory institution, and got drunk on the way. He wandered into the Tabernacle one Sunday for rest, being broken down physically and mentally by drink, and heard Mr. Sankey sing, " Waiting and Watching." This set him to thinking about his mother; and, if there was any word that would touch his hard heart, it was that word "mother." All Sunday night he paced the street, unable to think of any thing except of his mother in heaven watching and waiting for him. On Monday he went to Farwell Hall, and was there converted. He had had nothing but happiness since that. He had found that the blood of Jesus had power to cleanse from all sin.

Mr. Isaac R. Diller, a prominent politician, also in another of the meetings rose and made this statement, —

" I believe no one can be a politician without being

tempted to use intoxicating drinks. I found myself, by
reason of my associations, going on from bad to worse,
and almost breaking the heart of my wife. I have
attended these meetings a good deal. The first time I
heard Mr. Moody was at the Park-avenue Methodist
Church some years ago. When he asked those who
were Christians to stand up, I did not rise : now, thanks
to God, I know that I am a Christian. The first inti-
mation I had from God's Spirit was when I heard Mr.
Sankey sing, ' Jesus of Nazareth passeth by.' It was
at the Tabernacle ; the hymn came home to me most
powerfully, and I began to wonder if Jesus had passed
me by. But to-day I can say he has not passed me by.
I am here on the Lord's side."

Thus, through the potency of truth sweetened by
song, the kingdom of God is set onward.

"Men untouched," observes " The Moravian," " by
any thing that Mr. Moody says, break down under the
song-question, ' Oh ! what shall the harvest be ? ' They
feel that they cannot face the awful reaping of what
they have been sowing ; and they go into the inquiry-
rooms to learn how they may see better things. One
evening as we sat behind nine or ten thousand people,
the words of the hymn were distinctly borne to us over
the heads of the multitude, —

' No room, no room! Oh, woful cry, " No room!" ' '

And we felt, as we have seldom done, that the day is
indeed coming when the door will be shut.

"As the song, 'Scatter seeds of kindness,' is being sung, we watch the faces before us; and when the words, —

> 'Ah! those little ice-cold fingers,
>   How they point our memories back
> To the hasty words and actions
>   Strewn along our backward track!' —

sound out, we are startled to see how the arrow goes home. These are but instances of the general power of Mr. Sankey's singing. Scarcely a day passes without a letter or a conversation which records a conversion through the same song-word, made sharp by the Spirit in the heart of the king's enemies."

"I do not know," says Dr. Talmage, "how we shall stand the first day in heaven. Do you not think we shall break down in the song from over-delight? I once gave out in church the hymn, —

> 'There is a land of pure delight,
>   Where saints immortal reign.'

An aged man standing in front of the pulpit sang heartily the first verse, and then he sat down weeping. I said to him afterwards, 'Father Linton, what made you cry over that hymn? He said, 'I could not stand it, — the joys that are coming.'"

Sometimes these precious songs have proved a source of consolation to the sufferer on the dying bed. In the touching services held in the Free Assembly Hall, Edinburgh, on the last night of the year 1873, Miss Maggie

Lindsay, an interesting young lady of seventeen years, was converted; and on the twenty-seventh day of January, 1874, she was fatally injured by the wreck of a train near Linlithgow. She was reading, when the accident occurred, the hymn-book of Mr. Sankey; and there was a leaf turned down at her favorite hymn, "The Gates Ajar," by Mrs. Elizabeth Baxter, —

> " There is a gate that stands ajar,
>   And, through its portals gleaming,
> A radiance from the cross afar,
>   The Saviour's love revealing."

"At one time," says the minister who attended her in her dying hours, "when we thought she had fallen into a sleep eagerly wished and prayed for by us, we moved away out of her sight; but in a few minutes we heard her in low, gentle tones, singing to herself the words, —

> ' Nothing either great or small
>   Remains for me to do:
> Jesus died, and paid it all, —
>   All the debt I owe.'

"She also sung, before she fell asleep in Jesus, Mr. Sankey's hymn, ' For me, for me.' "

Another very touching account is given by an English writer, of the dying hours of a girl about ten years old, who was greatly pleased with the hymns of Mr. Sankey. "Oh, how I love," said she, " those dear hymns!" naming especially that by Fanny J. Crosby, —

> "Safe in the arms of Jesus,
>   Safe on his gentle breast."

"'When I am gone,' said she, 'mother, will you ask the girls of the school to sing the hymn, —

> 'Ring the bells of heaven! there is joy to-day
>   For a soul returning from the wild;
> See, the Father meets him out upon the way,
>   Welcoming his weary, wandering child.'

"The night before her death she said, 'Dear father and mother, I hope I shall meet you in heaven. I am so happy, mother! You cannot think how light and happy I feel.' Again, 'Perhaps Jesus may send me to fetch some of my brothers and sisters: I hope he will send me to fetch *you*, mother.'

"Half an hour before her departure she exclaimed, '*O mother, hark at the bells of heaven! they are ringing so beautifully!*'

"Then closing her eyes a while, presently she cried again, 'Hearken to the harps! they are most splendid. Oh, I wish you could hear them!'

"Then shortly after she spoke again, —

"'O mother! I see the Lord Jesus and the angels! Oh, if you could see them too! He is sending one to fetch me!'

"She had been counting the hours and minutes since she had heard the mill-bell at half-past one, P.M., longing so earnestly to depart, yet expressed a hope she might see her dear father (then absent at work) before she went.

" At last, just five minutes or so before her expiring breath, she said, —

"'Oh mother! lift me up from the pillow, — *high*, high up! Oh, I wish you could lift me *right up* into heaven!' Then, almost immediately after, — as doubtless conscious that the parting moment was at hand, — 'Put me down again, — down quick!' Then calmly, brightly, joyously, gazing upward, as at some vision of surprising beauty, she peacefully, sweetly, triumphantly breathed forth her precious spirit into the arms of the ministering angel whom Jesus had sent to fetch her; and so was forever with the Lord she loved."

But what effect, it may now be asked, is this new style of hymns and music to have on the service of song in our churches? It may perhaps be safely said in reply, that it will be the means of introducing into it more of Christ and his precious gospel. The Psalms of David are indeed most excellent and dear to every Christian heart; but it must not be forgotten that they were written under the old dispensation. I have in mind an aged Christian who will tolerate nothing but the psalms and hymns of Dr. Watts; overlooking the fact that David had the thoughts and spirit of the old dispensation, and perhaps not knowing that Dr. Watts has given us nothing more than a loose paraphrase of the Psalms. Some of them are minatory, and inapplicable to the times in which we live. In his version Dr. Watts infused into them as much of Christology as he dared to do; and for it was severely criticised by the rigid Hebraists of his day; but the churches wanted Christ, and so accepted, against much opposition, the new paraphrase. In every fresh revival more of Christ was wanted, and the Psalms by slow degrees gave way to hymns founded on some passage of the gospel. It is interesting to observe that from the day of Watts down to "The Songs for the Sanctuary," the church hymn-books, both in England and America, present in less and less proportion versions of the Psalms of David. The revival hymn-book of that earnest and successful Christian armor-bearer, the Rev. A. B. Earle, does not contain a single psalm; and I am not aware that more than one or two are ever sung in the Moody and Sankey meetings. The reason is that Christ and him crucified is the grand central theme of Christian song; and David had but dim foreshadowings of his work or power. As the Church advances on its conquering way, it will turn more and more to Jesus as its king and counsellor, and will consequently demand more and more of him in its song. One result, then, of the new departure in hymnology will be to introduce still more of the new, instead of the old dispensation, into the worshipping assemblies.

But has the gospel scope and variety enough to supply the church with song? Dr. Johnson intimates in his unfair life of Dr. Watts, that, from the paucity of the topics, no one can excel in sacred lyric poetry. He had not sounded the depths of that word "grace." In its relations to man, as a sinner, as a Christian, and as au heir of immortality, the gospel gives unnumbered topics to the sacred poet's pen. The redeeming love of Jesus is a sea without a bottom or a shore. Some of the grandest lyrics written since the days of Dr. Johnson have been inspired by the advent, work, and death of Jesus Christ. Cowper, Heber, Lyte, Montgomery, Kelly, Smith, Hastings, Bonar, Palmer, Crosby, Adams, and Bliss have proved by their precious hymns that the subjects clustering round the cross are inexhaustible, and adapted also to the higher demands of poetry. But nobler strains are yet to come, and the Church will wisely press them into its service of song.

This new style of singing may bring into the sabbath services of the church more of what are called *teaching*, in contradistinction to praising hymns. We have already, in our church manuals of song, many didactic hymns, or such as convey some knowledge of doctrine; but they are often so spiritless and prosaic, as to produce but little or no impression on a congregation. There are needed in our public service hymns that in the way of a story, or of illustration, teach some gospel truth, or enforce some religious duty. Let a congregation drawl out the words to some such heavy minor tune as "Burford," —

> " Naked as from the earth I came,
>   And crept to life at first," —

and then break into the stirring song that tells and teaches something heartily, —

> "Ho, my comrades! see the signal
> Waving in the sky," —

and the spirit of the people changes instantly from torpor into joy. Such songs as "Hold the Fort" might not be always appropriate; but could they not, indeed will they not, occasionally come in between the Psalm of David and the dull didactic hymn, to arouse, if nothing more, the audience from its somnolence? Why should the sabbath school and the revival meetings have all the best of the music?

Such, then, again, is the wonderful effect of this new style of sacred song in the conversion of sinners, that it will doubtless be the means of bringing more of singing, and that congregationally, into our public worship. As a rule we sing too little in our sabbath services. Worship is in form threefold or triplicate. It consists in preaching, praying, singing; but the people join actively only in the last-named service. Since, then, it may be so effective, since it may combine prayer and to some extent preaching also, should not more of time be devoted to its practice? Will not the marvellous results of the singing of the modern revivalists, as well as of the "Service of Praise" introduced by Dr. Tourjée, have a tendency to lead the people to demand more of song in stated worship in the sanctuary?

So again (and here will be the greatest benefit), the singing of Mr. Sankey and other revivalists may tend to break up in some degree the cold formality, which is indeed but solemn mockery, that prevails to a lamentable extent in this part of worship in the house of God. The end of church music is to lead sinners to Jesus, to quicken the spirit of devotion, and to glorify God. But in too many instances the singers perform their parts to glorify themselves. Sitting far apart from the minister, and having but little sympathy with him or his preaching, they but too often spend the time he occupies, in looking over books, or in listless inattention: they sing expressly for a musical effect, and nothing more, except for the pay which they receive. Now, this is simply sacrilege; but the people encourage it, the churches tolerate it, and hence one source of their spiritual weakness. The objective end of the singing of the revivalists, and of their hymns also, is the conversion of souls and the glory of God. Hence the rich fruits that follow. The people see this, know this, feel this; and hence we may be sure that a kind of revolution in our church psalmody is at hand, and that music will be made ere long to fulfil its grand mission for the advancement of the Redeemer's kingdom.

But can the methods of the revivalists in song be practised and sustained in the churches? Perhaps not. A Sankey is not found in every congregation; solo and chorus cannot always be performed; and it is strictly Biblical that psalms and hymns, as well as what are called revival melodies, should be sung,—just as St. Paul says, "teaching and admonishing one another in psalms and hymns and spiritual songs." But the people can sing congregationally; the children can blend their sweet voices with them if the sabbath-school pieces are sometimes brought forward; the choir can sing to lead and teach and praise; and the whole, as the apostle beautifully enjoins, can sing with "grace" in the heart "to the Lord." This is the perfection of praise.

So whether we sing the mighty psalm, —

> " Before Jehovah's awful throne,
>   Ye nations, bow with sacred joy :
> Know that the Lord is God alone;
>   He can create, and he destroy," —

or the tender hymn, —

> " There is a fountain filled with blood
>   Drawn from Immanuel's veins ;
> And sinners, plunged beneath that flood,
>   Lose all their guilty stains," —

or the spiritual song, —

> " Ring the bells of heaven : there is joy to-day,
>   For a soul returning from the wild ;
> See, the Father meets him out upon the way,
>   Welcoming his weary, wandering child," —

we are still exalting our Redeemer's name, extending his dominion over this sinful world, and training our voices for that fair song-home, —

> " Where the saints of all ages in harmony meet,
>   Their Saviour and brethren transported to greet ;
> While the anthems of rapture unceasingly roll,
>   And the smile of the Lord is the life of the soul."

ILLUSTRATIONS OF MR. MOODY.

ILLUSTRATIONS OF MR. MOODY.

CHOICE SAYINGS, INCIDENTS, STORIES, AND ILLUSTRATIONS OF MR. MOODY.

Christ Conquering. — The Net. — Realities. — God here. — Feeling.— Jesus. — Mysteries. — Knowledge. — Purgatory. — The Blood. — Feeling and Faith. — Morality. — Consequential People. — The Devil in Church. — Down Grade. — Thankfulness. — Judas. — Nearness to God. — Book of Wonders. — Strength. — Juniper-Tree. — Reason for Faith. — Lost. — Faith. — Three Steps. — Garibaldi. — Laziness. — Wesley. — Bravery. — Rushlight. — Dead Sea. — Adversity. — Workers. — Missing Stone. — A Smile. — Conversion. — Roll-Call. — Light. — Prairie on Fire. — Love. — Not Me. — Duty. — A Lie. — Your Life. — Law. — The Earth. — The Law. — Man a Failure. — Chain and All. — Scarlet Thread. — A Resolve. — Infidel. — A Substitute. — The Crown. — The Surgeon. — " Blazing." — The Soul. — Burden-Bearer. — God and the World. — The Shadow. — God's Love. — Now. — Life-Boat. — Heart and Head. — The Rescue. — A Lady Converted. — Belief. — Norwegian Boy. — The Worm. — A Want. — The Bible. — Not Enough of Them. — One in Christ. — Money. — Higher Up. — Sympathy. — The Check. — Silence in Heaven. — Eleventh Hour. — Prayer. — Enthusiasm. — A Line. — A Scotch Woman. — Trust. — Pride. — The Bible. — Run upon the Banks.

"The heart of the wise teacheth his mouth, and addeth learning to his life." — SOLOMON.

"Sometimes he tells them stories and sayings of others, according as his text invites him ; for them also men heed and remember better than exhortations." — GEORGE HERBERT.

CHRIST CONQUERING. — It is said of Julian the Apostate in Rome, that, when he was trying to stamp out Christianity, he was pierced in the side by an arrow. He pulled the arrow out, and, taking a handful of blood as it flowed from the wound, threw it into the air shouting, " Thou Galilean, thou hast conquered ! "

CAUGHT IN THE GOSPEL NET. — A man told me the other day that he came to see the chairs. He said he heard there were ten thousand chairs all in one hall, and he thought they must look so strange. He had a curiosity to see them. Thank God, that man got caught in the gospel net that very night! and I hope some others that came just out of curiosity this evening will get caught with the old gospel net.

REALITIES. — I believe heaven is a city quite as real as London is. What we want is, to make heaven real, and hell real, and God real, and Christ real, and live as if we believed these things to be real.

GOD IS HERE. — We have abundant manifestation that his influence from heaven is felt among us. He is not in person among us, only in spirit. The sun is ninety-five million miles from the earth, yet we feel its rays. God has a dwelling-place, God has a home, God has a throne.

FEELING NOTHING TO DO WITH BELIEVING. — A great many are saying, " Do you feel this and that ? Do you feel, do you feel, do you feel ? " God does not

want you to feel: he tells you to believe. He says,
"When I see the blood I will pass over;" and, if you
are sheltered behind the blood, you are perfectly safe
and secure. Suppose I say to a man, "Do you feel
that you own this piece of land?" He looks at me a
moment, and thinks I must be crazy. He says, "Feel?
Why, feeling has nothing to do with it. I look at the
title: that is all I want." Do you see? all you have to
do with is the title.

A SIGHT OF JESUS. — One Christian asked another
what he expected to do when he got to heaven; and he
said he expected to take one good long look of about
five hundred years at Christ, and then he would want
to see Paul, and Peter, and John, and the rest of the
disciples. Well, it seems to me, one glimpse of Christ
will pay us for all that we are called upon to endure
here, — to see the King in his beauty, to be in the
presence of the King.

BIBLE MYSTERIES. — Supposing I should send my
little boy to school to-morrow morning, and when he
came home I should say, "Can you read, write, and
spell? Do you understand all about arithmetic, geome-
try, algebra?" The little fellow would look at me,
and say, "Why, what do you talk in that way for? I
have been trying all day to learn the A B C." Supposing I replied, "If you have not finished your education,
you need not go to school any more." Well, there is

about as much sense in that as in the way that infidels talk about the Bible. They take it up, read a chapter, and say, " Oh! it's so dark and mysterious, we cannot understand it."

KNOWLEDGE OF CHRIST WILL NOT SAVE. — A great many persons flatter themselves they are going to be saved because they know a great deal about Jesus Christ. But your knowledge of him will not save you. Noah's carpenters probably knew as much about the ark as Noah did, and perhaps more. They knew that the ark was strong, they knew it was built to stand the deluge, they knew it was made to float upon the waters : they had helped to build it. But they were just as helpless when the flood came as men who lived thousands of miles away.

PURGATORY. — I am told that in Rome, if you go up a few steps on your hands and knees, that is nine years out of purgatory. If you take one step now, you are out of purgatory for time and eternity.

THE BLOOD OF JESUS. — There is no condemnation to him that is in Christ Jesus. You may just pile up your sins till they rise up like a dark mountain, and then multiply them by ten thousand for those you cannot remember; and, after you have tried to enumerate all the sins you have ever committed, just let me bring one verse in, and then that mountain will melt away, — " The blood of Jesus Christ his Son cleanseth us from all sin."

FEELING. — I like to have people's faith grounded, not on feeling, but on some strong text of Scripture. If you feel, feel, all the time, you have no firm ground to stand on. It is true, it is better to know God says a thing than to feel it. Do not be waiting to feel it. If a man invited you to his house to a feast, you would not talk about feeling, would you? The question for you to consider is, Do you want to be at this feast to which God invites you? If you do, come along, and your feelings will take care of themselves.

MORALITY NOT ENOUGH. — Nicodemus stood very high: he was one of the church dignitaries; he stood as high as any man in Jerusalem except the high priest himself. He belonged to the seventy rulers of the Jews; he was a doctor of divinity, and taught the law. There is not one word of Scripture against him: he was a man that stood out before the whole nation as of pure and spotless character. What does Christ say to him? " Except a man be born again, he cannot see the kingdom of God."

CONSEQUENTIAL PEOPLE. — I pity a man or woman that has got an idea that the world can't get along without him or her.

THE DEVIL IN CHURCH. — Many say, "Oh, yes! I am a Christian: I go to church every sabbath." There is no one who goes to church as regularly as Satan.

He is always there before the minister, and the last one out of the church. There is not a church or a chapel, but he is a regular attendant of it. The idea that he is only in slums and lanes, and public houses, is a false one.

THE DOWN GRADE. — I was on the Pacific coast some time ago, and there they were telling me about a stage-driver who had died a little while ago. You that have been there know that those men who drive those coaches make a great deal of the brake, for they have to keep their feet upon it all the time going down the mountains; and, as this poor fellow was breathing his last in his bed, he cried out, "I am on the down grade, and can't reach the brake!" As they told me of it, I thought how many more were on the down grade, and could not reach the brake, and were dying without God and without hope.

THANKFULNESS. — One reason why we don't have more answers to our prayers is because we are not thankful enough. The divine injunction is, "Be careful for nothing; but in every thing by prayer and supplication WITH THANKSGIVING let your requests be made known unto God." Some one has well said there are three things in this verse, — careful for nothing, prayerful for every thing, thankful for any thing.

THE KISS OF JUDAS. — Judas got near enough to Christ to kiss him, and yet went down to damnation.

NEARNESS TO GOD. — If you want to introduce sinners to God, you must be near to God and to the sinner too; and, if a man is near God, he will have a love for the sinner, and his heart will be near that man. But until we are brought near to God ourselves, we cannot introduce men to God.

THE BOOK OF WONDERS. — A man once wanted to sell me a " Book of Wonders." I took it, and looked it over, and could not find any thing in it about Calvary. What a mistake ! — a book of wonders, and the greatest wonder of all left out !

STRENGTH IN GOD. — When God wants to move a mountain, he does not take the bar of iron, but he takes the little worm.

The fact is, we have got too much strength. We are not weak enough. It is not our strength that we want. One drop of God's strength is worth more than all the world.

THE JUNIPER-TREE. — Many of the Bible characters fell just in the things in which they were thought to be strongest. Moses failed in his humility, Abraham in his faith, Elijah in his courage — for one woman scared him away to that juniper-tree ; and Peter, whose strong point was boldness, was so frightened by a maid as to deny his Lord.

A REASON FOR OUR FAITH. — I like a man to be able to give a reason for the faith that is in him. Once I asked a man what he believed, and he said he believed what his church believed. I asked him what his church believed, and he said he supposed his church believed what he did. And that was all I could get out of him.

"I AM LOST!" — A man got right up behind me, and he trembled as he said, "I am lost: I want you to pray for my soul." And I said, "What if Noah had heard that? He worked a hundred and twenty years, and never had a man come to him and say that; and yet he didn't get discouraged." And I made up my mind then, that, God helping me, I never would get discouraged: I would do the best I could do, and leave the results with God; and it has been a wonderful help to me.

FAITH. — Faith says "Amen" to every thing that God says. Faith takes God without any ifs. If God says it, faith says, "I believe it;" faith says "Amen" to it.

THREE FATAL STEPS. — There are three steps to the lost world. The first is neglect. All a man has to do is to neglect salvation, and that will take him to the lost world. I am on a swift river, and lying in the bottom of my little boat; all I have to do is to fold my arms, and the current will carry me out to sea. All a man has to do in the current of life is to fold his arms, and he will drift on and be lost. The second step is refusal. The last step is to despise the love of Christ.

GARIBALDI. — Although I don't admire his ideas, I do admire the enthusiasm of that man Garibaldi.

It is reported, that, when he marched towards Rome in 1867, they took him up and threw him into prison; and he sat right down, and wrote to his comrades, "If fifty Garibaldis are thrown into prison, let Rome be free." That is the spirit. Who is Garibaldi? That is nothing. "If fifty Garibaldis are thrown into prison, let Rome be free." That is what we want in the cause of Christ.

LEANNESS AND LAZINESS. — A good many people are complaining all the time about themselves, and crying out, "My leanness, my leanness!" when they ought rather to say, "My laziness, my laziness!"

WHAT JOHN WESLEY SAID. — I believe in what John Wesley used to say, "All at it, and always at it;" and that is what the Church wants to say.

BRAVERY. — There is a story told in history in the ninth century, I believe, of a young man that came up with a little handful of men to attack a king who had a great army of three thousand men. The young man had only five hundred; and the king sent a messenger to the young man, saying that he need not fear to surrender, for he would treat him mercifully. The young man called up one of his soldiers, and said, " Take this dagger, and drive it into your heart; " and the soldier took the dagger, and drove it into his heart. And, calling up another, he said to him, " Leap into yonder chasm; " and the man leaped into the chasm. The young man then said to the messenger, " Go back and tell your king I have got five hundred men like these. We will die, but we will never surrender; and tell your king another thing, — that I will have him chained with my dog inside of half an hour." And, when the king heard that, he did not dare to meet them, and his army fled before them like chaff before the wind; and within twenty-four hours he had that king chained with his dog. That is the kind of zeal we want.

A FARTHING RUSHLIGHT. — Some one said, " I cannot be any thing more than a farthing rushlight."

Well, if you can't be more, be that: that is well enough. Be all you can.

THE DEAD SEA. — What makes the Dead Sea dead? Because it is all the time receiving, never giving out any thing.

Why is it that many Christians are cold? Because they are all the time receiving, never giving out any thing.

ADVERSITY. — John Bunyan thanked God more for Bedford Jail than for any thing that ever happened to him.

WORKERS WANTED. — It is not enough to come to these meetings: we want ten thousand workers in New York City.

We want ten thousand men and women that are willing to say, " Lord, here am I ; use me."

Ten thousand such people would revolutionize this city in a little while.

THE MISSING STONE. — I remember hearing of a man's dream, in which he imagined that when he died he was taken by the angels to a beautiful temple. After admiring it for a time, he discovered that one stone was missing, — all finished but just one little stone ; that was left out. He said to the angel, " What is that stone left out for ? " The angel replied, " That was left out for you ; but you wanted to do great things, and so there was no room left for you." He was startled, and awoke, and resolved that he would become a worker for God ; and that man always worked faithfully after that.

THE POWER OF A SMILE. — Won to Christ by a smile. We must get the wrinkles out of our brows, and we must have smiling faces.

The world is after the best thing ; and we must show

them that we have got something better than they have
got.

How some are Converted. — A good many men
are converted to a church. They say, "I like that
church; it is a beautiful church, and there is beautiful
singing. I like that quartet choir, and the grand
organ; and there is a good minister." And so they are
converted to the church, and they are converted to the
singing, and converted to the organ, and converted to
the minister, or they are converted to the. people who
go there. But that is not being born of God, or being
converted to God.

The Roll-call of Heaven. — A soldier lay on his
dying couch, during our last war, and they heard him
say, "Here!" They asked him what he wanted, and
he put up his hand and said, "Hush! they are calling
the roll of heaven, and I am answering to my name."
And presently he whispered, "Here!" and he was
gone.

Light shining. — A friend of mine was walking
along the streets one dark night, when he saw a man
coming along with a lantern. As he came up close to
him, he noticed by the bright light that the man had
no eyes. He went past him; but the thought struck
him, "Surely that man is blind!" He turned round,
and said, "My friend, are you not blind?" — "Yes,"

was the answer. "Then what have you got the lantern for?"—"I carry the lantern," said the blind man, "that people may not stumble over me."

Let us hold up our light, burning with the clear radiance of heaven, that men may not stumble over us.

THE PRAIRIE FIRE.—Away out on the frontier of our country, out on the prairies, where men sometimes go to hunt or for other purposes, the grass in the dry season sometimes catches fire; and you will see the flames uprise twenty or thirty feet high, and you will see those flames rolling over the western desert faster than any fleet horse can run. Now, what do the men do? They know it is sure death unless they can make some escape. They would try to run away, perhaps, if they had fleet horses. But they can't. That fire goes faster than the fleetest horse can run. What do they do? Why, they just take a match, and they light the grass from it, and away it burns; and then they get into that burnt district. The fire comes on, and there they stand perfectly secure—nothing to fear. Why? Because the fire has burned all there is to burn.

Take your stand there on Mount Calvary.

CHRISTIAN LOVE.—The morning I was converted, I went out doors, and I fell in love with the bright sun shining over the earth. I never loved the sun before. And, when I heard the birds singing their sweet songs,

I fell in love with the birds. Like the Scotch lassie who stood on the hills of her native land, breathing the sweet air, and when asked why she did it, said, "I love the Scotch air."

If the church was filled with love, it could do so much more.

ANY ONE BUT ME. — There are few now that say, "Here am I, Lord; send me." The cry now is, "Send some one else. Send the minister, send the church officers, the church-wardens, the elders, but not me. I have not got the ability, the gifts, or the talents." Ah! honestly say you have not got the heart; for, if the heart is loyal, God can use you. It is really all a matter of heart.

It does not take God a great while to qualify a man for his work, if he only has the heart for it.

LOVE ABOVE DUTY. — I am tired of the word "duty," tired of hearing, duty, duty, duty! Men go to church because it is their duty. They go to prayer-meeting because it is their duty. You can never reach a man's heart if you talk to him because it is your duty. Suppose I told my wife I loved her because it was my duty — what would she say? Once every year I go up to Connecticut to visit my aged mother. Suppose when I go next time, I should tell her that I knew she was old, and that she was living on borrowed time; that I knew she had always done a great deal for me, and that I came to see her every year because it was my duty. Don't you think she would say, " Well, then, my son, you needn't take the trouble to come again "? Let us strike for a higher plane.

A Great Lie. — One of the greatest lies that has come out of the pit of hell is that Christ is a hard master. It is a lie, and has been so from the foundation of the world.

Oh, young men! I beg of you, do not believe the Devil when he says that God is a hard master. It is false, my friends; and to-night let me brand that excuse as one of the Devil's own lies, that he has been retailing up and down the earth for these six thousand years.

Your Biography. — If you want to read your own biography, you need not write it yourself. Turn to the third chapter of Romans, and it is all there written by a man who knows a good deal more about us than we do about ourselves. Christ was the only one that ever trod this earth, that saw every thing in the heart of man.

The Law our Looking - Glass. — The law is a looking-glass, just to show a man how foul he is in the sight of God.

How Earth looks to One near Heaven. — When men going up in a balloon have ascended a little height, things down here begin to look very small indeed. What had seemed very grand and imposing now seem as mere nothings; and, the higher they rise, the smaller every thing on earth appears: it gets fainter and fainter as they rise, till the railway-train, dashing along at fifty miles an hour, seems like a thread, and scarcely appears to be moving at all; and the grand piles of buildings seem now like mere dots. So it is when we get near heaven : earth's treasures, earth's cares, look very small.

Failing to fulfil the Law. — My father once told me that in England the archers used to shoot at a ring, and, if any archer failed to shoot all his arrows through the ring, he was called a sinner. Now, suppose I should take ten arrows, and try to send them through a ring at the other side of the building, and should only get one through: I should be called a sinner. And suppose Brother Taylor should take as many arrows, and send nine through, one after the other, and just miss the ring with the last one; why, he would be a sinner too, just like me.

Man a Failure. — One man says, " Give me more money ; " another, " Give me a seat in Congress; " another, " Give me a bottle of rum." Ah ! it is easy to condemn the Israelites, it is easy to smile; but beware that you are not guilty of the same sin. Man was a failure under the judges, a failure under the prophets, and now for two thousand years under grace he has been a most stupendous failure. Walk the streets, and see how quickly he goes to ruin; how many are hastening down to the dark caves of sin! Man in his best day, under the most favorable circumstances, is notning but a failure.

CHAIN AND ALL. — In the North there was a minister talking to a man in the inquiry-room. He said, "My heart is so hard, it seems as if it was chained; and I cannot come." — "Ah!" said the minister, "come to Christ, chain and all." And he just came to Christ; and Christ snapped the fetters, and set him free, right there.

THE SCARLET THREAD. — The grace of God brings grace down to men. Substitution! If you take that out of the Bible, you can take the Bible along with you if you wish to. The same story runs all through the book. The scarlet thread is unbroken from Genesis to Revelation. The hymns that have the scarlet line running through them will never be lost.

A GOOD RESOLVE. — I made it a rule that I wouldn't let a day pass without speaking to some one about their soul's salvation; and, if they didn't hear the gospel from the lips of others, there will be three hundred and sixty-five in a year that shall hear the gospel from my lips. There are five thousand Christians here to-night: can't they say, " We won't let a day pass without speaking to some one about the cause of Christ " ?

The Infidel. — When we were in Edinburgh, a man came to me, and said, " Over yonder is one of our most prominent infidels in Edinburgh. I wish you would go over and see him."

I took my seat beside him, and I asked him if he was a Christian. He laughed at me, and said he didn't believe in the Bible. " Well," said I, after talking some time, " will you let me pray with you? will you let me pray for you? " — " Yes," said he : "just pray, and see if God will answer your prayer. Now let the question be decided." — " Will you kneel? " — " No, I won't kneel: who am I going to kneel before? " He said it with considerable emphasis. I got down and prayed beside the infidel. He sat very straight, so that the people should understand that he was not in sympathy at all with my prayer. After I got through, I said, " Well, my friend, I believe that God will answer my prayers ; and I want you to let me know when you are saved," — " Yes, I will let you know when I am saved," — all with considerable sarcasm. At last up at Wick, at a meeting in the open air one night, on the outskirts of the crowd I saw the Edinburgh infidel. He said, " Didn't I tell you God wouldn't answer your prayer? " I said, " The Lord will answer my prayer yet." I had a few minutes' conversation with him, and left him; and just a year ago this month, when we were preaching in Liverpool, I got a letter from one of the leading pastors of Edinburgh, stating that the Edinbugh infidel had found his way to Christ, and found the Lord. He wrote an interesting letter, saying how God had saved him.

THE SUBSTITUTE. — Napoleon Bonaparte once sent out a draft. A man was drafted who didn't want to go. A friend volunteered to go in his place. He went into the army, and was killed. A second draft was made, and by some accident the same man was drafted again; but he said to the officer, " You can't take me: I'm dead; I died on such a battle-field." — " Why, man, you are crazy," said the officer. " You are not dead: here you are alive and well before me." — " No, sir," said the man: " I am dead. The law has no claim on me: look at the roll." They looked, and found another name written against his. They insisted; he carried his case before the emperor, who said that he was right: his friend had died for him. Christ died for me.

How TO GET INTO THE KINGDOM OF GOD. — The only way to get into the Kingdom of God is to be born into it.

THE CROWN. — When you are in London you may go to the Tower and see the crown of England, which is worth millions, and is guarded there by soldiers; but bear in mind that your eye will never rest upon the crown of life except you are born again.

THE SURGEON AND HIS PATIENT. — When I was in Belfast, I knew a doctor who had a friend, a leading surgeon there; and he told me that the surgeon's custom was, before performing an operation, to say to the patient, "Take a good look at the wound, and then fix your eyes on me, and don't take them off till I get through." I thought at the time that was a good illustration. Sinner, take a good look at the wound to-night, and then fix your eye on Christ, and don't take it off. It is better to look at the remedy than at the wound.

BLAZING. — When a man goes into the wilderness to hunt, he takes a hatchet with him, and cuts the bark off the trees, — they call it "blazing," — and thus he can find his way out. So God has blazed the way along: he has gone up on high, and he says, "Follow me." Just come now, and follow the Son of God, for there is life there.

LOSS OF THE SOUL. — We hear of a man who has lost his health; and we sympathize with him, and we say it is very sad. Our hearts are drawn out in sympathy. Here is another man who has lost his wealth, and we say, "That is very sad." Here is another man who has lost his reputation, his standing among men. "That is sadder still," you say. We know what it is to lose health and wealth and reputation; but what is the loss of all these things, compared with the loss of the soul?

CHRIST OUR BURDEN-BEARER. — A minister was moving his library up stairs. His little boy wanted to help him: so he gave him the biggest book he could find, and the little fellow tugged at it till he got it about half way up, and then he sat down and cried. His father found him, and just took him in his arms, big book and all, and carried him up stairs. So Christ will carry you and all your burdens.

GOD AND THE WORLD WITH HIM. — Some men have an idea when they get converted, that they have got to keep Christ and themselves too. It is all wrong. I remember one time my little girl was teasing her mother to get her a muff, and so one day her mother brought a muff home; and, although it was storming, she very naturally wanted to go out in order to try her new muff. So she tried to get me to go out with her, I went out with her, and I said, "Emma, better let me take your hand." She wanted to keep her hands in her muff, and so she refused to take my hand. Well, by and by she came to an icy place: her little feet slipped, and down she went. When I helped her up, she said, "Papa, you may give me your little finger." — "No my daughter: just take my hand." — "No, no, papa: give me your little finger." Well, I gave my finger to her, and for a little way she got along nicely, but pretty soon we came to another icy place, and again she fell. This time she hurt herself a little, and she said, "Papa, give me your hand;" and I gave her my hand, and closed my fingers about her wrist, and held her up, so that she could not fall. Just so God is our keeper.

FOLLOWING THE SHADOW. — When I was a little boy I used to try to catch my shadow, but I always failed. Many a time I might try to see if I could jump over my head; many a time I tried to see if I could not outrun it; but it always kept ahead of me. But I turned around, and faced the sun, and, lo and behold! my shadow was coming after me. And so we want to look towards Christ, and peace and joy and happiness will come in turn.

GOD'S LOVE DISPLAYED. — The best title you can have to salvation is to find out that you are lost. It was Adam's fall that brought out God's love. God never told Adam, when he put him in Eden, that he loved him. It was after he was lost. It was that very thing that brought out the love of God.

NOW. — I heard some one in the inquiry-room telling a young person to go home and seek Christ in his closet. I would not dare to tell any one to do that. You might be dead before you got home. If I read my

Bible correctly, the man who preaches the gospel is not the man who tells me to seek Christ to-morrow, or an hour hence, but NOW. He is near to every one of us this minute to save. If the world would just come to God for salvation, and be in earnest about it, they would find the Son of God right at the door of their heart.

THE LIFE-BOAT. — I read a number of years ago of a vessel that was wrecked. The life-boats were not enough to take all the passengers. A man who was swimming in the water swam up to one of the life-boats that were full, and seized it with his hand. They tried to prevent him, but the man was terribly in earnest about saving his life; and one of the men in the boat just drew a sword, and cut off his hand. But the man didn't give up: he reached out the other hand. He was terribly in earnest. He wanted to save his life. But the man in the boat took the sword, and cut off his other hand. But the man did not give up. He swam up to the boat, and seized it with his teeth. Some of them said, "Let us not cut his head off," and they drew him in. That man was terribly in earnest; and, my friends, if you want to get into the kingdom of God, you will seek your souls' salvation to-night.

THE HEART RULES THE HEAD. — If your heart is all right, your head will be also, for out of the heart proceeds all evil. Let the reservoir of sin be broken up and emptied, and all the rest of you will come around right.

To the Rescue. — May God wake up a slumbering church! What we want men to do is not to shout " Amen," and clasp their hands The deepest and quietest waters very often run swiftest. We want men to go right to work : there will be a chance for you to shout by and by. Go and speak to your neighbor, and tell him of Christ and heaven. You need not go a few yards down these streets, before you find some one who is passing down to the darkness of eternal death. Let us haste to the rescue !

The Conversion of a Lady. — When Mr. Sankey and I were in the North of England, I was preaching one evening, and before me sat a lady who was a sceptic. When I had finished, I asked all who were anxious, to remain. Nearly all remained, herself among the number. I asked her if she was a Christian ; and she said she was not, nor did she care to be. I prayed for her there. On inquiry I learned that she was a lady of good social position, but very worldly. She continued to attend the meetings ; and, in a week after, I saw her in tears. After the sermon I went to her, and asked if she was of the same mind as before. She replied that Christ had come to her, and she was happy. Last autumn I had a note from her husband, saying that she was dead, that her love for her Master had sustained her.

Belief precedes Good Works. — You cannot do any thing to please God until you believe. Suppose I should say to my little girl, " Emma, go and get me a glass of water," and she were to say, " I don't want to do it, papa." She goes into another room, and some one gives her a cluster of grapes, which she decides to give to her papa. Do you think these grapes would be acceptable if she did not want to get the water? I should say, " I do not want the grapes until you have brought the water."

She goes out of the room again, and some one gives her an orange. If she brought the orange to me, do you think I should want it? No, and that child cannot do any thing to please me until I get the water. You cannot please God until you believe on his Son.

The Norwegian Boy. — I was in a Boston prayer-meeting a number of years ago — but I ought to say that I have lived for a number of years out West, a number of years in Chicago; and you know that that part of the country is made up principally of young men. At any rate, the prayer-meetings were for the most part made up of young men, — I hardly saw a gray-headed man in them at all. So while I was in Boston it was quite a treat to see old, gray-headed men in the assemblies. Well, in that meeting, a little tow-headed Norwegian boy stood up. He could hardly speak a word of English plain, but he got up, and came to the front. He trembled all over, and the tears were all trickling down his cheeks; but he spoke out as well as he could, and said, "If I tell the world about Jesus, then will he tell the Father about me." He then took his seat. That was all he said; but I tell you, in those few words he said more than all of them, old and young, together. Those few words went straight down into the heart of every one present.

"If I tell the world,"—yes, that's what it means to confess Christ.

THE WORM THAT DIETH NOT. — I believe that worm that dieth not is our memory. I believe that what will make that lost world so terrible to us is memory. We say now that we forget, and we think we do; but the time is coming when we will remember, and we cannot forget.

There are many things we will want to forget, especially our sins that have been blotted out by God. If God has forgotten them, you would think we ought to forget them. Every sin that has been so taken away and covered up except the blood of his own Son will come back to us by and by.

WHAT IS WANTED. — If you can only convince the greatest blasphemer and infidel in New York that you really love him, you can reach him.

What we want, therefore, is this love; and that is the work of the Holy Ghost to impart; and let us pray to-day that the love of God may be shed abroad in all our hearts.

THE TRUE IDEA OF PREACHING. — The true idea of preaching is to cry down yourself and the Devil, and to preach up no one but God.

THE BIBLE ITS OWN INTERPRETER. — If you just take the Bible itself alone, without any other book to help you to interpret it, one passage will explain another. Instead of running after the interpretations of different men, let God interpret it to your soul.

NOT BIBLES ENOUGH. — People do not have Bibles enough. Once in my own Sunday school, I asked all the children who had on borrowed boots to rise; no one rose. Then I asked all those who had on borrowed coats to rise; no one rose. Then I asked all those who had borrowed Testaments in their hands to rise, and they all went up; and I said, "I want you all to bring your Bibles with you." And about two months after that, it would have done your soul good to see every child come with a Bible.

ALL ONE IN CHRIST. — The blood of Christ makes us one. During the days of slavery in America, when there was much political strife and strong prejudice against the black men, especially by Irishmen, I heard a preacher say, when he came to the cross for salvation, he found a poor negro on the right hand, and an Irishman on the left hand, and the blood came trickling down upon them, and made them one.

There may be strife in the world, but every one Christ has redeemed, he has made one. We are blood relations.

MONEY FOR CHRIST. — When men go up in balloons they take with them bags of sand for ballast; and when they want to rise higher they throw out some of the sand. Now, there are some Christians who before they rise higher will have to throw out some ballast. It may be money or any other worldly consideration; but, if they wish to rise, they must get rid of it. If you have got overloaded, just throw out a little money, and you will mount up as on eagle's wings. Any minister will tell you what to do with it. I never saw any department of the Lord's work that did not want some money.

HIGHER UP. — Not long ago there lived an old bed-ridden saint, and a Christian lady who visited her found her always very cheerful. This visitor had a lady friend of wealth, who constantly looked on the dark side of things, and was always cast down, although she was a professed Christian. She thought it would do this lady good to see the bedridden saint, so she took her down to the house. She lived up in the garret, five stories up; and, when they had got to the first story, the lady drew up her dress, and said, " How dark and filthy it is! " — " It is better higher up," said her friend. They got to the next story, and it was no better; the lady complained again, but her friend replied, " It s better higher up." At the third floor it seemed still worse, and the lady kept complaining, but her friend kept saying, "It is better higher up." At last they got to the fifth story; and, when they went into the sick-room, there was a nice carpet on the floor, there were flowering plants in the window, and little birds singing. And there they found the bedridden saint, — one of those saints whom God is polishing for his own tem-ple, — just beaming with joy. The lady said to her, "It must be very hard for you to lie there." She smiled, and said, "*It is better higher up.*" Yes; and if things go against us, my friends, let us remember that "it is better higher up."

SYMPATHY FOR SUFFERING. — I remember when our war was going on, I took up the morning paper, and read of a terrible battle, — ten thousand men killed; and I laid the paper down, and forgot it. At last I went into the battle-field, and helped to bear away the sick and wounded. After I had been over one or two battle-fields, I began to realize what it meant. I could hear the dying groans of the men, and their cry for water; and, when I heard of a battle, the whole thing was stamped upon my mind. I can tell you how a little child suffered, and it will bring tears to your eyes; but I tell you how the Son of God suffered, and some of you will go out laughing.

THE CHECK. — When Moses said, " If they ask

me who sent me, what shall I tell them?" God said, "Say, I AM sent me." And, as some one has said, that was a blank check, and God told him to fill it out; and when they were in the desert, and wanted water, he filled out the check, and drew water from the rock; when he wanted bread, he filled out the check, and God gave him bread from heaven.

SILENCE IN HEAVEN. — They never knew the Son of God when he was here. He would hush every harp in heaven to hear a sinner pray. No music would delight him so much.

THE ELEVENTH HOUR. — Somebody has said, "The thief on the cross was saved at the eleventh hour." I don't know about that. Perhaps it was the first hour. It might have been the first hour with him, I think. Perhaps he never knew Christ until he was led out to die beside him. This may have been the very first time he had ever learned the way of faith in the Son of God.

PRAYER. — If things do not always please you, don't complain: JUST PRAY.

A STRAIGHT LINE. — When I was a boy I used to try to describe a straight path through the snow in the fields by looking down at my feet. The way to make a straight path would be to look at an object beyond

So in this passage we are directed to have our eyes on the mark at the right hand of the Master.

THE SCOTCH WOMAN. — Some one said to a Scotch woman, " You are a woman of great faith."

" No," she says : " I am a woman of little faith ; but I have got a great God."

TRUSTING. — My little Willie I once told to jump off a high table, and I would catch him. But he looked down, and said, " Papa, I's afraid." I again told him I'd catch him ; and he looked down, and said, " Papa, I's afraid." You smile ; but that's just the way with the unbeliever. He looks down, and dare not trust the Lord. You say that would be blind faith, but I say it wouldn't. I told Willie to look at me, and then jump ; and he did it, and was delighted. He wanted to jump again ; and finally his faith became so great that he would have jumped when I was eight or ten feet away, and said, " Papa, I's a-comin'."

PRIDE IN ERROR.—You cannot find a man who holds any false doctrine of religion who is not proud of it.

TRY THE BIBLE A NEW WAY. — If we will only take our Bible, and make up our minds that we will depend upon our own study of the Bible, He will help us understand it. If we try to study it in one way, and we find we do not like it, let us take up another ; and. if that fails, try another.

Some time ago, my wife was very anxious that I should learn to like tomatoes. She liked them, and she wanted me to like them. So she got me to try them, first raw, with vinegar and sugar and pepper, but I could not bear them: then she fixed them another way, but still I could not eat them. One day I came home, and she said, "I have cooked the tomatoes a new way." Well, I tried them again, once more, and I thought they were the best things I ever tasted. So if you take up the Bible one way, and don't like it, take it up another way, and keep trying until you find a way in which it will unfold itself to you.

A RUN UPON THE BANKS. — God wants you to come right to the throne of grace, and to come boldly. A while ago I learned from the Chicago papers that there had been a run on the banks there, and many of them were broken. What a good thing it would be to get up a run on the bank of heaven! what a glorious thing to get up a run on the throne of grace!

www.ingramcontent.com/pod-product-compliance
Lightning Source LLC
Chambersburg PA
CBHW032013120726
47902CB00013B/700